Kathy,
Can't
Continued

, reaction.

MW01131150

DOING UNTO

OTHERS

The Golden Rule Revolution

Mike Bushman

ALTFUTURE PUBLISHING
NAPERVILLE, ILLINOIS

AltFuture Publishing
932 Commons Road
Naperville, Illinois 60563
www.mbushman.com

Publisher's Note: This is a work of fiction. Names, characters, places, and incidents are a product of the author's imagination. Locales and public names are sometimes used for atmospheric purposes. Any resemblance to actual people, living or dead, or to businesses, companies, events, institutions, or locales is completely coincidental.

Book Layout adapted from ©2013 BookDesignTemplates.com
Cover Design: Mike Bushman
Cover Photographs ©www.royaltystockphoto.com and Oleg Zabielin

Doing Unto Others/ Mike Bushman. -- 1st ed.
ISBN 978-0-9883369-8-8
Library of Congress Control Number 2014921180

To Lisa Ryder, Bill Bushman, Amy Foster, Eric Bushman and Christine Hudzik for proving with each passing year the true value of growing up in a large family.

"Therefore, whatever you want people to do for you, do the same for them, because this summarizes the Law and the Prophets."
—MATTHEW 7:12

"Never impose on others what you would not choose for yourself."
—CONFUCIUS

"As you would have people do to you, do to them; and what you dislike to be done to you, don't do to them."
— MUHAMMAD

"That which is hateful to you, do not do to your fellow. That is the whole Torah; the rest is the explanation; go and learn."
—RABBI HILLEL

"Hurt not others in ways that you yourself would find hurtful."
— BUDDHIST UDANAVARGA 5:18

"One should never do that to another which one regards as injurious to one's own self. This, in brief, is the rule of dharma. Other behavior is due to selfish desires."
— BRIHASPATI, MAHABHARATA (Anusasana Parva, Section CXIII, Verse 8)

1   INTERRUPTION

It's irritating to Professor Stark that he's even considering opening the message. He's stretching his arms around the only woman to simultaneously capture his mind, body and soul. Only the space where her spine curves more than his slightly inflated abdomen provides any physical separation. If he could, he'd get rid of even that space.

It's not the first time Jill has led him to her bed, but it may as well be for all the sensations, emotions and thoughts interrupting his every attempt to sleep. Even so, he pulls away.

"Damn it, Juan," he mutters as he throws his legs over the edge of the bed, sitting upright to reach his glasses and open his playing-card-sized Lifelink all-in-one identification, computer and communications device. While numerous people warrant audible alerts that override sleep mode on Professor Stark's Lifelink, only three are set to trigger the alert with a single message. One is in deep, contented sleep next to him. The second is in the White House. He never calls at night. It must be Juan. *a (Jill)*

It's the Professor's own fault. Juan never asked to be treated differently than any other academic candidate. Given their history, though, Professor Stark has self-adopted responsibility for Juan.

He holds his left pinkie over the fingerprint sensor to activate the camera, then takes a fast-flash photograph of his right eye to release the device's secondary security.

The time illuminates: 3:05 a.m.

The date also displays: 02/20/2041.

After a quick burst of frustrated exhale accented by the sound of popped vertebrae, Professor Stark creaks slowly toward the bedroom window overlooking the north Capitol Hill neighborhood, doing his best to avoid the noisiest of the stained pine floorboards with which he has only recently gained familiarity. Pulling aside the room-darkening shade to let in light only away from the bed, he stares out at a neighborhood caught mid-cycle between beautiful renovation and stark dilapidation. Jill's is the only townhouse in the row that fits neither description, though it at least shares red brick encasing with every other neighbor.

Professor Stark shakes his head into what counts for alertness at this hour, holding the Lifelink between the shade and the window to minimize how much light reaches the bed. He doesn't want to give Jill—the strong, sharp-witted and sensual woman he somehow convinced to engage in more than conversation—any reason to believe she isn't first on his mind, even as he reads a message so critical it was sent in the middle of the night.

Flipping to the message that triggered the alert that cut short his sleep, the University of Chicago professor and nationally renowned integrated culture and policy expert checks a message from Juan Gonzalez, a message certainly failing to warrant immediate attention and almost certainly not intended by Juan to demand it.

"If just about everybody believes it, why doesn't our country already follow the Golden Rule? Is there any government that expressly follows the Golden Rule—now or ever?" Juan asks, questions no doubt triggered by the President's address to Congress the previous night.

Professor Stark cracks his neck, moving his head from side to side while contemplating his response. He unfolds the playing-card-sized device: up once, down once, all three levels to the right, then all three levels to the left before locking it into flat-sheet mode. He can't dictate a response without waking Jill, so he triggers the keyboard and starts hunting and pecking with his right hand while his left holds the Lifelink steady.

"1) Too many believe Golden Rule applies just to personal behavior. Concept of 'doing unto others as . . .' is critical to government, since politicians often create separate rules for their games. 2) Not aware of any government operating with Golden Rule devotion, though some laws based on Golden Rule principles. It's why God's Law idea President announced is important. 3) Interested in helping?" Professor Stark asks, before shutting off the sleep alarm override for messages from Juan for the night.

Peering around the room, Professor Stark contemplates whether the response is complete enough. He's too tired to respond further. Before the light on the device fades as he climbs back into bed, he realizes his love handles have expanded from pinch-sized to full grip mode. He grabs at his side: "Ughhhh."

After staring at the ceiling fan whirring lightly overhead, he rolls back behind Jill and reaches one arm under her pillow and the other around to gently rest at her waist. He struggles, unsuccessfully, to shut down his thoughts.

Starks response on
Golden Rule

no just personal
no current in govt
Would Juan Gonzales like to help

Spy? Abdullah Raheem sent to find Gen. Timur who has nuke material in Russia

2   MISSION

Abdullah Raheem — Arabic Speaker. Lives in Russia. (owns bookstore) Translates to English. Spy?

Gen Timur, Locate. Has nuclear material in 300 mi radius

Closing time just behind, Abdullah Raheem is in the midst of blending tahini paste, a squirt of lemon juice and diced, stove-flame roasted red peppers into his mashed chickpeas when he hears an alert. Walking over to the back window, the only natural light in his studio apartment above the most admired antique bookstore in Russia's Kazakh province city of Almaty, he checks to be sure no one outside can peer or listen in. He does a quick security sweep, checking for cameras and bugs, before opening his device to check the contents of a far-too-infrequent instruction. After scanning and confirming his fingerprint, eyeprint and facial structure into his communicator, Abdullah clicks in his memorized forty-nine-character security code.

A message scrambles onto his screen with a fifteen-second countdown before it expires. Normally, Abdullah would have time to re-read instructions before they disappear, but he has spent so long immersed in Kazakh and Russian while trying to retain Arabic fluency that his brain takes time to recalibrate to native English.

"Target: Gen. Timur," the message states. Thirteen seconds.

"Directive: Locate only. Zero contact." Ten seconds.

"Priority: Highest. Only." Eight seconds.

"Search range: Estimated within ~300 miles radius of current location." Three seconds.

"Key Risks: Traveling with nuclear material . . . ," the message concludes, evaporating from his screen before Abdullah can read the remainder.

Though he read slowly, he thinks he understands his new orders. He certainly noticed the word nuclear.

Abdullah takes another look around, checking to be sure no one is in the stairwell and looking back out the window for any sign of nearby motion. He launches into a cleaning frenzy to be sure no traces of his real mission are discernible in either his modest storefront antique bookstore or his upstairs apartment—just in case he's unable to return.

After walking six blocks to the Al-Hamid Mosque where he has joined *salat* at least once daily since opening his store, Abdullah removes his shoes at the entrance to the simple, but elegant House of Allah. It is time for the fourth of five daily prayers, the Maghrib sunset prayers. He takes an extra look around after entering the prayer room, then rubs his fingers up against an elegantly paneled pillar near its back. He inserts what appears to be a blank, folded piece of paper behind. Only if his contact here discovers it will he know to put the note over heat to reveal the one word written in lemon juice: "Timur?" At the corner away from the mosque, and outside the range of its security cameras, he kicks a small stone into place to alert his contact that a message is waiting.

At a nearby hookah bar, Abdullah sits comfortably talking and smoking with a group he has joined after salat many times over the years. "*I'm heading to the mountains to read and meditate,*" he tells the group in Kazakh, ensuring that at least some in city government will know why his bookstore is closed and perhaps deter suspicion during his absence. Reaching under the thick, wooden table, he shoves another note up with the same message, this time written in Arabic. This note is intended for a source who smokes once every week in exactly the seat Abdullah occupies now. While the language is different, the message is the same: "Timur?"

DOING UNTO OTHERS

As darkness overtakes Almaty, Abdullah walks through a meandering course to the four other locations set as emergency contact points with his sources. As he turns each corner, he checks to be sure he isn't being followed. At some corners, he'll reach down and tie his shoes. As he turns other corners, he steps into open shops or pretends to read restaurant menus, taking moments to check for faces that appear more than once during his walk. On some blocks during daylight, he walks with a book up to his face though he's rarely actually reading the words on the page.

At each of the four locations, all containing tiny, nearly unnoticeable slits in the modern buildings that dominate much of Almaty thanks to the oil wealth that created both its boon and the bane of its re-control by Russia more than a decade earlier, Abdullah inserts his small pieces of paper inserted with the same message in appropriate primary language for each intended recipient. As he proceeds, he also inserts six sealed straws containing rubles at separate pre-agreed spots. Each time, Abdullah marks the deposit with a symbol known only to its target recipient, often as simple as a rock turned to display dripped paint or a sound activated near a specific high-rise entrance that can be heard only by someone nearby tuned to the specific frequency.

"Hopefully, someone will know something when I get back," he tells himself as he returns to his bookstore, loads his backpack and strides to a diesel-powered car parked in a garage on the edge of the city.

Once fully packed, Abdullah departs for *Uryl'*, the town he had long ago decided he would head toward if he was being hunted. Just east of Uryl' are passable border crossings into China, Mongolia and non-provincial Russia.

In his excitement to be part of what seems to be a critical mission, he ignores that he should be sleeping soon.

[handwritten margin notes: "4 recipients additional. Speakers of other languages. 6 payments" and "diesel-powered car / backpack"]

3 STIMULATION

"Nothing," Professor Stark mouths as he tries moving the fingers on his left hand. "Nothing." He tries flexing his wrist but can't muster any movement. Still, Professor Paul Stark gladly trades awkward tingles stretching to his fingertips for the sensations penetrating the rest of him.

After an exhausting night ending an arduous year in which almost everything was risked and nearly lost, Professor Stark gazes to his left. With the battles behind, he has everything that matters to him now. Jill's head rests fully on his biceps, crushing down as a temporary tourniquet on the arteries and veins tucked inside.

Her left hand repetitively, involuntarily caresses tufts of chest hair. She has to be exhausted, he reminds himself. I need to let her sleep.

For years, Professor Stark's toughest mental battles have all been fought alone—separating fact from fiction, identifying internal biases, confronting distorted perceptions. Now his toughest barrier to rational behavior cuddles next to him, softly scrambling every attempt at logical consideration of his next steps.

He believes in her, trusts her and thoroughly adores her. But can he restrain his desire, even for just the short time until she wakes? It has been decades since he's had both minds fully activated simultaneously. One of his internal control agents, though, is conniving against the other's efforts to at least consider Jill's sleep desires.

"Let her sleep," he audibly but softly directs himself in an early morning self lecture, the sound being a consequence of having spent too many years alone combined with learning through trial and error that he's more likely to remember what he verbalizes and hears.

"Huh?" Jill opens her eyes, lifting her head ever so slightly from his biceps. "What did you say?" she asks, before licking the inside of her mouth and her lips to remove the dry coating inside.

"Sorry," he replies. "Go back to sleep. You have another thirty minutes."

Hearing this, Jill slides her head upward, resting it on Paul's chest. She's one of the few who calls him Paul. Everyone, at her insistence despite her position, calls her Jill. He wiggles his fingers, trying to restore blood flow above his neck without disrupting her movement. Reaching slowly, she wraps her left arm fully around his chest, turning to slide her left leg between his calves.

As her leg encounters resistance, she looks down before lifting her head just long enough to connect her eyes with his. "I take it you're awake," she says with a smile.

Paul Stark — (important but goes by first name)
Jill

Meet- Cesar Castillo
    Gen. Raúl Hernandez
Cartel / military

Meet - JT Alton
    Ally Steele Pilot
Company/ New Rite
Meet- sex slave victim
at Cartel- Abril DeSesus

~~Gen.~~ Pres. Phillipi
attacks Drug compound
in Sinaloa eminent

danger- Nukes.

2 prong attack
    bullets + Bombs

Day after the
Presidents address
Ch. 11

Cartel cover- (industrial
    truck train)
Cartel-
Drugs + military
Leader Cesar Castillo

Known by US
but not politically
responsible to destroy
- people wouldn't understand-

4 RETALIATION

When the Castillo drug cartel's Sinaloa Province compound was
designed, its chief architect assured now deceased cartel leader Cesar
Castillo that it would look just like any other expansive power
generation and industrial park. A power plant sits at the west end of
the property, sapping up generous amounts of the Gulf of California
to cool its nuclear processes. Dozens of manufacturing plants—some
owned by the cartel and some built in the compound only following
estímulo or, more accurately, threat—sprawl over nearly fifty square
miles. Industrial truck and train traffic shrouds the cartel's
underground drug production and military operations, as do
thousands of workers entering daily from surrounding communities
and thousands more housed in on-site single-unit and barracks-style
homes.

Despite well-designed cover, U.S. intelligence and drug enforcement
agencies have long known that the cartel's main operations center is
buried beneath this industrial park. They haven't been confident,
however, that they can destroy cartel operations without significant
collateral damage. Even when Mexican leaders approved U.S.-led
attacks against the cartel compound in an effort to rid their country

JT Alton founder New Rite - COLORADO Co. Gaming / Weapons had gathered data it drug killed brother

of the cartel's overwhelming political and economic influence, senior U.S. politicians stopped these operations, fearing backlash from America's large Hispanic voting population if innocent civilians were killed or nuclear plant damage triggered an environmental catastrophe.

New Rite, a global survivalist gaming and weapons development company headquartered in Colorado, amassed extensive data on the compound over the years as part of its founder's clandestine mission to destroy the cartel responsible for the drugs that killed his younger brother. Even with founder JT Alton putting most of New Rite's extensive profits into creating in-house intelligence and special operations capabilities, he never had the military depth to orchestrate a successful compound attack. For years, New Rite waited for cartel leaders to stray to less secure locations or to the compound's outer edges to be captured individually. Patience and restraint are now neither necessary nor warranted.

Fear of collateral damage during a compound attack disappeared in the mind of U.S. President Marc Phillipi in recent days when nuclear weapons entered the cartel's attack and blackmail strategy.

After failing in a massively orchestrated and violent attempt to drive America's Southwest states to secede, cartel military leader General Raúl Hernández proved unwilling to accept conventional defeat. When the secession effort ended and invading forces were repelled, he ordered nuclear bombs planted inside five American cities with a kill zone covering thirty million Americans. This action, even more than secession support and invasion coordination, earned White House wrath.

Despite knowing he is enemy number one to the United States, General Hernández is hardly worried. Nuclear weapons are his security blanket. Fear that Hernández might trigger the nuclear weapons hidden in Los Angeles, San Diego, Phoenix, Dallas and Houston has already led U.S. President Marc Phillipi to accept Hernández as the unelected President and essentially dictator of Mexico. Mexico's former President stepped down to prevent the cartel from exploding a sixth nuclear bomb in his hometown, where his family is held prisoner by the cartel.

President Marc Phillipi no longer fearful - Attacks

Gen. Raúl Hernandez try to get SW states to secede. 5 nukes in SW cities

With five nuclear weapons on U.S. soil, the trigger for the weapons with him at all times, and security beefed up on the compound surface fifteen hundred feet above his office, General Hernández refocuses on shoring up remaining coalition partnerships with several nations and a collection of terror organizations. He takes time out from coalition partnership work only to pursue his basest of pleasures. *U.S. Cartel*

As he seeks his pleasures near the depths of the compound, ground-level security forces unaware of his nuclear security blanket nervously scan the land, the ocean and the skies, though they see no hint of trouble hovering above even as they remain certain an attack will come. *Cartel*

They can't repel what they don't see.

Gecko-like aerial skin camouflage developed by New Rite is particularly effective when background scenery changes slowly as it does on this relatively clear day with only slow-moving clouds. To cartel security troops, that camouflage obscures more than nine hundred Advanced Propulsion Blend attack (APB) fighters hovering thirty thousand feet above the cartel compound. Cartel ground and air defense troops don't see any threat. Sophisticated heat masking and signal absorption and redirection technology fools every other intruder identification technology operating at the compound near where the Gulf of California runs into the Pacific Ocean.

"Okay, go," U.S. President Marc Phillipi orders, once informed by New Rite pilot Ally Steele that troops are all in place. He rides with her rather than the military pilots operating the rest of the APBs because she is the only pilot with APB combat flying experience.

Marksmen on board the floating fighters respond instantaneously to the go signal, shooting rifle-sized launchers that release missile-backed bullets able to take down targets well outside the range of conventional rifles. For surface-level Protection Corps soldiers, as the military wing of the cartel is known, death is mercifully rapid as bullets create wide paths through victims on impact, knocking the soldiers guarding the cartel compound down faster than mobile homes in an EF5 tornado. Less than a second separates the first fallen Protection Corps soldier from the last.

New Rite Pilot — Ally Steele

missle-backed bullets

MIKE BUSHMAN

As crews on the APBs survey their handiwork, a handful of cartel military survivors scramble toward buildings now known to house stairwells or elevators into the compound's underground network. New Rite Special Operations Leader Ally Steele relays the President's order to launch phase two. U.S. Air Force bombers drop tunnel-burrowing bombs that impale through layer after layer of the cartel's sophisticated underground operations, precisely in the spots suggested by New Rite intelligence and a detailed map sent by a high-level cartel insider who feared that General Hernández was planning to trigger the cartel's nuclear weapons regardless of whether the United States acceded to his demands.

Tunnel-burrowing bombs concentrate the devastation of its explosions downward, following each other in a series of precisely timed detonations in the exact GPS-designated spots built into the weapons. To get down fifteen hundred feet below ground, the depth at which the cartel's leadership is believed to be operating, fifteen of these bombs detonate in precise sequences that take just thirty seconds to reach the maximum depth needed for sub-surface combat entry.

The U.S. military could have blown deep holes in the industrial compound more quickly using large conventional bombs. These explosions, though, would create enough air displacement to careen many of the floating APBs into each other and would certainly have created intense collateral damage, including the potential to destroy the nuclear power plant. Those bombs also might destroy hope of finding connections to remaining nuclear weapons believed stockpiled by the cartel.

More than one thousand feet below ground, Abril DeJesus's face is buried in her now blood-soaked sheet, her head driven relentlessly into the wall by the worst of her captors. He's the man in charge; the one who took her first, always compounding her moral devastation with a physical beating that leaves her back torn. During each fresh beating, Abril's scars convert in appearance from gravel-pit texture to still-cooling lava pit. The man whips her between deeply penetrating strokes to lengthen his enjoyment, compound her pain or cause some combination of the two.

Perverse

Recalled Abril's abuse *In art history also shown* *Horrid* *Explated*

Throughout world history, sex savagery has been a prize valued by violent aggressors, a lesson painfully endured by Bosnian Muslim women at the hands of Serbian militias, by Nigerian Christian girls under the fists of Boko Haram and by Yazidi women behind the guns of the Islamic State of Iraq and Syria. General Hernández doesn't discriminate in his pursuit of debasement, taking it from whomever he desires.

Abril usually bears the physical pain General Hernández and others deliver by mentally departing for another world, the one she came from where kneeling on pews and scrubbing floors were her worst discomforts, ones easily endured in the service of Jesús Cristo. Deep in her artificial existence as concrete sections break from the ceiling above, it takes Abril moments to reconnect to physical reality. At least he's not stoning me, she thinks as she looks up to see several pieces of concrete separating from the ceiling and falling to the bed to which she's chained.

Unsure why the ceiling is disintegrating, the man behind her stops whipping, then pumps faster and faster until he releases and drops onto her open wounds. Abril screams in agony, infuriating the man everyone calls "General." He whips her one last time before pulling on his pants, threading his belt and running away.

"Please swallow me up in your earth, God," Abril cries out in Spanish, as other girls around her scream to be saved and the remaining soldiers race from the sex slave pit to the sounds of the attack siren and collapsing walls. *"I'm ready to be taken into your arms, Lord,"* she calls out, dropping to her knees. *"Please God, I beg for your mercy."* *Sad*

⊙≫≪⊙

Less than a day before the compound attack, President Phillipi stood in front of a joint session of Congress calling for a bold new initiative to win the post-secession peace and restore America's greatness. He has a name for his proposed new constitutional amendment to require application of the Golden Rule to every government action: "God's Law." His name for the proposal generates its own controversy. The President's hope is that proper use of the Golden Rule will reunite a nation torn apart by generations of divisive politicians seeking advantage through segregating the nation by race, religion and income for partisan advantage.

"The God's Law concept is not an attempt to create a national religion," the President argued in his address to Congress the night before the Sinaloa compound attack. "Far from it. Religion must not run government. Faith is part of our humanity, but reason is a gift we must exercise in conjunction with faith. I believe we must consider our faith in the context of a deep, studied understanding of what it takes for societies to survive and prosper for millennia. Only then, building from faith and reason, can we take the steps to build a better, lasting society."

The President didn't mention that he was leaving from the joint session to personally participate in launching a new war, a retributory attack on the Castillo cartel's Protection Corps military and several terrorist groups and national militaries lingering in Mexico after their conventional defeat in the Southwest. Every group being attacked is identified by intelligence sources as contributing to Hernández's placement of nuclear weapons in the five Southwest cities.

Lying back on Professor Stark's now sweat-moistened chest, Jill bolts upright as her emergency alert warning blares.

"What's going on?" Professor Stark probes, swinging his legs around the edge of the bed, but not missing the opportunity to check out Jill's bare, dimpled backside as she stands.

"Damn it. Emergency alert. It's only gone off twice. Not good," Jill replies with almost stoic resignation. Jill, officially Congresswoman Jill Carlson, grabs a robe that hangs at the edge of her bed, double checks to be sure the window shades are fully closed and paces quickly down to the kitchen counter where her mobile all-in-one device rests.

"What is it?" Professor Stark yells down from the top of the stairs.

Jill Carlson
Congresswoman

Jill comes back into the bedroom, looking every bit as if she had just lost everything that mattered in her life. "We're back at war," she states, her lips beginning to tremor.

"What? Who attacked this time?" Professor Stark asks the woman who first captured his attention less than a year earlier.

"No one. We started this one," Jill replies.

Professor Stark exhales heavily, drops his head and shakes it side to side. "Damn it!"

"President Wilt is asking for a war powers vote this morning," Jill continues, reading further down in her congressional alert system message.

"Whoa, whoa, whoa. . . . President Wilt?" Professor Stark inquires, now standing straight, but with his mouth agape.

Jill looks up, realizing what she has just read. "President Phillipi has taken leave. This says he's personally leading the attack."

Professor Stark clasps his hands behind his head, pulling it toward his chest. "Oh my flippin' God," he exclaims, before blowing into his hands as he presses them flat together in front of his mouth.

"Paul, you need to head home. As soon as we vote, we're being taken into protective security," Jill tells him while scrambling to pull herself and her stuff together.

"Can't I go with you?" he asks, not wanting to separate from Jill after finally making a connection he wants to last a lifetime.

Jill walks toward him, puts her arms around his chest and lifts up slightly to kiss him on the lips. "Only immediate family," she says. "Sorry."

"Too slow again," he mumbles audibly before reminding himself that he needs to stop instructing himself out loud.

"Too slow," Jill questions, turning to look into the Professor's eyes.

Professor Stark has the engagement ring in his coat pocket. He had hoped for permission to ask Jill to marry him on the House floor after last night's Presidential address, but the Secret Service denied his request. When he had asked President Phillipi to intervene, Professor Stark had not received any response. Now he knows why. The President clearly had more important issues on his mind.

"Never mind," Professor Stark comments. "I'll walk you to Cannon and grab the Metro from there."

"I love you, Paul," Jill states emphatically.

"I love you too, Jill," he replies as he again envelops her in his arms. "Why does this have to happen now?"

"I know. It's almost too much to handle," she replies, deciding she has time for a quick shower—alone.

Recalled engagement

Stark ready to propose to Jill — delayed

was act by on Pres. Phillips Sinaloa drug cartel puts Pres. Wilt in power & calls congresswoman Jill to vote war powers act.

Meet — ousted Mexican Pres. Daniel Suarez
he traveled with Alley Steele and Pres. Phillipi
during attack.
7 nations involved in Cartel also being attacked
simultaneously.
Lower into compound to ^cartel control room

5 INCURSION

Pres. Phillipi + pilot Ally Steele ^ousted
US led New Rite Co.
assault on Cartel Compound
involving 7 other nations along with Mexico
Mex. Pres. / Suarez make a Military to sieze control room.

Recently ousted Mexican President Daniel Suarez sits next to officially incapacitated U.S. President Phillipi, hovering in one of hundreds of New Rite-designed APBs. Because New Rite special operations leader Ally Steele is one of few pilots with APB combat flight experience, she has drawn the presidents as her passengers, a responsibility that brings with it de facto on-site mission command.

Ally spots a tunnel breach deep in the tunnel center that seems to have a stable landing area. From above, it appears that a meteor slammed into the cartel's compound, carving a precise five-hundred-foot-diameter hole straight into the earth. Walls near the perimeter of the hole are still crumbling as the first wave of APBs approach surface level, but the attack team has been assured that any parts of the structure that haven't collapsed within sixty seconds will remain stable. Coordinating the attack was facilitated immensely once engineering plans to the compound were obtained, a gift from an American involuntarily propped into cartel leadership by General Hernández.

Fifty APBs land in a two hundred and fifty foot perimeter around the hole, with marksmen on board driving stakes into the ground to

hold their roped harnesses as they sprint to the edge of the hole, drop
to prone sniper position and search for live targets around the hole's
perimeter. Each sharpshooter has his or her assigned depth levels to
search. After two minutes of clearing cartel survivors from the edges
of the hole, Ally leads a group of ten APBs to the compound's new
interior courtyard floor. Unworried at the prospect of incinerating anyone below as they land, Ally pulls in the APB's blades and rotates
the rocket propulsion system so she can immediately re-launch if the
landing area gives way.

"Mr. Presidents, ready for tunnel insert," Ally clicks back to
presidents Phillipi and Suarez. Just weeks earlier, President Phillipi
thought President Suarez had been leading the United Nations-backed
invasion to support Southwestern U.S. state secession. After General
Hernández deposed Suarez, forcing him to resign under threat of
having his hometown obliterated by a sixth nuclear bomb, President
Phillipi became convinced that Suarez's actions were driven solely by
a desire to protect his nation. General Hernández, it turned out, had
directly conspired with several anti-American nations to turn a U.N.
peacekeeping mission into an attempt to liberate four Southwest
states and move them toward his control.

"Proceed," the U.S. President-on-leave responds, an order Ally relays through official U.S. military command. Phillipi and Suarez
recheck their weapons and grasp their cover shields as they prepare to
bolt from Ally's APB fighter, a highly maneuverable jet/helicopter
cross whose capabilities were known until recently only by the New
Rite weapons development and special operations teams.

After a series of mistakes for which he feels he must atone,
including a bureaucratic-incompetence-covering lie about inviting
United Nations troops onto U.S. territory that General Hernández
used to gain tactical advantage, President Phillipi demanded a
physical role in the deep tunnel attacks. While this attack is
underway, full-scale military assaults are also launching against
targets in seven nations that still have troops in Mexico supporting
Hernández's theft of that nation. President Phillipi knows enough
about history to understand the risks the United States endured when
it had Cuba implementing the Soviet Union's bidding from just ninety

miles offshore. If these seven hostile national militaries remain in Mexico, all from single-religion theocracy or dictatorial-communist nations, the United States will endure constant survival threats.

Ally drops her APB straight down at a pace so rapid that Phillipi and Suarez check to make sure their organs remain inside their skin. Just shy of landing, she yells out directions to the Presidents and the other four soldiers assigned to both lead and protect them.

"Insertion point thirty paces to my left when we hit ground. Everyone clip in. We should find a circular stairwell to the bottom with kill zones along the way. Shields up, Presidents," Ally barks out.

Shortly after Castillo cartel Protection Corps General Raúl Hernández replaced Suarez as President of Mexico—a move Phillipi tacitly endorsed while trying to locate and disarm cartel-delivered nuclear weapons inside U.S. territory—the General moved Mexico's military command center to this Sinaloa Province Protection Corps headquarters. Hernández had been a general in Mexico's military until leaving to form the cartel's Protection Corps. The Protection Corps, along with allied anti-American forces from several nations, remains America's most immediate global threat. President Phillipi refuses to give these failed invaders time to rearm.

Ally jumps from her pilot's seat to lead the assault into the compound interior and down, clipping in with her carabiner before beginning a rapid drop through the center of a circular stairwell located exactly where it was expected. Two bulletproof semi-circular shields are latched to her feet to deflect any shots coming up at the descent team. Three other military veterans follow Ally before the Presidents clip on for descent; all helping to clear shooters lined along stairs and crumpled walls during the assault. Another wave of troops follows behind, breaching tunnels at every level through the intricate, maze-like compound built over the past decade to run the cartel's near-monopoly illicit-drug operations into the U.S. and Canada—and plan its protection and retribution schemes.

President Phillipi clips together his surround shield, protecting him from normal bullets from four sides, but leaving him still vulnerable to shots from above and below. Suarez carries an identical shield for his descent, a protection insisted on by the U.S. Defense Secretary before

Mendoza?
Chapter 7

allowing either President to take part in this retribution assault. Technically, Phillipi won't resume the presidency until his part in the assault is over and he is within immediate communications reach of the government. Before leaving the U.S. Capitol following his State of the Union address just twelve hours earlier, the Chief Justice had privately sworn in the Vice President to take over during the President's incapacitation throughout battle.

"Oh God," Phillipi yells out during the initial stairwell descent, again feeling his stomach thrusting at his tonsils, creating an immediate rush of nausea Phillipi struggles to control. "Whew, whew," he breathes out, trying to regain control of his senses.

The automated, motorized carabiners used by the two politicians control their descent, allowing them to focus on holding their shields and preparing their automatic weapons. Hitting bottom, they follow Ally and the rest of the assault team as they search for the control room where they expect to find General and now self-proclaimed Mexican President Hernández.

*Meet- General Timur - Russian terrorist, military, &
  supplies Nuclear material + opiates to Cartel/Ger.*
                                          Hernández
★ *(Timur friends Hernandez for access to enemy)*
  Timur ousted from Islamic Republican of Iran
  Meet Ramon Mantel - Cartel, US map provider
   Software engineer, blackmailed w/ family. Hates
Hernandez nuclear destruction ideas. Escapes in
Hernandez tunnel

6 REACTION

see end page

In Russia

Deep in the mountain steppes south of Almaty, in Russia's Kazakh province, another general is alerted to the U.S. attack. The Castillo cartel has been General Timur's largest opiate customer for more than a decade, helping finance Timur's enormous personal wealth and his rapidly expanding terrorist activities. Timur had also provided material for several of the nuclear weapons Hernández recently placed inside U.S. borders, helping Hernández to steal control of Mexico.

More important to Timur, alignment with General Hernández provided him a new state sponsor, this time with ready access to his primary enemy.

"Who attacks?" he asks the messenger, one of his most loyal soldiers, in their shared Persian language.

"The Great Satan," the messenger replies.

"Then we must make our own plans. Allah wills it," he states, calling his select group of loyal troops together inside the cave they have frequently hidden in since the general was ousted from control of a large branch of the former Islamic Republic of Iran military.

❦

MIKE BUSHMAN

Castillo cartel leader Ramon Mantle, the provider of detailed compound maps to the U.S. military, watches as the assault breaches the cartel's perimeter defenses. "You can't leave any competitors standing, even me," Ramon's message to U.S. leadership reads. He wants the cartel fully destroyed, even if it means his life ends as well.

Only days earlier, Ramon had decided he was ready to die to prevent the world from facing nuclear catastrophe at the hands of Hernández and the rest of the cartel's military wing. Known to the world primarily as a brilliant software engineer and, until recently, head of one of the world's largest and most important automation control companies, Ramon had for more than a decade also worked for the Castillo cartel. For most of that time, his cooperation was involuntary, with his father held hostage by General Hernández and the remainder of his family under constant threat of death if he tried to escape the cartel's control.

As his own death approaches, Ramon's survival instincts kick in. He easily breaks through the security code into General Hernández's personal office suite, a two-thousand-square-foot oasis of comfort nearly two thousand feet below the earth's surface. Even as the cartel's new boss, Ramon's compound accommodations aren't nearly as luxurious, perhaps a reflection that Ramon's employment was compelled under constant threat from General Hernández, even as he has been named the cartel's official leader. Ramon provides the intellect the cartel needs, but Hernández has always controlled its military and its money.

Searching through the office, Ramon inspects Hernández's exercise center, looking for buttons, levers or pulleys that might open a hidden escape route. Ramon is certain that Hernández would never go down with the troops he orders into battle, having worked with him long enough to know that Hernández's first order of business is always protecting his own personal safety and ambitions. He searches through the gold-plated handles in the bathroom, around the desk and through the communication display wall. Ramon presses up on the ceiling and kicks along the floor before finally coming to the liquor cabinet of a man who had simultaneously imprisoned and protected him for more than a decade.

DOING UNTO OTHERS

Hidden in Hernández's liquor cabinet is a latch Ramon finds and twists, pulling the cabinet forward and allowing Ramon to slide into the dark, desolate tunnel. He closes the liquor cabinet entrance to minimize risk of being followed, twisting the lock shut from inside the tunnel. After just a few seconds, Ramon realizes he has no light. He feels around, hoping to find a switch or something else to generate light. After a minute of searching, he realizes the tunnel is just three feet high and three feet across. He can't find any light source and begins to panic. As he moves forward to try reopening the liquor cabinet, he hears grenade-like and machine gun sounds outside and decides to face his fears. At least at this depth he's unlikely to encounter spiders, snakes, scorpions or other dangerous wildlife.

Ramon backs away, doing an army crawl in short increments before reaching around to find a light source. "What a horrible tomb," he tells himself as he contemplates this tunnel being his final resting place. Maybe if I surrender, he considers, but realizes that both Hernández and the U.S military would shoot first and ask questions later, if ever.

With one hundred feet between him and the tunnel entrance, Ramon's army crawl hits something solid. He hears whatever he just hit start to roll. He approaches the sound slowly, reaching an inch at a time until he locates it. It's a cart on wheels. He can use it to propel himself quickly through the tunnel. That must be its purpose.

As Ramon secures himself on the cart, a flash of light coming from the tunnel opening shocks his pupils. Several minutes of absolute darkness had already started to disorient Ramon so the light is welcome, until he hears a voice.

"Who's in my tunnel?" General Hernández screams out in Spanish before quickly closing the door, though leaving it unlocked and allowing some light to still enter.

Ramon knows it's General Hernández and contemplates whether to respond. Before he decides what to do, Hernández shoots down the tunnel. The bullet skims the back of Ramon's ankle and the edge of his buttocks as he lay on the cart face down.

"Soy yo. Soy yo," Ramon yells. No longer sure what to do, he sees a flash of brighter light again as the tunnel door is pulled back open.

Ramon reveals himself Hernandez shoots and wounds

Hernández dies of a grenade whilst harrassing Ramon Mantel in his escape tunnel (handwritten annotation)

Hernández turns to shoot at whoever is entering. Ramon takes this as his cue to move away as quickly as possible and starts propelling himself on the cart as fast as his toes and hands will propel him. In seconds, he moves hundreds of feet away before hearing the sounds of a grenade being tossed into the tunnel.

Hearing the clink of the grenade against concrete, Ramon thrusts with every ounce of energy. Hernández's body absorbs the grenade's direct impact, sending shredded body parts careening toward Ramon, an undeservedly rapid death for a man best known for his enjoyment of extended, excruciating tortures. While the hits from Hernández's body parts aren't debilitating to Ramon, the odor of seared flesh creates immediate nausea to which he succumbs.

Ramon quickly accelerates as he hears part of the tunnel collapsing behind, burying Hernández in what was designed as a personal escape path. This buys Ramon the time to evade whoever took down his long-time colleague and captor.

Still trapped in darkness, with no food and water, Ramon's only comfort is that the tunnel walls, floor and ceiling are all reachable with his hands. He rips off pieces of clothing to stop the bleeding on his ankle. His butt wound isn't deep enough to cause much pain, but it makes it uncomfortable to roll onto his back when his body tires of pushing along in downward facing position.

The combination of exhaustion and fear presses at Ramon's composure. He contemplates going back. At least he knows that if he digs through the rubble there's an opening on the other side. He can't imagine, though, that Hernández had a tunnel dug without an escape hatch. He stops and says every prayer he can remember, getting the Our Father only partially right and completely butchering his Hail Mary. Still, simply taking a moment to reflect on something other than his current misery gives his mind a chance to regain control over his emotions. Hours later, Ramon's arms and legs move beyond sporadic cramping to persistent pain. He contemplates turning around to use different muscles, but fears he'll forget which direction he should push and end up going back-and-forth over the same path.

Ramon's disorientation in the darkness is nearly complete, tears beginning to form in the corner of his eyes as he struggles to find the

dehydrated

energy to move. He presses upward and forward, alternating between using his arms and his toes now that he has lost the energy to use both simultaneously. He tries licking his lips to moisten his mouth. His tongue has no moisture to give.

comes to gravel

What seems to be hours later, Ramon feels the cart rolling over a bumpy, gravelly surface. It slows his momentum enough that when he bangs his head into a wall the ache is inconsequential compared to other throbbing pains. Rolling off the cart, Ramon lies on his back. Catching his breath, he waits for the energy to test whether his journey has ended.

For the first time in hours, he feels something besides concrete. Perhaps it's not an end.

Find a wall, a bar,

Struggling, Ramon rolls over and pushes up on his knees. He reaches around until he finds something other than flat wall; a metal bar, roughly two feet off the ground and jutting out from the wall. Slowly, methodically, he continues to reach around. Minutes later, he finds another bar, then another above it and another above it. A ladder.

Cursing out, he screams that he can't even stand, no longer caring whether anyone hears him. After collapsing in pain, he pushes himself to move. He can't give up now. Ramon pulls upright, one bar at a time until he stands inside a thin opening. Each step takes several minutes. An hour or more later, he reaches the last rung, braces up two more and feels for what's up there—two feet of flat concrete. Then nothing. Damn it. Slowly, he pulls himself forward until the concrete bottom disappears. He can't go up. The sides are concrete. Down is the only direction. Carefully, he reaches down. As he feels around, he finds one. A rung. He reaches another rung, then another before sitting back up and realizing where he has to go. Down a ladder. Agonizing pain and a missed rung that drops him the last four feet enable Ramon to reach bottom.

Looking at a floor panel, the only spot he can see that isn't solid concrete, after pain from the fall subsides Ramon clasps his fingers around a latch. He tries pulling it up. It doesn't move. Then he twists the latch and hears it unlock. Ramon can hear every breath and every heartbeat now. His heart is racing, excited by potential escape. Ramon says one more prayer. Then he lifts.

The light that enters the tunnel is no more than the light on a cloudy night in the middle of a desert, but feels nearly blinding to Ramon. Ramon considers whether he is looking at a mirage, even as he closes his eyes to give his unused sense time to adjust to the light. Minutes later, Ramon's eyes adjust enough that he is able to look directly at what is below the latch. He stares down and quickly determines it is dark water below. More metal rungs are built into the wall down to the water.

After moments of reflection and recovery, Ramon climbs down the rungs. He screams as his ankle hits the water, searing him with pain. He reaches into the water with his hand, scoops it to his mouth and confirms what he suspected. Salt water. Nothing he can use to quench his incredible thirst and constant pain for yet-to-scab wounds.

Sitting on one cheek hunched over with his feet hanging down just above water level, Ramon contemplates his next move. The tunnel reaches a dead end just a few feet past the latch. If he goes back, the other end is now collapsed with Hernández buried inside. The water escape is likely his only way out.

Ramon waits, giving his eyes further time to adjust to the bit of light that seems to be coming up from deep below. The light must be the escape route. There is no alternative. Ramon assumes the path below will take him out to the Gulf of California. The tunnel compound was just ten miles inland from the shoreline. It seems he could have rolled long enough to get to the coast and closer to its surface. Hernández's office was on the western edge of the compound—at its deepest point.

Wait. That means I could still be below sea level, Ramon realizes. The cart path was not that steep. How far above sea level was the compound surface he wonders, trying to recall if he ever encountered that elevation in any schematics.

Ramon sits on the edge and stews, saying several more prayers, this time coming closer to the originals. It's funny how trauma always brings him back to the rituals of youth, praying to a God he has long

remembering prayers in his trauma

believed had no more than passing interest in his life or those of just about anyone else.

Finally, Ramon decides to take the plunge. The initial saltwater impact on his ankle has already inflicted the worst pain. His butt wound doesn't seem that deep and, with scattered nerve endings, he'll easily absorb pain there. Ramon steps down the metal bars, dipping his injured foot first into the cool, but easily tolerable saltwater. He holds there for several seconds until the searing dulls. Not sure what he'll find below, he drops his body into the water, but holds the last step with both hands. He kicks around and finds that the opening widens below the water level.

Just before dropping in, he finds a pressurized oxygen-scavenging mask hanging to the side of the last step. These masks are something he heard about but never used. He inserts the mask into his mouth and fumbles to figure out what to do with the other loose piece before deciding it's meant to clip over his nose. If it works right, the mask has enough power to pull oxygen from the ocean for one or two hours of swimming. Realizing he could have a long swim, he mentally notes that he'll need to descend and ascend slowly to keep from exploding his lungs. He prays that whoever left the mask understood and prepared for pressurization requirements for the pool's depth.

Finally, after several deep breaths, Ramon inserts the mask, drops into the water, spins to dive downward and consciously swims slowly toward the dim light.

Birth?
We can all relate

In this
Chapter
meet Rámon Mantel
reluctant software engr.
of Cartel escaping US led
~~cartel~~ (attack on) Cartel
+ Gen. Hernandez bullets
through Hernandez escape
tunnel, Hernandez
killed ~~by~~ US grenade,
Mantel in water,

Meet US Def. Secty Mendoza — ch5 insisted on
shields for Pres.

Revealed — Ramon Mantel software
engineer developed software system
controlling American Vehicles.
Revealed + clarified — Ramon supplied Cartel
compound maps to US
through Stark. (Ch.6)
maps.
Meet Margone, is prostitute / sex slave abducted
Revealed — Abul others extracted, One asks to go home.
Revealed Abul is a noviciate — convent to
become a nun.

see end

7 INDIGNATION

Ally's orders are to allow President Phillipi and President Suarez no more than a taste of battle. The tunnel Ally's team is breaching should be one of the least guarded entrances into the cartel compound, given its depth below the surface and information contained in forwarded compound maps. Leading up to the raid, Secretary Mendoza tried ignoring President Phillipi's demand to personally take part. When simply ignoring the order failed, Secretary Mendoza added a separate planning exercise to minimize risks to the President during battle.

On hearing that the cartel's General Hernández had placed nuclear weapons in San Diego, Los Angeles, Phoenix, Dallas and Houston, Ramon Mantle decided that he would need to risk losing his life and that of his immediate family to stop General Hernández from igniting a level of destruction Ramon couldn't even contemplate allowing. He hadn't joined the cartel to kill. Technically, he never actually joined the cartel, at least not voluntarily. Ramon's pride and wealth came from personally developing the software system used to control hundreds of millions of American vehicles. A law mandating that his software control any vehicle operating on roads built using federal

Goals achieved MIKE BUSHMAN *power to control vehicles (weakness) exploited*

funds made him extraordinarily wealthy. That control mandate was sold as a means of increasing fuel efficiency, reducing environmental damage, and substantially improving highway safety. It had accomplished these goals, but also gave Ramon's company enormous power to control vehicle movement around the country.

When *Cesar* the Castillo, cartel's founder, discovered Ramon's extraordinary technology capabilities during Ramon's drag racing days, he had General Hernández's Protection Corps take Ramon's father hostage to force Ramon's compliance with cartel demands. Where Ramon's technology expertise and creativity had once been the purpose for confining him, it finally is contributing to the cartel's demise. Days earlier, Ramon used his tech savvy to break into the cartel's operating system, steal maps of the tunnel compound and send them to University of Chicago Professor Paul Stark to relay to the U.S. government.

Ally had the map largely memorized and was using it to lead the now one hundred troops gathered at the stairwell bottom through a perimeter sweep of the tunnels, aiming for the parts of the system used for drug production and distribution. She is under clear instructions to keep President Phillipi away from the military wings of the compound tunnel system.

Reaching an unguarded thick steel door, Ally calls out for her long-time friend and detonation expert to blow the door off its hinges. With all troops back around the corners, and the presidents additionally hunched behind their protective shields, her colleague Clint blows the concrete and steel frame around the door.

As Clint and others pull the door and frame forward, first shots ring out from inside the production room. Ally and others return fire, killing dozens of guards perched on metal walkways layered over the production floor. Shots are exchanged. Ally and other nearby soldiers push the Presidents back behind their shields, restraining them until the gun battle subsides.

"I'm ordering you to allow me into that battle right now," President Phillipi yells at Ally and the others.

"Sorry, sir," Ally responds. "Commander-in-chief ordered you away from any intense action."

"I'm commander-in-chief, damn it," the President barks back.

"Not at the moment, sir. At least not 'til we're out of here safely," Ally replies without even a quick glare at the President. "Then, I'll take whatever abuse you decide to dish out."

President Phillipi bangs his fist on his shield.

Finally, a soldier calls out the "all clear" and the Presidents are allowed to enter.

President Phillipi stops at the entrance, staring in disbelief.

The production floor is at least forty feet high, four football fields in length and two football fields wide. Reinforced steel beams dot the open room, with metal walkways connecting the edges of the room to each beam and circular walkways running around each beam. Dozens of dead guards lie on these walkways. U.S. soldiers and a handful of New Rite special operations team members make their way through the walkway system to tie up each body, just in case one still carries a pulse. Long whips lie next to bodies of some guards. From the walkway, more soldiers release ladders down to the production floor and sub-floor cells and round up hundreds of unarmed production workers and sex slaves in corners of the main floor.

President Suarez asks if they have time to find out what's been going on here. He translates for President Phillipi.

"This woman was abducted by the cartel when she was thirteen years old and used as a sex slave and prostitute for many, many years. When clients stopped being willing to pay top dollar for her, she was brought here and has worked here ever since," Suarez says. *She doesn't know*

"How old is she now?" President Phillipi asks. *her age*

"I asked. She doesn't know how long she's been here," Suarez says.

Shaking his head, the President asks, "She doesn't go home?"

"This is their home," former President Suarez relays after asking several more questions. Other women are released from their chains and cells, but rounded up in a corner of the floor for extraction.

"I have a home," one woman, having overheard the discussion, yells in near-perfect English. "I have a home. Can I go home now?"

"Yes. Soon," President Phillipi says, turning to a woman whose broad smile captures his eyes even under these conditions. "These men here will help you get home."

"To my convent?" she asks.

"Your convent?" the President asks. "Are you a nun? Are you American?"

"I was getting ready to go to America, to be a nun," she replies.

"What's your name, señorita?" President Phillipi asks.

"Abril," she replies haltingly, doing her best to not let crying drown her voice. "My name . . . is Abril."

Suarez turns to the first woman, thinking she must be in her 40s or 50s, but suspecting she's much younger. Her nose and jaw appear to have been broken and badly reset. She stands in a hunch, shoulders forward with her back arching forward. Her skin is an almost ghost-like pale, crinkling along the forehead. Suarez asks her where she lives. Maria points to grated openings on the production floor.

"Below, she says," Suarez states. "Under the floor, aquí."

"Do you want your freedom?" Suarez asks Maria in Spanish.

Maria drops to her knees, begins wailing and kisses Suarez's boots.

It's only then that both Presidents see the bloody welts on her back. President Phillipi turns back to look at Abril as she is shuffled away to a corner with other women and girls. Even from the distance, he can see blood coating the bottom half of her loosely fit shirt.

President Phillipi's sorrow for the women quickly turns to rage. He drops his shield, turns and sprints through the tunnel, searching for cartel soldiers to kill. Suarez tries to join, only to be restrained by Maria's firm grasp. She won't let him go.

Ally and others assigned to protect the President pursue him, catching up just in time to join a hallway firefight with eight Protection Corps soldiers running for an escape tunnel.

The President is trapped inside a door jam, taking fire from down the hall. Intermittently, he reaches around the corner of the door jam to fire back. Ally calls for a New Rite missile bullet rifle, drops to the floor and shoots, hitting her first target four hundred feet away with such deadly force that two other Protection Guards go down behind him. She rolls across the hallway floor and locks in on a cartel soldier as he peeks around the corner. When she fires, the missile bullet locks onto its target, rounding the corner to follow him and explode away any thoughts.

Another Protection Corps soldier starts a suicide sprint down the corridor, firing aimlessly forward until President Phillipi drops to the ground and fires up at his chest as he passes.

The last two guards throw their weapons down. "No me shoot," both yell out. "No me shoot."

President Phillipi runs at the men with his weapon elevated and throws the first up against the wall, his adrenaline running higher than he can ever recall. By the time he has the first man shoved chest and face first into the wall, Ally and her team are at his side. Video recorders on their helmets record the President taking the two soldiers as prisoners; just as they earlier captured his first combat kill. Ally turns her head to look at the guard felled by the President, kicking away his weapons and tying his remaining arm to his opposite foot in hog-tie fashion, just in case.

President Suarez joins the group in a small side room and starts interrogating the men. As the prisoners share what little they know of the cartel's battle strategy, Ally opens a message.

Mexican, Egyptian, Iranian, Russian, Pakistani and Saudi jets that had been parked in Mexico just south of the U.S. border after the United Nations pullback are scrambling, some toward the cartel compound and some appearing to leave the country. The battle is moving back to the air.

"Back up," she yells at the team. "Incoming jets."

The group starts a full-speed sprint up the stairwell to evacuate, everyone doing their best to avoid twisting ankles traversing the concrete wall and ceiling chunks shattered across most of the floors. In places, the wall crumble is complete enough that the compound's thick steel beam structure is visible. Both Presidents keep up for the first few stories before slowing, creating a gap between the lead and trailing groups. As the separation grows, Ally and her team jump in front of the Presidents to provide protection, alternating between looking for threats in their path and turning back to ensure they remain closely in front of the Presidents. Thirty stories up—it seems much farther going up—President Phillipi stops, bends over the railing and hurls down the center of the spiral staircase, catching some of the soldiers behind with spray chunks.

typo Phillipi

We found out Ramon Mantel cohersed into help Cartel. His Software Engr. use his Software to contrle US Vehicles. Kooperated w/ US giving maps to Cartel to Stark. Breached compound. Attack. Found slave workers + sex slaves. met allys coworker Clint. Found out

name ? US Secry Def. Mendoza. Phillipi shot, medics on plane now; ? simultan cores attacks

"I can carry you for a while, Mr. President," Ally yells back as more than an offer. As she squats to throw the President over her shoulder, President Phillipi pushes back.

"I'm fine," he yells, pride re-triggering his adrenaline. "Let's go."

The group continues its ascent. Occasional fire from the sides and below is quickly suppressed.

With ten stories to go back to the APB, a thin wall sliver suddenly opens, with automatic weapon fire spraying the U.S. troops. Ally drops to the side, lifts her handgun into the corner of the hole and starts shooting through the slit. Seconds later, the attack stops.

When Ally turns back to lead her group forward, she sees President Phillipi down, a stream of blood dripping from his gut toward the stairwell.

"Medic," a dozen soldiers yell out simultaneously.

One of four medics assigned to stay within range of the Presidents sprints forward, inserts a clotting pack into the open wound, injects a pain-killing dose of morphine and starts questioning the President.

Through the shock, President Phillipi attempts to direct his treatment. "I can't . . . move . . . my legs," he says softly between hard bites on his bottom lip.

"Stretcher," a medic screams.

President Phillipi is raced up the stairs on a stretcher, two soldiers below hold the back end of the stretcher over their heads while two others hold low from the front to keep the President flat. Ally sprints ahead to get back to the APB and get it ready for quick ascent.

Once President Phillipi is on board and tied in, joined now only by medics and one sniper, Ally shoots her APB straight up two thousand feet and turns toward the ocean. Ally turns toward Camp Pendleton, racing to save the President's life.

"There's fifty units of the President's blood behind the medical kit," Ally calls back to the medics, none of whom were the medic on board her APB when it arrived.

Ally, one of the best evasion flyers in the world, turns on her APB camouflage skin and hopes it works if they encounter enemy jets. Too many evasive maneuvers would, at the very least, permanently paralyze President Phillipi. That may be the best-case scenario.

Ch. 7 - Ramon Mantel -goodguy. Software Engr. ~~knows~~ cooperative w/ Stark giving him Cartel Compound maps. Hdqts breached. Workers, Slaves rescued. Simultaneous attacks in 7 countries. Counter attack launched via air. Pres. Phillips shot. ~~was~~ New Meet - Abril-nun candidate - Sex slave, Clint - Allys co-troop. Meet - Maria sex slave

8 PROTECTION

Ramon gets to a safe cave.
water, food, rest

It's seems like hours before Ramon reaches the bottom of the saltwater pond under the tunnel. His oxygen-scavenging mask generates enough good air to keep him breathing, but the intense work of propelling through the escape tunnel and then swimming down what seems like hundreds of feet leaves him fighting fatigue, soreness and a foot cramp so intense he can't pulls his toes far enough forward to diminish its searing agony. *dehydrated*

He closes his eyes as he approaches the increasingly brilliant light at the bottom of the saltwater pool, only now realizing that it's a man-made light source. Fighting panic, Ramon's pulse surges. His heart dominates surrounding sound as much as a loudly banged bass drum would overtake a flute. He fears this dive leads him nowhere. Ramon fights to regain control of his emotion, knowing that his body needs more oxygen to fight every second of panic.

He stops in the water, floating without moving. Ramon thinks about his little sister jumping triple toe loops and flawlessly executing camel spins on ice. He thinks about the last time he ate dinner together with his whole family, looking over the ocean on the back patio of his Punta Mita vacation estate. Even then, his mind wanders to the cartel's soldiers who surrounded the dinner to make sure Ramon couldn't escape with his family.

Calmed by memories of his family, Ramon closes his eyes briefly as he swims the last meters down to look at the light. Looking around once at the light, he spots a series of reflective signs, invisible from above, but clearly meant to capture attention from here. Checking the gauge on his mask, he realizes he's running out of time. Still, he swims over and follows reflective signs through a tunnel, the brightness of the reflections dimming the further he swims. Soon no more signs are in sight, but there's also no more ceiling to the tunnel. After an initial upward burst, Ramon reminds himself that moving too fast will punish him with the bends, resulting in almost certain death with no medical support to be found. He slows his upward swim substantially, struggling to control intense panic, hoping he won't use the last oxygen while still underwater.

Squinting the last five meters as he sees another light above, Ramon explodes out of the water, grabbing at water's edge only to feel parts of it move away from his shriveled fingertips. He looks up to realize that the sun is piercing through a small hole in the cave ceiling, with no other opening in the dark, crumpled walls that are his new confines. Not sure what occupies this space normally, Ramon has no other option but to pull up onto land. Instantly, shivers send his body into a series of convulsions. He reaches down in vain endeavor to unfold an again-cramping foot.

As Ramon's eyes adjust, he sees a well-equipped, secure location, complete with a small noise-activated light, fresh clothing obviously sized for General Hernández, three cases of bottled water, three bottles of 40-year-old single malt scotch, a fishing pole, a knife and enough dehydrated food to hold Ramon for at least a month. He's not alone. Dozens of insects roam the surface and walls of the cave.

Despite continued cold, starting a fire is out of the question, certainly during the day. Throwing off his soaked clothing, Ramon puts on a dry set of clothes and battles his sheer exhaustion to do pushups and hop on one leg to warm his body.

Twenty minutes later, with his energy returning, Ramon listens intently. He hears waves. The cave can't be far from shore.

With time to contemplate next steps, Ramon decides that staying put is his best option. The U.S. military is destined to be searching miles around the cartel compound for surviving combatants. It's easier to find a person in motion than one holding still. Motion captures the human eye, as well as most mechanical eyes. Still, Ramon worries that heat-sensor or motion-sensor scanners might find him here. "Am I safe from discovery?" he questions, already talking to himself just to hear a voice.

Ramon's pleasures had always come from fast cars, well-built women and technology breakthroughs, though not necessarily in that order. Surviving outdoors had never been a desire. But he did know that the cartel's compound was built to avoid detection by U.S. technology. Heat-sensing technology had to have depth limits, and he had to hope that Hernández had considered those limits in selecting this cave. If he had, Ramon's greatest caution had to be avoiding triggering the noise-activated light at nighttime, when the unusual light source might be spotted through the tiny gap in the ceiling that let bits of sunlight in during the day.

Ramon guzzles a large bottle of water, downs a bag of dried food and starts blowing up the air mattress inside. Only minutes after covering himself in a blanket, Ramon falls into deep, exhausted sleep.

9

CONFUSION

Even among Professor Stark's prize pupils, Rachel Cruz and Tamika Jackson are standouts. Both women combine keen intellect, emotional maturity and a willingness to struggle past any hurdle to achieve their goals. A series of events in the past year brought them closer to Professor Stark than he typically allowed. For university professors, getting too close to attractive students of the professor's gender preference often triggers the collegiate bureaucracy rumor mill. Professor Stark had worked too hard for too long to allow his career to be undermined by inaccurate perceptions. But his relationships with Rachel and Tamika are too important to shunt aside just to quell rumors.

Fortunately, Rachel and Tamika are now as connected to Jill as they are to him. Besides, Rachel is engrossed in what appears to be a serious relationship with one-time secession spokesman Juan Gonzalez, enough so that Rachel frequently endures cradle-robbing jokes highlighting their three-year age difference.

With the latest war announcement, Professor Stark decides to skip public transportation and rents a car to drive home to Chicago—the old-fashioned kind he can manually control when he wants. Juan takes him up on his offer to join him for the drive to Chicago, undoubtedly attracted by the chance for an impromptu visit with Rachel.

Deciding that too many Americans will try to again escape urban areas in the midst of another potential war breakout, with a massive bottleneck already developing around Breezewood, Pennsylvania, Professor Stark re-routes through the mountains of Western Maryland. As they traverse the heavily forested, mountainous Cumberland Gap, a finally awakened Rachel responds to Juan's message that he's on his way.

"Professor Stark is driving me," Juan tells Rachel.

After a short pause, Professor Stark hears Juan's next comment.

"Yes, he's actually driving," Juan states.

Another pause.

"He said it's safe."

Another pause.

"Yes, I told him I'd feel better on auto-pilot."

"You know I can hear you, Juan," Professor Stark finally says, his patience with his driving skill being attacked nearly exhausted.

"Rachel wants to talk to you. I mean us," Juan says. "I'm putting her on speaker."

"Fine."

"Good morning, Rachel," Professor Stark says, turning his face toward Juan before realizing he needs to keep his eyes fixed on the road.

"Good morning, Professor. Well, morning anyway. Hey, do you know anything more about what's going on with these attacks than what's being reported?" Rachel asks, no longer bashful about pursuing the answer to any question that intrigues her.

Professor Stark sees a long upward mountain climb ahead and pushes his foot down hard on the gas pedal. "No, though I'm not sure I could say anything even if I did," he notes as Juan wraps both hands around the shoulder restraint when he briefly veers into the adjoining lane.

"Well," Rachel continues. "Then what do you think about this?"

"What do you both think is happening?" Professor Stark asks back, instinctively turning to the Socratic method that dominates his teaching style.

"I think it's horrible," Juan interjects, grabbing his Lifelink back with one hand while the other continues to strangle the seatbelt across his chest. "Some of my relatives are in Mexico."

"So are mine. Half of my Dad's side still lives there," Rachel adds.

The summit of the highway mountain climb reached and surpassed, it takes several seconds and a serious increase in downhill speed before Professor Stark eases his foot off the accelerator. Juan points at a series of S curves ahead. His skin turns a ghastly pale, fearing death in his first time riding in a car not being driven by computer. Professor Stark sees his panic, taps his brakes and rolls down Juan's window in case he needs to puke.

The burst of fresh air seems to help. "How can we go to war against our family and neighbors?" Juan asks as his skin returns to its naturally well-tanned tone. "This is exactly why I wanted peaceful separation—to avoid getting to a point where people die over our differences."

"Is this truly a declaration of war against Mexico or retribution against the cartel?" the Professor questions, as he holds his left arm out the window, cupping his hand to direct more air toward his face. Juan holds both hands in front of him on an invisible steering wheel in a vain attempt to get Professor Stark to focus on driving. Professor Stark smiles again.

"Well, from what I'm reading as we talk, it's against Mexico and all the other countries with troops still in Mexico," Rachel replies.

"I never wanted it to get to this point," Juan adds, leaning forward in his seat with hands folded in front of him and looking down at the floorboard to avoid seeing as Professor Stark weaves around several cars.

"This isn't about America having a problem with Mexico. Is it? It's about the cartel and terrorists stealing Mexico from its people. It's not like we won't give the country back to the people as soon as the terrorists are taken out, right?" Professor Stark half-states, half-asks.

"I don't know what to think, other than it just sucks. I'm so tired of this," Rachel remarks, directing her next comment to the Professor. "Sorry, I know you think that using that word is a cop-out."

Professor Stark slows down and moves to the center lane, away from the cliff ledges that alternate between being on the left and right of the highway. "You know, Rachel, as we've worked on this God's Law amendment, I've been struck by how important the Golden Rule is to making the right decisions in government as well as in our personal interactions."

"Do you ever just talk like a normal person?" Rachel asks, a question she never would have posed during her initial classes with Professor Stark.

"Is that a serious question or just an effort to dodge the one I propounded?" the Professor asks.

"It's serious. It was serious," Rachel replies. "Anyway, it's a lot easier to apply the Golden Rule when only one of us has to decide what's right and wrong, instead of needing to get a majority of Congress and the President and five Supreme Court justices to agree on a definition of right and wrong."

"Easier, yes, I'll agree with you on that," Professor Stark notes as a vehicle behind approaches rapidly. "But that's because the more people involved, the more important it is to gain common collective knowledge of the situation, to engage in more active imagination of what doing unto others as we would have done unto ourselves means and to trust each other to act with sincerity and integrity."

"You're talking about the concepts from those books you gave me," Juan comments, turning a mirror he sees as unusually placed in the top center of the windshield toward him to see how he looks.

"I need that to drive," Professor Stark points out to Juan before shifting the mirror back and turning back to the main conversation. "Recognize that the challenge is compounded from what Professor Gensler and others describe when you take the Golden Rule into government. I can't possibly know what President Phillipi knows that made him decide to go into war," Professor Stark suggests, looking toward Juan only to see Juan point his eyes back toward the road in front of them. "Maybe there was another attack coming. Maybe the terrorist risk is still real."

"I suppose," Juan replies, pointing to a car stopped on the side of the road ahead to be sure Professor Stark sees it.

Realizing that he's too focused on the conversation, Professor Stark sets the car into autopilot mode, verbalizing his home address as the car's destination. Once the autopilot is set, Juan releases the death grip on his shoulder harness.

"Maybe," Juan remarks, "the fact that the President is putting his own life at risk tells us there's something truly serious here. It scares me, though."

"It should scare you both," Professor Stark notes. "With this many countries involved, if we don't stop what we're trying to stop quickly, you're both in the draft-eligible age."

"Draft?" Rachel exclaims. "Seriously, when does life get to be normal again?"

Professor Gensler) p. 91
Ethics & The Golden Rule

10 DISTINCTION

President Phillipi's vital signs slip rapidly as Ally drops the APB down at Camp Pendleton. A massive medical team rushes the President immediately into surgery, with the White House surgeon—flown to Camp Pendleton as soon as the compound attack launched—overseeing a team of specialists gathered from the area and rushed by military choppers to the camp hospital.

Ally and others who returned early from the compound battle wait outside as the surgical team begins a spinal graft and the tedious process of reconnecting hundreds of severed nerves. The procedure has been in use for nearly a decade, but it's not clear whether the President's treatment began too late to restore full use of his lower body.

"Will he make it?" Ally asks the Camp's medical director, a woman who has been given the duty of maintaining constant communications with the White House on the President's condition.

"If you're asking will he live, I'd say the odds are better than decent," the medical director responds. "But I'll be surprised if they're able to restore all of his function."

MIKE BUSHMAN

"Well, living is a start," Ally responds, only now realizing she can remove her helmet and straighten her hair. "We'll just have to pray for the rest."

By the time surgery concludes six hours later, Ally has spoken with interim President Marcia Wilt, Defense Secretary Xavier Mendoza and Ally's direct boss, New Rite Founder JT Alton. She watches with amusement to see the mix of truth and fiction being reported through national media on the success of the cartel attack, as well as attacks on nations and terrorist groups believed to be directly involved in the cartel's latest strategy. Video of President's Phillipi's battle engagement is replayed every few minutes, carefully edited to exclude his multi-story vomit.

Just a week ago, America's Southwest was held under military control by a broad United Nations coalition. Most of the nations involved were lured into what turned into an invasion by intelligence that General Hernández provided and interpreted as proving that the U.S. military planned a genocidal attack on anti-federalist Hispanics in Texas, New Mexico, Arizona and California del Sur. These four states were believed to have voted the prior November to secede from the United States, votes only recently proven to have been computer manipulated in part by Ramon Mantle.

The U.N. invasion, sold as a peacekeeping mission, had been supported by then Mexican President Daniel Suarez to protect Mexico from what he had been convinced was a planned U.S. invasion. Battles in the Southwest were the first step in Hernandez's plans to make the cartel's Protection Corps the strongest military in the world.

Manipulating Cesar Castillo, the cartel's recently deceased founder, into expanding his ambition had been easy enough for Hernández. Since taking the Protection Corps job, General Hernández built the cartel's military capabilities through cooperative agreements with wealthy terror groups and national militaries from nearly two dozen nations intent on either distracting the U.S. military or destroying the Great Satan—as leaders in several nations call the United States routinely in private and, increasingly, in public.

Media reports suggest that military strikes in Iran, South Yemen, Egypt, Northern Sudan, Iraq, Afghanistan, Pakistan and Somalia have had their intended effect, though massive explosions are believed to have resulted from the attacks in Pakistan and South Yemen with deadly civilian consequences.

China and Russia issue formal objections to these raids as do several other nations. None intervene militarily, with many of the most powerful nations embarrassed at having been lured into participating in the U.N. invasion of America's Southwest on the basis of largely fabricated intelligence.

Ally dozes off in a chair, slinking her strong, medium-height, well-defined body into a blanket-covered ball that conceals her strength. Even in this state of rest, though, her eyes remain directed straight through the waiting lounge door to the surrounding austere, sanitized hallways.

It's been a long, complex, intense series of missions for Ally. She doesn't think she can fully rest until she knows whether the President has survived and her mission is accomplished, but exhaustion quickly sends her into deep, open-mouthed sleep.

"Ms. Steele," she later hears a voice call out.

"Yes, ma'am," Ally replies, jumping up as Camp Pendleton's medical director rapidly approaches.

"The President would like to see you," the director states.

"The President?" Ally asks, surprised that he's both out of surgery and alert after just a few minutes.

While Ally checks the time, the medical director spots her. "You've been out for a while. He's being re-sworn as we speak."

"And?" Ally asks with eyes widened and hands turned up.

"And the surgeons are optimistic," the medical director responds. "He better make it. The video of him, and you I might add, engaged in that battle is all over the media. There are already a half million people surrounding this base, waiting for news of his condition. He wants to see you before anyone makes any announcements."

Ally takes a deep breath as she stands. I hate crowds, she thinks to herself, partially comforted that at least she can leave up and over the mass of people.

Ally slows her pace as she nears the President's room, laboring to make sure her mind is fully engaged before entering. Twelve fully armed guards blocking the entrance to the hallway pull aside after being ordered by Secretary Mendoza to allow Ally to enter.

Vice President Wilt appears on screen in the President's recovery room, linked from the White House Deep Underground Command Center. She remained secure while Secretary Mendoza raced to Camp Pendleton on hearing of President Phillipi's wounding. Secretary Mendoza prepares himself to face the national media and the million Americans surrounding the base. They don't have time to establish a sound system that can reach that many people, so Mendoza is relying on most participants having their Lifelink multi-function devices with them to listen in to the broadcast.

President Phillipi pushes out a weak smile as Ally enters the room. He invites her to come closer. Ally instinctively reaches out and holds his hand, before looking to the White House surgeon to make sure her move is okay. The doctor nods.

"I just wanted to thank you personally, for what you've done for America above all, but also for what you've done to protect me," President Phillipi says in intermittent spurts, a bit of color returning to his face from when Ally last saw him.

Ally finds herself choking up for one of few times in her life. She's startled by her reaction.

"Service to my nation and justice is all I've ever sought," Ally replies, speaking slowly and softly to be sure her words reflect more than just the emotion of the moment. "I can think of no greater honor than serving with a commander-in-chief willing to risk his life beside his troops."

"The honor is mine. May I call you Ally?" the President asks.

"You may call me whatever and whenever you want," Ally replies, tensing her face in a futile effort to prevent tears from noticeably extruding. Wanting to stop further exertion, the surgeon steps between Ally and the President, encouraging Ally and the others to leave the room to allow the President to rest.

Minutes later, Secretary Mendoza takes to the makeshift stage built to handle the media hordes streaming into Camp Pendleton while ensuring he can be seen by as many of those surrounding the base as possible. Ten New Rite-designed APBs hover about the compound with expert marksmen armed with the latest missile-bullet rifles on board surveying the crowd. Every detection device known to the U.S. military is in use, searching for potential attackers. Fifty of New Rite's Cooper's hawk drones fly above the crowd and around the base perimeter, scanning for unusual movement. Secretary Mendoza takes the stage.

"The President of the United States . . . of America . . . is alive," Secretary Mendoza says to an extraordinary cheer that takes several minutes to subside. "Surgeons believe the President . . . will make a substantial recovery."

With that, Secretary Mendoza walks off the stage.

Hastily assembled components of the U.S. Marine Corps Band play "Hail to the Chief."

11 RENOVATION

For <u>Abril</u>, the trip through a multitude of partial tunnels and up a series of half-destroyed stairwells creates a <u>nearly debilitating array of</u> <u>emotions</u>. Days spent <u>waiting underground</u> while American troops secured the entire compound and industrial park had been traumatic. To be close to freedom, without actually being free, frightened her. How devastating would it be to have salvation in sight and not be able to get there? Can she really trust that these men and women won't use her or torture her, just in a new place?

It's not until the soldiers leading her group open a door at surface level and a flash of sunlight penetrates the stairwell that Abril senses she might finally go home. Hundreds of other women, some seeing the sun for the first time in years, join Abril in a collective breakdown. Hugging. Kissing the rubble-strewn ground. A few others also kneel in prayer. Some collapse thinking again of parents and brothers or husbands and children slaughtered as they were taken. Struggling to follow directions, <u>Abril</u> loses herself in rumination. <u>Despair</u> at having her life destroyed. <u>Fear</u> at needing new work. <u>Anger</u> at her attackers. <u>Embarrassment</u> at who she has become. All of this <u>pain is</u> tempered only marginally by excitement at feeling warmth from the sun and relief that this horrible phase of life may actually be over.

When the time comes to board buses to take them wherever they want to go, Abril can't bear the thought of returning to the convent. She also doesn't want her parents to know what happened to her. She needs to heal physically and emotionally or they'll be devastated.

"Puerto Vallarta, por favor," she says when she finally decides which direction to head. Asked if she knows an address, all Abril can muster is "Tía Juanita."

Home in Chicago didn't provide much respite, particularly in the immediate days after the cartel compound attack as Professor Stark awaited news that Members of Congress would be released from confined seclusion.

He's tired of interesting days, having had far too many in his life already. But today, as he returns to D.C. for the first time since the compound attack, promises to be another challenge for Paul Stark. Though he is one of the nation's most highly regarded university professors, Professor Stark doesn't look the part most days, alternating between flannel shirts and jeans in cold weather and t-shirts and hiking shorts in warm weather on any day he's not in the national media spotlight.

Professor Stark pulls down a grey and black t-shirt, stopping only after realizing the neck opening is scraping shaving cream. At the mirror, he notes he forgot to actually shave the left side of his face again, having lost concentration on that mundane task while considering what to share with the President.

"Damn it," Professor Stark says after finishing his shave. He looks at his t-shirt and realizes he also scraped white deodorant on the outside as he pulled it down. He's done this enough times that he knows the deodorant won't wipe away cleanly. He goes to a backup, emblazoned with the white oak logo of singer-songwriter Tree. The t-shirt is more than twenty years old, battle-worn and long overdue for wastebasket residency, as Jill regularly reminds him.

Professor Stark carefully backs out, exhilaration and trepidation heightening his focus. For most of the past decade, government-mandated and Ramon-created automation software controlled almost every vehicle movement. On rare occasions to feel some measure of freedom, Professor Stark paid exorbitant fees and taxes to rent an antique convertible, keeping his driving skills fresher than for most.

Congress loosened these automated control restrictions after the nation learned that Ramon's company enabled the secession attempt by shutting down all non-invasion traffic in the four secession states.

It's not clear how many Americans want to drive their own cars, but Professor Stark certainly is not going to pass up the opportunity to drive when and where he wants. He became one of the first to purchase an optional-drive convertible—a car that lets him drive with the top down and also lets him choose between software-managed and manual driving.

The return to manual driving control, with national system vehicle tracking disabled to boot, will test states and municipalities. During the past decade, most government units disabled their highway and street traffic police forces, only rarely needing to handle speeding and vehicle accident issues.

Automation software prevented speeding—at least with the exception of cartel drivers—and contained automated safety control devices that nearly eliminated vehicle deaths. Ramon's software identifies where all the vehicles are on every road, adjusting safety distances between vehicles depending on braking conditions. Visibility no longer matters. Automation software ensures controlled cars can move rapidly even in heavy fog without increased risk of accidents. Wet and icy roads, however, add to the braking distance needed between vehicles. The automation system automatically adds to the safety cushion between vehicles when wheel sensors detect such conditions.

With all the benefits of government-mandated automation software—increased safety, reductions in traffic police, improved fuel efficiency by optimizing miles driven and fuel use per mile, and reduced road construction requirements as the optimization software allows more vehicles to safely travel on existing roads and highways—

amending these requirements didn't end up being the slam dunk sponsors had expected after the secession effort was repelled.

Everyone knows the horror stories of families stuck in Texas, New Mexico, Arizona and California del Sur. When the invasion launched, Ramon's Perfect Logistics Company—with hidden Castillo cartel ownership—shut down the software systems in all four states to give U.N. troops unfettered ability to control the streets. For hundreds of families, the inability to escape by vehicle back to U.S. controlled territory was fatal. Texan Bob Lee was killed first when cartel thugs came to kidnap his wife Charlotte to punish her for her anti-secession proselytizing during the prior November's secession referenda votes. Charlotte's slaughter was one of hundreds of gruesome punishments inflicted at the direction of General Hernández. Once Charlotte's mangled remains and those of dozens of others were visually captured and disseminated nationally, support for the Southwest secession to create the Republic of Alta Texas dipped sharply.

Professor Stark saw those pictures and knows he doesn't ever want to lack escape alternatives if a government entity turns against him. He was first in line in Chicago to buy the newly approved versions of automation-to-manual convertibles.

As he prepares to back out of his garage, he puts the top down. It might seem a bit chilly to drive with the top down, but he can't wait to feel the burst of fresh air against his face.

His anxiety fully displays on his face as he reaches city traffic. Since most other vehicles on the highway are still automation controlled, his merge space leaves little room for error. It's not long before Professor Stark realizes that, even though he is in physical control of the car, he is highly restricted in his ability to speed up or slow down by the vehicles in front, to his side and behind him.

Drivers, or at least the people being transported in surrounding vehicles, look at him in horror. The man in the car in front of his convertible swivels his seat around, taking a break from consuming what Professor Stark can only assume is something coated in maple syrup. The woman in the car on his right takes a break from pumping and pedaling away at the exercise system add-on in her vehicle to glare at him. Behind, another driver looks over the top of his communications device with an expression of clear concern that his life could be imperiled by the vagaries of human driving. Clearly, Professor Stark's driving with the top down, and actually driving, is a fear-generating distraction to everyone traveling around him.

Realizing he can't truly drive in this much traffic even without the distraction of passengers, Professor Stark reaches over, pushes on the automation system, and leans back as the software takes control over the vehicle's direction. At least the sun is out, so he might even capture a bit of Vitamin D before he reaches the airport. He closes his eyes, reclines back and feels the sun beating into his pores, warming his face and hands. The wind captures the front of his hair and keeps it pressed backward, ensuring his forehead remains fully exposed to evenly distribute whatever tan he can gather. Cool gusts of air circle around quickly enough that, despite the beating sun, he never warms enough to sweat. Still, it's glorious to know he at least has the option to drive free.

Just two weeks after surgery, President Phillipi returns to the White House to complete his recuperation. Nerve regeneration begins taking hold and the President's therapist pushes him to aggressively work his leg muscles while upright. Held up by a harness, the President spends sixty minutes three times a day regaining control of his legs, holding parallel bars tightly as he slowly, painfully propels each foot forward. With his popularity at a nearly inconceivable high for modern-era Presidents, Phillipi realizes he needs to move quickly to push his legislative agenda and reform government policy if he wants to create a stronger governing platform for America's next hundred years.

Between physical therapy sessions, the President sets up preparation sessions on his top agenda item, passage of the "God's Law" constitutional amendment and attached legislation to enact its intent. Congressional leaders have set another joint session exactly one month after the State of the Union to allow the President to push agenda items lost in news about the retaliatory attacks and the President's recovery.

During his State of the Union address the night before the cartel compound raid, the President previewed his second term focus: "I hope everyone now sees that protecting our liberties is government's paramount obligation. But it's not enough. We must also repair the foundation of our nation, the laws upon which we are governed. We have a legal code so riddled with loopholes, subsidies, evasions and uncertainties that we, the people, have lost faith in the decency and integrity of government. Too many run businesses and programs in legal terms, asking questions such as: Is it legal? If not, am I likely to get away with it? Instead, we need to ask these questions: Is it ethical? Am I acting with integrity? Is it fair? Would I be okay if someone did this to me?

"In simpler terms, we must be a nation where we do unto others as we would have done unto us," the President continued, without showing any sign of distraction at the idea of leaving straight from the speech to join the front lines of the cartel attack. "Some of you may see this as mixing religion and government. I see it as creating an environment in which this government succeeds for its people, not at the expense of its people. So, in the coming months, I will turn this concept into a sweeping reform of our laws I will refer to as God's Law."

Although the American Civil Liberties Union and a number of atheist and extreme liberal organizations began orchestrating an attack on the "God's Law" concept simply based on its naming, most commentators in the initial hours after the President's State of the Union took a "wait-and-see" attitude in their immediate post-speech wrap-ups. Little did they know that the President would follow his success in breaking apart the United Nations coalition invasion in the Southwest with personally participating in an attack on the cartel and its remaining coalition.

The President knows that pressure to attack the God's Law concept will grow with each passing day. He needs to get out front and clarify its meaning before opponents mischaracterize its intent.

Professor Stark is a regular White House visitor during this time. Concepts developed by Professor Stark and one of his classes provided the inspiration for the God's Law concept. Jill Carlson, the congresswoman from Indiana who shares the President's independence from any political party, also takes part in many of these preparation sessions. The relationship between Jill and Professor Stark occasionally makes debate sessions entertaining for reasons beyond the President's intellectual enlightenment.

During one of several preparation sessions held in the Oval Office, after Professor Stark contests a point Jill made about required clarity needed to separate church and state, Jill turns to him and threatens, "Are you sleeping on the couch or the recliner tonight, Paul?" Startled she would make that comment in front of the President, Professor Stark contemplates meekly acquiescing to her threat. Instead, he decides to up the ante. "By the time you've finished eating what I've planned for dinner and I've finished massaging your feet, I'm pretty sure that both of those options will be forgotten," he blusters.

Jill blushes fully and President Phillipi decides to interject: "You two realize you are in the Oval Office, and that I'm here with you, right?"

They glance at each other with sheepish smiles and apologize to the President for the inappropriate comments.

"Actually, don't apologize. It's refreshing to see actual passion. Everything I see in life is sanitized before it reaches my desk," the President admits, a clear sadness in his tone as he pats the top of his desk.

"Still," Jill acknowledges, "we owe you our best advice and thoughts, so I hope you don't mind that we argue."

"I certainly don't mind," President Phillipi responds, surprising everyone in the room by slowly standing up from behind his simple, wooden desk and walking around to rest his backside on its front with only the aid of a cane. "My commitment to the American people is that I'll allow facts to interfere with my opinion, even if those facts suggest I screwed up."

"You realize that you have much more leeway than most presidents after the leadership you've shown and the sacrifices you've made," Professor Stark suggests.

"Perhaps. Perhaps. But I can't let myself think that way. We've stopped a small group of evil people, but the ideas behind them will linger if we can't find a better way to live together," the President replies as he lifts up to walk toward a closet door, steps in and returns with a beer. "Anything for either of you?" he asks before straining back to his seat. Everyone declines, recognizing he has no other hands available.

The President uncaps his beer and takes a couple of quick swigs, an old habit returning with increased regularity since he stopped taking post-surgical pain killers. "What we're going to try to do here is create a more thoughtful, considerate way of governing so America is again seen as a nation to emulate, rather than one so many want to decimate."

By the time the post-attack joint session occurs, the President still struggles to walk more than a few steps at a time without help. He needs to be pushed to the floor of the House of Representatives by wheelchair, but enters from behind and to the side of the Speaker's podium to avoid public visual evidence of his struggle. Railings are set up along the short path he will walk. The President refuses to be seen publicly being pushed in the wheelchair or aided by a cane.

As the door opens, he receives a standing ovation from members of Congress and other high-level government officials gathered for the speech. He grabs the parallel bars on both sides of the path and slowly, methodically makes his way to the stairs up to the podium, cameras adhering to strict direction to only show him from shoulders up. As he ascends the stairs, he turns his head away from the audience to hide each grimace. Using stairs is still more painful than walking on a flat path. He stops at the first plateau of steps, turns to the audience and raises his right hand to wave to the crowd, which only elevates the level of applause and cheers coming from those gathered. As they cheer, he grabs the back bar with his hand and ascends to the top of the podium, where an elevated seat allows him to speak from normal height without needing to stand.

Once in place, the President claps back, waves at his wife and family and points at several specific people in the audience, including Jill in her congressional seat and Professor Stark up in the gallery.

"During the past months, we have secured several important victories for these . . . United . . . States of America. We have been able to stop a Castillo-cartel-led and United-Nations-backed invasion into our territory with loss of life limited to the thousands, losses I point out that are still painful and shocking to the friends and families of those affected. We have also exacted retribution against the cartel and other terror-sponsoring nations who used a United Nations desire to prevent a fabricated concept of genocide against our Latino and Latina citizens as cover for a full-scale invasion and attempted takeover of all of the military bases in our Southwest. I don't need to rehash the issues here, but I do need to take this moment to tell you why we attacked the cartel to thoroughly destroy its military capabilities," the President says, leaning further in toward the cameras as he goes.

"In the days leading up to the State of the Union, cartel General Raul Hernández informed me that he had planted nuclear bombs in Los Angeles, Dallas, Houston, Phoenix, San Diego and the hometown in Mexico of since-restored Mexican President Daniel Suarez. With the aid of a private entity, the U.S. military found these nuclear bombs and disarmed them just hours before the attack in which I participated. I could not, in good conscience, watch these attacks from afar when I did not know as we began whether we would succeed in disarming the nuclear weapons. It is with God's grace that we succeeded. Our attacks on targets in seven other countries were aimed at capturing or destroying other potential sources of enriched uranium used by the cartel in creating nuclear weapons."

Many members of Congress and the entire audience who had been unaware of the nuclear threat display stunned reactions. Professor Stark sits with his mouth open, looking down at Jill. Jill also had not been fully briefed on the nuclear threat and held her hands in Christian prayer fold over the front of her lips, a behavioral vestige of her youth.

"Though this is now our past, it does provide us with cause to be vigilant in the pursuit of our national defense. Yes, other nations may threaten our survival. Yes, avowed terrorists clearly threaten our survival. Yes, others who harbor ill will toward the United States are threats to our survival. But I believe the biggest threat to our survival is still from within. We must not allow ourselves to again be divided by politicians and others in the pursuit of power and self-interest," the President says, adjusting his seated position as he feels discomfort growing around his surgically repaired spine. Recognizing a line they had better be seen as applauding, everyone in the chamber stands to deliver an extended ovation. Very few even consider that the President's admonishment might be directed toward them.

"I ask again, how do we create a better America, one that shines as a beacon of democracy, capitalism and opportunity in which we truly ensure that our citizens have the potential to achieve their greatest capability? Government has become so intrusive and so overwrought in our rules, regulations and bureaucracies that we have stopped becoming a nation of decency and fairness, and turned instead into a nation of cronyism and segregation."

The House Speaker and Senate Majority Leader, seated behind the President, race to be out of their chair first to lead applause. Democrats, Republicans and independents compete to see who can cheer the loudest, doing their best to make it seem as if they agree more with a leader whose popularity is at levels that usually only follow death.

The President halts, grabbing both sides of the physical podium that hides view of his elevated seat, and leans forward. "The concept of God's Law as a constitutional amendment is simple. The amendment I propose reads simply: 'Congress and the states shall not make and agencies of government shall not administer laws that fail to conform with the principle that we must do unto others as we would have done unto ourselves, given acquired knowledge of the circumstances and ultimate effects of our actions.' I call this God's Law because the Golden Rule concept provides at least a partial foundation to every major religion in world history, though you could just as easily refer to it as natural law. From Confucianism to Buddhism, Christianity, Judaism, Hinduism and Islam, this concept has been consistently advocated even if not consistently followed by those who have administered the world's faiths over the millennia. Yet the concept does not require a religion to make sense. It is the foundation of a peaceful society for atheists and agnostics. It is unquestionably the foundational principle of human decency."

Jill looks up from her seat on the House floor and finds Professor Stark. It isn't long before he feels her eyes on him and looks down at her, sharing a knowing, content smile before they both turn their eyes back to the President.

President Phillipi details his God's Law plan over the next thirty minutes, spelling out a system of justice based on the real Golden Rule, a dramatic shift from the long-followed perspective of many people and governments that, "he who owns the gold, rules."

in which Ramon escapes his cave hide-out

12 PREPARATION

Ramon slowly, methodically scrapes a shoreline map into a portion of the cave wall, using an extraordinary visual working memory to illustrate a path taking him one hundred miles away from his existing spot. Using the sharpest point of a rock found inside the cave, he scrapes slowly and quietly against the ancient volcanic wall during daytime, marking X's in spots along the shore where small villages and fishing homes should be located. He moves slowly and quietly to minimize his noise, just in case a shore patrol is nearby. At high tide, Ramon feels free to be less cautious, given the staggering noise of waves crashing against a not-too-distant shore. But at low tide, Ramon is careful to avoid generating sound.

If U.S. scanner drones continue disciplined, patterned survey of the terrain, eluding capture will challenge Ramon. Unwilling to rely on luck, Ramon crafts the most secure escape route possible given his knowledge of the coastline. He needs to leave while he still has enough food and water to stay hydrated and fed through several days of contact-avoidance hiking before he has any chance of blending into surroundings without being captured by U.S. or Mexican troops.

For once, Ramon is grateful for General Hernández's extraordinary preparation, precision and diligence. For nearly a decade, those attributes made it impossible for Ramon to escape cartel control. It's ironic, he considers, that these same attributes applied to creating this escape cave may be just what allows him to start life anew. But even the general underestimated the length of time this cave would need to serve as sanctuary. Ramon's mental stability is eroding with each passing hour of solitary self-imprisonment in the near-shore cave. Perhaps worst of all, the noise-activated light in his temporary dwelling is beginning to lose its strength.

In an effort to keep his mind sharp, Ramon presses his ear for several minutes every waking hour toward the bottle-cap-sized opening near a top corner of the cave, listening to the sound of the waves. After estimating the height of the waves from his aural assessment, Ramon measures the depth of the pool below him to establish a correlation. Unsure whether this exercise will ultimately produce any valuable insights, Ramon continues the effort nonetheless, just to occupy his mind.

Ramon's clothes are tattered, bloodied and now oversized as he is only cautiously consuming food left in the cave, though still not as oversized as the clothes that had been stored in the cave. Still, his silk shirt, tailored pants and expensive leather shoes—at least what remains of them—would stand out if Ramon were to walk in a crowd. To avoid this in case his escape path encounters an unforeseen populace, Ramon rubs his clothes between rocks to wear the fabric down and give them an impoverished, repeated hand-me-down appearance. The rubbing, combined with bloody stains and holes he can't remove, should discourage most people from approaching a man clearly strained by intense poverty.

Ramon has less than a week's worth of water and food left. He can't wait until he runs out to make his escape down the coast. The shoreline will likely be empty for at least twenty miles and there's no telling how long it will be until it is safe for him to be spotted by another person. Ramon's newly grown, but heavily matted beard and mustache should obscure his otherwise youthful appearance.

DOING UNTO OTHERS

It's time for Ramon's final preparation dive. He can now hold his breath swimming up to more than two minutes. When the pool beneath him runs low, he believes he has his best chance of swimming underground to the outside shore. Weeks earlier, he found an underwater path that went the opposite direction of the path from the tunnel. He swam as far as he could before shortness of breath caused him to spin around and head back to his cave. Since that day, he has been working on improving his strength to propel him through the second underwater path, as well as on breath and anxiety control to allow him to survive it. Efforts to find a replacement power source for the oxygen generation mask, something he assumed the general would have thought to keep here, have turned up empty.

Before Ramon swims through this path with his clothes and the remaining water and food attached behind him in the blanket left with supplies in the cave, he wants to prove to himself that he can physically make it. At some points, the path to the shore may be too narrow to allow Ramon to turn with his food and water.

Ramon sits on the edge of the pool to finish undressing and tie flippers and paddles he had fashioned from plastic strips cut from the water bottles to his hands and feet. Ramon tested the flippers and paddles and found they let him go roughly thirteen percent faster than swimming without them.

Taking a deep breath, Ramon dives straight down into the pool. Very quickly Ramon is at the entrance to what he hopes is an exit tunnel, feels the perimeter of the entrance with an elbow to make sure he's going the right direction, then propels himself forward.

Counting in his head, Ramon reaches thirty seconds just after entering the path.

The width of the path is good enough to swim with his arms nearly fully extended to the side and to kick with his feet.

Forty-five seconds.

The light brightens ahead. He must be getting close.

Sixty.

Ramon's right hand paddle hits a wall. This is already farther than Ramon has made it in his prior attempts. It's the point of no return.

He can hold his breath for two minutes. He pulls both arms in, kicking now serving as his only propulsion.

Seventy-five seconds.

The light is strengthening ahead. He thinks he can see it. Finally, a spot to ascend. He pushes off the ground with his feet, moving upward swiftly. He can't push his head up through the rocks. The openings aren't big enough.

Ninety.

Not here. Not like this.

Ramon pushes back down. When his feet hit bottom below, he pushes off, hoping he is still going away from the cave.

One hundred and ten. Just ten seconds left, Ramon realizes.

He struggles to keep his adrenaline from usurping the last of his oxygen, fighting a mental battle nearly as challenging as his physical contest. Two minutes. It's too late to pray. Ramon sees another splash of light above, and kicks up, he hits his head on a rock, not being able to get his body through the small hole. He flips his head backward and his nose sticks just above the water line.

One hundred and thirty five seconds.

He pulls his body flat enough to get his mouth and nose above water, gasping loudly and furiously trying to refill his lungs with air. Any concern about going undiscovered is long since past. His flippers and paddles are broken. He can't swim back. He can't imagine making it back here with his gear.

Naked save for silk boxer shorts, exhausted and frightened, Ramon holds the boulders above, contemplating his next steps. Finally, he realizes he can stand with his head held backward and continue to breathe. His eyes struggle to adapt to the intense bright light. He can't keep them open for more than the time of a blink without feeling blinded by a thousand flashes. His eyes had grown accustomed to the intense darkness of the cave, with the noise-triggered lighting inside the cave for minutes at a time and truly bright light entering through the top of the cave for only minutes each day.

Ramon feels the coolness of the water, but that coolness is not much different than the temperature inside the cave. Pushing at the rocks to try to get easier access to oxygen, he feels one move. It's too light to be a boulder. Ramon is able to move it easily. He blinks his eyes open to see where he is and realizes he is indeed along the Gulf of California shore. He'll have to stay here until dark.

By the time darkness comes, Ramon's eyes begin to recover. Still as night falls, he sees as well as others might during daytime. He pushes the unusually light, seemingly near hollow boulders aside and pulls himself from the water. Shivering, shriveled and exhausted, he sits amidst a pile of boulders gathering his thoughts. He can't make it back to food and water through the underwater path. Perhaps from above, from the bottlecap-sized light hole above the cave. Could he open it from above? If he does, Ramon realizes, satellite algorithms will soon discover a change in the earth formation and send a search party to figure out what happened. They'll realize a survivor has been holed up here, trace the tunnel back to the cartel compound and start a massive manhunt.

He has to go on. Nearly naked. No food. No water. He can make it moving at night without water for a few days, as long as he can find cover to keep from having his hydration sapped by the sun. Ramon's search starts with the basics: water, food, clothing, shelter.

With the moon providing substantial light, Ramon stands on the shoreline and faces the water. He turns left and starts climbing rocks down the shoreline until he reaches a flat path of sand. Walking as quickly as he can, Ramon scans his surroundings for signs of humans. Anyone who may have roamed here in the past scrambled away when the Battle of the Castillo Compound launched. Looking north, he spots the industrial park's nuclear power plant steam stack miles off in the distance.

The shoreline is desolate. Ramon is not yet hungry or thirsty. But he is cold, nearly to the point of numbness. He holds his hands in front as he pisses on them, urine running down onto his feet to provide temporary warmth. Quickly, he wipes the moisture off his body with sand, before the dampness attracts more cold.

An hour or so into his hike, Ramon hears the first artificial noises he had no hand in creating in more than a month. A boat patrols the shoreline, perhaps five hundred yards west of the shore. Ramon drops to the ground and rolls on the rock- and shell-infused sand until he reaches the water line. He rolls into the water, with only the top of his face jutting out above the shoreline.

Every four seconds, a wave covers Ramon. He holds his breath until it recedes, then gasps, listens and holds again.

13   OPPOSITION

Dark hair plugs embedded in rows atop House Judiciary Committee Chairman Will Henry's head belie him as twenty years younger than his actual age, particularly when those plugs combine with biweekly colorings of clinging natural hair around the sides and back of his head. An expanding paunch, sagging jowls and multi-layered neck contrast sharply with the Chairman's more youthful, artificial hairline.

It's not, however, appearance, charm or charisma that attracts Washington swarms to his door. It's power. Power held. Power perceived. Power exercised—bluntly, clearly and even, at times, maliciously.

After more than thirty years representing a largely rural Tennessee district, Chairman Henry is among the House's longest-serving members, and certainly among its most powerful and feared denizens. Over decades, he has proven adroit at maneuvering through even the most densely packed of political minefields.

Few expected the Chairman to survive the first elections after the Political Freedom Amendment became Constitutional Amendment Twenty Nine. In fact, he was thought by many to be a specific target of the reforms. As Professor Stark led the Political Freedom drive, he used Chairman Henry to exemplify the problems created when corrupt behaviors were legally endorsed and protected by the nation's political system. Professor Stark had not been alone in expressing both contempt for Chairman Henry's practices and admiration at his skill in using them to his advantage. To many long-time Capitol observers, Chairman Henry's political career epitomized all that had deteriorated in American politics over several generations. It's unsurprising, then, that Chairman Henry resents both the political reforms that prevent him from accumulating an intimidating war chest well in advance of filing deadlines and the man most responsible for securing these new Constitutional restrictions.

With Professor Stark back before his committee, supporting the addition of another amendment to the Constitution, Chairman Henry now has another opportunity to destroy a man he considers both arrogant and egg-headed.

"This proposed constitutional amendment is like trying to teach a dog how to meow," Chairman Henry states as he opens his committee's hearing on the proposal to embed the Golden Rule as an amendment to the U.S. Constitution. "You may find a dog somewhere in the universe that can bark out something one might claim to be the equivalent sound of a meow, just as you might find a government somewhere in the world that accidentally produces policies that fit some fool's interpretation of the Golden Rule, but neither of these events can be consistently replicated. The Golden Rule is something that applies to personal behavior, not to government policy and even individuals find it impossible to follow. It's foolish to think our massive government can do what a single individual cannot."

Every seat in the Judiciary Committee's Rayburn hearing room is filled with legislative staff, lobbyists and a few tourists anxious enough to get in that they began lining up at 4 a.m. Dozens of late-arriving staff tightly pack against the back walls. The only empty seats in the room are on the dais, the seats of committee members roaming in and out of the hearing as their turns to speak and question come and go.

"I'm a firm believer that Ralph Waldo Emerson was right when he wrote that 'consistency is the hobgoblin of small minds,'" the

Chairman continues. "Our duty as legislators is to understand the various circumstances that should be considered as we pass each policy measure and then write legislation that takes into account these different circumstances in a way that people unexposed to conflicting concepts might not be able to understand or meld. People may be able to apply the Golden Rule to their own behavior," he adds, "but governments have to be nimble and flexible enough to adjust the rules we impose to various circumstances. That is our role as representatives of the people. I will not cede our interpretations to review of the unelected judiciary. This proposed constitutional amendment, in my view, shifts the balance of power inside our government in a manner inconsistent with the effective governance of our democracy."

"Having made my views clear, I would like to welcome the experts testifying on this panel today, as well as our first guest, University of Chicago Professor Paul Stark," Chairman Henry continues. Long-time followers of the Judiciary Committee know that Chairman Henry intentionally did not describe Professor Stark as an expert, continuing a personal feud dating back more than a decade. After Stark subtly ridiculed Henry at a hearing last year, the Chairman made it known that he would never allow Professor Stark in his hearing room again. Only the intercession of Stark's girlfriend and Judiciary Committee member Jill Carlson forced Chairman Henry to break that vow. Even that intercession required Jill to secure tripartisan signatures from two-thirds of committee members on a private letter demanding that Professor Stark be allowed to testify given the importance of the subject and his ties to the President's initiative.

"Thank you, Mr. Chairman," Professor Stark says as he straightens his tie and sits straight to begin, seeking and gaining permission to have his written testimony entered into the record so he can counter some of the misdirection pursued by Chairman Henry.

"I would agree with those who suggest that 'foolish consistency is the hobgoblin of little minds,' as the quote from Emerson reads in full, because the Golden Rule does not suggest enabling foolishness," Professor Stark begins. "It is, however, about discouraging hypocrisy and encouraging consistency, a consistency that has for too long been absent from the laws imposed by Congress, enforced by the Executive Branch and adjudicated by the courts. I applaud President Phillipi and others working to embed the Golden Rule into our constitutional processes, since treating people equally and fairly without regard to race, gender, religion, sexual orientation or type of employment is fundamental to both natural law and an underlying, but oft-ignored precept of all of the world's major religions."

Typically, those testifying in congressional committees are given five minutes of uninterrupted time to make opening remarks, but Chairman Henry can't restrain himself. Chairman Henry doesn't like listening to Professor Stark's policy views on a normal day, but when Professor Stark begins his remarks by correcting the Chairman's use of the Emerson quote, he sets off the long-simmering, powder-keg-shaped lawmaker. Chairman Henry's anger is quickly apparent as his face reddens and his plugged hair flips away from its normal part.

"I'd like to remind the Professor that the Chair will not tolerate insults directed at himself or other members of this committee," Chairman Henry states loudly between gavel bangs.

A bit taken aback that Chairman Henry launched an attack so quickly, Professor Stark acts nonplussed by the interruption. "I have the greatest of respect and admiration for members of this committee," Professor Stark says, "and would never want my comments to be interpreted as insulting these members."

Soft, but audible snickers are heard from the audience. Several committee members drop their heads down or turn away from the hearing cameras to prevent their reactions from being seen. Jill bites hard on her lip. Her eyebrows elevate instinctively as she crosses her hands in front of her. She had begged Paul to be nice to the Chairman and knows this was his way of being as polite as he can be while being honest if incomplete in his statements.

"We certainly appreciate this," Chairman Henry replies, not considering that Professor Stark's reference to members of the committee could have been meant to exclude the Chairman in much the same way as the Chairman had purposely excluded Professor Stark in his reference to experts.

"Thank you, Mr. Chairman. I understand that President Phillipi has chosen to refer to the Golden Rule as God's Law because its concepts are embedded consistently in all of the world's major faiths. The President could have just as easily have referred to this concept as Natural Law or Man's Law, because the concept of treating others as we would want to be treated in similar circumstances is well-accepted as the cornerstone of a healthy society even if not well-practiced," Professor Stark continues. "I'd like to address a couple of the most important objections to the proposed constitutional amendment. First, a strong concern has been expressed by several members that the idea of treating others as one would want to be treated under similar circumstances is a religious concept and, therefore, runs contrary to the church-state separation that is part of our national foundation."

Of the several members who raised this issue in their opening statement, two still remain at the hearing and turn to listen.

"I don't believe the church-state issue to be a problem for two reasons," Professor Stark continues. "First, the Bill of Rights references to freedom of religion are intended to ensure that the federal government neither imposes a national religion nor supports one faith to the advantage of another. It is not intended to prevent common moral concepts from being used to govern the nation. As I said earlier, the underlying concepts of the Golden Rule are embedded in Christianity, Islam, Hinduism, Judaism, Buddhism, Christian Science, Confucianism, Taoism, Zoroastrianism, Sikhism, Unitarianism and the Baha'i Faith, along with most of our land's native spiritualties. Equally important, it is a sensible, practical concept accepted by most secular humanists, including most atheists and agnostics. It is not simply a concept of faith, but is most certainly a common concept of human morality."

One member who had raised the church-state separation issue shakes his head rapidly while sternly looking down to take notes.

Professor Stark ignores the reaction: "More than anything, the Golden Rule promotes consistency, a concept that clearly aligns with our nation's belief that all are created equal. Embedding the Golden Rule in our Constitution would ensure, for example, that the Congress would not be able to pass laws from which it exempts itself, since a core concept of the Golden Rule is that one should not do unto others that which it would not wish for itself."

Chairman Henry tries to restrain himself from interjecting again, but self-restraint is not among his core capabilities. "So you think that Congress is breaking the Golden Rule when passing laws that don't govern Congress. I, for one as a man of deep faith, find this comment particularly insulting," Chairman Henry argues.

Professor Stark straightens his tie as he briefly contemplates his response, particularly given what he's almost certain is an absurd claim of religious rectitude: "I would suggest to the Chairman that I certainly mean no insult by this remark, nor would I suggest in any way that I have never broken the Golden Rule. The idea of treating others as we would want to be treated under the same circumstances requires that we acquire knowledge about those who we are impacting and actively imagine what it would be like if we were to find ourselves in their situation, as well as the situation of everyone they impact. My comments are meant to suggest that I don't think it is possible to comply with the Golden Rule if one is creating separate classes of people to which laws are applied."

"I would suggest to the professor," Chairman Henry brusquely responds, "that you have not yet used your knowledge or imagination to understand what it's like to be inside a member of Congress or you would have come to the conclusion that this God's Law idea makes no sense."

Over a period of several seconds, nearly every member of the committee gets out of their chair and walks rapidly to the anterooms behind the committee, keeping their faces pointed away from the audience. Jill and Professor Stark bury their heads in their hands, faces instantly reddening, as many in the audience attempt to stifle laughter. Chairman Henry bangs his gavel furiously in an attempt to get the room under order as a staff member leans forward to explain to him why everyone is laughing.

Ramon Mantel breaks in
fisherman's(?) home
Gets clothing, food, gun
leaves.

14   EVASION

Cool nighttime gulf winds hit Ramon. While the winds may softly caress a dry, clothed beachcomber, they send shivers through Ramon in his barely clothed state. His full body shake doesn't match the rapid twists of a drenched longhaired dog, but the intensity of hair slapping at his face is the same. Deeply chilled, Ramon decides he needs to run to warm up.

In the two months since Ramon last went for styling, his hair grew well below the shoulder length he maintained for years. Ramon's beard, grown only during the past five weeks since his tunnel escape, is matted, unkempt and a bit sporadic in coverage. Under water during daylight, Ramon's eyes confirmed what he thought he was seeing in the cave, that his efforts to conserve food and water while building strength to swim had left him far leaner than before, rib bones protruding, providing a gulley between each rib through which his fingers can now draw lines. None of that matters now as Ramon runs south searching for an abandoned home, an old car he can steal or anything else that helps him get away from where he walks. Rebuilding his life away from the confines of the cartel and outside the custody of any government almost certainly requires permanent relocation and a dramatic shift in lifestyle.

As he jogs for stretches and walks quickly in others, Ramon's feet feel the sting of too many shell fragments and too many sharply pointed rocks. It's worse when he plants a heel-first step, forgetting that his bullet-grazing injury is still not fully recovered. Blisters form on both soles, but it's the cold Ramon feels that has him most concerned. He can't stop and start a fire, and doesn't know how to start one in any case. He needs to find shelter.

The moon and its reflection off the water light his path. Not seeing anything ahead along the shore, Ramon considers turning inland in search of shelter. As he does, Ramon hears a vehicle in the distance and crouches down to assess it. From the vehicle, searchlights pan the horizon in all four directions. Ramon rolls to a cluster of rocks, edges up next to them, kneels and bends over, his buttocks pointed upward and his hairy head wedged under his arms for cover. He listens carefully as the vehicle edges nearer, careful not to move as light pushes through his closed eyelids. A deep shiver takes control. Ramon panics that he might be spotted now. Briefly, he contemplates standing and running, but knows his best chance is remaining still.

Finally, he partially opens his eyes, attempting to peer sideways under his arm. A light traces back and forth. Suddenly it turns off. Ramon's attempt to relax fails when he hears an eerie growling snort on the other side of the rocks. He flinches at the sound of an explosion before recognizing that shots are being fired. Ramon drops flat and turns his head to spot a wild boar racing across the flat sandy surface. He hears another shot and sees the wild boar roll in a head first dive over itself as a bullet disables it. Trying his best not to move, Ramon watches as a uniformed man grabs the boar by its tail, pops a pistol shot through its skull and secures help from two others in lifting the boar onto the back of the transport vehicle. Minutes later, the group is gone. Ramon lies still on the ground, unwilling to move and—at least for the moment—unable. The vehicle turns inland.

After gathering his wits, Ramon wanders back to the shoreline, figuring he has just a few hours of night remaining. At least the adrenaline surge seems to have helped warm him. Ramon needs to find cover, somewhere he can hole up for the day and avoid being noticed. Ideally, he'll find water, food and clothing as well.

With hope running low as the first rays light the top of the sky, Ramon spots potential salvation. He sees a small, dilapidated boat and fishing gear and nets tied up in a small cove. A shack-like home sits just a few hundred yards away—almost certainly the fisherman's home.

If he steals the boat now, he'll have just a short time to get away from the shore and will need to travel in daylight. He's shivering even as he moves, and his thirst now controls his focus. Floating on the boat in gulf water largely naked in the hot sun is certain to invite extraordinary sunburn pain later in the day. More importantly, it is certain to invite a long series of questions from anyone who sees him on the boat, and a bullet through the head or at least a severe beating if the person who finds him owns the boat.

Ramon dismisses the boat-theft option. Instead, he finds a spot away from the shack from which he can watch the boat and at least partially view the shack. He decides to wait, curled up under rocks with only a small bit of direct sun exposure, hoping today will be a fishing day for whoever lives in the house. Until then, he simply shakes uncontrollably. The adrenaline surge has passed.

As dawn breaks, Ramon's desires play out. A small man, shorter than Ramon by a half-foot, ambles down toward the boat cover. It's too dark to see his appearance fully, but Ramon notices that he hunches over as he walks. Perhaps he's older, perhaps simply injured. Just as well. After fifteen minutes of set-up, the man opens up a door Ramon had not noticed and rolls out an engine on a hoist to place at the back of the boat. He adds fuel to the engine, unties from the small, hand-built pier and pushes the boat away before starting the engine. Ten minutes later, the boat is out of Ramon's view.

Not sure what to do next, Ramon walks past the cover to check out the door, the pier and anything else he can see, then walks the edge of the shoreline to approach the house from the opposite direction.

Uncovered and nervous, Ramon concocts a story of having had his boat hijacked and being tossed overboard as he cautiously approaches the house. He pretends to seek help by yelling "Ayúdame" to try avoiding startling anyone inside.

Reaching the shack, still without drawing anyone's attention, Ramon knocks with one hand while covering the flap on his boxers with the other. No answer. He yells more loudly, letting anyone inside know he means them no harm and just needs food, water and clothing. No one answers. Slowly, carefully he enters.

Though a shack on the outside, the home is clean, reasonably or- derly with a surprising number of modern amenities easily visible. No permanent walls separate the perhaps six-hundred-square-foot cabin, though a slightly rusted steel beam stands in its center. A flat-screen monitor covers a large portion of the ceiling above the man's bed, tempting Ramon to find a news channel to learn what is happening. Ramon searches for any security cameras, now concerned that this place might be under surveillance, stopping every two minutes to check that the fisherman isn't returning. Feeling a small floor imper- fection with his feet, he lifts up a thin throw rug to see a recessed keyhole in the floor. He tries to lift and pull, stops to check for the fisherman, and tries to put the throw rug back in exactly the same spot.

Panicked that the owner of this shack might be more sophisticated or cartel-connected, Ramon grabs a rag and starts wiping down his fingerprints.

Hoping to avoid his theft being noticed, Ramon pulls out pants from the bottom of a drawer and puts them on. Too short by several inches, they fit easily around his waist. That will have to do. A tat- tered shirt from a pile of clothes inside a small closet carries with it a pungent, salty aroma, but it will also suffice.

Hurriedly, Ramon finds a container of water and consumes more than he intended, eyes still intently focused on the shoreline. Dried beans and smoked fish refill his belly, easing hunger pains that had grown in intensity in just a day.

Ramon grabs a lighter, some additional food and a large container of water. He decides he needs to be far away from the shack by the time the man returns. Several rifles are stored on a rack above the bed. The man will know someone broke into his home.

Starks students debate personal belief weighted as much as societal & Stark explains impact on others.

Starks announces Rachel will work for president Domestic Policy implementation

15 ILLUMINATION

Tamika appointed legislative assistant to passage – Jill Carlson Congresswoman Indiana will be house lead. Five together

"I hope you all saw the fruits of your intellect reflected in President Phillipi's national address," Professor Stark notes in opening his Integrated Policy master's program session. Several teasing comments during his early morning flight home about his prior-day exchange with Chairman Henry have him on edge.

Professor Stark is among Chicago's most famous professors, recognized nationally for leading passage of a constitutional amendment to substantially reform the political system. After maintaining a much lower-key presence for nearly a decade following passage of that constitutional change, Professor Stark's national profile reemerged throughout 2040 when he became embroiled first in a dispute over whether the United States needed to have a common official language and then as a firm opponent to Southwest secession attempts.

National engagement detracts little from the attention Professor Stark pays to his students, many of whom enter the unique undergraduate and master's program at Chicago primarily for the opportunity to be taught and mentored by him. His appearance during class contradicts official University policy, but Professor Stark's appeal in attracting the nation's best and brightest public policy minds means he gets away with his minor affronts to University standards. Many former students are already building substantial careers in Washington, D.C., New York City, Brussels, Beijing, Delhi and other global government and corporate centers, sending portions of their growing income back to their alma mater.

Refusing to keep up with modern trends to correct most eye issues through simple surgery, Professor Stark's glasses are at least partly an appearance-enhancing adornment. The glasses magnify eyes that otherwise appear too small for his face, while also hiding dark sub-eye circles derived from nearly continuous exhaustion. With the winter trimester nearing end, Professor Stark's puffiness makes clear he has added back more than his usual full-schedule weight gain. On days he teaches, he starts his mornings at Heart and Soul Café, consuming more fats and caffeine than his age and health dictate as wise.

As this penultimate class of the trimester starts, all of the students recognize the risks and opportunities that come with a nationally broadcast class session. Professor Stark wears a tweed jacket, something he does only on days when his classes are being monitored by journalists or recorded for use in one of the Professor's lecture-series ventures. It's his deal with University administrators.

As class begins, Professor Stark relieves the stretch on his jacket button by undoing it, letting his slight gut hang over pressed khaki slacks. Several students are repeats from his undergraduate course. There are always a few who fail to believe that the intense workload and turmoil he inflicts on undergraduates could possibly be enhanced at the graduate level.

Rachel Cruz is among those punishment gluttons. An energetic brunette from Fresno, North California, her academic focus tumbled recently when her father and boyfriend found themselves on opposite sides of the secession battle. Rachel's father emigrated from Mexico before marrying and working extraordinary hours to provide a better life for his family. Rachel's white, once-provincial mother had her life thrown into tumult when abandoned by a father drawn to overseas work and the women in those countries.

Rachel's parents, strengthened through their own challenges, raised Rachel to fight through every obstacle thrown in her path. Rachel's obstinate insistence on having Professor Stark for this master's course, after suffering through the intense workload and expectations of his undergraduate course, reflected a belief that the only way to ensure no one questioned her success was to follow the most direct, intense route possible. Professor Stark willingly provides such a path.

Tamika Jackson, another repeat masochist, was born, raised and lived most of her life without ever leaving Chicago. A high school debate and basketball star, Tamika was raised by a single mother who dedicated herself to ensuring that Tamika didn't repeat her mistakes. It hasn't always been easy, but Tamika prospered under her mother's single-minded focus. The two transitioned into best friends through Tamika's college years, a shift Tamika would never have expected during repeated spats over Tamika's high school priorities. In a city and neighborhood where hard work and dedication often confronts random violence and utter indifference, Tamika's mother was able to keep her from losing focus. Despite now being able to afford to live on campus with her teaching assistant stipend, Tamika still commutes to class from her south side apartment, though she frequently ends up staying with Rachel and other friends when studies run too late.

"So, Tamika, how does society adapt to this uncertainty?" questions Professor Stark, maintaining his long-held adherence to the Socratic method. Any student displaying any hint of less-than-complete preparation is mercilessly peppered with questions until embarrassment causes them to beg forgiveness for shirking work.

Tamika looks up, eyebrows elevated and fixated on Professor Stark. She has been listening to the discussion, of course, but with this being the last pre-exam day of class with Professor Stark, she is more concerned about finishing her thesis than gaining public attention for her views. Professor Stark undoubtedly spotted her eye glaze. He made it a habit to pick on those trying to evade attention. But he was kind to Tamika. He wasn't above tossing his foam football rocket at students drifting out of the discussion.

Tamika refocuses mentally on the class debate, benefitting from a life-long ability to maintain multiple fields of awareness.

"I'm not worried about adjustments. Even without this, our laws constantly face court challenge. I mean, we're still battling over the

Constitution and the Bill of Rights. The Golden Rule Amendment, as I believe our work should be called, adds an overarching concept that is simple enough to understand, live and evaluate laws against," Tamika says, happy to see Professor Stark shaking his head up and down rather than side to side.

Professor Stark sips away at his hazelnut coffee, an aroma that has become all too familiar to his students. Peering around the chairs, he sees Rachel with her forehead buried in her hands.

"Rachel," he says. "A migraine?"

"No. No. Just thinking."

"About?"

"About how we have 250 years of laws put in place that may or may not conform to this consistency concept in daily application and how long it will take to unwind all of the garbage in our laws and regulations," Rachel says.

"Is that really what you were thinking about?" Professor Stark asks, a bit of smirk on his face since he finds her response both unusual and somehow believable.

"Yeah. Really. I'm worried we aren't thinking through the implications of taking a rule meant to govern personal behavior and embedding it into our national government," Rachel states, twisting her hair behind her. "If individuals improperly interpret the Golden Rule, a few people get hurt. If our government interprets the Golden Rule the wrong way, we can all suffer immense harm."

"How so?" Professor Stark asks.

Tamika doesn't wait to be given the floor: "Just consider how relativists will try to suggest that someone else's beliefs are just as important as general societal beliefs. The courts could then use the Golden Rule to say, for example, that if I were a David Koresh-type religious leader, I would want to be able to have sex with young teen or pre-teen girls as a divine right. A relativist interpretation of the Golden Rule would suggest that he has that right to force himself on young girls because that's his belief and all belief systems have equal value. Can you imagine the social chaos and damage to society from this type of interpretation?"

"That's an important point, Tamika," Professor Stark replies, leaning back against the edge of his desk and pausing for effect. "We know that the Golden Rule doesn't just consider what the other person wants or what we would want if we were them, but also considers the impact on others. So, for example, would a judge let a child rapist go free because she would want to go free if she were a criminal if that judge also considers whether she would want her daughter or granddaughter to be that criminal's next victim, or whether she would have wanted to be raped at that age by someone claiming to have a divine right to that rape."

"Exactly," Tamika replies. "But do you really think our government and our society is sophisticated enough to think at that depth?"

"I do," Professor Stark replies. "Of course, it will take time to get it right and require more thoughtful political discourse than the type that takes place today."

"There is so much work to do, maybe more work than we can possibly even contemplate, if Congress passes and the states ratify this concept," Rachel interrupts, her hand reaching up, grabbing her long, straight black hair and twisting it into a knot behind her head so tightly that she flinches as her hair starts to pull.

"Hmmm," Professor Stark says.

"Hmmm, what?" Rachel asks.

"Well, I'm going to pause our livecast for a few minutes to do something I had planned to do after class," Professor Stark states as he pulls up the control panel on his desk, pauses broadcast of the class and quickly enters and sends a couple of messages.

Every student fully fixates on Professor Stark now. They've only seen Professor Stark pause a broadcast three times since this double trimester class began in the fall. All three times, one of their classmates had their intellectual hides peeled, tanned and hung out to dry so completely that physical flaying might have seemed preferable. Surely, he's not about to do that to Rachel, not with the course almost completed and with her being one of the elite students in the class.

As the seconds pass without further word from Professor Stark, several begin to sweat. He wouldn't tell anyone they have failed the class in front of everyone. Would he?

"Rachel, stand up," Professor Stark tersely states, though no visible emotion is detectable on his face.

Rachel stands up, her knees shaking instantaneously.

Not now, she thinks. Not when I'm this close.

She purses her lips, taking deep breaths to control her rapidly accelerating anxiety. Her pupils fully dilate.

"Tamika, stand up," Professor Stark adds, changing nothing in his tone or dour appearance.

Rachel looks over at Tamika. Tamika looks back at Rachel. The two have been best friends for some time and are seated next to each other. Tamika reaches over and briefly clutches Rachel's hand. Tamika's face shows none of the nervousness so clearly etched into Rachel's features. Both know better than to ask questions or argue with Professor Stark now. Once he's angry, if that's what this is, it's better to just let him get it out and calm himself down.

"Rachel, I know you've been considering entering the PhD program here next year so you could be in the same city as your boyfriend if he decides to go here," Professor Stark says. Everyone in America knows that Rachel is dating Juan Gonzalez, once seen as a key national leader despite his youth in the Spanish-only language movement and later in Southwest secession referenda. If it hadn't been well known nationally, Professor Stark wouldn't have mentioned this relationship. "I'm afraid, though, that the two of you might need to trade cities instead."

"What?" Rachel asks, realizing she has asked a question she could have phrased with better clarity.

Professor Stark smiles broadly, self-satisfied at his ability to keep a straight face this long. He knew Rachel and Tamika would panic at being called out with the cameras off and enjoys playing with the anxieties of his strongest students.

"Rachel, the President of the United States has asked me to offer you a position on his domestic policy staff as part of the team charged with ensuring passage of and then pursuing implementation of God's

Law. If you accept, you will be charged with working through the implementation challenges that worry you so much," Professor Stark says.

Rachel's smile makes clear her response, but is followed by a tear running down from the outside of her right eye.

"Really?"

"Really."

"This isn't some kind of sick joke," Rachel continues.

"Not in the least," Professor Stark replies.

"Thank you, Professor, I need to do this," Rachel says. "I hope Juan will understand."

"Why the moisture, then?"

Rachel pauses, doing her best to maintain control.

"I guess I just can't wait to share this with my parents; for everything they sacrificed for me to make this happen," Rachel finally comments. "I think they would be so proud."

As Rachel speaks, Professor Stark reaches for the control panel and displays on the wall a live feed of Rachel Cruz's parents celebrating and hugging inside their living room. "I didn't cut off the feed for everyone," Professor Stark admits.

Rachel tries to hold herself together, but turns away from the camera for several moments. Professor Stark tells Rachel to turn on the messaging part of her Lifelink to see a message from her parents.

"Now, Tamika," Professor Stark continues.

"Yes, Professor Stark."

"As you know, the President has appointed Jill as the House lead for God's Law passage," Professor Stark says. "Jill has authorized me to offer you a position as her legislative assistant dedicated to passage of this constitutional amendment, if you are interested."

Tamika pumps her fist, and smiles broadly. Still beaming, her emotion catches her off guard as she sees her mother blowing kisses at her on the screen. She rolls her lips between her teeth and bites down to prevent her real emotions from being displayed. Public displays of emotion are not Tamika.

"Last piece of news," Professor Stark says. "Jill has a townhouse near the Capitol that has a downstairs apartment big enough for two people to share. You are welcome to stay there as long as you need until you can get settled."

On realizing that they will live and work together, Rachel and Tamika can't believe their good fortune.

"Congratulations ladies. You've both earned these opportunities," Professor Stark tells them with the entire class joining in a standing ovation.

Once the ovation calms down, Professor Stark brings Rachel and Tamika back to reality.

"Just so you understand, you will spend the next several years in a constant state of exhaustion getting this done," he says. "But when you succeed, and I say when on purpose, you'll feel an immense sense of pride and the nation will owe you a debt of gratitude. With that happy news out of the way, I'm going to start our broadcast again. We have our last ninety minutes in class together and I don't want any of it going to waste."

*Starks Class 10 important areas
of govt focus for societal success, p. 91
Rachels 100 most important issues*

*Ramon heads to Puerto Vallarta
and is beat up in Cabo
for his Morelia
logo on stolen shirt.*

16 CONFRONTATION

General Timur, ex-Iranian military leader turned opiate dealer and nuclear terrorist, runs through an inventory of nuclear materials and nuclear weapons still in his control. Every morning, his two closest aides join him as he writes down the locations, security codes and organizational control responsibilities for every ounce of stolen enriched uranium, every nuclear weapon and every missile system within his control. Seconds after finishing each list, Timur burns it himself in a fire maintained for warmth inside the cave system in which he and his leadership team now hide. It's a process he follows to ensure the only record that exists is one his enemies can never find.

Stuck holding out in a cave network near the Kyrgyzstan/Kazakh border, Timur is afraid to step into daylight. While his security team roams the area surrounding the cave—hunting, gathering food and ensuring perimeter security—they aren't among the most sought after people on earth. The team dresses like local hunters and herders, only leaving and entering the zone around the cave in darkness to avoid drawing satellite attention to Timur's location.

Timur is certain the Americans will come after him now that they have attacked General Hernández and many of his other allies.

Timur starts his list, identifying the location of his stolen submarine systems:

"Issyk Kul, Bay of Bengal, Caspian Sea, Gulf of Aden, Sea of Japan . . ."

Next, he turns to explosion-ready nuclear devices.

"Scratch out the bombs held by Hernández," an aide tells the general. *"We haven't been able to get anyone into the compound to see if the Americans found them."*

"No, we keep them on the list until we know Satan has them," Timur responds in an angry tone that tells his aides the debate is over.

He writes down six other sites, then adds "Sinaloa" with a backwards question mark.

Finally, he writes down locations for 624 kilos of highly enriched uranium.

"How much do we think is still secure?" Timur asks his aides, a question that draws nothing more than shrugs in return.

With his classroom broadcast restarted, Professor Stark returns to his typical role as questioner in chief.

"So, Rachel, what are you thinking needs to be done to unwind all of the garbage in place in our laws and regulations?" he asks.

Rachel's hair is back twisted in a knot.

"You know you'd make a terrible poker player," Professor Stark contends, turning toward Rachel.

"Why's that?" she asks.

"You're twisting your hair behind you," he replies. "Everyone here knows that's your 'tell' that you're anxious."

Rachel looks at her hand and realizes she didn't even know she was twisting her hair.

"Maybe I am really anxious now. It's one thing to conceptualize an issue's complexities. It's wholly another to know you have to fix these issues. Oh, God," Rachel admits, taking a deep breath before continuing. "I guess I need to memorize this book," Rachel adds, holding up a copy of Professor Harry Gensler's *Ethics and the Golden Rule,* "and the rest of our Golden Rule readings."

Rachel's right hand reaches up, involuntarily twisting her hair.

"To answer your question, Professor, there are hundreds of issues that must be tackled. I'd start by listing the one hundred most important issues, getting input from as large of a group of sources as possible, and then start working on the top ten. Even trying to do ten things at once might be too much to handle and overstress everyone involved."

"Great, and good segue," Professor Stark notes. "Can we finalize our list of the top ten national priorities to restore America that we began work on a few months ago?'

As a class, Professor Stark had initiated discussion on the ten most important areas of government focus for societal success. Professor Stark had started the debate after seeing that no plan was in place to win the peace even if the Southwest secession and associated invasion were repelled. Throughout history, wars not quickly followed with plans to win the peace either led to repeats of the wars or complete societal breakdowns. Broadcast discussions of the classroom debates on the list's creation had attracted the attention of President Phillipi and led to the President's launch of the God's Law effort.

Professor Stark puts the remaining, modified concepts up on the board as they last stood.

1. Provide for national defense.
2. Protect liberties, particularly those constitutionally granted.
3. Treat others as we would want to be treated in similar circumstances, enabling hope and opportunity to pair equally with responsibility and accountability.
4. Ensure competition—in science, business, religion, education, government and weaponry—necessary for societal survival, advancement and prosperity.
5. Protect property rights so hard work is rewarded.
6. Root out evil, particularly those who unfairly harm others in their quest to achieve or maintain power.

7. Relentlessly battle the intrusions of bureaucracies, whether government, corporate, union or otherwise.
8. Embrace our role as stewards of the future.
9. Contribute to the advancement of others.

"We talked about a top ten list. We have nine critical elements of focus. President Phillipi is taking number three and running with it as God's Law. Numbers one and two technically are already covered in our Constitution," Professor Stark notes. Stark faces away from the class, grabs his tattered foam football rocket and tosses it over his head. Unlike the bridal bouquet toss at a wedding, students instinctively try to avoid contact with it, unless one of them already knows what he or she wants to say. Rachel knows.

"How do we deal with inclusiveness, or creating a sense of belonging for everyone inside a country?" Rachel asks.

Rachel's sensitivity to the topic was heightened during the secession referenda debates and the U.N. secession invasion. At the outbreak of that invasion, Rachel's father, an American of Mexican heritage, was detained out of fear that he might fight for Mexico and other secession supporters. Instead, her father had been heading to the temporary border to fight to defend his family. That the United States repeated an error it had made one hundred years earlier with the Japanese American internment during World War II made the arrests all the more difficult for Rachel to tolerate. "After all, the re-segregation of America over recent decades was what led to this stupid war, allowing our country to be divided by politicians who found their self-serving interest tied to creating a sense of hate and anger between races, ethnicities and classes."

Another student brings in work done by former Harvard Professor Niall Ferguson that identifies the six "killer apps" of western success as being competition, science, property, modern medicine, consumerism and work ethic. He questions how Ferguson's ideas fit with Professor Stark's list.

Professor Stark takes a crack at responding: "Professor Ferguson did some very interesting work. To some extent he identifies the same challenges, but categorizes them differently. Another professor of note,

Jared Diamond, contemplated the thirteen thousand years of world history for which we have written and archaeological records and suggests that geographic proximity to competing nations spurred food production, weapons development and other technology in an advance-or-be-overtaken pattern."

"Whom else should we look to for research that points us to the right areas of focus?" a student asks, with chewing gum dangling from his mouth as he speaks.

"I wish we had time to work further on this, but we need to reach a conclusion today. Focus for now on what makes sense to you," Professor Stark urges the group.

With several days having passed since he left the cave sanctuary along the shoreline, Ramon has traveled nearly two hundred kilometers from the cartel's Sinaloa Province compound. He keeps the beard and vagrant look to avoid arousing any suspicion, but that filth-coated appearance and associated odor draw unwanted attention from Puerto Vallarta residents.

Ramon evaded most towns throughout his journey, but his last stolen food was consumed two days ago. The irony of the situation isn't lost on Ramon. As Ramon Mantle, he's a multi-billionaire with money ensconced in dozens of banks around the world. But he's almost certainly on the most wanted lists by now of both the U.S. and Mexican governments. Anonymity is his best option at least until he can figure out if he has any friends.

Less than a handful of people know that Ramon prevented the nuclear explosions planned by General Hernández. Even among those in U.S. government who know he sent the cartel's nuclear weapons location maps and the headquarters compound schematics, Ramon isn't sure that he'll be treated fairly. Ramon continues to believe his best hope of survival is to gain access to some of his money and disappear untraced. For that to happen, he'll need to be dead to his family and dead to the world. A bank in Cabo San Lucas is his best hope for cash and anonymity. Until he gets there, he needs to simply survive. Puerto Vallarta offers his best hope of catching a boat ride to Los Cabos without being identified.

Clothes stolen from a clothing line thirty kilometers north aren't much of an upgrade from the clothing stolen from the fisherman. At least they fit: long pants in a muted tan speckled by occasional oil drops, likely the clothing of an antique auto repair mechanic. An unfortunate Morelia logo on the sleeve of the loose, synthetic shirt he stole is certain to draw objection from fans of Guadalajara and other nearby Primera teams. The logo alone, worn in the wrong place, could cost Ramon some abuse. He goes out of his way to hide it.

As he walks through side streets north of Puerto Vallarta, his best efforts to avoid notice aren't succeeding. A group of teens trails Ramon. No point in running, Ramon knows he doesn't have the strength to get away. He struggles to have the energy simply to walk. He steps around three corners, circling only to find the group has circled behind him. It's clear. They're following him. Ramon walks through a bar and out its back door. Turning, he sees the group still following him. The lone girl in the group starts yelling at the boys, "*What are you waiting for. Teach him a lesson,*" she yells in Spanish.

"Damn it," Ramon says under his breath as he sees the gang running toward him. He turns toward the boys. "No tengo nada," he yells, trying to let them know he has nothing to take. It doesn't matter. Soon, Ramon is crouched on the ground in a ball, covering the back of his head with his arms and hands. The boys take turns. Hitting. Kicking. Stomping.

Ramon fends off many of the blows before his body goes limp. Finally, one of the boys convinces the others to move on.

"*He knows better than to be here now,*" the boy says in his native language, adding an insult to Morelia that makes clear to Ramon that he should have stolen a different shirt.

As they start to walk away, Ramon looks toward the group. The girl turns back and stares at him. Around blood dripping from several openings on the top and back of his head, Ramon stares back. His nearly perfect, single-glance memory has always been a great intellectual asset. He'll remember her face, though not for any intellectual pursuit.

17 IRRITATION

Fireworks at the first God's Law hearing, particularly between Professor Stark and Chairman Henry, creates extraordinary interest in round two, a hearing the media widely portends as the Chairman's retribution session. In announcing the hearing, Chairman Henry suggested he would subpoena Professor Stark if necessary to get him back in front of the House Judiciary Committee, a threat quickly unveiled as empty when Professor Stark released his pre-announcement email to committee staff saying he would happily appear anytime, anywhere.

Chairman Henry built his long-term success on dogged pursuit and destruction of his enemies, particularly those who tried to take his congressional seat or his power base in Congress. With the subpoena comment, he leaves little doubt that he plans to crush a man he has publicly derided as a narcissistic utopian, and privately castigated as a bullet-free, satanic revolutionary.

Three-quarters of hearing room space is absorbed by credentialed media, with the last seats taken by lucky winners of the lottery conducted of lobbyist seat holders and tourists waiting in line at midnight for the chance to sit and try remaining awake through the all-day hearing.

When the hearing finally gets underway at 10 a.m., several Internet news networks begin live coverage. Even the historic national networks break into regular programming to alert viewers that an entertaining debate on President Phillipi's most important national priority is about to begin.

While calling the hearing to order, Chairman Henry carefully brushes his hair plugs, making sure he's as well put together as he can be at this age. He's studied hard for this hearing, wanting to be sure Professor Stark is unable to better him and carefully planning a questioning attack strategy with the team of legal scholars he has assembled as his committee staff.

"How in God's name can anyone believe it makes sense to have a constitutional amendment mandating we follow God's Law when our Constitution requires separation of church and state," Chairman Henry begins this hearing.

Jill, a member of the Judiciary Committee, leans to a colleague and whispers in his ear: "I wonder if the chairman even understands the irony of his question's wording."

"You should say that in your remarks," he responds.

Jill grabs a semi-clear flexible mask, holds it in front of her mouth and dictates notes at an extraordinarily rapid pace to be transcribed and organized automatically into bullet points by the computer function of her Lifelink. The mask protects taped dictation from being captured by parabolic microphones while also stymying those who've learned that lip reading and upside-down reading skills confer powerful advantages to the capable.

As Jill concludes recording into the mask, the system arranges her comments into five key themes with several supporting points associated with each theme. Once she approves, the computer searches the Internet for compelling facts and quotes supporting her comments, as well as listing key objections to her arguments based on global searches. Jill's already prepared remarks were contained in her Lifelink before the hearing started, but she frequently continues editing her remarks right up until starting delivery.

As she works her thoughts, Chairman Henry continues expressing his views. "With the President's attempt to impose the Golden Rule concept on government, or God's Law as he calls it, I see a man desperate to impose his morality on others. Since I would never want someone to impose their morality on me, it's clear I must not impose my morality on others, so the concept is inherently flawed from the start. It's like we're trying to train a wolf to herd sheep. We might even be able to train it for a while, but eventually that wolf is going to get hungry and it's going to destroy what it was developed to protect," the Chairman contends. "So it is with this God's Law. The concept, though it might be designed to protect us, will end up destroying our very society by imposing an absence of true morality and clear definitions of right and wrong that this Congress establishes as law. The type of lawlessness that society would be forced to endure as Golden Rule concepts are adjudicated is simply intolerable, in my very humble opinion."

Because of her leadership role in promoting God's Law in the House, the coalition of Republicans and independents caucusing together as the minority allows her to speak first after the chairman concludes his lengthy remarks.

Jill shakes her head side-to-side as the chairman concludes, then focuses on making sure she presents her best case. She's making her argument to the American people, not just to other members at the hearing. Convincing the chairman to change his mind is a far more difficult task than swaying the nation, particularly once an issue becomes personal, as this one clearly has become.

"Mr. Chairman, I appreciate you conducting this hearing, and particularly appreciate the irony of you asking how 'in God's name' we can justify passage of God's Law in a nation that values the separation or church and state," Jill begins, careful to smile regularly as she speaks. Jill long ago learned that the majority of people respond more to how a politician looks while speaking than to what they actually say. "Your point, however, is a critical one, so I'll focus my opening comments here and perhaps beg some of my colleagues for their time to supplement thoughts on other areas," Jill states, taking a moment to look over at colleagues who have unusually agreed in advance to cede as much of their time to her as she needs.

"It may come as a surprise to some that separation of church and state meant something very different to our founders than what we often hear preached today. Our founders did not object to moral influence on society. In fact, they both insisted on a core morality and, I believe, perhaps even assumed its continuance. Written into the Declaration of Independence is the idea that men 'are endowed by their Creator with certain unalienable Rights.' To me, this is the most crucial statement in either of our founding documents—the idea that certain rights are granted to us by a higher being, not subject to theft or disruption by any form of government including our own form of government under which you most certainly are, Mr. Chairman, imposing your morality on others. This Declaration statement, the unifying principle that caused our predecessors to fight for our independence, makes clear the belief that a higher power exists who watches over us, judges our actions to be right or wrong and promises to hold us accountable for our failings even if we manage to escape accountability on earth. The concept of religion was deeply embraced by the founders, even if many of those founders believed that many organized religious sects were seriously flawed."

Chairman Henry's irritation at being specifically called out by Jill is apparent in his red-faced, surly expression, as well as in the rapid movement of committee staff inputting arguments into his electronic notepad that he can use against her.

"Our founders were deeply concerned that the nation would force its citizens to follow a single religion," Jill continues, providing a history lesson that fills in gaps of what many are taught in the public schools. "Remember, many of the founders were of English descent. Many came from families that left everything they had ever known to escape religious persecution when they refused to swear allegiance to the Church of England. That did not mean they did not believe in a higher power, as is clearly evident in the documents they constructed."

Jill stops again for a second, smiling toward the massive media section, wanting to convey the impression that her argument is the one that restores success and decency to the nation. She learned from years working in the media and studying history that style can overcome even obviously superior substance. Certain her substance is right on this issue, she focuses on also creating the right image.

"Since I have limited time, let me get to why morality must be embraced in our society—not a single religion imposed and enforced by the states—but a morality common to the multitude of religions that helped our society advance and prosper. If you'll indulge me, I'm going to quote research from Professor Stark that is not covered in the opening remarks he submitted to us last night," Jill states, only to be interrupted briefly by smirks from some of her colleagues from all parties who find the tabloid-style coverage of their relationship entertaining. A recent story about their relationship on one entertainment show highlighted the extent of celebrity style interest in their relationship. "Would you let your man shove you in a box and roll you through the streets?" the headline read with a picture of the pair in the background.

Professor Stark patiently waits his turn, continuing to take notes as committee members run through opening remarks. He came here knowing he'll need to listen carefully to facts and arguments stated by other witnesses that he might need to refute. He is on the last panel of the day.

Down Pennsylvania Avenue, President Phillipi has made it his personal mission to track down Ramon Mantle. After neither Ramon nor any of his body fragments were found inside the Sinaloa Province compound, President Phillipi turned to New Rite and its founder JT Alton for help tracking Ramon down. With CIA assistant director Branch Whitney having already worked directly with New Rite, the President makes Branch the government's contact with New Rite.

After weeks of turning up no information, JT visits the White House to directly discuss the President's demand that Ramon be found. President Phillipi, Defense Secretary Mendoza, Branch and JT gather privately in the Oval Office.

"Is there any chance we were played by Ramon?" the President asks JT. JT's New Rite intelligence and special operations group had tracked Ramon's movement for years as part of its investigations of the Castillo cartel. Despite initial research showing that Ramon's cartel involvement appeared limited to technology development that enabled the cartel to out-compete other drug vendors, New Rite still tracked Ramon with hopes he would lead them to Cesar Castillo.

More than twenty years earlier, JT had decided to avenge his younger brother's overdose death and had been successful enough with his survival-based company to fund massive investments in intelligence gathering directed at the cartel. When his intelligence arm showed promise and his company continued to expand, JT invested further in creating a special operations unit of some of the military's elite, retired special operations personnel.

"We haven't seen any evidence of a new drug operation taking over distribution of the Castillo cartel," JT replies to a secure video conference call question from the President. "Our intel shows that drug operations are at a standstill in dozens of major markets with limited supply available. Prices are skyrocketing now. If Ramon is really playing us, he'd align himself with another group capable of filling supply gaps. He's smart enough to have planned for this, in our estimation."

"What are the chances, Xavier, that he's dead and we just haven't found the body?" the President asks Secretary Mendoza, who is joining from his Pentagon office while pedaling away at the exercise bike he had installed under his desk.

"If he was near the compound, we would have found him or at least had his DNA turn up in some of the remains. We've tested everything now that looks like human remains," Mendoza replies, a small bit of sweat accumulating at the crest of his eyebrows. "If he's clever enough to have somehow evaded our satellite tracking and wasn't in the compound, we may never find him."

New Rite's JT interrupts: "Mr. President, if you get any word from the intelligence community that Ramon has been spotted, let me know. We'll move resources from our broad international search to focus on a particular area as well when we have a better chance of finding him in our visual net. But, to the Secretary's point, I believe he's clever enough to pull off anything he wants to pull off."

DOING UNTO OTHERS

The President fiddles around inside his desk. "Branch, be sure to keep JT in the loop. I don't care who finds Ramon. He is likely the one person alive who might fully understand the extent of our remaining nuclear threat," the President states, before cautiously standing and walking away from his desk. Several minutes later, all of the other participants agree that the meeting has ended.

While the President fixates on finding Ramon, Judiciary Committee debate continues inside its Rayburn hearing room. Jill gains another block of speaking time after several supporters of God's Law agree to give up their opening statement time, unusual acts of congressional selflessness when cameras are rolling.

"Let's look at history," Jill says as she continues her comments. "Professor Stark's historic research found that the most sustainably evil societies are typically nations that ban religion outright or single-religion theocracies intertwining government and religious leaders and bureaucracies. Our founders insisted on preventing the United States from becoming a single-religion nation, in part through personal knowledge of persecution, but also because they understood that evil perpetrated in the name of God or a group of gods ramps up when government and a religion exclusively intermingle. At the same time, our founders no doubt realized that God-less societies are usually led by people so corrupted by power that there are no earthly abuses they won't impose in order to maintain their power."

Sweeping several roaming strands of hair away from her eyes, Jill continues: "Single religion nations are a threat to human peace. God-less nations are threats to human survival. It's only through competition among religions and governments, competition based on peace, that we have a chance. Many religions begin with self-serving, egocentric focus that flawed individuals in the cleric bureaucracy class seize for personal aggrandizement. I believe that my religion is superior to others. That's why I follow it. This gives me, in my view, the right to talk about my faith and live it fully as an example. It does not, however, give me a right to impose my faith on others as clerics often demand once they become embedded in single-religion government."

Chairman Henry's fidgeting betrays his impatience. He uses his ability to control the hearing room sound system to cut Jill off.

"Is this single-room schoolhouse lecture going anywhere relevant to consideration of this constitutional amendment?" the Chairman asks in obvious exasperation.

Jill raises her eyebrows, doing her best to not respond to the Chairman's ridicule. "Ridicule is man's most potent weapon," Saul Alinsky argued in *Rules for Radicals*, a guidebook for community organizers based on Alinsky's experience in organizing the radical Congress of Industrial Organizations wing of the labor movement. Chairman Henry's operating methods as a politician closely follow Alinsky's recommendations, a consideration Jill continuously takes into account.

"Yes, Mr. Chairman. I'm starting my argument with why I believe pluralistic, unified societies are superior to segregated societies in order to explain why I think we need to embed moral concepts that we all agree make sense into our system of government," Jill states, annoyed by the chairman's interruption, but smiling in any case.

"That's wonderful news. Perhaps you aren't hearing what you're saying. You've just gone into great length to suggest that atheists and agnostics should be eradicated from the planet, blaming untold mortality on people who put science ahead of religion," Chairman Henry replies, "and coming close to arguing that it's best that we just execute everyone who doesn't follow a religion or ban them from public office to save ourselves later grief."

Straw man arguments are a staple of Chairman Henry's belligerent approach. Whenever he's unhappy with the direction of a debate, he suggests his opponents are arguing for an outcome they've never suggested and would almost certainly oppose, then proceeds to skewer his false interpretation of their views rather than their actual arguments. Jill entered the hearing fully aware that her arguments would be mischaracterized at some point during the debate. Still, she struggles to hide her annoyance.

"If you're going to interrupt my remarks, Mr. Chairman," Jill responds, face turning bright red, "you might want to turn your hearing . . . Uhm. You know, I'm not going to stoop to this. Clearly, you have not understood my comments. I'm arguing that government must be extraordinarily cautious in preventing people from following our individuals faiths and requiring us to act in contradiction to our beliefs, unless actions we take based on faith would cause irreparable harm to others."

"But it's okay to interfere with atheists?" Chairman Henry interjects, waving his arms for exclamation.

Jill calms and reminds herself to smile. Remember, appearance matters, she thinks. "The same caution applies to all belief systems. One doesn't require belief in God to have a belief system. Atheism itself rests on as many unproven beliefs as every other faith. You argue atheism is based on science, but there is no scientific evidence proving that a God does not exist."

"But you think organized religions are superior, isn't that right, Congresswoman?" the Chairman blusters. "Particularly Christianity, if my memory serves me right."

Jill smiles again before responding, looking toward the Chairman in a way that several commentators note as giving the Chairman a visual pat on the head. "No belief system is superior when unchallenged and intermingled fully with government. I won't argue for a minute that religions don't have flaws. Sometimes, true evil is masked as service to a God or gods. I'm personally wary of religions that say God only welcomes true believers of a particular religion to after-life. In the Catholic crusades and Islamic jihads, what better justification for men to kill than the idea that they would help convert non-believers destined to burn in hell for eternity to the only religion that gives people a chance at eternal life. Europeans wiped out native populations throughout the Americas emboldened and nourished by this pretense," Jill continues.

Chairman Henry fidgets relentlessly, holding his gavel in the air and pointing toward Jill to be sure she sees that her time is exhausted. Jill continues nonetheless, looking only at the audience and cameras.

"As I was saying, history is filled with actual and would-be rulers who justified killing millions in order to have the chance to 'save' some souls. The most evil assert power and control by using racial, religious, ethnic, sexual preference, wealth and other differences as excuses to kill, maim and deny basic freedoms. So single-room schoolhouse lesson one, Mr. Chairman, is that belief in the superiority of a certain type of people holding a defined set of beliefs attracts exploitive leaders who will use that belief to control, dominate or eliminate others—and it is those evil exploiters who must be stopped."

Chairman Henry turns to a staffer, screaming at her to get Jill under control. After having her microphone turned off, Jill speaks in her loudest voice, still heard in a hearing room thrilled that they are already getting the contentious battle they predicted and sought.

"God's Law will embed in our constitution the principle that we would treat others as we would want to be treated after gaining knowledge and insights to enable a sound decision. If I were a Catholic, if I were gay, if I had a handicap, how would I want to be treated?" Jill loudly states.

"The gentlewoman's time has clearly expired," the Chairman says, banging his gavel loudly and staring at Jill to let her know she is testing his patience. "And I must say that you have fully convinced me that religion brings great evil, which is why I am opposing your God's Law proposal to create a national religion for America."

Jill turns to look directly at Chairman Henry. "I apologize, Mr. Chairman. I focused too much time explaining why pluralism is an asset to America and not enough time explaining why God's Law is a necessary constitutional supplement to prevent the state from effectively imposing a single national religion, your religion of government as all-powerful giver and taker."

"Jill, I think you're letting your emotions get the best of you and becoming disrespectful to the Chairman, something I cannot allow," Chairman Henry vociferously responds, inciting Jill to open her eyes widely and grasp the desk in front of her firmly with both hands.

After a second to filter her immediate reaction into a calm reply, Jill replies: "So tell me, if you agree that the facts are all accurate as presented, under what conditions do you suggest that emotion contributed to my conclusions? Or is it just because I am a woman that I must not be able to think straight when in the wafting zone of abundant testosterone? Is that it?" Jill snipes before the Chairman waves one hand to suggest she is misrepresenting his comment, while slamming the gavel repeatedly.

18 ALTERCATION

Ramon regains a foggy, physically constrained version of consciousness.

He opens his right eyelid just enough to peer out and spot a tongue wagging near his face. Unable to focus, he can't tell what type of animal licks rapidly at blood crusted across his face. He can't generate the strength to move. A surge of adrenaline pumps into his blood vessels, shrinking them and opening air passages as he fights to endure the intense pain overwhelming every one of his senses.

He moves his arm toward the animal and attempts to move his face away from what he now sees is a dog. He peers at the surroundings through the small slit of the one eye he's able to see through. Rocks. Dirt. Crumbled, faded walls. Metal bars over a nearby door. Bags and boxes of rotting, stinking garbage spill over and block the rest of his view.

He tries lifting his head to better determine his location. Seconds later, Ramon collapses back to the ground, again unconscious, the Morelia logo on his stolen shirt fully soaked in blood.

Four hours into the Judiciary Committee hearing, the final panel, including Professor Stark, is invited to present its testimony.

Professor Stark has heeded Jill's advice for the occasion, ditching his traditional tweed sport coat for a more traditional suit and tie. "Everyone already knows you're a professor. You don't need to appear a caricature of the role when you testify," she had prodded him earlier. "Besides, you need to give some in the media something easier than the substance they can focus attention on. You can't wear the same clothes every time you testify."

"But it's my lucky jacket," he had replied. "Well, I'll give it a try, but if it doesn't go well, I'm buying a tweed bathing suit for our next vacation."

"I'd love to see that," she had told him, not actually meaning what she said.

Once seated, Professor Stark is asked to present his opening statement. As he has done traditionally, he eschews his prepared remarks and starts talking off the cuff. Chairman Henry is fully attentive, searching for his opportunities to pounce.

"Thank you Mr. Chairman, for welcoming me again today to testify in front of your committee," Professor Stark begins. "I realize my last exchange with you in front of your hearing might have seemed contentious to some, but I always welcome the opportunity to engage in thoughtful dialogue with you."

"I appreciate that, Professor, though I'm sure my attempts to cajole you at our last session won't suddenly create a tamer witness," Chairman Henry replies, a jovial expression on his face making clear that he enjoys the sport of attacking this particular witness. "I look forward to some good entertainment today, and perhaps seeing if there is something I can learn from you."

"Thank you. I do as well," Professor Stark replies. "The concept of God's Law is being taken by opponents as all about religion, when in fact the concept is all about creating a society that fits with a concept of human decency that is either embedded or at least appears in almost every major faith and has proven essential to human survival and prosperity throughout history. I appreciate that Congresswoman Carlson and others have discussed the failings of single-religion nations as well as of God-less nations, because understanding these extremes is important to understanding the value of creating a pluralistic society in which the Golden Rule simply provides an important unifying moral element. Let me spend a few minutes talking about why religion is important to humanity."

Uncomfortable already in a newly purchased suit and a shirt buttoned tightly enough that a bit of neck fat rests on his shirt collar, Professor Stark fidgets in his chair as he continues.

"It's my view that organized religion can be a source of both great good and great problems. Strong religious views, particularly the belief in an afterlife dictated by how one behaves in this life, can have a powerfully calming effect on a population. The concept that 'blessed are the meek, for they shall inherit the earth' as written in the Bible's New Testament Gospel of Matthew provides a rationalization for those suffering in this world—physically, economically or socially—to believe this suffering will eventually bring reward. To the extent this provides comfort during times when hope and opportunity are stifled, these religious views aid social stability. In addition, religions often provide and encourage charitable works, providing a reason for people to give what they have earned to aid others who need their support. However, religions can also create problems. Justifying evil, by making people of certain race or nationality or disability or sexual orientation appear to be ungodly and unworthy of decent treatment, is the greatest of these problems. Beyond this, I'm concerned that some organized religions discourage people from making the most of their God-given talents, with the consequences of this failure shared by all."

Professor Stark looks up to be sure the Chairman isn't preparing to interrupt. Seeing the Chairman fully reclined, he continues: "You've already heard about the problems created when a single religion is imposed on society, offering no opportunity for competition of ideas among the religions to create a platform for progress. So let me focus on the responsibility government has to avoid relying on individuals believing that suffering today necessarily earns later reward. Life, of course, will never be fair. We all must endure and overcome our own individual trials and tribulations. But our responsibilities extend beyond self-centered, narcissistic compulsions. The concept that doing unto others as we would have done unto ourselves describes these responsibilities and is the precept behind the God's Law constitutional amendment."

"It sounds," Chairman Henry interrupts, his interest now drawn, "like we agree, Professor, that government needs to take from some people to give to others to prevent self-centered, narcissistic behaviors from destroying our nation. Is this what you are saying will be enabled by God's Law?"

"You may have missed my point," Professor Stark responds.

19   REORIENTATION

New Rite's Colorado compound rests on tens of thousands of acres founder JT Alton purchased from the National Forest Service when the U.S. government reached the nadir of its debt repayment crisis. New Rite's office, research and meeting space layers nearly 250 stories from near mountaintop to deep below Byers Peak. JT's favorite living space, a home built to provide him with 360-degree views of the surrounding area as well as to provide multiple escape paths, connects by tunnel to the office operations.

JT has shared this living space and a passion for destroying the Castillo cartel with Ally Steele, commander of the Special Forces organization JT built to destroy Castillo. To most who worked at the offices, however, Ally had been known only as the survival camp and training director for New Rite's Colorado operations. JT's meticulous protection of New Rite's special operations team minimized leaks about New Rite's drug cartel destruction work.

Ally steps slowly into the headquarters' most secure meeting room, situated more than two thousand feet below the mountain's top surface. She moves sideways until standing with her back pressed against the wall, surveying the faces of corporate types for any reason to believe they'll have a shared mission going forward. The shadows are Ally's comfort zone, a place where she can observe the world without being noticed herself.

Ally's ability to move through society unnoticed was permanently destroyed by a series of national media reports in recent months, highlighting her exploits in leading the assault on the world's most dangerous cartel military organization with President Phillipi in tow. Quickly recognized by New Rite's corporate leaders, Ally is surrounded with requests to sign autographs for an assortment of immediate and extended family members and friends.

With New Rite's special operations team now publicly exposed by their role in the cartel attack, JT added Ally to his expanded corporate leadership team. Ally joins the heads of New Rite's online gaming, survival training, competition management, military weapons research and weapons production business units, along with the heads of finance, human resources, law and corporate relations. Weapons development business leaders are meeting the survivalist training and gaming business leaders for the first time. Until a few weeks ago, the online gaming, training and competition unit leaders were unaware that their extraordinary profits were being largely invested in real weapons development, not just in creating life-like models for gaming use. By remaining a private company, JT enabled New Rite to avoid the financial scrutiny that would have exposed New Rite's full scope.

Two business unit leaders know Ally from her dual reporting "day job" as Colorado survival compound and training leader. These roles and the dual-reporting relationship allowed Ally to disappear for days or weeks unnoticed. Even those who know Ally are awestruck to be around one of the nation's newest heroes and its latest recipient of the Presidential Medal of Freedom.

"First, let me thank everyone in this room and your teams for the extraordinary work you've completed over the last several months against nearly insurmountable odds. In a matter of months, following years of preparation, we've crushed every gauntlet thrown down in front of us," JT begins the meeting. "However, I want to start this meeting by taking a minute to silently remember New Rite team members who paid the ultimate price to ensure our success, along with, perhaps more importantly, the survival of the nation."

JT's New Rite organization is the world leader in online combat training and survival competition games. At elite levels, New Rite survival competitors install expensive 20-by-20-by-12-foot competition pods in their homes. Competitors hook themselves into a harness system that allows them to simulate running, jumping, swimming, sniper insertion and full hand-to-hand combat with walls and flooring that continuously adjust to changing terrain. The competition environment is displayed on the 360-degree surround projection floor, ceiling and wall.

Battle competitions can last up to twelve hours per day, a limit New Rite imposed to ensure gamers sleep between competition days. While competing, though, competitors can draw water and food from tubes tied into their helmets, minimizing their need for breaks. Feed replacement bags are specially designed to provide a constant revenue source for New Rite. Oxygen enrichment technology built into the system allows combatants to compete for longer periods of time without tiring and also requires buying new filters monthly. The best online competitors win free entry into New Rite's weekend-long survival competition battles, globally telecast events in which a set number of participants are let loose in the wild with weapons modified to identify when death would have occurred had the weapons been real. Competitors who do not earn their way into these battles through online battle victories often pay tens of thousands of dollars each to compete in single-weekend tournaments.

After New Rite's special operations team involvement in destroying the Castillo cartel and stopping its attempts to detonate nuclear weapons inside U.S. borders became known, New Rite's online gaming and compound training membership doubled in just the first month. Absorbing that rate of growth is a technological challenge, but one the team appears to be pulling off.

While business performance is better than ever and JT's personal fortune is certain to soar in value in coming years, he faces a more critical challenge, one he isn't sure he can overcome. For two decades, New Rite's business was driven to support JT's nearly single-minded obsession with killing Mexican drug lord Cesar Castillo and destroying his drug cartel as revenge for the death of JT's younger brother. JT blamed Luke's death on the Castillo cartel after he discovered the cartel had both supplied and employed him. JT was in the early stages of comfortable business success with his survival training sites and online survival gaming when Luke died. Since then, he had taken a sizable portion of New Rite's annual profits and invested it in weapons development, intelligence gathering and creation of a special operations team to kill Cesar Castillo, an objective finally reached months ago and followed up even more recently with the U.S.-military-aided destruction of nearly the entire cartel.

"We have three major challenges we need to address," JT says in opening of the strategy session. "First, we need to ensure that we absorb rapid gaming and survival compound growth without any service deterioration. Our physical systems and our hiring must continue to demand extraordinary attention to excellence. No drop off in quality. Same standards. Agreed?"

Heads nod around the room. New Rite achieved success by hiring talented people who were fully committed to what they knew of the company's mission.

"Second, the U.S. government now fully understands most of the weapons we had in the gaming testing stage. I've been told that Justice Department bureaucrats think they can confiscate, or at least shut down, our military weapons development unit. A few careerists are even threatening prosecution for engaging in undisclosed and unsupervised military weapons production, completely unaware of the tremendous service you've all provided to this nation. Since I know you've heard or seen these rumors, I'll tell you that I'm convinced presidential pardons will prevent these consequences if anyone tries to pursue criminal charges. Let your families and teams know there is no cause for legal concern," JT continues.

New Rite's legal team might have phrased JT's comments to his team a bit differently. While JT is confident he can protect his team, the reality is that some of New Rite's activities have breached U.S. law for most of the past 20 years. JT is convinced that the ends achieved by New Rite excuse the organization and that he will successfully convince juries to nullify prosecutions any government agency might pursue, with pardons as the ultimate escape hatch. The legal team isn't willing to make the same success commitment.

"Third, and perhaps most importantly, I need to come clean with most of you. While I've been driving the business, I have to apologize that I had not been able to tell you all my full motivation. Those who knew me from the early years I'm sure have had your suspicions, but I've been reinvesting almost everything our publicly known businesses have made into creating the weapons and teams needed to destroy the cartel that destroyed my brother. I've also been insisting that the weapons developed for our survival competitions and online gaming be as realistic as possible in order to minimize the number of people I needed to actually produce real versions of these weapons for combat use. I've lied to many of you, some of you for twenty years, to protect you from legal consequences for my actions," JT states, beginning to choke up as he speaks. "If this betrayal is beyond your ability to tolerate, I'll understand and will accept your resignation and pay for you to have time to transition to another company."

JT stops and looks around the room to see if anyone wants to bail.

"If you aren't sure you want to be here, I need you to leave the room now," JT continues. "Decide to stay later and I'll fill you in on what we discuss. But I can't have anyone here who might even contemplate leaving."

JT looks around the room. "I'm committed," Ally says, a statement repeated by everyone else in the meeting.

"Since we've now succeeded in accomplishing everything I wanted to achieve against the cartel, I've been struggling with what's next, if anything, to motivate me, to motivate us I mean," JT continues. "More importantly, I think it's time to be sure we're all working toward the same purpose beyond simple financial success, rather than me hiding my true intentions from so many of you. So, what is our purpose for existing, beyond thrilling our customers and feeding our families?"

Ally is the first to talk. Ally established her reputation as the best Air Force elite operations pilot, a reputation enhanced and spread by her leadership in the attack on the Castillo cartel's Sinaloa Province compound.

"With all due respect, JT, I know I speak for the rest of special ops when I say our mission isn't complete," Ally states. Wearing a jacket over her tight-fitting t-shirt, fatigues, boots and necklace, Ally would be a misfit in almost any other corporate leadership team meeting. That she is welcomed here perhaps explains her commitment to New Rite and its old mission. She believes any new mission that New Rite can take on could be even more important than achieving JT's revenge desire.

"I joined New Rite because I knew you were gonna make the world a better place. We've done that, at least as far as the cartel goes, but I don't believe we're done. Now that the media found us, there's a lot of cartel people we might not even know who want to kill our brothers and sisters, our parents, your children, your spouses. Not all of those who deserve to be punished have been brought to justice and we need to hunt them down before they find us," Ally contends to the assembled leadership team.

JT looks around the room, again seeing heads nodding from everyone there. He brushes his left thumb and index finger through his thick, well-groomed beard, resting his chin on the outside of his hand.

"You're right, of course," JT finally states. "If we really want to make the world a better place, there's plenty of evil remaining, and we don't even know where it all lives. The question I have is can we find it, prioritize targets and take them out without covering ourselves in the blood of innocents?"

"We could, if we could lurk unnoticed until ready to strike," Ally adds, "but New Rite isn't unknown any longer. We're gonna need to worry even more about security and protecting the people in this room and particularly about separating New Rite from any new mission."

Ally opens her Lifelink, tapping to an online alert she received just before entering the room.

"It looks like we might be able to get some help with target identification from a recent friend," Ally says as she shows JT that a military officer they had initially known only as Branch was just named CIA deputy director. Colonel Branch Whitney had been assigned to work with New Rite in a recent set of military attacks. Branch, a long-time protégé of Defense Secretary Xavier Mendoza, is a highly capable ex-military officer and now trusted friend of the New Rite special operations team.

"Well, this is certainly interesting," JT whispers to Ally. "If the President and Secretary Mendoza don't know or can't give us information directly, Branch might be a tremendous information source for us. He could give us the clues we need to focus our mission."

"I understand you've had your retribution, in a sense JT," Ally adds. "I hope you understand that we need ours now, for Sarah and the others."

JT decides to rename New Rite's national online combat competition in honor of Pete Roote, a gamer turned combatant who had made the ultimate sacrifice while rescuing Juan Gonzalez from cartel captivity. He also renames New Rite's globally televised outdoor survival competition after recently deceased New Rite special operations commando Sarah Osborne, who survived her single-woman sinking of a Pakistani nuclear sub in U.S. waters only to die while also freeing Juan. Later in the day, he flies to Washington, D.C. to meet with President Phillipi and Attorney General Betty Cooke to finalize details of pardons promised to the New Rite team.

Ramon's face is still covered in blood, his clothes torn and tattered, with lumps and bruises distorting his features to make him appear almost grotesque. He doesn't know how long he has been lying in this back alley when he feels a stick poke at his stomach.

"Señor. Hola. Señor," the woman's voice repeats. Ramon hears her, but can't bring himself to move or respond.

She pokes him slightly harder with the stick, clearly trying to determine if he's a corpse before getting any closer, triggering his brain with sharp-shooting pain. "Señor. Señor."

"Si," he responds in a guttural, whispering tone she barely hears, his face still largely hidden into the corner where the building's wall runs perpendicular to the dirt road that is soaking up so much of his blood. The beating hadn't stopped until he'd been able to push his face into the corner. Even then, he'd taken one last kick to the back of the head before blanking out. The position may have also helped protect Ramon from the roaming dog—who fortunately had been either recently fed or was naturally attentive to human needs.

She pokes him again. "Señor?" she utters again, though this time in more quizzical tone.

"Yes. . . . Si. . . . What? Donde . . . estoy?" Ramon finally replies with enough energy to be heard, trying to figure out where he is and muttering weakly enough that it takes some time for the woman to interpret his words.

The woman finally tells him he's in an alley, providing one of the few answers to his question that Ramon had already surmised. No, what city, he asks in garbled Spanglish.

"Are you okay?" the woman asks in English after realizing his Spanish was flawed, kneeling down next to him and pulling his hair away from his face to reveal a shredded, swollen mask worthy of the worst of Halloween horror movie trolls.

As Ramon struggles to sit, she gains full view of the damage: the mass lump on the right side of his forehead, a shattered jaw, bruising and coagulated blood coating most of the exposed portions of his body and shredded skin from repeated cuts outlining a hideous mosaic of remaining skin on his face.

One eye swollen shut, Ramon tries to see through the sliver of the other to figure out whether this is the girl who ordered his beating, back to finish the job. He tries to move, only to groan as rib cage bones, shattered by the beating, poke erratically at skin and organs sharply enough to collapse Ramon back to unconsciousness.

20 CONTEMPLATION

Clarissa Coleman's fifteenth birthday passes unnoticed—perhaps the best part of the day as far as Clarissa is concerned. All the lights are off in her bedroom. The door is shut and locked. Clarissa's head is buried in her pillow, her body sealed flat against her mattress.

Six weeks after returning to her Flagstaff, Arizona home from the New Rite Utah compound, Clarissa's daily high school life continues to deteriorate.

Long-time friends Dezbah, Catalina and Angela have barely talked to Clarissa since she returned, even turning to walk away as she approached on several occasions. At first, Clarissa thought they were angry that her family had gone north when Arizona, New Mexico, Texas and California del Sur, or South California as it is back to being called, were trying to secede from the United States.

Clarissa had served a watch role with her family along the border during the short, but intense confrontation with everyone in her family except her grandfather. Grandpa Coleman, refusing to give up his guns as part of martial law declared in the secession states, was attacked by local police and killed, one of several traumas Clarissa endured through the battle.

Clarissa had struggled with depression for years, but had until recently found enough of a comfort zone with her three friends that she thought she belonged somewhere.

With another miserable school day many hours past, Clarissa messages Dezbah, a Native American and Clarissa's best friend out of the group over the last year or two. Whenever Clarissa fell into a deep funk, Dezbah's sense of humor and adventure pulled her out. That close friendship appeared severed in recent weeks. Dezbah not even saying "Happy Birthday" made it clear to Clarissa that the separation is no accident. In her message, Clarissa asks two simple questions: "Are you angry? Why?"

Clarissa is already home when she receives a response. She doesn't like what she reads. "I can't be friends with racists," Dezbah writes back.

"What are you talking about?" Clarissa pleads.

Dezbah replies: "Everyone knows what your Grandpa said that made the police kill him."

"Knows what?" Clarissa asks.

"What he said?" Dezbah notes.

"IDK what you're talking bout," Clarissa messages back, now hunched over her Lifelink and responding furiously to each bit of information.

"Don't lie to me too," Dezbah demands.

"WTF"

"How long have you thought I was a prairie n#*@r?"

"What?" Clarissa asks, now furiously trying to figure out who is making up what.

"Yeah, we know."

"Know what?" Clarissa probes. Between each text, she grabs around at her sides, pinching furiously. During the long delay before Dezbah's next reply, Clarissa walks to her closet, bends down and grabs a bottle behind the boxes stacked in the back corner. She takes several deep swigs before sitting down on her bed, staring at her Lifelink, hoping for a response and slicing at the inside of her thighs. "Know what?" she messages again.

"Know your family r racist haters. Police tell us horrible things your grandpa said before they knocked him out," Dezbah finally replies. "I can't be friends with someone who hates me for who I am."

"Ridiculous," Clarissa messages as fast as she can. "You're my friend. I don't hate you."

"Too late. You're blocked."

Over the next fifteen minutes Clarissa sends message after message to Dezbah, with no reply. After the first few, she receives an "undeliverable message" response. She really did block me, Clarissa says to herself.

Clarissa folds her body over in a lump, crying almost uncontrollably but unnoticed by anyone in the house over her loud music. Fifteen minutes later, Clarissa grabs the vodka bottle from the back of the closet, a pair of scissors from her desktop and her Lifelink. She pulls her blankets over piles of pillows and clothes arranged to mimic the arc of her body to anyone peeking into the room.

Convinced no one will know, Clarissa walks to the bedroom window, pulls out the screen and puts it under her bed. She drops her backpack down with the scissors, vodka and a tranquilizer gun, seconds after pulling her Lifelink out and putting it under the covers to avoid being tracked. She looks down at the six-foot drop to the ground from her split-level home bedroom on the upper floor, sits on the window ledge, leans her head out past the window and jumps to the ground.

Minutes later, Clarissa heads toward Humphrey's Peak, taking well-worn trails she has used numerous times over the years.

An hour into her run-hike, Clarissa pulls over into a patch of spruce trees and pulls out the vodka bottle. She takes a swig. Then another and another and another. Dropping her head down onto her knees, she decides she has had enough, pulling out the scissors. She uncouples the blades, holding a single blade in her hand, placing it up just beneath the bottom center of her ribs. Looking up at the stars, Clarissa says the only prayers she can remember, asking for forgiveness. She twirls the blade around, then pulls off her sweatshirt. Seconds pass as Clarissa contemplates what to do next. She takes a couple more swigs of vodka, then puts the blade up again under her ribs. Twirling. Twirling.

Tonight marks a first. Never in his history as a professor has Professor Stark travelled to meet a prospective student for the student's convenience. But Professor Stark has a couple of ulterior motives. Meeting Juan Gonzalez over dinner in Washington, D.C. buys the Professor another night of travel at university expense, giving him a chance to spend another night with Jill. It won't cost the university much now that he's spending his nights with Jill but it does give him a chance to pass on a flight change fee to his expense account. His second ulterior motive is perhaps equally innocuous. He wants Juan as a student and he didn't seal the deal on their last travels together.

Ever since Professor Stark gained fame for providing the intellectual leadership behind the Political Freedom Amendment, a constitutional amendment that instituted the most sweeping political reforms in the nation's history, he has gained a national reputation for developing many of America's leading young public service and political minds. Never, though, has he had a student enter one of his classes with a well-established national reputation that arguably equals his own.

Caught up in an employment dispute as a senior in high school, Juan became the public face and voice behind a Spanish-only language requirement in Arizona that sparked national debate on whether the Southwest states should secede. When secession appeared within reach, Juan accepted an offer from the Honor to Mexico national advocacy organization to delay starting college for one year to become the national spokesman for secession. In return, Juan received a four-year college scholarship provided, ironically, by the company whose employment denial sparked his political activism.

At nineteen now, Juan is ready to choose his university. The University of Chicago is his leading candidate, though Juan's interest in studying under Professor Stark is tempered by contemplation of

Chicago's frigid winters. Juan first encountered Professor Stark in media and political debates on both the language mandate and secession issues. When Juan unexpectedly found his life threatened last fall by people he thought were on his side, he turned to Professor Stark for help largely out of lack of options. Professor Stark's intervention saved him, leading to an almost parent-child bond between the two that should make Juan's university selection choice an easy one. Juan, though, grew up in West Nogales, Arizona. He'd traveled to Flagstaff's higher elevations during winter months on several occasions and found the cold there almost unbearable. He's nearly certain he'll freeze to death during Chicago's winters.

At a small restaurant with a highly eclectic menu inside D.C.'s Union Station, Juan quickly spots Professor Stark and the two exchange a handshake and a hug before starting their discussion.

"Are you willing to try something new?" Professor Stark queries Juan.

"Sure," he replies. "Just so long as I don't go hungry."

Within minutes, an appetizer of garlic-and-butter-poached shrimp arrives at the table. Professor Stark remembered that Juan loved shrimp he had tried for the first time at a meeting the prior year. He's pulling out all stops to make sure the nation's most prominent young leader joins his program.

When dinner arrives, two platters are put in the middle: One contains a chicken pad Thai covered in crushed peanuts and shredded Thai chili peppers. The other platter is a fourteen-ounce blackened filet mignon with a charred butter spice crust. Sides of corn relish, twice-baked potatoes and grilled vegetables are also spread on the table between them. In the year since Juan became a national figure, exposure to diverse and abundant flavors expanded his enthusiasm for food.

"Juan, it's clear that the University of Chicago wants you as part of our school and we're prepared to do something unique for you that is far outside the bounds of normal," Professor Stark says, elbows now propped up on the table as he leans toward Juan over the slightly oversized table. "We're prepared to offer you a two-in-one deal. Two years of credit in one year."

"Two for one?" Juan asks.

"To be clear. Two in one, but you still have to pay for all the credits, which won't be a problem with the FirstWal scholarship," Professor Stark responds.

"How does that work?" Juan asks around the pad Thai he continues to savor.

"The experiences you've had over the past year qualify you to quickly earn credit for many of our basic and some advanced coursework. Teaching you public speaking when you've already spoken in front of tens of thousands and to national media audiences doesn't seem necessary. Several general studies professors have agreed to grade you based on your previous and current work, filling in any knowledge gaps through individual, focused sessions." Professor Stark continues, breaking his sentences amid bites. "We'll do the same for three public policy courses for which we believe you have already achieved near mastery based on your personal experiences."

"So I can be done in three years?" Juan asks.

"With your undergrad, yes. A fourth year if you decide to also obtain a master's degree," Professor Stark suggests. "But before I go any further on what Chicago can do for you, what I really want to know is what do you want to accomplish with your life? No amount of education makes sense if it doesn't help you achieve your life goals." It's not just paternal instincts kicking in. Professor Stark asks his question of nearly every student he gets to know.

Juan stops chewing for a bit, guiding pieces of filet to the side of his mouth as he prepares to respond.

"What I've learned more than anything is that I want to do something that makes people's lives better. There are a lot of politicians who focus their time on what they need to do to get elected and reelected. I'd like to be in a position where I can advocate what is right, whether it's popular or not," Juan responds.

"An admirable objective, to be sure," Professor Stark notes. "Some might argue a bit naïve, so tell me more about what this role looks like."

Juan doesn't notice that many of the other diners are taking pictures of the two until one diner interrupts them with an actual print copy of the Professor's latest book. She implores him to sign it, a request he gratefully accepts. Professor Stark had remained well aware of potential threats and was relieved that the woman who stared as they entered and ran from the restaurant when they sat had only bolted to find hard copies of his *The Elements of National Destruction* and *The Bastardization of Acquired Democracy* books.

Emboldened by the interruption, several other diners request that the pair sign e-book covers or pictures of Juan that many of the younger girls in the restaurant kept on their all-in-one system devices. The attention wanes quickly enough to let them get back to their discussion.

"You know that I've actually been listening to you and following your class even as I've been arguing with you in public," Juan replies.

"That's clear. Each time we've debated, the intensity of your challenge to my arguments has amped up," Professor Stark notes.

Juan wipes his lips with his cloth napkin. "I'm glad to hear that you think that. I certainly do my best."

"Your hard work and preparation level in our debates and in other public venues is the primary reason Chicago is ready to make an exception for you on our standard practices," Professor Stark acknowledges.

"I appreciate that, on an individual level," Juan states. "But for the nation, we still have deep flaws that hurt people. I want to help eliminate that. So for me, my decision is all about what best helps me figure out how to help and gives me the tools to succeed."

Professor Stark thinks about offering Juan the remainder of his beer bottle before reminding himself that Juan isn't yet twenty-one. Cameras are everywhere. "Okay. That's admirable and something I know many people would like to do. How do you expect to achieve that goal?"

"I'd help define the expectations of a society that gives people the chance to succeed," Juan responds.

"Sounds similar to what the President is trying to do with the 'God's Law' constitutional amendment," Professor Stark contends.

Juan shoves another over-sized piece of filet to his cheek to enable him to speak. "Perhaps, though how it plays out once politicians have put their hands around it isn't clear," he mumbles around the meat in his mouth.

"Fair enough. You're supporting my belief that you have a far deeper than base understanding of our political system," Professor Stark notes.

Juan thanks him for the compliment, knowing from Rachel that compliments have to be earned from Professor Stark. "I think my best chance of influencing our national future while in college is to be part of your program. You've had a clear impact on the President's thinking and, really, that of the whole nation so maybe some of my ideas can filter through as well."

"You, of course, have other methods of sharing your views, dating a key presidential advisor or through friendships with a leading congressional staffer," Professor Stark notes, reminding Juan that the Professor really does know him well. "The challenge for you will be to focus on your education at the same time as you try to impact public policy. So tell me what issues bother you the most."

Juan sits up straight, finishes chewing and takes a drink of water as he contemplates his answer. "As much as I fight to not let it affect me, it still bothers me to see how hard my Mom had to work just for us to survive, when so many people have lives that are so easy by comparison," Juan says. "I mean, we literally were scraping our last food out of bags and boxes some days, or going to neighbors to borrow a meal until Mom got paid. She worked her tail off and then came home at night and badgered me until I had everything done for school."

"Why do you think she badgered you so hard?" Professor Stark asks. "And why do you think you worked so hard to be a great student?"

"She didn't want my life to be as hard as hers," Juan replies. "And, to tell you the truth, I want something more for my life and for Mom than what she was able to get."

"So, you worked hard to avoid some of life's harshest difficulties?" Professor Stark asks.

Juan pushes his plate to the side, taking a few more sips of water: "Yes. I mean, the media seems to think that I've been lucky, but I think I've worked very hard for what I've achieved, and you know as well as anyone it has come with a lot of pain."

"So the challenge becomes," Professor Stark interjects while nodding his head in agreement, "how does society ensure that people have help they need to overcome challenges and secure a good, productive life without making failure so easy to endure that it becomes acceptable and common." Professor Stark has talked too much, and trails behind in getting through dinner. He cuts into the quarter-portion of the twice-baked potato he decided was all the starch he could handle without gaining any more weight.

"I get that, but I'd just like life to be fair for everyone," Juan exclaims.

"I won't argue for a minute that life is fair," Professor Stark says. "But let me ask you a question. Knowing how you've turned out and what you've already accomplished in your life, I'd like you to ask your mother a question. Is there anyone in the world she would trade lives with? Not, are there things she doesn't like about her life, but would she trade lives and who would she trade with?"

"Well, I know she wouldn't trade," Juan says.

"Why not?"

"Because she's proud of what she's accomplished. I just wish someone had been there to help her through it," Juan says.

Professor Stark looks at Juan, putting food aside. "I bet if you asked, she'd tell you that she had help, from her church, from Honor to Mexico's social services group, and perhaps even a friend or two along the way," he contends. "That doesn't make it right, of course, that she had to struggle so much, but it does help. I've started some discussions with Tamika that you should be part of on how we can revamp government away from bureaucracy and toward people-focused, mentor-based service and support for families and individuals in temporary need of a helping hand."

"I'd like to hear more about this," Juan says. "Maybe I can add some different perspectives."

"I have no doubt that you can," Professor Stark says as he internally self-congratulates for having piqued Juan's curiosity.

Ramon regains consciousness, looking up at bright lights overhead. He tries moving, but feels restraints around his body. Perhaps he is simply too weak to move yet, he considers. His eyelids spread far enough apart he can tell he's no longer in the same alley. Ramon tries moving his head but he can't twist it around. A metal device holds his head in place.

"Hello," Ramon calls out. "Hola?" he follows, trying to figure out what language to speak. He spoke English regularly in his business and political dealings from his pre-cartel-leadership home base outside of Dallas, but Spanglish is his primary social language. Besides, last he knew, he was in Mexico.

Minutes later, a nurse ambles toward his bedside. She leans over the top of him so he can see her face, clearly aware that he is immobile.

He tries asking her for information about his physical condition. She tries first finding out who he is.

"¿Como se llama usted, señor?" she asks.

Ramon contemplates whether to identify himself. Surely they checked his picture against system records. That means they couldn't find him if she doesn't know his name. Perhaps the beating distorted his appearance enough that he can't be identified even from facial recognition scanners that increasingly permeate civilized society.

"Je ne sais pas," he finally replies, using one of the French phrases he learned working with the Quebec government in trying to sell his automated vehicle control technology. He's hoping the nurse doesn't know any French. He needs to fool her long enough to get out of here before his identity is discovered.

"English?" she asks.

"English, yes, I can speak English," Ramon replies before realizing he's lost his chance to remain silent.

"What . . . is . . . your name?" the nurse asks, trying to remember an old English lesson.

"My name? My name? My name?" Ramon repeats. "I don't know . . . . Where am I?"

"Hospital. Puerto Vallarta. México," she responds after checking the translation program on her device to be sure she understands what he asked.

"How long?" Ramon asks.

"Cuatro. Four dias," the nurse replies. She lowers Ramon's bed so he can more easily see her as they talk. Ramon looks at her. She's solid. Her uniform runs flat down her body. Her hair is cut just above her shoulders, with sharp bangs. He can see her warmth, even hidden behind more than a few developing wrinkles. She's much older than Ramon, or wears her age far more obviously. Perhaps it's the end of a long shift, Ramon says to himself, seeing no signs of grey in her hair.

"Four days until I can leave?" Ramon asks.

"No, no, no," replies the nurse, whose name he can now see is Juanita. "You, aquí, four days."

"Can I leave now?" Ramon inquires, a question Juanita obviously finds amusing once translated because she smiles broadly before responding.

"No, no, no, señor. Muchos días. You here many, many days," she says in stuttering pace. "How pay you?"

"I, I, I don't know who I am, even," Ramon says, realizing that his beating may give him the chance to create a new life if he can get out of the hospital and get access to his money.

"We tried find you with photo," the nurse slowly tells him, speaking to Ramon with the help of her translation program. "Perhaps send fingerprint to France to you find."

"Please don't," Ramon begs. "How do you know that whoever did this to me won't come back to finish killing me if they find me. I need to hide until I find out who I am and why people tried to kill me."

Juanita asks Ramon to repeat. The second time, she tapes Ramon's comment and runs it through her translation program. She looks at the screen, then looks back at Ramon.

"Yes. Maybe right," Juanita replies, again prompted by the translation guidance.

"You won't stay here long if can't pay. Maybe girl who brings will take in you," Juanita says. "She come back each day to check."

Ramon is hopeful she is right.

Juanita comes back later that night to feed Ramon through a straw. She pulls his gown off in sections, giving him a sponge bath. She starts with his face, then gently works on his arms, under his chest. When she gets to his waist she stops and then works from his feet up. Finally, she reaches under the gown to gently wash around Ramon's genitalia. "Your body. Works now," Juanita says to Ramon. "You no do *ayer*."

A bit embarrassed, Ramon tries to control himself as Juanita turns his body to wash his back.

"Save energy to healing," Juanita tells him as he focuses on the pain he's feeling. "If cannot pay, must release. Girl bring you came back. She take care you until okay."

"Can I walk?" Ramon asks. Juanita checks her translator again.

"Maybe. You weak," Juanita says, sitting Ramon up and pulling a badly scratched walker over to the bed. "Practice tonight. Slowly."

As Juanita helps him sit, the pain in Ramon's fully wrapped ribs focuses his mind elsewhere.

"How long until I can function?" Ramon asks.

Juanita looks at him and asks him to repeat, again recording his comment so she can be sure she understands his question.

"Many weeks," she finally replies, "Until you not need help."

"What if no one comes for me?" Ramon asks, realizing as he tries to stand that he isn't even mobile enough to acquire food and water without help.

"I pray for you. You okay," Juanita says. "I trust girl."

"How can you be sure?" Ramon asks, realizing he is helpless as Juanita translates his comment and gets help with her reply.

"The girl who checks on you," Juanita replies. "She is nice."

"Nice?"

Juanita types into her translation program: "Uh, niece."

"She will be nun, so you must be good man," Juanita says, pointing toward Ramon's mid-section. "Put away or I take it away," she says, making a slicing motion with her hand. Juanita chuckles at her comment. Ramon closes his eyes and passes out again from exhaustion.

21 INITIATION

It's not so much her rich, pumpernickel skin color or upbringing in a struggling, single-parent household that causes Tamika to stand out in her new job as Jill's Judiciary Committee legislative assistant. What makes Tamika an oddity among Judiciary Committee staffers is that she isn't a lawyer and harbors no law school ambitions. Top congressional staff roles are often a springboard to a lucrative law firm or lobbying career, but a law degree adds particular value to staffers launching from a Judiciary Committee support role.

Tamika is one of a handful of congressional staffers to ever start a new aide's job in neither Washington, D.C. nor the lawmaker's home district. Jill, Congresswoman Carlson, didn't come to Chicago for an onboarding session with Tamika. But while spending Saturday night and Sunday with Professor Stark, she takes an hour to prepare Tamika for a workload that will start at hyper-sprint pace on Tamika's first day and accelerate from there.

After months of indoor-insulated incubation, spring fever grabs a powerful hold on Chicagoans. Jill and Tamika meet at "The Bean" in Millennium Park, as the whimsical reflective steel structure created by Anish Kapoor is known. Tamika arrives early, circling the bean and looking at the Chicago skyline reflecting around her as she loops around the sculpture. Not long after, Jill arrives, greeting Tamika with a hug.

"It's interesting what you see when you see the world from a different perspective," Jill states as she releases Tamika from the hug.

"It's funny. I grew up and spent my whole life in Chicago and I don't ever recall the city looking this magnificent," Tamika replies, eyes still glued to the arched mirror view of dozens of skyscrapers surrounding the park. "This is a different part of the city than what I saw as a kid."

"I'm hoping you can do that for me, Tamika. Show me a different perspective. Let me know a view of the world that I might not see," Jill says, comfortable that the hundreds of strangers weaving around them are completely ignoring their conversation. "I grew up in different circumstances from you so I want you to challenge me on the direction we take with God's Law."

"I think I can do that for you," Tamika replies, looking slightly down at Jill, even with Jill in heels and Tamika wearing flats. A former high school basketball star and debate champion, Tamika was ensconced in after-school activities throughout her academic career. Jill grew up on a dairy farm, milked in the morning, spent an hour on a bus to school each direction and worked when she came home to keep the family farm afloat, often through difficult times. "I'm not sure that we aren't much more similar than you might think."

"How's that?" Jill asks.

"I may be city and you definitely are country, but neither one of us ever had anything handed to us from what I've read about your life," Tamika says.

"Well that's certainly accurate," Jill says.

"Tru dat," Tamika says. "Isn't that your generation?"

"True that?"

"Dat. Dat. With a d. That's old school to say, 'well that's certainly right," Tamika says, doing her best to imitate Jill's tone and smiling as she speaks. "Some of the differences are just surface stuff, looks, words. From when we first met and from what I've read and watched of you, I think we share similar souls. That's why I'm so thrilled to work for you. So, I'll challenge you. I may give you a different perspective. But I know in the end that I can trust that you'll do what's right for all people."

Jill nods her head at Tamika and takes a few steps with her toward nearby water cascades: "I hope I can live up to your expectations." A few steps later, Jill adds: "I really appreciate your confidence."

Tamika pulls out her Lifelink, flips it open to screen view and pulls up a recent class submission to share with Jill. "This piece gets at what I consider the most important issue to make this a better country. I'd be curious to hear your thoughts on how this fits with the God's Law work."

Jill sits on a park bench, takes the Lifelink from Tamika and starts reading:

"Your plan misses the mark when talking about 'allowing differential rewards.'" Tamika wrote in her critique of a list of critical federal responsibilities being created in Professor Stark's class. "While conceptually reasonable, in and of itself, it must be expanded to add 'but ensure equivalency of opportunity.' A human being born into deep poverty, educated in terrible schools, lacking the support of family and detached from opportunities to find their talents has far less chance of success than someone born of wealth, schooled by the best, supported by family and with every opportunity to find their passion. Government can reduce these discrepancies, but not in the way done today."

Jill nods her head as she finishes reading, and Tamika takes back her Lifelink. She quickly taps on two spots, and pulls up the questions posed to her by Professor Stark: "The only fair way to provide total equivalency is to remove children from the care of parents at birth and expose all children to development through the state. North Korea and Russia did this for generations, and not to desirable outcome. Would the benefits of this approach to the disadvantaged outweigh the societal harm caused by removing the loving bonds of parents and children? If we are to leave children with their parents, is there a role for government in promoting parenting skills? Can the government go so far as to forcibly prevent people from having children until they have passed requisite skill and disposition tests? Starting from where we stand today, what is the first change you would make to reduce the discrepancies in opportunity that exist in the world?" Professor Stark wrote in his usual litany of questions demanding that each student dig further in finding answers.

"Well, that certainly sounds like Paul," Jill comments. "He's always taking my concepts to an unintended extreme as a means of pointing out their limitations."

"I get that," Tamika replies, comforted somehow that the professor's classroom approach carries over to his personal life, "but my point is we have to do better. Life maybe never will be fair. I get that. However, people provided with responsibility and accountability must also see hope and opportunity—and vice versa. You got this from your parents from what I've read. My Mom broiled this into me. But I saw a lot of kids who never were inspired to believe in themselves."

"It's interesting that you say that," Jill remarks, leaning toward Tamika as she speaks. "I remember thinking it was unfair that so many kids had it easier than I did when I was a kid. It wasn't until I lost my Mom that I realized how fortunate I really had been."

"I can see that," Tamika replies as she works to maintain an even emotional keel. "I hadn't realized it when I was younger, but nearly everyone faces some kind of struggle. The problem is that when a group decides that no effort can be enough to let us live a better life, anger and resentment grows. When anger and resentment builds in a sizable population, the spark of revolution ignites."

Jill lifts her eyebrows and huffs: "Tell me about it."

"So you agree with this idea?"

"Yes, uhm," Jill says, an uncomfortable look on her face. "True dat," she says in shrinking volume.

"Oh, God. That's hysterical from you," Tamika laughs, taking several moments to return to her core concerns. "You probably shouldn't ever say that again."

"I could tell that while I was saying it," Jill replies, shaking her head in recognition of a failed effort to sound young and hip.

After substantially trimming his beard, inserting prosthetic implants to his cheeks and nose, encasing his eyes in pupil-distance-distorting contacts and situating one of his sets of cosmetic teeth over his own, General Timur sneaks out from the Kyrgyzstan mountain cave in which he and his men are ensconced, circles one of his guards and asks what he thinks. A drawn automatic weapon gives him the answer he hoped to receive. His appearance is different enough to not be instantly recognizable.

"*You did not know it was me,*" he laughs, completely unfazed at having a loaded machine gun point toward his chest as he pulls out the cosmetic teeth and cheek implants. "*I'm ready.*"

"*Ready?*" his guard asks.

"*It is time?*" the Iranian commander turned terrorist replies.

"*Time.*"

"*Time for the world to feel Allah's wrath.*"

"*Allahu Akbar,*" the guard says, looking toward the heavens.

"*Allahu Akbar,*" Timur replies. "*We leave in ten minutes. The infidels failed us, so we will deliver Allah's punishment ourselves.*"

Tamika and Jill continue walking toward Buckingham Fountain on their way to a path running alongside Lake Michigan. A breeze repeatedly blows Jill's hair across her face as they walk until she is annoyed enough to pull her hair into a ponytail. Having discussed the surroundings for several minutes, Tamika turns the discussion back to her social justice concerns.

"I think that resentment, or at least failure to believe in equal opportunity, is what drove the secession effort. Some political leaders act in the best interest of the people they lead, but far too many act in their own self-interest. I think political leaders like George Washington, Martin Luther King Jr., Nelson Mandela, Mahatma Gandhi and Abraham Lincoln led and sacrificed for the cause of the people rather than simply to achieve and hold power. After the revolutionary war, many of his officers wanted George Washington to become king. He saw the hereditary passage of power as failing the ideals of the liberty movement that created our independent nation and refused."

"So what's your point, Tamika? How can we work together to help address the disparities in our society?" Jill asks.

"You know what I think it is?" Tamika states. "Each individual has different needs, different capabilities, different dreams. What I see in government programs is an effort to fit people into boxes, to make people easy to administer, rather than to provide resources we need to become our greatest selves."

"I think you've hit something here," Jill suggests, leaning forward over the edge of the park bench with her face turned toward Tamika.

Jill asks Tamika to walk with her as she contemplates what Tamika is telling her. "I'm wondering, given your clear, deep interest in fixing our anti-poverty systems, whether working on God's Law is a good use of your time?" Jill questions.

Tamika worries that she may have focused too much on what she wants to accomplish, and not enough on finding out what Jill wants her to do. "Sorry, Jill," Tamika says as she invites Jill to sit next to her on a bench facing the lake.

"Don't be sorry," Jill replies. "This is extremely interesting."

"Even so, I'm babbling about what I've been thinking about, but I haven't tied it back to your work. I think it's all related, the idea that our laws should reflect how we would want to be treated if we were in similar circumstances. I wouldn't want a lifetime of handouts and I don't know many people who do. But the programs today punish people when we try to get ahead. You have to be confident that the short-term losses of having government assistance cut off when you work will pay off in the long-term. When you come from an area where you see a lot of misery, it's sometimes hard to believe you can make that payoff happen. So, I'm thinking that once the idea of Golden Rule government is in our Constitution, it'll force Congress to fix these programs to make them work the way people would want them to work if they found themselves in similar circumstances. Right now, I feel like everyone is just battling for political advantage and our real needs are being ignored."

22 SENSITIZATION

Juanita pushes Ramon in a wheelchair down the hallway to the Puerto Vallarta hospital entrance. Without identification or any way to pay for hospital services, Ramon isn't allowed to remain.

Swelling around Ramon's jaw and forehead is receding enough that he is beginning to look somewhat like himself, but hopefully not close enough to be identifiable.

"You sure you don't want re-check your identification?" Juanita asks with translation. "You look better."

"No. No," Ramon replies, putting on his best French accent. "Merci beaucoup. I mean, uh, muchas gracias señorita."

"De nada," Juanita replies. "Uhm, welcome."

Ramon doesn't want to be recognized. Juanita had bought clothes for Ramon from a local charity store, a gift Ramon knew he must someday repay. Throughout the stroll, Ramon kept his head down, just in case any hospital cameras might pick up a clean image of his face. At the door, the girl from the alley—the one who helped him—awaits.

"Hola, Tía Juanita," speaks a young woman with the most striking face Ramon has seen in months. Her smile is relaxed, her eyes wide and nearly transparent.

"Buenas días, Abril," Juanita replies.

Ramon tries to say hello, but instead simply stares at the pair. He identifies small patches of resemblance, particularly shared shapes of their lips and noses. Abril's thin, youthful appearance though projects an effervescence and sense of mystery and tension that holds Ramon's attention. If Juanita's touch began to engorge him, it will be nearly impossible to force his above-neck brain into maintaining control around Abril.

"My aunt tells me you'll need help for a week or two before you'll have the strength to go back on your own," Abril says as she pushes Ramon down the street in the wheelchair.

"Wait, isn't this a hospital wheelchair?" Ramon asks.

"Sure, but my aunt trusts me to bring it back."

"How far are we going?"

"Not far. My little apartment is just around the corner. We'll be there in a few minutes," Abril informs him. At the complex, Ramon sees he'll need to walk up stairs to Abril's unit. Abril walks in front. Ramon is torn between watching his steps and memorizing the firmness and shape of Abril's buttocks. He looks up her skirt as she walks slowly in front of him, almost as if taunting him by having her thighs fully exposed. Ramon forgets about the stairs, stumbling and recovering to move faster as Abril quickens her pace toward the door.

A breeze blows the back of Abril's skirt upward, exposing panties wedged tightly up with the bottom third of her cheeks uncovered by lace or anything else. Ramon tries to control himself, but has lost all ability to manage his impulses. If he could move quickly, he would grab and control her, caressing her while shoving his tongue down her throat. But he can't move quickly, and he still has a steel mask holding his jaw in place.

Finally, Ramon reaches the apartment and sees it is a single room. A tattered mattress rests on the floor, with a sink, shower and toilet behind a long, hanging towel. The two windows are near head height, pushed open to allow fresh air into the room. A small refrigerator sits in a corner with just an electric fry pan and a microwave to cook with. A few minutes of assessment later, Ramon realizes this room had once been a janitor's closet.

"Take a drink of water," Abril tells Ramon, "and take this pain pill. My aunt tells me you'll need these for a few more days."

Ramon complies and lies down on the bed as Abril tells him she'll return the wheelchair to the hospital and leaves the room. Minutes later, Ramon is sound asleep.

Jill is thoroughly engaged in her discussion with Tamika, the hour they agreed to spend together at Millennium Park having long passed.

"You make many great points, Tamika. We agree that social stability requires people to be able to meet basic needs, live safely, and have the real opportunity to pursue goals. You've raised some interesting points about how our social welfare system works, or maybe doesn't work. There's no doubt our safety net has become so program-focused and bureaucratic that the vast majority of resources aren't reaching the people who need them and certainly not in the way those resources can be most helpful," Jill says. "Am I understanding correctly what you're saying?"

Tamika agrees that Jill has summarized the issue fairly and then outlines reform constraints that Tamika, Rachel and several others had agreed on in a discussion with Professor Stark. First, any new system must provide better outcomes for those in need, they concluded. Second, it must not discourage movement toward self-reliance and ultimate escape from government programs. Third, the safety net must minimize the potential for corruption. Fourth, it must allow for competitive solutions to emerge that provide better fixes than currently envisioned. Fifth, it must ensure that parents maintain or develop responsibility for their children, whenever possible.

"That all sounds reasonable," Jill agrees. "Put what you think we need to do into practical terms for me."

"My mom was a young, single mother raised by another young, single mother. She would be the first to tell you that she didn't know everything she needed to know about being a good mother when she had me. But she knew she wanted to be the one to break the cycle of poverty and didn't want to live her life begging for handouts from everyone else. So she studied a lot and learned. But wouldn't it have accelerated the pace of her growth as an income earner and mother if she could have had someone to be her life coach? Take all, or maybe just a chunk of the government dollars that go through government bureaucracies today, and give it to her to spend as she and her life coach agree will help her achieve her goals, including the proper raising of her daughter as long as she makes progress toward independence."

"That puts a lot of power in the hands of a life coach," Jill states, expressing a concern that Tamika has certainly considered given the many ways she's seen people exploited during her life.

"Sure, but right now that power is spread into hundreds of people who don't know and can't possibly care at more than a superficial level about the success of everyone they encounter. So you make sure that you have life coaches who truly see serving in these roles as a calling," Tamika contends.

"That's interesting Tamika," Jill interjects. "One of the reasons people argue for religious institutions to provide more social services rather than government is that the people who work on religious programs are more likely to see their work as a calling."

Jill suggests that one way to mitigate excessive control by the coach is to give each recipient a quick appeals process. Life coaches would be evaluated based on outcome improvements and family evaluations.

"I still see a system with potential for real abuse. The life coach could funnel business to his friends for insurance or rent or whatever," Jill notes.

"Agree," Tamika replies. "This new system would have imperfections and be subject to abuses that need careful monitoring. But I can also see how we could get better outcomes as a result. The current system already is abused, so I'm not sure we could possibly be worse off. This would be fundamentally different from the system we have today. I wonder if there is anywhere in the world that this type of comprehensive social service system has been tried and whether there are any lessons we can learn from them."

"Tamika, I like where you're headed here," Jill says.

"I'd like to flesh this out more," Tamika says. "Can we talk about it some more on my first day in DC?"

"I look forward to it," Jill replies.

When Ramon wakes, he has again lost control of his mobility. It takes a few minutes to realize the inability to move results from shackles and stretched chains attached to his wrists and ankles, with a metal belt used to bolt his waist to the floor.

He tries looking around the room, but can only swing his neck so far and can't lift his head without poking the metal jaw bars into his collarbones. Making it even worse, the ends of the metal jaw bars now have sharp points, so Ramon punctures through his skin before settling his head back to the floor.

"What's this?" Ramon asks in Spanish as loudly as he can, forgetting his pretense that he could only speak English and French.

"This," Abril states as she straddles over the top of Ramon, *"is an interrogation."*

As she says this, Abril bends over and caresses her breasts. Ramon quickly realizes his pants have been removed. Abril turns and looks. Not quite.

Abril smiles at Ramon: *"You're almost there, big boy. Perhaps you need just a little more encouragement."*

"Let me guess," Ramon says. *"You aren't really studying to be a nun."*

"Oh, no," Abril says. *"I was studying to be a nun."*

Abril sits on Ramon's chest, rubbing herself on Ramon until she hears him scream.

"Ahhhhhhhh," he screams with a high pitch and fear that makes Abril smile widely. *"What's that?"*

"Just a piece of glass set just a few inches above your little spear," Abril replies. *"Of course, on the side facing you, I've glued some rusty nails and razor blades and shattered glass."*

"Why are you doing this to me?" Ramon asks. *"Don't you see how hurt I am already?"*

"Oh no, you haven't even begun to suffer. Certainly not for what you did to me and to everyone else," Abril replies through quivering lips.

"What do you mean?" he pleads.

Abril stares directly into Ramon's eyes: *"I know who you are!"*

"I don't know what you're talking about," Ramon contends, remembering that he has to continue to claim amnesia to be safe from the U.S. military and whoever remains in the cartel's Protection Corps.

"Sure you do," Abril contends, now fully clothed and with no hint of a smile remaining. *"It was your men who stole me from the convent and raped me every day, at least twenty times a day for the most hellish months of my life before your prisons and drug halls were destroyed by the Americans."*

"I don't know what you're talking about," Ramon pleads again.

"Yes, you do. You know, Señor Mantle. I know who you are. And I know you know who you are. Now I'm going to pay you back for what you and your men have done to me."

Ramon starts to break down, realizing the futility of his situation, but decides he can never admit that he knows who he is, no matter what.

"You wimpy, slobbering bitch," Abril yells at him. *"Now you know what it feels like to have absolutely no control over your life. Perhaps if you're a good boy, I'll give you a break from your beatings. Isn't that what you used to think was the only dream I had the right to pursue?"*

With rage thrusting adrenaline through his veins, Ramon yanks to dislodge his chains only to find Abril inserted several spikes into each of the chain cuffs. Blood now pouring around his wrists, Ramon watches as it rolls down his arm, pooling on the inside of his elbow before dripping to the floor.

"Did baby hurt himself, Mr. American?" Abril asks. She stands up, stepping backward down to Ramon's feet before kneeling on the floor and starting to rub the inside of Ramon's calves.

"Want me to take care of you?" Abril asks.

Ramon is tormented, not sure whether he's totally infatuated or in complete dread of Abril. She works her way up with her hands, rubbing his knees, then his lower thighs, then moving higher.

Ramon does everything he can to think about anything besides Abril's touch. He tries to envision her touch as first cuts from General Hernández while skinning Ramon alive, one of many tortures Ramon had been forced to watch the general inflict on cartel deserters, law enforcement agents and other enemies. His envisioning attempt fails.

As Abril's caress reaches inside his upper thighs, Ramon loses focus. Her face and body reappear in his mind, forming an unassailable enemy to self-control when combined with Abril's tender, massaging touch. Ramon fights to keep blood flowing to his brain. Abril's touch is having her intended effect despite Ramon's efforts to combat his physical attraction. Abril leans over, moving her lips below the glass plate. She blows soft wisps of air between Ramon's thighs. Ramon reacts in her intended manner until he again feels the cut of glass shards and sharp needles, as well as nails he hadn't noticed before. He tries twisting his hips to move himself away from the pain, only to be sliced by layered razor blades set to punish him for attempting to escape. As he screams, Abril shoves a towel in his mouth, holding it there until he quiets down with tears streaming down the sides of his face. Finally she pulls out the towel.

"I never hurt anyone. I don't know who you are and I don't know who you think I am, but I can assure you that I never hurt anyone, ever, ever in my life," Ramon pleads haltingly, eyes still watering from a combination of pain and abject fear.

"If you don't know who you are, how can you know you never hurt anyone?" Abril asks, pleased with her interrogation skills.

"Please, please, I just know. Please just let me go," Ramon begs, doing his best to keep himself from sobbing loudly.

Abril looks at Ramon, a hint of satisfaction on her face. *"What will you do for me if I let you go?"* Abril asks.

"What? What do you want me to do for you?" Ramon pleads, a whimper taking over his normally confident voice.

"When you can answer that on your own, you might be ready to go," Abril replies.

Abril walks to the mini-fridge, pulling out a few items that Ramon can't quite see without again impaling the spikes attached to his facial mask into his shoulder blades. Minutes later, Ramon hears the sound of something cooking. He begins to smell peppers, spicy peppers, cooking in oil. As time passes, he realizes how hungry he has become. His stomach growls loudly. Abril laughs at him.

She sits in a chair next to Ramon, eating out of a bowl, making sure he can see the food, but being equally certain to ensure he can't see her tears. She's saddened by what she's doing, but she can't think of anything else. Ramon's mouth had been so dry his tongue felt stuck to the roof of his mouth at times. This aroma, though, triggers his saliva, moistening his mouth in anticipation of a bite Ramon prays will come. Abril wipes her eyes with a towel before walking back to Ramon.

Sitting above and looking down on him, Abril feeds Ramon several bites of beans, rice, peppers and tomato, before washing the food down by slowly dripping from a glass of water into his mouth while standing over him.

As Ramon's thirst subsides, his eyes move away from catching the water to looking up Abril's skirt. He quickly closes his eyes to avoid being cut again if his mind again loses control of his hormones.

Abril watches as the water misses Ramon's mouth, seeing he has closed his eyes.

"Open your eyes and look," she tells him, switching to English she had learned and practiced in the convent in preparation to be sent to work in the northern United States.

Ramon keeps his eyes closed until Abril bends down and slaps him across the face.

"Open and look," she orders, grabbing a loose piece of chain in her left hand to let Ramon know what will happen next if he disobeys.

Abril sees him open his eyes, and hears him scream again as she turns to see that her body is having its intended effect on Ramon.

Ramon is screaming in anticipation of the pain he's about to feel, failing to stop himself from reacting.

Finally, Abril relieves his misery.

"Don't worry, Ramon," she says. "I moved the glass plate. I need to clean you or you'll be deathly ill soon enough."

"Ramon?"

"Yes, you know it, Ramon."

Abril pulls a bowl over to the sink, fills it with warm water and soap and grabs a soft cloth. Turning back to Ramon, she sits beside him and begins to clean his bloody wounds, first from his shoulders, then his wrists and arms, and then from his mid-section. She is soft and gentle with her touch. Ramon feels blood rushing away from his head and lies fully extended on the floor as Abril cleans him, then slowly dabs anti-bacterial cream on all his wounds.

Ramon's pain is both exhilarating and debilitating. As he begins to feel an explosive pulse, she stops.

"Be a good boy now," Abril says. "I'll see you tomorrow."

"Please, please, don't leave me," Ramon says as he hears Abril walking toward the door.

"I'll be back."

Ramon hears several locks latching from outside the door. Then he hears the windows above closed and locked from the outside.

"Please God," Ramon begs between weeps. "Forgive me for my sins. I won't abandon you again. Never again."

The work part of Jill's Chicago weekend concluded, Professor Stark pulls up with the top down on his convertible. After two attempts to park manually in the street parking spaces with just twelve-inch clearances in the front and back, Paul gives up and triggers automated parking on the car—allowing the wheels to be turned at ninety degree angles straight into the spot.

A weak whistling attempt fails to draw Jill's attention up from her reading so he gets out and sneaks up from behind Jill to wrap his arms around her waist. Fortunately for him, he's still quick enough to move his face out of the way of a strong elbow swing.

"Hey, hey. It's me," he yells out as he jumps out of the way.

"Well, then, don't scare me like that."

"You're right. I should be a little more sensitive to being snuck up on," he acknowledges, thinking about the four muggings he endured a decade ago. "Sorry. I wasn't thinking."

"Ready?" she asks.

"Dinner will be ready when we get home," he remarks as he opens the door for Jill, runs to the driver's side and enters his home as the destination. He knows Jill is skittish about his driving skill and decides he's annoyed her enough for one hour, so lets the automation program take them home as Jill recaps her discussion with Tamika and tries to keep her hair from covering her face.

Walking from the unattached garage to the back kitchen door of Professor Stark's south side home, Jill is immediately captured by the aroma spilling outside.

"Wow," she remarks. "Whatever you're making smells great. That's a strong garlic smell."

"I figured if we both smell like garlic, it wouldn't matter. Homemade sausage lasagna, with everything fresh including the pasta and sauce," Professor Stark announces, drawing a surprised smile from Jill. "Well, I did buy the sausage, mozzarella and ricotta, so it's not all homemade."

23 REVELATION

For more than an hour, they sit across from each other enjoying a candlelit dinner of lasagna, roasted garlic crostini and a radish, roasted beet and goat cheese salad tossed in a homemade basil, oregano and balsamic vinaigrette. A bottle of Chianti extends the dinner along with continued conversation about their multitude of common interests and connections.

As the bottle empties and it's clear dinner is coming to an end, Professor Stark starts to sweat, even though the temperature inside his thoroughly renovated south Lake Shore home would be perfectly comfortable any other day.

"Is something wrong, Paul?" Jill asks, seeing beads accumulate on his brow just as she is ready to suggest that it's a bit too chilly.

"Not wrong. No," Professor Stark replies, any pretense at maintaining a confident disposition clearly destroyed by cracks in his voice, drips from his forehead and a sudden inability to look Jill in her eyes. "But I've known for a while that I needed to show you something about me that you probably won't like and I keep putting it off and I promised myself I would show you this weekend. So, this," he says as he wipes with his napkin, "is me dreading your reaction."

"Well, whatever, it is, just show me and we'll figure it out," Jill replies, trying her best to be reassuring, while wondering what could possibly have him so worked up. She couldn't have completely misjudged him, could she?

"Okay," he replies, taking her hand and walking her toward the stairwell. Passing the entrance to the upstairs, he takes her around to the door to his basement. "You haven't seen this and I think you need to see it to really know me, scars and all."

"Okay," Jill murmurs as she follows him into what appears from the stairwell to be a typical unfinished basement, with chips crumbling out of the concrete floors and walls and several boxes stacked to the right of the stairs. Tiny crumbs of salt circle the water softener and a half-dozen clean air filters sit to the right of the furnace with a sizable pile of dirty filters stacked behind them.

"Ewww. Why don't you throw those out," she says as she sees the pile of air filters.

"Oh, those," he replies. "They're reusable. I just never get around to washing them out. But I will. I will."

"That's what you were afraid to show me," Jill says, not seeing anything else of note in the basement.

"No. No. I wish it were," he replies, grabbing Jill's hand and walking her to a storage shelf against the wall behind the stairs. "It's this," he says as he drops to the floor, pushes books aside, pulls aside a small wall panel and twists to push the shelf and the wall into the rest of the concrete wall.

Jill lets go of Paul's hand and takes several steps back toward the stairs. He lets go easily and moves away from her to make sure she isn't scared by his presence. Jill is nearly back to the stairs, sidling backward and peering toward the opening before she can see inside. Professor Stark steps down six stairs and turns on the lights inside the hidden room. As he steps further in, Jill walks slowly back toward the entrance, still keeping her distance. With Professor Stark outside her view, Jill steps toward the entrance, looking around to see if anyone or anything unusual is around her.

"What . . . is . . . this, Paul?" she asks as she peeks in and then takes her first steps down, still keeping a hand on the opening door.

"This. This. This was my bedroom for much of the last decade."

"What?" she asks as she steps the rest of the way in. To her right, she sees a queen-sized bed. On the left are thirteen monitors, twelve that show security views inside and outside the home and the last situated at eye level beyond a desk at the foot of the bed. To the left of the thirteenth monitor is another stairwell leading upward.

"Where do those go?" Jill asks as she looks between Professor Stark, the stairs across from her and the stairs behind her.

"To my garage," Professor Stark replies. "I know. I'm a freak. I spent so long being afraid to sleep in my own bed. After the attacks, I built this and started hiding here at night."

Jill looks at him for a few minutes, trying to gauge whether this is what he was hiding, or this is the control center for what he was hiding.

"There's not, like, women buried behind these monitors—or girls or boys or anything, right?" she asks in what is attempted as a half-joking voice, all while stepping backward as she speaks.

"No. God, no. I'm not that crazy. Just. Just. Just. You know. Just maybe paranoid about someone else wanting to get rid of me," Professor Stark states. "It took me a long time to get over it, you know, the muggings, so I hid here when I didn't feel safe and after awhile, I just got into it being my routine."

"Did you build this?" Jill asks, eyes and head still rotating constantly searching for signs of danger.

"Well, this structure was here. This house used to have a store with living quarters above and this back area as storage space. I did the remodeling to hide it and seal it and make it comfortable," Professor Stark admits.

"This is what you were so afraid to show me?" she asks.

"Nobody else knows about this. Nobody," he replies. "I know I'm nuts. But I think you need to know who I am, flaws and all. I just don't think anyone else needs to know."

He stops talking and stares at Jill, waiting for a response. She looks at him for several moments, twitching her lips back and forth while contemplating her response. Then, she reaches over and grabs his hand.

"Let's go to bed," she says with a smile, pausing for several moments before adding: "Just not this creepy one."

As he starts to follow toward the stairs, she stops and turns back around.

"Aren't you going to turn off the cameras?"

"Yeah, of course. Thanks for reminding me."

Walking up the stairs from the basement, Jill turns back around and looks down at Professor Stark: "You haven't recorded us before, have you?"

He looks up at her and smiles, eyes wide open and eyebrows elevated: "I hadn't even thought of that."

"Well don't. Or you'll need to lock yourself in there to stay alive."

"I know. I know," he replies. "I may be a little odd, but I wouldn't ever do anything to hurt you."

Ramon's sleep only comes in still painful fits and starts before Abril returns. The windows are opened first, letting light in the room along with some fresh air. Then, Ramon hears the locks near the door opened one by one.

Finally, Abril enters.

"If you lie to me today, you'll pray to God it was yesterday," Abril says, reverting back to Spanish. *"If you want to live, you'll start telling me the truth."*

Ramon can't stand the thought of another day like yesterday. *"Anything, anything. I'll tell you anything you need to know,"* Ramon says. *"Please God, just don't hurt me anymore."*

Abril pulls the blanket off of Ramon she had put on the night before, leaving him again exposed. She reinserts the glass cover over his man mind, making sure to show Ramon the glass shards, nails and razors before setting it down.

Then Abril unbuttons the top button on her shirt and leans over.

" You're name?" she asks.

"Ramon. Ramon Mantle," Ramon admits, having decided that if she is going to kill him, he'd just as soon get it done. *"But I'm begging you, please don't tell anyone I'm alive. There are so many people who want to see me dead."*

"How do you know I'm not one of them, *Señor Mantle?"* Abril inquires. *"Especially given what you and your men did to me."*

"I swear. I swear. I don't know who you are," Ramon pleads. *"I'm sure I never hurt you."*

"Your men took me captive and raped me every day, twenty or thirty times a days in your drug tunnels," Abril says, slapping Ramon violently as she speaks. *"You tore my soul from me and now you want to tell me that you never did anything to me."*

"You have to realize that I was a captive there too," Ramon says, a statement that draws another violent slap from Abril and then a whip into his ribs with the loose chain. *"I'm not lying. Just listen to me and kill me if I'm lying to you."*

"I may kill you anyway," Abril says, knowing though that killing Ramon would complete her descent into hell.

"General Hernández held my family at constant gunpoint. If I did not do whatever he commanded, he promised to kill them," Ramon states. *"I had no choice when he moved me to Mexico."*

Abril stares at Ramon, trying to detect from his eyes whether he is lying. Finally, deciding he must be lying, she whips him in the ribs with the chain again.

"I'm telling the truth," he implores, tears welling up from the pain.

"The leader of the Castillo cartel was a prisoner?" Abril asks, striking Ramon a third time with the chain. *"Impossible."*

Ramon struggles to decide what to say next, not wanting to be beaten and wanting to convince Abril he is telling the truth.

"So, did you ever meet General Hernández?" Ramon asks.

"He was the first one to rape me, right when I first arrived, and then he raped me every day until . . ., until we were rescued," Abril says.

"Did I ever touch you? No. Because I never did that," Ramon pleads.

"I didn't see you on me, but so many took me without me even see-ing their face. I don't know what's worse, looking at you, or just being

treated like an object, a thing, a piece of meat," Abril replies, a tense, pained expression accentuating her words.

"If I was really so powerful, wouldn't I want to look into a face as beautiful as yours while we made love," Ramon says, drawing a slap across the face, followed by Abril's spit.

"Love? That's what you call love? You destroyed me. You shattered me," Abril replies, tension contorting every feature of her face.

"I never saw you, let alone took you against your will," Ramon says. *"If I was really the powerful leader, wouldn't I have been told at least about the most beautiful women in our entire command center?"*

Abril slaps Ramon again, though not as hard as her earlier blows.

"I would have done anything to be with a woman as beautiful as you these last miserable months," Ramon pleads. *"Don't you see how I can't even control myself around you when I know that pain follows my desire? If I'm the rat in your experiment, I'm the rat who can't turn away from pain if it means looking at you."*

Abril turns her head away.

"I'm telling you, I never would have let you be hurt if I had any control," Ramon says. *"I would have demanded that you be with me and begged you for your permission to caress your lips with my own."*

Abril leans forward on her chair. Ramon looks up to see her head bobbing forward and backward. Then he feels it. A tear drops onto his neck.

24 EXAMINATION

The back table at Heart and Soul Café—several blocks south of the University of Chicago's Hyde Park campus—has no assigned seating, but owner Margie blocks off Professor Stark's preferred table near the back exit on days she knows he'll be on campus.

Over the years, Margie has taken to personally seeing to his service, in part because she enjoys the occasional banter and in part because he is one of their most loyal customers—and not above showing a bit of financial appreciation for high quality service. Rather than deal with constant back-and-forth to refill Professor Stark's cup over the two hours he typically takes to linger through breakfast and complete his preparation for the day, Margie keeps a carafe on hand solely for the Professor's use.

As he walks in this morning, she fills the carafe, grabs a half glass of skim milk and places it in front of the seat with his back to the back corner that he always takes.

"Good morning, Paul," she greets him. "So happy to have you back. I was starting to feel neglected without my ray of sunshine to start my day these past couple of weeks."

"I've missed you too, if it's any consolation," Professor Stark replies while looking directly into Margie's eyes. "It's been a crazy couple of weeks."

"Oh, Paul. It's been a crazy year for you," Margie replies. "Well, and for all of us, for that matter."

"No question about that, but all this stress seems to make you just younger and more beautiful," he replies.

"You keep flirtin' with me like that and my husband's going to start showing up to keep an eye on you."

"I'm pretty sure your husband isn't the least bit concerned about losing his dream girl to some saggy-bellied bookworm," Professor Stark says, looking over at the daily specials to see if there is something besides one of his usual meals he wants to order.

"You're hot enough for America's princess from what the Celebrity Channel tells us, so don't you go on with this modesty business. Besides, maybe it'd be good for my husband if he did have just a little bit of concern," Margie replies. "I might get a little extra of his attention."

"Sure, but I'm pretty certain I lose all the way around in that scenario," Professor Stark says as he turns off the menu built into the table.

"So what can I get you today, sunshine?"

"Oh, good God. Please don't call me sunshine, certainly not this early in the morning," Professor Stark pleads.

Margie smiles at him and puts her hand on his shoulder the way she always does when she wants him to know she's just teasing him. "Okay, sweetheart. What can I get for you?"

"I know my doctor would tell me to get the asparagus and sun-dried tomato egg white omelet, but I can't pass up the sweet potato and sausage hash special, can I?" Professor Stark states. "Since I'm being bad, why don't you throw a sunny-side egg on top. Make sure the cook keeps the yolk runny for me."

"You got it, Paul."

For the next hour, Margie leaves him alone, knowing he prefers to focus on class preparation until he's comfortable that he's ready. She can always tell when he feels comfortable, because that's when he shoves his Lifelink device back into his pocket, leans back in his chair and does a bit of people watching around the café. That's Margie's cue to go back and talk a bit more, sometimes about life, sometimes about his work and sometimes just talking about their futures.

This morning, though, Margie spots a younger woman walking to join him, pulling up a chair across from him while Professor Stark's Lifelink is still open.

"You're that Professor dude, aren't you," the young woman says as she sits down, leaning forward so that her breasts push up off her forearms to expose even more of already displayed, ample cleavage. Straight, blond hair falls past her shoulders, blue eyes and a wide smile sparkling enough at him to at least offer modest competition for his visual attention.

"I am a professor," he responds, elongating the "a" sound. "I don't know that I'm that professor dude, though."

"Sure, sure you are," the young blond replies. "Wow, you're way better looking in person."

"Then you're definitely looking for someone else."

"Professor Stark, right?" she asks.

"That's correct, and your name is?" Professor Stark asks.

"Cindy. Cindy Colorado," she says as she leans over the table to shake his hand, her shirt dropping down even farther, leaving parts of her areola exposed.

"Uhm, well, uhm, nice to meet you Cindy Colorado."

"I can't believe I just shook Professor Stark's hand. My twin sister is going to be so jealous. She has such a total crush on you."

Professor Stark looks around for cameras, then realizes that pin cameras are so small, he might not be able to spot them. Keep your eyes up, he reminds himself. There has to be cameras in her shirt, trying to catch you looking.

"Where are you from Cindy? And what brings you here?" Professor Stark asks.

"My sister and I came up to Chicago for vacation. We're from Texas," Cindy replies. "Sandy's going to be so mad she slept in. Can I get my picture with you? She'll never believe me otherwise."

"I guess that's okay," Professor Stark says.

Cindy asks a waitress to take a picture, then steps around the table to stand next to Professor Stark. As he puts his hand around her waist, he realizes that her shirt has almost no back. He also realizes that Cindy doesn't have any boundaries as she shoves her hand down his back pants pocket.

"It looks like you're doing a lot of work so I won't take your time this morning, but can I ask you for a huge favor?" Cindy asks after turning to stand directly in front of him again, eyes open and eyebrows elevated.

"What's that?" he asks, looking around to see who's watching and realizing that nearly half the restaurant is looking to see what's going on.

"Sandy is going to freak if she doesn't meet you. When are you done with classes and all for the day?" Cindy asks, rubbing her hand up on his elbow as he ungracefully tries to back away.

"I'll be done on campus by four or so, at the latest," Professor Stark says, still wondering where this is going and wondering how to cut this off without being rude.

"Is there any chance I can talk you into meeting us for a drink at the HydeSpree Hotel bar? You'd just make Sandy's and my twenty-first birthday something really special to remember."

"You're twins?"

"Yeah, identical twins. I'm sure we'd have a good time if you could meet us," Cindy says. "We'll be waiting at the bar."

Cindy bends down to grab the little purse she brought with her to the restaurant before heading back to the counter to order two coffees and two yogurt parfaits to go.

Professor Stark fights the temptation to stare, assuming there must be cameras trained on him for some kind of investigation. After she walks out, he clasps his hands on the back of his head and leans over the table.

Margie can't wait a moment longer to find out what just happened.

"It's bad enough to know you're cheating on me with your Jill," Margie says as she reaches the table. "I better not find out you have a baby doll on the side too or you're going to make me jealous."

Professor Stark looks up and starts laughing.

"What the hell is going on?" he asks, not really expecting a reply.

Margie shrugs her shoulders: "What do you mean?"

"You remember that guy that sat down with me a couple of weeks ago, the last time I was here?" he continues.

"Oh yeah, he was a real hot one. All of us girls had our eyes on him," Margie notes. "We were a little disappointed that you didn't introduce us to him."

"Well, I don't think he was your type," Professor Stark contends.

Margie shakes her head side-to-side and makes a soft guttural sound. "Trust me, a good-looking young man like that. We all could think up all kinds of things we could'a done to him."

"Yeah, but it didn't seem to me that you're all his type," Professor Stark informs her, setting Margie's eyebrows to uncontrolled elevation.

"Are you saying I'm not attractive enough, Paul, 'cuz I'll bend you over my knee if I hear something like that comin' out of your lips."

Professor Stark rests back into his seat. "No, I'm saying that he invited me out to dinner and made it clear he was physically interested in me."

"Well, now there you go just ruining several weeks of fantasy," Margie states, a wry smile and eye glint letting Professor Stark know she's having fun with this discussion.

"Sorry, but, look. Something's up. I've gone more than forty straight years of never having a stranger come up to me and express any sexual desire for me. Then, twice in two weeks," Professor Stark says. "That's clearly not coincidence. And then to throw twenty-one-year-old twins on top of that."

"You already named those girl's breasts the twins? Shame on you, Paul," Margie states, shaking her finger at him.

Professor Stark laughs at the goofiness of the entire exchange. "No, no, no. She told me she has an identical twin sister and she wants me to meet them at the HydeSpree bar this afternoon."

"Do you think, maybe Jill just wants to test you to make sure you're not going to play around on her?" Margie asks. "I don't mean to be offensive, but, you know, sometimes a girl just needs to be sure."

"Even if I was interested, I'm not going to mess up the best thing that ever happened in my life for a one-night romp," Professor Stark emphatically states.

"Just keep yourself away from danger and that girl is definitely danger," Margie replies. "I knew it the minute she walked in the door."

"Yeah, but why me?" Professor Stark asks, still trying to make sense of it all.

"Hell, I sure don't know," Margie replies. "Can you think of anyone who wants to ruin you or, better yet, has something to gain from controlling you?"

"I hadn't thought about that second question," Professor Stark replies. "But why now? And who?"

"I get that our government is better than many others," Tamika says in reply to a comment from another aide who suggests that Tamika must not think much of the nation to believe a fundamental change like the Golden Rule constitutional amendment is necessary. The exchange takes place during Tamika's first formal Judiciary staff drafting session, just five days after moving to D.C. with three suitcases, her Lifelink card and her friend Rachel.

During closed drafting sessions, committee members try to achieve consensus on at least some modifications to the God's Law proposal from President Phillipi. More importantly to Chairman Henry, the session is intended to smoke out amendments that could be proposed in public markup in order to organize the chairman's opposition or support, whichever best suits his purpose of being seen as the legislative victor.

The committee staffer's look of disdain encourages Tamika to explain.

"Your reverence for the Founding Fathers is far greater than mine," she adds. "Remember, some of my ancestors were property to many Founding Fathers. The Constitution let slavery continue, so you can't possibly expect me to think it ever was a perfect document."

Rachel Cruz, Tamika's former University of Chicago classmate, sits along the outer rim of the rectangular meeting sessions under strict instruction to remain an observer. Two days into her White House employment doesn't qualify Rachel as a trusted team member, but Jill had specifically requested that the White House send Rachel for this meeting. Rachel's job is to identify threats to the President's language and work back through the Attorney General and others on the ad hoc God's Law team to propose position adjustments to the President.

"Go get 'em," Rachel whispers under her breath as Tamika considers pursuit of a verbal assault against a pretentious, Yale-educated aide to a New York congressman when he argues that the God's Law constitutional amendment is completely unnecessary and unworkable even if it was needed.

"Don't misinterpret my comments," the New York aide finally argues back to Tamika. "I'm not saying the Constitution was a perfect document. What I'm saying is that the founders wisely created an amendment process that allows the nation to change without revolution. Historically, nations required war to undergo the dramatic change we've seen here."

Tamika leans forward on her chair, sweeping her eyes around the room to connect with everyone taking part in the discussion.

"So, even with their extraordinary gift of the Constitution, we had a brutal Civil War and our recent secession battle. Perhaps this gift was less perfect than you imagine," Tamika replies. "Perhaps it is a bit like giving a child a bicycle for Christmas but not having the foresight to include the pedals. It's still useful and has value. We can sit on the bike and propel ourselves forward with our feet, even without pedals. But the speed we can move forward as a society means we need to add the pedals. That's what this Golden Rule amendment does. It adds the pedals to the Constitution . . . in our view, of course," Tamika adds, making clear that she is speaking for Jill.

Despite this being her first full staff meeting since joining Jill's team, Tamika isn't the least bit intimidated by the knowledge and experience of other staff in the room.

"Let me put this another way," Tamika interjects after another fifteen minutes of debate involving other staffers in the room, "Do we all agree that the United States has imperfections?"

She waits for several seconds, looking around the room until all the heads are nodding agreement.

"Do we think that government policies sometimes run contrary to the fair treatment of our citizens?" Tamika asks.

Again, heads nod and shoulders shrug in agreement.

"Do we think that individual citizens sometimes take advantage of others in society and escape accountability because of legal loopholes when everybody knows the legal outcome is not equivalent to the moral outcome?" Tamika asks.

As most nod in agreement, Tamika sits back down and pulls her chair up closer to the long, rectangular table around which the staffers gather.

"So, if we acknowledge these flaws," Tamika continues, "why would we not want to use the process the Founding Fathers 'wisely' provided to us to make this a better society, where morality and legality intertwine rather than plow divergent paths?"

Rachel closes her fists and lightly, quietly pumps both hands.

"Tamika, right," the New York aide interjects. "It's pretty clear to me now that Jill chose wisely in hiring you. You're a strong advocate for her views but constitutional amendments are too important to pursue without taking time to fully think through the consequences."

"I agree," Tamika responds, before the committee staff director makes her first comment of the day from a spot sitting up on the congressional dais and looking down on the debate.

"Wells is right," the staff director says, nodding toward the New York congressman's legislative director who had been arguing with Tamika. "We must thoroughly explore the unintended consequences of turning this 'God's Law' concept into a constitutional amendment. Why doesn't somebody put together a list of potential flaws?"

A committee aide opens her system device and opens a program that records the conversation, automatically summarizes verbal comments into a list and projects the list against any solid surface. While the Lifelink program does this automatically, it allows for the owner to manually adjust the contents of what is projected as well, making computer control of list creation a true advantage. Everyone in the room agrees to have the contents of the discussion from this point recorded.

Wells, the round-faced, cherubic New Yorker, starts off the discussion.

"Ambiguity is clearly the biggest obstacle to success of this as a constitutional amendment," Wells says. "Given the vast divides in how various judges interpret even relatively straightforward, specific language, it's almost inconceivable to me that the American people will be able to rely on the courts to consistently interpret the amendment's requirements."

"That's a fair concern," Tamika replies, "particularly when we have all seen that changing even a single member of the Supreme Court can lead to radically different decisions as to what are the laws of our land. We have a judiciary that often sees its role as creating policy, rather than implementing policy, but adding one more constitutional amendment to the mix of laws to be followed won't magnify these disparate outcomes."

"Do you find that acceptable?" the committee staff director asks, part of a concerted effort by Chairman Henry to kill or distort "God's Law" in a way that ensures its defeat at the committee level.

"I do and here's why," Tamika replies, again leaning forward to ensure she can make eye contact with everyone around the table. There's no doubt that Tamika's high school debate training affects the way she presents. "The constitutional amendment gives courts the right to determine that laws are unconstitutional if those laws violate the 'do unto others as you would have done unto yourself' concept. That means, the courts will be deciding on the constitutionality of a law itself and, if the law is constitutional, on ensuring that enforcement of the law is being done in a constitutional manner."

"So, you don't see this as being used by a criminal defendant to get a sentence reduced if the judge treated them unfairly?" Wells asks.

"That could be an outcome only if the courts decide that a sentence directly contradicts the Golden Rule because of how a law is written. It's not the main purpose of the amendment, but it would be a welcome improvement if people have a way to challenge the constitutionality of laws that create unreasonable consequences, perhaps completely unintended consequences."

"So what are the limitations of this proposal?" another aide asks, having not really studied the issue in advance of the drafting session.

"Perhaps an example will help," Tamika replies. "Over the course of time, Congress has passed numerous laws to which it has exempted itself, its members and its employees. Because Congress is doing unto others what it is unwilling to do to itself, these laws will be inherently unconstitutional."

"Are you serious?" the staff director asks, having also personally not really thought a great deal about the proposal in advance of this session. "Do you have any idea how many laws Congress has passed while exempting itself or ensuring that its members are treated differently? All of these laws will be thrown out as unconstitutional. Our bosses will be subject to libel and slander laws when they speak on the floor. How in the world can we pass new laws to replace all of this?"

"Fair question," Tamika responds. "We've thought about this. Congress will have three easy choices: 1) amend existing law to include Congress and its members as covered entities, 2) pass a new law written in a way that Congress is comfortable it can comply, or 3) allow the law to be removed from the books. Options one and three can be accomplished quickly. Only option two takes substantive time and work from Congress."

Hours later, Jill calls Tamika to her office to de-brief Tamika's first committee drafting session. As Tamika sits down, Jill pours a cup of coffee for her and hands her a sugar packet. "How did you know that I take my coffee this way?" Tamika asks, trying to think whether she has ever had coffee with Jill before. "Last year, dinner with your Mom at your house," Jill replies. "Some details just stick in my mind of truly memorable days. Don't ask me why. So, on to a more important topic: how did the drafting session go?"

Tamika straightens herself almost involuntarily, an outgrowth of years of debate training and practice.

"I think it went well. Rachel was there, so I'm sure you'll get a report from the President's staff, but I think we made progress with some of the reluctant members," Tamika notes. "The further we went into debate, the clearer it became to many that the language as presented actually will accomplish what it's intended to accomplish."

"Is it settled, then? No amendments?" Jill asks.

"Definitely not settled. The staff director, Martha?" Tamika says, trying to be sure she caught the staff director's name properly. Jill nods. "Well, Martha wasn't happy in the least with how the debate was progressing, so just before the end of the discussion she rattled off a list of questions the Chairman needs to have answered before we can move forward," Tamika says. "I sent them to you in a message right after the session ended," Tamika adds, with Jill opening her Lifelink, finding the message and opening it to read the notes.

"Very well," Jill replies. "I think we can handle these."

"I do too," Tamika responds, "but one issue did come up during the session that I think bears mentioning."

"What's that?" Jill asks, folding her hands together.

"God's Law ensures that laws are not created that violate the 'do unto others' concept, but are we sure this will do anything to allow redress of individual cases when people are treated unfairly?"

"That's not as clear," Jill replies. "I've been thinking about this quite a bit. What are the primary sources of un-redressed injustice in society? Sometimes, government is abusive in treatment of our citizens, in part because government employees are often protected from liability for even malicious mistreatment. At other times, people can be bankrupted or otherwise destroyed by relentless pursuit from criminal prosecutors or trial lawyers, even when it turns out they had done nothing wrong. When the courts determine that these people never engaged in any criminal or inappropriate behavior, their lives can remain destroyed even when they are legally vindicated. That's clearly not right. That's not justice. How do we help people who have been so unfairly attacked recover what remains of their life, in part to help them recover and in part to ensure that prosecution of others is pursued only after fair, thoughtful consideration?"

Tamika nods her head, stopping to sip from her coffee cup before proceeding. "That's the type of issue some people were raising. Didn't matter if they were Democrats, Republicans or other independents.

The questions were about whether this would accomplish everything that needs to be fixed," Tamika notes.

Standing up to leave, she stops and turns back toward Jill. "I would add one more issue to the mix that wasn't specifically raised. Even in areas where we have sentencing guidelines, there can be wide discrepancies in how people are treated by the courts for the same crimes. A prosecutor might agree to a plea bargain to a lesser crime in one jurisdiction that would never have been agreed to by another prosecutor. One judge might sentence someone who bilked investors of ten million dollars to two years in a federal penitentiary in one case, while a case with an almost similar set of facts attracts a ten-year sentence for another defendant. How do we make sure that the punishments handed out to criminals are consistently applied, so that race, religion and other issues aren't distorting justice?"

"Good questions. We'll have to get to those issues, but I'm not sure that we can take this all on now. Do you think Chairman Henry is trying to complicate the issues and expand the scope of the proposal so it sinks from overweight?" Jill asks, standing up and walking with Tamika toward the door between her office and staff offices.

Tamika folds her hands in front. "Good question," she replies. "Good question. I don't know. I hadn't thought about that."

"Let's connect again tomorrow," Jill states, "before I leave for the weekend."

25 DESECRATION

Abril's deep brown eyes peer intently into Ramon, searing him even through their tear-soaked covers. *"How could you not know what was going on there?"* Abril asks, thinking it is clear her question is intended to be rhetorical. Abril's hands press together in front of her face, fingers and palms flattened against their opposites just as she had been trained in the convent.

The Castillo cartel raided Abril's Sacred Heart convent just a few months earlier, kidnapping nearly all of the girls and young women training to be nuns. Rather than serve their Lord, they were repurposed to sexually service the rapidly expanding Protection Corps militia based at the cartel's Sinaloa Province deep underground compound. Abril had been fortunate to still be a virgin when sent by her family to study at the convent at the age of 11. Her father had diligently worked to keep her safe from marauding cartel members, but knew he couldn't keep Abril at home any longer when he caught a Protection Corps soldier in his yard with his hands all over Abril. Abril didn't know, but her father paid the soldier more than a month's wages to leave his daughter alone that day.

Her father wasn't naïve. He knew it wouldn't be long until the soldier returned, alone to extract more money or with friends to extract Abril.

Until her kidnapping, Abril's separation from her family had been her greatest trauma. Abril's parents accompanied her on three buses over twelve hours to the gates of the convent. A nun held Abril's hand at the gate until Abril realized that the bus taking her parents away wasn't coming back. That moment is etched in Abril's mind, the moment she realized that everything she ever knew was driving away.

Twice a year, Abril's mother or father had visited her, letting her know she was loved and missed. It was as often as they could afford to visit. Not often enough for Abril. Certainly not often enough for her parents. But enough to allow Abril's heart to have recovered before the kidnapping. Healed. Just in time to be destroyed.

Eight years later, Abril had been nearly ready to take public vows and be sent to work at a U.S. convent facing a shortage in nuns when she was kidnapped.

Her first hours inside the cartel compound had been the most hellish experiences in her life. General Hernández had all the sisters-to-be stripped and lined up for his inspection. It was clear immediately that the general was in charge.

He walked up and down the line, grabbing wherever he wanted to grab, pulling the women's lips apart to see their teeth, and rubbing himself on them at will. When he made his choice, he had the others girls chained to the wall to watch, and had the other soldiers leave the room.

Abril was left unchained. A moment of praying that she would be freed passed quickly as he shoved her to her knees, ripped open his pants and inserted himself, grasping her hair violently and thrusting away. Gagging and crying, Abril tried to pull away only to be choked until she submitted. When he tired of raping her mouth, he bent her over the table and continued his assault from the back.

The other nuns screamed in horror, in part because their friend's chastity was stolen from her and in part because they knew their turn would come. When General Hernández finished with Abril, he dragged her to her chain and untied another girl, the youngest girl in the convent whom Abril had considered to be her little sister. Watching the general impose his horror on her little sister was even more traumatic to Abril. She prayed for God to let her die, along with any of her sisters who desired the same fate.

When General Hernández finished with his third victim, he dressed himself and walked out. Seconds later, the thirty soldiers who had raided the convent and captured Abril and her sisters came in, grabbing and tearing at each of the girls, entering in places they had never contemplated and beating them fiercely whenever they resisted. After what seemed an eternity of this abuse, a soldier sprayed them all with a cold water hose, threw small bars of soap for them to wash, and then walked each of the girls individually to their small bed areas, where they were chained for twenty two hours a day until the U.S. attack on the compound led to their freedom.

During two hours a day, the women and girls were allowed to exercise and clean themselves on one of the drug production floors, with guards on the floor with them and on metal walkways overhead armed with automatic weapons to ensure their compliance. Abril had watched some of the more experienced girls during these hours use their sexual prowess on guards to get additional food and comfort for their rooms, including protection against beatings by the most violent guards. At first repulsed by these girls, Abril soon studied to learn how they manipulated the guards to get what they had wanted. She used some of what she had learned to torture Ramon.

"How could you know who I am if we never met?" Ramon asks, praying that Abril will either kill him quickly or release him from his miserable confinement now that he is telling the truth. Abril decides she wants to practice speaking her near-fluent English with him.

"You came by on the overhead walkway, walking next to General Hernández," Abril replies. "No one else walks next to General Hernández. I knew you must be important man. I prayed you would come to me to protect me from General Hernández. I stared at your face and prayed every night I would see it again and escape my hell."

"But I didn't know you were there," Ramon contends.

"So you never came, even from behind?" Abril asks. "I wanted you to save me."

MIKE BUSHMAN

"I was not in the compound for very long," Ramon assures Abril, explaining the long story of how he came to be involved in the cartel, how the general always held his life in his hands and how he was head of the Castillo cartel in title only after Cesar Castillo had been assassinated. "From the time I was a teenager, my life had been owned by Cesar Castillo and General Hernández. So I know how you feel."

Abril surprises Ramon with a vicious slap, a slap that takes Abril by surprise as much as it does Ramon. For minutes, Abril stands over Ramon, feeling herself tremble. Abril races out of the room, throwing a long shirt on as she runs outside. She races down the steps making it only part way down before spraying vomit over the last several steps and the ground below. Stepping around the stairway pools, she wanders toward the edge of the lot before collapsing into fetal position against the brick piles that serve as a fence. Disgusted that she can hurt someone like this, Abril takes several minutes to recompose before returning upstairs.

"How could you possibly know how I felt?" Abril screams loudly as she reenters the room with a long-dormant tough demeanor back on display. "Did men rape you every day, all day and removing every ounce of life from your soul? Did you pray for death to bring relief? No. You can't possibly know how I felt."

"I'm sorry. I'm sorry," Ramon responds, well aware that he is chained and at Abril's mercy. "I just wanted you to know that mine is not the life I would have chosen either."

Abril reaches toward Ramon's face. He tries to duck to avoid another slap, puncturing his shoulders again with the metal bars attached through his jaw.

"I'm not going to hurt you," Abril assures him, loosening screws that held the metal bars in place and removing the bars. Seconds later, she unlatches the plate that held the bars to his jaw. "My aunt told me that your jaw is okay without this. I asked her to leave this in place to make you easier to control," Abril admits.

Slowly, Ramon moves his head in a circle, stretching his neck, feeling the muscles around it pull as he moves. His vertebrae crack. With his arms, feet and waist still chained, Ramon is hardly free, but feels a sense of relief nonetheless.

He looks at Abril, searching for any sign of her next intention. "How did you escape the tunnels?" Ramon finally asks as she washes her hands and face.

"Americans freed us, after they killed or captured all the guards," she responds. "They gave us food, water and salves and bandages for our wounds and let us go. I decided I could not go back to the convent. I have too much hatred in my heart now to be any use to God."

Ramon stares again at Abril. It's easy to see why General Hernández chose her first. Long, tight legs leading up to a fully curved posterior that didn't even require high heels to appear fully contracted. Her breasts pushed out buttons on her shirt, appearing disproportionate to a constricted waistline that likely had shrunk beyond normal during her captivity.

Despite the abuse she endured, Ramon could see a spark in Abril's eyes, even if that spark seemed fully triggered by talk of revenge. Abril's only smiles had appeared when she wanted Ramon to believe he could have her. She had learned how to appear interested without needing to feel any actual desire. Abril's cheeks were sunken, with a hint of dimple in each. A small birthmark under her right ear appeared the only permanent, pre-cartel blemish, though it is clear that several cuts around Abril's shoulders and deep scars on her back need substantially more time to heal.

"You wanted me to come to you to protect you," Ramon suggests. "I know you wanted that in the tunnels, but perhaps God had plans for you to find me here."

"Crap. Just bull," Abril replies. "How can you protect me when you couldn't even protect yourself from a street gang?"

"That's a fair question," Ramon responds, taking a minute to gather his thoughts before continuing. "It won't be easy."

"Genius," Abril interjects. "I have found a genius."

"No, I have money stashed in banks around the world. I need to get some of that money without having it disclosed that I'm alive," Ramon says. "I'll need to think about how to make that happen."

Abril debates for hours what to do next with Ramon. If he's telling the truth, perhaps he can help her. If not, he'll likely kill her. Either outcome, she ultimately decides, is acceptable. She can't bring herself to hurt him anymore, now that he seems to be human and not an animal who had tortured her.

Abril takes Ramon's picture and tells Ramon to wait patiently while she walks down to the lobby of a nearby hotel. At the hotel, she finds a public computer and creates a new private profile for Abril Sinaloa. She uploads a picture of Ramon as well as selfies she took with Ramon in chains in the background. She sets the profile to go public in forty-eight hours if she doesn't enter a code to extend its privacy. Only resetting her privacy requirement will keep the pictures from being easily found by intelligence agency searches. She adds enough information to her profile that anyone searching for Ramon Mantle will be certain he is the man in the picture.

On returning to the room, Abril tells Ramon what she has done to protect herself, then unchains his hands and feet. Finally, Abril says a prayer and then throws the key to Ramon to unchain his waist. Sitting, praying, Abril puts her head down and waits to find out how Ramon will respond.

She tenses her hands and arms as she feels Ramon's fingers penetrate the hair on the back of her head, gripping her head firmly in his palm. As she prepares to be beaten, Ramon bends over and kisses her on her neck. Abril's heart slows. She exhales loudly. He grabs her left hand, lifts it up to his mouth and caresses it against his lips.

"I'm so sorry for everything that was done to you," Ramon says. "I'll do my best to atone for both of our sins."

Abril can't speak. Her tears say everything.

"We have to find a way to bring the various religions and secularists together to avoid ridicule on the church-state issue," Professor Paul Stark tells President Phillipi in a weekly strategy discussion on pushing God's Law passage. "Calling it God's Law isn't really helping our cause, particularly with the media."

"I'm sure that's true. I guess I settled on that in the post-secession heat, wanting to remind America that there is something greater than other people to which we are accountable," President Phillipi replies.

"I realize not everyone believes this but we were founded on the belief that a Creator has provided us with unalienable rights and I believe that concept is correct. To me, the Golden Rule is the missing right, the right to be treated with consideration and consistency. But I get your point, Professor. I should have thought through the impact of the label on the ability to get it done."

Professor Stark is the only strategy discussion participant not physically in the Oval Office. The President, Jill and the rest are gathered there. Professor Stark's face and voice project from a clear screen resting on an automatically adjustable platform that moves his face height to the average height of other faces in the room, a feature that becomes awkward as some participants stand or others enter or leave the room.

"The challenge, Mr. President, is that you're trying to unify the country and your opponents are afraid to let that happen. So we have to anticipate all the ways opponents will seek to divide the nation," Jill remarks, contributing to the discussion as leader of the House passage effort. "The most obvious is the church-state issue, but don't think for a moment that some in Congress and elsewhere won't try to use this to create or deepen animosities between religions. There's no doubt that some scriptures and cultures appear more closely aligned with what we believe the Golden Rule means than others. Chairman Henry, for one, will try to use differences in how the Golden Rule is interpreted to create animosities between faiths."

"Some people are telling me that some faiths might not expressly believe in the Golden Rule," President Phillipi interjects. "I thought all of the major faiths have it built into their beliefs."

"Yes, major faiths certainly," Professor Stark replies. "All of them. Scarboro Missions and many scholars documented this extensively. Of course, there are some small exceptions. Some Wiccans may not agree, for example. Some white and black nationalist faiths with small congregations, and radical wings of even some large faiths, don't even pretend to believe in peaceful coexistence. I think we can dismiss the concerns of at least most of the faiths expressing public opposition because they don't advocate peace among people. I'm not sure how to deal with whole faiths that think it's their job to create a world in their exact image."

"Is it really possible to find common ground between all of these competing faiths?" asks Vice President Marcia Wilt.

Professor Stark fidgets away from the desk seat where he is being filmed, grabbing several books and opening them to folded pages.

"Not on everything, of course. But emphasizing what all people have in common is far better than antagonizing our differences. Finding common cause even just between the world's two largest faiths is always a challenge," Professor Stark replies. "That challenge took on great urgency after Pope Benedict's Regensburg lecture, which then led to the Common Word letter from Muslim clerics, but maintaining unity between faiths is difficult. Bureaucrats, and in every religion you find clerics who act more as bureaucrats than as faith leaders, will inevitably advocate what they believe is in the best interest of expanding their power and their bureaucracy."

"Sounds like government bureaucrats," the President interjects, drawing the type of laughter that powerful leaders can always count on from people dependent on them for their own success.

"Perhaps," Professor Stark replies after the laughter subsides. "That's my point. Bureaucracies inevitably beget bureaucrats."

Jill holds up a finger, catching Professor Stark's attention as he surveys the parts of the Oval Office that appear on his screen.

"That's what makes it doubly dangerous when religion and government become one and the same and why we need to be careful to ensure that church and state are not overlapped here," Jill says. "When church and state are too close, there is no one left to challenge individual men or women who distort faith or government to serve their own purposes."

"That's right, Mr. President," Professor Stark adds. "If you take a look through history, the most dangerous types of governments are those that are God-less, whether in the format of atheistic communists or operating under a structure in which the national leader is deemed a living God. But equally dangerous to God-less nations are single-religion nations."

"Explain this to me in a way I can explain it to the public," President Phillipi requests. "I've heard you talk about it before and it's all a bit complicated."

Jill looks at Professor Stark with a nod to make sure he recognizes she was right when she told him he needed to simplify what he has been saying on this topic.

"Okay, I'll try to simplify," Professor Stark states. "Let's look at history from the perspective of mass atrocities. Most people look back at the primary twentieth and early twenty-first century mass atrocities, most of which were caused by political regimes that promoted God-less religions. Look at communist incursions by Pol Pot in Cambodia, Joseph Stalin and others in the Soviet Union, Mao Tse Tung in old communist China and even the starvation and atrocities caused by North Korean leadership. It's not just communism though. Look at the atrocities created under Japanese empires from the late nineteenth century through World War II, when the people of Japan were taught that the emperor was a human God accountable to no one but himself. In all of these nations, the ruling class and the people believed that there was no higher non-human being who would ultimately hold leaders accountable," Professor Stark states.

"Equally troubling and likely to cause mass atrocities and outright genocides are the single-religion nations. Nazism and Hutu Power were thought of as political movements, but really were single-religion nations in the sense that no disagreement with the tenets of these movements was tolerated. Some argue that Adolf Hitler and the Nazis used Christianity to promote their message. In reality, they tolerated Catholic and Protestant church involvement in Germany only until the Nazis had accumulated enough power to eradicate any dissent within those faiths. Islamic crusades to force conversion throughout the Middle East, North Africa and into Europe began in 634 A.D. and have largely continued with only minor respites since then, typically driven by small percentages of Muslims. The Second Sudanese War, the Red Terror in Ethiopia and the Muslim Brotherhood-supported slaughters in Egypt are some of the latest examples. One of the great, but unknown mass slaughters in history took place under Timur, who is estimated to have killed seventeen million people or what was then five percent of the world's population to impose his faith. But clearly, it is not just Islam where single-religion states lead to atrocities. The Christian Crusades over two hundred years killed several million. The Thirty Years War created as many as eleven million deaths in the seventeenth century. But the greatest atrocity under the guise of Christianity took place in China, where Hong Xiuquan claimed to be the brother of Jesus and led a revolt to impose Christianity in place of Confucianism, Buddhism and other Chinese folk religions at a cost of at least twenty million lives during the Taiping Rebellion."

Vice President Marcia Wilt interjects, standing up to be sure Professor Stark gives her the floor: "I'm more than a bit disturbed by the anti-Islamic tone of this discussion. From everything I read about Islam and the Prophet Muhammad, the faith makes clear that the decision on whether or not to follow Islam must be a clear decision of the heart and never coerced. So the idea of these Islamic crusades seems a bit of fabrication."

Professor Stark is used to this kind of a response from those whose history exposure was confined to government-sanctioned texts designed increasingly around political consensus rather than historical exploration. "That's exactly my point," Professor Stark replies. "In the vast majority of cases where major religions contribute to or create mass atrocities, it does not have to be the teachings of the scriptures themselves that demand the atrocities. Instead, it is how men usurp the authorities of their faiths and select only portions of those teachings to suit their own political purposes. This usurpation grows even worse when a national government is de-facto ruled by the leader of a faith. When that happens, there is no competition between faiths to properly define right and wrong, no redress for adherents of the various faiths to challenge political leaders on moral grounds and limited opportunity to stop the perversion of religion to suit political power grabs without imprisonment or execution."

Vice President Wilt covers her mouth with her hand for several seconds. Then she shakes her head up and down before pulling her hand away and looking at Professor Stark. "Okay, I think I get it," she remarks.

26 IDENTIFICATION

Days later, Abril steps into Puerto Vallarta's Banderas Bay Bank wearing a newly sewn, long-flowing tunic and scapular similar to the one she had worn during her years studying to become a nun. Only Abril's face from her eyebrows to the bend in her chin remains exposed. Despite coverage of the form-driven aspects of her beauty, sightings of nuns inside the bank are rare enough that Abril still draws substantial attention as she enters.

Within minutes, Abril begins the process of leasing the largest safe deposit box the bank has on site. Following two hours of security measures, including fingerprint and retinal identification, Abril takes the deposit box key, memorizes her personal code and thanks all those who had helped her. She promises to return soon to make a second deposit.

At a small café along the waterfront, a re-civilianized Abril joins Ramon at a table facing Banderas Bay.

"As you suspected, your box is in the same room as my new one," Abril informs Ramon as he grasps her hand under the table and begins to rub her knee.

"Perfect," he replies, continuing to speak in English to minimize the risk of their conversation being both overheard and understood.

"Did the banker remain in the vault while you inspected the box?"

"No, complete privacy," Abril assures him.

"Then, tomorrow we will have our first chance at a new life," Ramon assures Abril. Abril pays for their food, tipping just enough to avoid triggering attention.

With Abril running low on pesos, she agrees to share a room with Ramon for the night. The motel is decent enough to sleep in, but dingy enough to ensure their interest in leaving as soon as possible. As they lie down on the full-size bed, Ramon rolls over and puts his arm around Abril's waist, a move from which she initially recoils before settling back next to him. He pulls her hair to the side and begins massaging her neck with his lips, then moves up to nibble on her ear. His hands begin to roam up toward her breasts, one of them cupped from the bottom by his thumb and index finger. Abril begins to feel Ramon pressing at him from below when he suddenly moves his mouth away from her, rolls onto his back and yells, "Ahhhhh."

"*What's wrong?*"

"*Damn it,*" Ramon says loudly. "*Everything is still cut up.*"

"*That's okay, I'm not ready for you anyway. God can forgive me for what I was forced to do. I'm not convinced he will forgive me if I chose to take a man without being married,*" Abril says, a statement that helps deflate Ramon.

"*But what about the way you were touching me while I was in chains?*" Ramon asks.

"*That was for your torture, not my pleasure,*" Abril replies, smiling at Ramon to let him know that she enjoyed how easily she could torture him.

"*So your God finds it acceptable for you to torture me, but not for me to provide pleasure to you,*" Ramon argues despite knowing he is in no shape to gain full pleasure himself without intense agony.

"*I'm sure God is sickened by what I've become and he's not alone,*" Abril replies. "*I can wait for your touch until it is right and I'm truly ready to believe it is for my pleasure.*"

"When will that be?" Ramon pleads, voice tinged with the timidity that accompanies begging.

"I'll tell you when I know," Abril replies. *"If I ever know."*

Ramon turns back to his side, staring at Abril, feeling even greater desire. It has been a long time since he has been forced to wait by any of the women he desired. His wealth had always been a powerful aphrodisiac. That he was attractive as well convinced him he was practically irresistible, except, he is discovering, to Abril. He rolls to his other side, staring at the streetlight streaming through the crack in the curtains.

"Tomorrow will be a better day," he finally says to Abril, gaining no response.

Abril lies on her side facing toward Ramon. Whenever she hears the bed creak, she closes her eyes. As she hears him begin a light snore, she sits up on the edge of the bed, grabs the bag of clothes Tía Juanita had bought for her and takes it into the bathroom.

Sitting on top of the toilet lid and reaching down through the bag, she finally finds it: Her English Bible, the only possession that survived her imprisonment. Abril turns to the Book of John. She reads out loud. "But if we walk in the light, as he is in the light, we have fellowship one with another, and the blood of Jesus Christ his Son cleanseth us from all sin." Abril turns her head toward the ceiling, clasping her hands together. "Please God," Abril prays out loud as she kneels on the broken tile bathroom floor, "guide me back to the light."

Abril waits for inspiration, trying to free her mind from her desire for revenge and open her heart to God's will. Thirty minutes later, her still-calloused knees begin to ache. The tile floor hasn't been flat in years. Several of the tiles stick up, excessively concentrating pressure in several spots on her bony kneecap. While noticeable, the pain is nothing compared to what Abril endured in the cartel's sex slave den. She continues to kneel and pray, hoping her answer will be clear.

Finally, as exhaustion forces her to fight dozing off, Abril decides to trust in her Lord that his guidance will come to her, flipping pages until she rests her finger on a random page. When she opens it, she looks at where her finger is pointed and begins to read: "Therefore all things whatsoever ye would that men should do to you, do ye even so to them: for this is the law and the prophets."

Resting her Bible on the sink, Abril clasps her hands back together and thanks God for his guidance.

Abril is again dressed in her white tunic and black scapular when Ramon finally wakes fully rested. Despite sleeping no more than three hours, Abril is alert and energized in a way she hadn't felt for months. She hands Ramon a fresh bottle of salve to help heal his wounds and tells Ramon she is ready to head to the bank. Abril packs her bag with heavy stones inside of boxes to stuff in her safe deposit box. The backpack she brings out of the bank with whatever is in Ramon's box has to be lighter than what she brings in.

After reviewing the plan, Ramon shows Abril one more time how to pick the lock on his box after she enters his security code. She can gain access to the room and he can provide the security code, but the bank will never give Abril the key. Picking locks was never among Abril's skill sets so Ramon has her practice repeatedly. Ramon is pleased the bank didn't verify identification electronically when he took out his box, likely because much of the old wealth stored there is deposited by individuals who don't want to be identified.

JT receives word from Central Intelligence Agency Deputy Director Branch Whitney that the agency's global facial recognition scanning database search has identified a possible match with Ramon Mantle from several security cameras in Puerto Vallarta.

Immediately, JT sends Ally out in one of New Rite's APB attack insertion fighters to speed New Rite's Cooper's Hawk drones into Puerto Vallarta. Slowing just above the city, Ally and her team drop dozens of these bird replica drones from the APB. Back at New Rite headquarters, the drone surveillance team begins flying the hawks in what appears to any casual observers as random directions but in reality is a patterned scan of the city searching for Ramon from the vicinity of where cameras last captured him outside.

Walking into the Puerto Vallarta bank with a heavy thick bag, Abril draws more attention than she had the day before. A bank manager asks if he can help her carry her items. Abril refuses as she asks for access to her safe deposit box.

Several minutes later, the door to the vault is closed behind Abril. She opens her box and empties the contents of her bag, placing the rocks carefully so they won't fall out onto her if she ever has to open the box again.

With that complete, Abril turns her attention toward Ramon's safe deposit box. Like her box, it is nearly a meter tall and more than a foot in width. She enters the code Ramon provided, popping open the outer security door. Pulling out the tools from her bag, she starts trying to pick the lock as Ramon instructed her. Several times, the picks drop to the floor as Abril's hands shake.

"Please God, give me the strength to open your vault," Abril says out loud, knowing that sounds are unlikely to be heard from outside the vault door. Minutes pass and Abril begins to sweat. She has heard just two of the clicks Ramon promised would tell her she was succeeding.

Finally, Abril takes a deep breath, begins to pray the "Hail Mary" and the lock opens. Closing her eyes, Abril takes a deep breath before opening the box. She opens her eyes, at first to see nothing, and then notices a thin glass or plastic card lying on the bottom of the safe deposit box.

"*What's this?*" Abril asks herself before putting the card into her bag and resealing both deposit boxes. "*Did he lie to me . . . about everything?*"

Waves roll gently up to the shoreline, claps followed by tremulous whooshes resonating repetitively as Ramon sits waiting. Seagulls caw and cluck at the shoreline and on the roof overhanging the patio deck. Ramon listens and watches the shoreline, watching shore birds attempting to secure their own mid-day meals. It has only been a few months since Ramon's hunger had driven him to consider shore birds and every other animal in sight as prey. None had been so unfortunate to sate his hunger.

The vast expanse west of the stained-wood deck on which he currently rests reminds Ramon just how miniscule he is in the context of this world, even more so when he contemplates how little time he might have left if the wrong people figure out he is alive.

With his eyes focused on the water as it glides up and soaks into the sand before retreating under the next incoming wave, Ramon misses the out-of-place movement. Even if he was watching carefully around him, he might not have known what belongs and what doesn't.

Within hours of beginning its patterned scans, a Cooper's hawk drone flying near the water line triggers an alert back to New Rite's intel team. Facial recognition match confirmed for Ramon. Remote surveillance team members take manual control of the drones, sending five to perch along all the possible exit routes from the coffeehouse where drone scans have now confirmed that Ramon is sitting alone. Hidden away from surface sight lines, each of the hawk drones has several feathers point up and separate. A tiny hatch on the back of each bird drone opens, releasing tiny wasp drones.

While the Hawk drones remain dormant, the surveillance team takes direct control of each of the wasp drones, flying them as quickly and surreptitiously as possible toward Ramon. Strong ocean breezes, those caressing Ramon's face and encouraging him to briefly close his eyes and soak in their relaxing touch, make the journey difficult for the drones. Power cells in the wasps aren't yet to full strength. After ten frustrating minutes for the drone control team, a wasp reaches Ramon from behind, stings him in the neck and pulls away quickly. The wasp flies back to the hawk drone hatch for flight back to the drone collection point. During the flight, the DNA sample captured by the wasp is analyzed, confirming from New Rite's old cartel files that the man in the coffeehouse is Ramon.

Cameras on a hawk drone perched fifty yards away on a roof provide continuous video as Abril pulls up a seat next to Ramon while he scratches at a fresh bite on his neck.

"What the hell is this?" Abril asks as she puts an identification system on the table. Lifelink cards are barely bigger than an antique 1980s playing card when folded up. Once opened—using fingerprint, DNA sample or facial recognition assessment depending on the privacy required for the application being used—Lifelink screens extend to the size of an old school paper sheet.

Ramon looks at the thin, nearly clear plastic card, turns its camera eye toward him and clicks to begin facial recognition assessment. When the device opens, Ramon gains access to the accounts of an alter ego he created years earlier while formulating potential escapes from the Castillo cartel. An account search shows that he has access to fifty million U.S. dollars, a screen shot he turns and shows to Abril.

Abril's face brightens immediately, converting from stern to smiling in no more time than it takes Ramon to blink.

"What is this?" Abril asks, pointing to the screen.

"You don't know what this is?" Ramon asks, turning the screen face toward Abril. "Don't you have these?"

"You forget where I have been the past decade. Christ's teachings don't require electronics to make sense," Abril instructs Ramon. "So how does this work?"

"This is my payment card, my new identification, my computer, all wrapped into a single card I can easily fit in my pocket. Which reminds me that I need to buy clothes with security code pockets to keep this safe," Ramon tells Abril, referencing now-common clothing lines that contain security code protected interior pockets to deter Lifelink theft. The pockets are designed to erase the devices inside if forced open. "Otherwise, this could be stolen and used by someone willing to cart around my finger, my eye and my blood," Ramon informs Abril.

As Abril and Ramon leave the coffeehouse, this time with Ramon leaving a meaningful tip, the hawk drone perched on a nearby rooftop follows them visually, only moving when necessary to maintain distant visual contact.

Inside a clothing store, it strikes Ramon that his face has healed enough that facial recognition scanners can identify him now. He buys half of the store's allotment of hats, putting the largest of them on his head as he leaves.

Recognizing that hats will only help so much in preventing him from being identified, Ramon finds a plastic surgeon, buys an assortment of non-surgical implants and gets the surgeon to overcharge in return for providing Abril with as many traditional pesos as he can access from his bank.

"Why are you so paranoid?" Abril asks.

"Because I know what I'm capable of doing, and I know that the men who want to find me are highly motivated to use those capabilities," he replies, whispering in her ear, then blowing into it, grabbing her face and pulling her toward him. It's the last image of the two Ally reviews on landing. With instructions from JT to bring Ramon in, Ally walks to the Veracruz Bar, a modern though empty tourist bar where Ramon and his female companion have been followed by New Rite's drones.

Before entering the bar, Ally transforms her look and identity from highly focused, elite military fighter to sensual but still highly toned beach volleyball competitor. In a short skirt showing off her thick, muscular thighs, a tight top and a thin, silk shawl wrapped covering equally toned upper arms, Ally pulls up a seat at the table next to Ramon and Abril, waiting for an opportunity to introduce herself.

Ordering a mango daiquiri, Ally sips slowly, being sure to look around the room as if waiting for someone to join her. She glances from time-to-time at Abril and Ramon, each time finding them fully entranced in each other's eyes.

Finally, she cannot sit alone any longer without being conspicuous.

"Disculpe. Hablas usted ingles?" Ally asks, looking between the two for whoever will answer.

"Si señorita. We speak English," Abril replies while turning her attention to Ally.

"Great. Thank you. Did you see another volleyball player in here earlier? I'm supposed to meet my partner here," Ally states.

"What does he look like?" Ramon asks.

"She. She is very tall, six inches taller than me, thin, strong, blond hair," Ally replies, with a strong accent on the first word. "Very nice body," she adds, cupping her hands in front of her to suggest her friend's breasts were bigger than her own.

"No, no one like that," Ramon replies, turning his eyes back toward Abril.

"Well, thank you anyway," Ally responds, turning back away. As Ramon and Abril talk again, Ally sends a fake email to herself from a fictitious account. The note tells Ally the fictitious sender will catch up with her that night at Veracruz.

After sending it, Ally opens up her account, adjusts the time stamp on when it was sent to that morning, then turns back to Ramon and Abril.

"Excuse me," Ally interjects, "This is Veracruz, isn't it?"

Abril looks at the email, covers her mouth with the tips of her fingers and looks back at Ally. "Are you sure she meant the bar and not the city? Veracruz the city is on the other side of the country," Abril questions.

Ally's jaw drops until she rests her entire head in her hands.

"Are you okay, miss?" Abril asks after several seconds.

"I'm so stupid," Ally replies. "There's no way she could have meant to another city, right," Abril says, opening up a fictitious calendar entry she had also just created. "Oh no, our next tournament is in Veracruz. I bet she already left."

Ally pretends to call a local hotel, loudly begging the hotel to let her stay that night and pay them later.

"Are you serious?" Abril says to Ramon.

"That's a bad day," Ramon adds while looking toward Abril, "though we've both had worse."

Ally buries her head back into her screen, pretending to try making flight arrangements and hotel reservations. After several minutes, she turns back to Abril.

"I know this is a lot to ask, so please feel free to say no, but I only have enough money to fly to meet my teammate tomorrow morning. I was supposed to fly out today. The flights tonight are already booked and I can't afford a hotel tonight," Ally says in her best sheepish voice. "Is there any way, and I understand if there's not, that I can stay with you tonight. I'll leave first thing in the morning."

Abril looks at Ramon, who fights every instinct in his body that wants to say yes immediately. As much as he is into Abril, spending a night with Abril and another attractive mystery woman would make the night perfect. Then he remembers that he's still not fully healed and wouldn't be able to enjoy fully even if everything followed his fantasy.

"I don't know that it's a good idea," he whispers into Abril's ear, "but I'll leave it up to whatever you think is right."

"We can't just leave her to wander around at night looking for a stranger to sleep with. How would I feel if I let something horrible happen to her like what has happened to me?" Abril says.

"Well, that's your call," Ramon replies. "I'm willing to do whatever you want," he adds, fully meaning what he said.

Abril quickly becomes drunker than she has ever been. Ramon is also fully inebriated, but Ally drinks slowly throughout the night, pretending to take sizable drinks but letting very little past her lips. When Ramon begins to insist Ally drink more, Ally buys the next two rounds of drinks and tips the bartender well to leave the alcohol out of hers. After socializing at the bar for another two hours, the three amble home.

In the hotel room, Ramon quickly passes out on one side of the bed. Ally thanks Abril again and offers to sleep on the floor.

"No, no, no, no," Abril says. "There's plenty of space aquí."

As Abril begins to undress, Ally considers delaying her extraction plans. "Wow," she says under her breath, as Abril pulls her dress over her head. "Wow."

As Abril turns to get into bed, Ally's "wow" turns into "Oh, my God."

She walks over, pulls the blanket aside, and stares at scars from repeated whip marks on Abril's back. She sees the scars extend down onto the top end of Abril's buttocks.

"Did he do this?" Ally says, standing and tensing her muscles to prepare to beat Ramon.

"No, no, no, no," Abril slowly replies. "A general. A dead general, I think."

Ally regains control of her anger. "Are you okay now?"

"Yes," Abril replies, "but I need to have this ointment rubbed into the wounds to help them heal. Can you do it?"

Ally's eyes widen. "Sure, uhm, why not?"

Abril turns onto her back. Ally squirts a bit of the medical salve onto her fingertips and begins tracing her fingers over the heavy lines of remaining scar tissue. Over years, the salve is supposed to convert the scar tissue into softer skin tissue by enabling surrounding cells to replicate and replace the scar tissue.

Ally works her fingers slowly over the wounds on Ally's back, beginning near the top. Softly, gently, her spreading lubricant soothes Abril's wounds. Methodically, she moves her fingers downward, following the scar tissue in its interwoven lattice pattern. Pulling Abril's panties down partially, she makes circular motions with her fingers around the embossed wounds, lingering a bit longer than she had on Abril's back.

"That's so mush, mush, mush . . . softer," Abril whispers, before passing out to sleep.

Ally looks up at the ceiling, exhales a soft "whewww" and then reaches to her side to grab her Lifelink, setting the alarm for her ear insert to go off in one hour. In one hour, Ramon and Abril should both be in deep sleep.

Ramon wakes to stare directly into Ally's eyes, seeing that she is fully dressed. The intensity in Ally's eyes betrays a seriousness of purpose that Ally hadn't displayed at the bar or when they first returned to the hotel.

"What's happening," Ramon asks, seeing now that his hands and feet are bound and that Ally fully controls his movement, shoving him up and walking toward the door while Abril trails behind similarly bound and attached at Ally's back. Outside the room, Ally leads the group up a stairwell, then further up to the top of a roof.

Ramon tries to stop the movement, wedging his feet into several stairs, only to have his legs go limp as Ally zaps him. With his legs losing function, Ally carries Ramon's full weight. Her pace of progress is barely impeded by the added weight.

On the roof, Ally grabs latches at the bottom of four ropes hanging down from the sky. Ramon looks up, unable to see anything above, and hearing only a mild whisper but feeling wind propelling downward at them at a violent, sandstorm pace.

Abril and Ramon quickly recognize the futility of attempting to scream, unable to break through the masks covering their heads. Abril flings her body in a rage of wild motion, doing anything she can to keep from being taken again. It doesn't work.

Wind briefly beats down on their heads from above until Ramon looks up to see an aircraft hovering directly above his head. He turns his head enough to see Ally hooking up to devices from the aircraft.

With the last of four latches connected, Ally calls out the clear signal and the three are lifted straight up at a rapid pace. Abril and Ramon feel their stomachs drop. With a clear view of all of Puerto Vallarta, Ally, Abril and Ramon hover for just over a second while their ropes are rapidly winched into the APB. The bottom of the APB sits open as they are pulled to the roof of the interior. As soon as their feet clear the bottom, the door shuts. Ally unlatches Abril, while another New Rite soldier restrains her into a seat. Ally ties Ramon in herself before jumping to the front.

"Welcome back to America, Ramon," Ally says as she buckles down for the accelerated ride home and pushes to open communication between all of the APB's occupants.

"Damn it," Ramon blurts. "Are you U.S. military?"

"I'm your best option," Ally counters.

"Who's the girl?" the APB co-pilot asks Ally.

"Not sure," Ally replies, "but I didn't think it would be safe for her if we left her behind."

Ally turns to look at Abril, clearly shaken by the events of the last several minutes and crying to the point her oxygen injection rate is having a hard time keeping her lungs and heart stable.

Ally unbuckles from her seat, takes two steps back to Abril, grabs her right hand and caresses it between her own.

"Don't worry," Ally says. "No one is ever going to hurt you again if I can help it."

27 DEVASTATION

Near the top of Humphrey's Peak just outside Flagstaff, Arizona, a tall, thin-hipped girl bends over a wood stick. Despite her baggy sweats, Clarissa attracts the attention of a stranger who can't figure out who or what is wandering so far off trail on this majestic hike.

Already on this day, fifteen-year-old Clarissa has the makings of a beautiful woman. She might not be a head-turner in high school terms, mind you, where beauty is defined as too much make-up, overly tight clothes, the right weight, perfect hair and other telling signs to a high school boy that a girl might gain portions of her self-worth or her own pleasure from satisfying his spear-motivated desires. Beautiful, nonetheless. A pleasant, disarming face highlighted by high cheekbones. The rest of Clarissa hides under a baseball cap and overly loose clothing covered in a desert camouflage pattern.

Clarissa hasn't filled in all of the parts boys seem to care about in tremendous disproportion to their long-term relationship satisfaction value. That, combined with being six-feet tall at an age when she looked down at most classmates, means Clarissa normally doesn't attract attention the way girls who are perky, busty or smiling happily and frequently are noticed.

In the course of just a few months, Clarissa's body has deteriorated from reasonably fit to unusually thin. Given her baggy clothes, the taut, sunken appearance of her cheeks provides the only outward clue to her approaching emaciation.

Clarissa turns her head up, slightly away from a stick wedged into the ground below. Her eyes show no fear, despite clearly exposing a thorough sense of despair as the stranger approaches. Clarissa manages to attract the stranger's focus away from majestic beauty of this stark wilderness only a short distance down from the mountaintop tree line. The old man suddenly realizes why Clarissa is bent over and sprints toward her, attempting to distract her.

It isn't a wood stick wedged into the ground. It's a rifle. Clarissa's mouth remains over the barrel as her head turns partially to watch the stranger with one eye.

Closing her eyes to refocus, she reaches for the trigger.

"This just in," cable news network announcer Brody Maguire says as he cuts off that hour's leading news story, an interview with a woman now infamous and far from contrite for repeatedly slapping fellow shoppers. "We're receiving word now that what appears to be a nuclear bomb has been detonated in the country of Armenia, in a city I believe is called Yerevan."

While the video feed cuts to satellite imagery of the explosion, Maguire discusses a history of Armenia cobbled together quickly by producers from several Internet sites. Production staff, White House and Pentagon reporters scramble to be first with any details on the bomb and its death toll.

As they gather details, Maguire talks about Armenia's history. "Scholars continue to argue over whether the 1915 slaughter and forced extrication of Christians from Armenia can be characterized as genocide, but dozens of nations have officially designated those slaughters and forced marches as exactly that despite strident opposition from the Turkish government. We all, of course, remember the more recent invasion and slaughters of Armenians at the hands of a renegade Iranian army battalion, making this the third time in less than 150 years that Armenians have been attacked. At this point, we don't know what actions taken by Armenia inspired this attack."

Maguire remains silent for a moment as he takes instructions from his producers. "While we gather information about the Yerevan attack, we're going to invite University of Chicago Professor Paul Stark to talk with us about religion, government and armed conflict. Professor Stark is a noted scholar who focuses his research on the intersections of religion, government, business and the media. He played an important role in last year's language policy and secession debates. Thank you for joining us, Professor," Brody begins.

"Good to be with you, Brody, though certainly not under these circumstances," Professor Stark replies. "Before we jump to your questions, I have to raise concern with a comment you made just a moment ago. You said that we don't know what actions Armenia took that inspired this attack. What could possibly justify a nuclear attack on innocent civilians?"

"Fair point, Professor," Brody replies. "I certainly didn't mean to intimate that this attack was justified, but simply was saying we don't know at this point what inspired the attack. So, Professor Stark, do you have any idea what could have been the reason for this attack?"

"Anything we say at this point is pure speculation," Professor Stark replies while still tightening a tie over an only partially buttoned shirt he scrambled to put on as the video connections were being made, "but what I do know is that the global nuclear threat has grown exponentially in the past generation. Brody, nuclear weapons technology now resides in the hands of dozens of governments and, my sources tell me, several non-government entities."

"By non-government entities, do you mean corporations or other criminal enterprises?" Brody asks.

Professor Stark smiles. It's never a surprise, but always entertaining to hear Brody's biases come out in the way he asks questions. "Criminal organizations, Brody. But I'll need to leave it at that."

"What do you think this detonation means for global peace efforts, particularly if it turns out, as many might initially suspect, to be an anti-Christian attack by Islamist extremists?" the famously well-groomed news network anchor inquires.

"It's difficult to say until we know more details, so I hate to even have this discussion absent evidence of what really happened," Professor Stark replies.

"So take this incident away. Can Christians and Muslims live peacefully together if nuclear weapons are now not just a threat, but actually in use?" Brody prods, trying to keep finicky viewers from changing channels if they aren't seen as providing the most intense coverage on what has to be the world's biggest news.

"Nuclear attacks certainly make it more difficult. It's very difficult to turn the other cheek after one's whole body is eviscerated," Professor Stark notes, "but I urge caution and beg Americans of all faiths or no faith to wait for the facts. I beg your viewers to protect neighbors who had no role in this senseless attack. It's quite possible, isn't it, that the explosion could have been triggered accidentally or been economically driven."

"I certainly agree with you, Professor, in asking our viewers to act with great restraint while the facts are gathered," Maguire states, almost involuntarily reaching up to push hairs falling near his eyes back into place. "I urge all our listeners to stay with us as our best-in-the-business news gathering team brings those facts to you."

28 PREVARICATION

Just thirty minutes after the nuclear explosion occurs, President Phillipi steps to the podium in the White House briefing room to make hastily prepared remarks. Every national news network and several entertainment networks cut to the press conference.

As he nears the briefing room, an aide stops the President, reminding him to tighten his tie and button his suit coat.

Stepping slowly to the podium and then grasping its sides to help with his balance, the President takes a deep breath to calm the incredible tension adding tremors to his already challenged balance.

"Those responsible or involved in enabling the nuclear attack on the peaceful, largely unarmed nation of Armenia will face retribution. The United States expresses its deepest condolences to the people of Armenia and descendants of Armenia, including many Americans of Armenian ancestry," the President starts.

"I rushed here this morning to prevent America's heroic and successful efforts to mitigate the Armenia disaster from being turned against us," President Phillipi firmly states, as cameras pan to reporters hurriedly rushed into the briefing room. The President pauses, wanting to be sure the audience absorbs his latest comment.

"Immediately on seeing a nuclear explosion in Armenia through our global satellite surveillance, we launched six submarine-based missiles to explode inside the mushroom cloud and absorb residual radiation from the attack. This technology was only developed in recent months to mitigate potential nuclear explosions on American soil, but these missiles were just deployed in recent weeks to also help protect our Middle East allies from attack. Of course, America could do nothing to prevent the immediate nuclear devastation, but initial drone reports of radiation levels shows these anti-radiation missiles, or Radabs for short, are mitigating the destructive attack residue."

"Mr. President, Mr. President," asks a reporter for the party-owned Republican News Network. "Can you tell us more about the technology, how and why it was developed, for example? As well as answer why disclose it now?"

The President nods toward the reporter, a sullen expression naturally taking hold. For a brief moment, he considers smiling, something he reminds himself to do frequently when he speaks. This isn't the time, though.

"I'll take the latter question first. I came down here immediately to announce this technology because we are sure that our enemies have satellite tracking of our missiles. We did not want anyone confusing our launch with the suffering Armenia is enduring. To your former question, I don't want to disclose too many details, but suffice it to say that the best and brightest science minds in the United States were extracted from their day work earlier this year when we learned that nuclear weapons inside our borders were outside our control. My instructions were plain. Invent whatever it takes to prevent and/or minimize the effects of an explosion if we aren't successful in preventing it," the President announces.

Reporters shout a multitude of questions; shocked that such a technology could have been developed and deployed without public knowledge. President Phillipi holds up his hand, encouraging patience.

"I am also announcing a major foreign policy directive. I am committing today, on behalf of the United States of America, that we will use this new technology to minimize the damage of a nuclear explosion on the soil of any nation, friend or foe," the President announces.

A reporter for MSDNC, one of two media outlets formally owned by the Democratic Party, is granted the next question: "Doesn't this new weapon give the United States a strong strategic military advantage, allowing us to restrict the damage of nuclear explosions when we feel like it while other nations face full nuclear threat? Shouldn't we just give this technology to every nation so they can defend themselves?"

President Phillipi grabs the outside of the podium with both hands and leans toward the wire-attached microphone dot hanging above.

"I don't know if you've scanned the U.S. Constitution lately, but my clearest, most important duty is to defend our nation. This technology aids our defense and its method of success must remain a carefully protected national secret," President Phillipi replies. "But I also recognize that America has an obligation, as a responsible nation, to help others. That is what I've just announced we will do."

"Don't we have a moral duty to humanity to turn this into open source technology so anyone can use it to minimize nuclear threats?" another reporter asks, building on the MSDNC question. "It's good and all that the U.S. is using this to help our friends in Armenia, but just the development of this technology could contribute to global destabilization."

The President's exasperation with the media shows in his rolled eyes. "Feel free to ask different questions from each other and perhaps to even consider the most important implications of today's actions," the President loudly admonishes the press corps, again frustrated at the group-think that dominates many open press conferences. He's sure his press secretary will remind him that he had recommended allowing no reporters in the room to prevent questions focused on secondary or inconsequential issues. "We have a nuclear attack, an attack that appears to have been launched by radical Islamic terrorists, an attack that is the single most brutal act of terrorism in the history of mankind, an attack that even with our mitigation certainly has killed hundreds of thousands and perhaps even more than a million, and you are asking me about whether America's new technology to save lives and the world environment during an horrific atrocity is destabilizing global peace?"

Staring intently at the reporter asking the question, the President adds: "Shame on you."

"Look at this video," the President continues, pointing to a screen against the wall now displaying a satellite view of the Yerevan explosion and showing the quick diminishment of the mushroom cloud as U.S. missiles explode inside. "This . . . is . . . our . . . enemy."

The President bangs his fist on the podium and walks away.

After several minutes of recapping the President's comments and asking for reaction from the network's White House and Pentagon reporters, anchor Brody Maguire returns to Professor Stark. "If this is the work of extremist Islamists as the President seems to have indicated, what next?" Brody asks.

"If it turns out this is a purposeful attack launched by radical Islamists as the President just suggested, it will again call into question the ability of non-pluralistic societies to peacefully coexist. Rash reactors will suggest solutions that conform to single-event exercises in game theory. Anyone who wants to consider why this won't work can read about the prisoners' dilemma game. We cannot see this attack as a single event, since religious and national attacks and counterattacks have occurred throughout world history."

"So what do you advocate as a response?" the anchor inquires.

"Clearly, reason rather than emotion needs to rule our decisions," Professor Stark replies while shuffling to get more comfortable in his seat. "Nations can be deterred by mutually assured destruction, but religious terrorists may not see destruction as a deterrent since destruction for many of them is the start in their minds of eternal bliss. So the options are simple, either we find a way to physically eliminate every person who believes they've been called to violence or we find a way to educate those who believe violence is the answer to understand that their beliefs are wrong."

"Which one do you advocate?" Maguire asks, not wanting to let the Professor get away with offering an either/or solution with such dramatically different implications.

"The elimination approach is fraught with peril since collateral damage tolls are likely to be high. The education approach almost certainly needs to start within a faith, particularly among those clerics and others who influence individuals at the outer edges of a faith," Professor Stark contends.

"There are some on the far right, Professor, who argue Islam has been a violent religion from its very inception, starting with attacks Muhammad led against Mecca and his approved slaughtering of Jews in Medina. Is there any validity to this assessment of Islam as a religion of violence rather than as a religion of peace?" Brody asks.

"There are many ways to read the Quran. Those who want to read it as commanding violent aggression can read it that way. Those who want it to read as a guide to peaceful, charitable, tolerant coexistence focus on the many passages that support that interpretation. The debate on what the Quran truly commands is an important one, but one I leave to religious scholars," Professor Stark replies, a bit of sweat appearing on his temples since this topic isn't one he enjoys dwelling on. Every discussion of Islam raises the risk he'll be victimized by some militant cleric's fatwa. "I live in reality, and the reality is that if even just one percent of Muslims believe the Quran commands them to pursue violent aggression, then we have nearly twenty million militants and potential terrorists roaming the earth."

"So, what are you saying?" Brody asks, arms out and palms up.

"I'm saying that Muslims must take control of their faith and I know it can be done," Professor Stark clarifies. "Italians in the United States had to marginalize and demonize the Mafia to not be defined by the tiny percentage of Italian Americans with ties to criminal behavior. The Mafia didn't shrink in significance until insiders and the broader Italian American community turned against it. Radical terrorist organizations also will be best torn apart from inside. But that destruction won't happen until fellow Muslims pressure for its collapse, shun anyone who uses violence in the name of Islam and aggressively self-police."

President Phillipi strides quickly toward the Deep Underground Command Center (DUCC), a subterranean command center attached below the White House and designed to protect the President and his top aides during nuclear attack or intense conventional bombing. As he moves, he demands connections to Defense Secretary Xavier Mendoza, CIA Director Roland Rand and several others. As he descends to the DUCC, Vice President Marcia Wilt travels to Andrews Air Force Base for a flight to one of twenty locations used to separate the President and Vice President during times of potential attack. At Andrews, twenty jets are crewed and fueled inside a massive hangar. Entering the hangar alone, Vice President Wilt enters one of the jets without knowing its destination. Once inside, the twenty jets depart for their separate final locations. Unbeknownst to her, Vice President Wilt is headed to the Great Lakes Naval Air Station.

After a split-second eye scan, facial recognition assessment, DNA analysis and code entry confirms his identity, President Phillipi descends at high speed to the depths of the DUCC, bypassing the multi-layered security interventions that slow the descent of other entrants. These same stops trigger deadly assaults for entrants failing authorization tests.

Inside the DUCC situation control room, the President directs the rest of the U.S. response, with everyone requested immediately joining except the CIA Director. New CIA Deputy Director Branch Whitney represents the CIA in the Director's place. A note on the President's screen reminds him of Branch's position and background.

"Trial by fire Branch. Who bombed Armenia? What's the next target? Why didn't we know? Go."

"Mr. President, I don't have answers yet. I can only provide speculation," Branch responds.

"Oh, by all means, let's just guess," the President replies in clear sardonic tone. "When can I get real answers?"

"We're rushing this as we speak. One hour, maybe two. Even then, I can't promise a definitive answer," Branch replies.

"Give me your speculation," the President commands.

"Best guess, a new terrorist offshoot of the Iranian military, led by someone upset by that country's recent move toward secularization and away from being an Islamic Republic."

"Names," the President barks.

Branch lists four generals, two recently fired, all deemed by the intelligence community as most committed to an Islamic national identity for Iran.

"Any chance it's government sanctioned?" the President inquires.

"Chance, yes. No evidence, though, in any surveillance."

"Why would you expect evidence? This isn't something you order in any traceable form."

"Understood. We're on it," Branch assures the President.

Turning to Defense Secretary Xavier Mendoza, the President continues his questioning barrage.

"Military options, Xavier?"

"I believe we need to move to DEFCON 1, Mr. President," suggests Secretary Mendoza. "No clearer evidence that we are at threat of imminent nuclear attack than the attack in Yerevan."

Adrenaline has the President moving at high pace, physically and in his questioning. "How will others respond, China, Russia, Germany, Mexico, Canada, if they see us go to DEFCON 1?"

"Worried for sure. We'll need to manage it," the Secretary says.

President Phillipi demands the Secretary of State be found and transported in order to connect securely.

"Immediate response recommendations?" the President asks.

"Radabs missiles appear to be doing their job," Secretary Mendoza notes, adding that Yerevan-area radiation levels are dropping quickly. "Nothing further on the defensive front. Also, recommend hold on offensive intervention until intel gives us something real."

"Agreed. Move to DEFCON 2, but give five minutes notice to key countries."

As the President is ready to wrap up the discussion, Vice President Wilt patches in and is brought quickly up to speed on decisions already made.

"Mr. President, one concern please," the Vice President states.

"Go ahead Marcia."

"We need to move cautiously in any further intervention in the Islamic world," the Vice President states.

"They unleash a nuclear bomb and we need to move cautiously?" the President barks back.

"Do we know who 'they' is?"

"Not yet, but ties to radical Islamists are our best bets now," Branch from the CIA interjects.

"But we don't know," the Vice President counters.

"An hour or two for certainty?" the President questions, looking toward Branch. "What's your point, Marcia?"

"We need to understand the Muslim faith. True followers of the Quran understand that its teachings mandate that violence can only be used in self-defense."

"Then what explains fourteen hundred years of Islamic crusades, forced conversion and mass genocides," the President replies. "If history is any judge, occupying any land some warlord Islamist wants is reason enough to attack in the supposed name of Allah."

"That's not what the Quran teaches," Vice President Wilt contends. "These invasions, as you call them, are the work of small groups of radicals who have a distorted view of the Islamic faith."

"And yet, nearly two billion peaceful Muslims have not risen up to stop this minority, Marcia," the President replies. "Not yet, anyway."

"I think you underestimate the efforts of peace-loving Muslims to disassociate from the radicals," Vice President Wilt replies.

"I think you overestimate the intensity of opposition. Peace-loving Muslims fear the terrorists as much as we do. Remember that these terrorists believe they have a mandate from God to kill anyone—including innocent Muslim women and children—to achieve their goal of spreading Islam. If peace-loving Muslims want to be left to practice their faith, they must be the ones who lead the fight and make the sacrifices to stop these terrorists. I would like nothing better than to see the peace-lovers in the Islamic community be in control. But that's not always the case, and Americans can't sit on our hands and wait to be destroyed ourselves."

"Are you saying you're going after Muslims?" Vice President Wilt nearly yells. "Because if that's what you're saying, I want no part."

"That's not what I said, but I do believe that we need to change our immigration policies to ensure that we're only admitting Muslims who believe that people of all faiths have the right to coexist in America and that Muslims have no right to forcibly impose their system of beliefs on others here."

Turning to the White House Chief of Staff, the President orders him to work with the Attorney General and the Department of Homeland Security to implement immigration changes.

"Muhammad only killed or allowed the killing of those he believed committed treason or were attacking him," Vice President Wilt argues.

"So the hundreds of Jews he sentenced to be beheaded deserved to die because we know all Jews are treasonous? And the caravan attacks? The Meccans didn't like him and were going to eventually attack him, so he might as well go attack and kill them first. Isn't that what we've learned of his life? If this is what self-defense means in radical Islam, then the only way to prevent radical Islamists from attacking is to maintain superior power. Even then, we're always at risk of attack because our power creates a risk to their objectives of global domination."

"That isn't what the Islamic faith stands for," Vice President Wilt replies. "I'm just begging you to calm down and not do something that invites another Holy War against the United States."

"I'm calm, Marcia," the President replies. "But we cannot let whoever nuked Yerevan get away with this atrocity. If we sit and let Armenians die, we have to wonder when it will be America's turn."

Abdullah Raheem has just finished a breakfast of shuzhuk horse meat sausages and shelpek flat cakes when a Lifelink alert lets him know he has a message direct from Langley, home of the U.S. Central Intelligence Agency.

It takes Abdullah more than an hour to politely extract himself from his conversation with the sheep herder who had found him sleeping in his vehicle and, at gunpoint, questioned him on his purpose for being alone in the herder's remote mountain grazing lands. That gun-point meeting led to a wonderful breakfast with the herder's sons. The meal took more time from Abdullah's day than he intended, but gave him a chance to practice his Kazakh and enjoy relative warmth.

The alert startled everyone during breakfast, including Abdullah. He had forgotten to turn the sound off on his alerts.

After showing his Lifelink and how some of it works to the eager eyes of the six male children, Abdullah excuses himself by saying that a signal from his cousin's phone places him in Uzbekistan and he needs to get there. Reluctantly, the family says goodbye to their new friend from Almaty, making clear that they would welcome a return visit. Abdullah promises he will come back with some books from his store once his cousin is safely found and returned to his home.

Once well outside the view of the herder, Abdullah pulls back to a small side road, opens his message and decodes it:

"Target: Same"

"Location: Last seen in Yerevan."

"Directive: Return to Almaty. Await further instructions."

Pulling out of the side road, Abdullah starts to turn back. Realizing he might encounter the herder going that direction, he turns back around and searches for an alternate route to Almaty.

With the White House strategy session concluded, President Phillipi initiates a series of short discussions with top world leaders, including the Premier of China, Russia's President, Mexican President Daniel Suarez and several others. China agrees to join the United States in co-leading a new anti-genocide coalition operating separate from the long impotent and now militarily restricted United Nations.

Motivated by its own secession challenges from a large Muslim population in its western provinces, China sees the chance to create a global containment policy that conforms to its own internal security objectives.

In a statement issued just an hour after President Phillipi and the Premier of China conclude their discussions, the countries state: "If the world's top superpowers unite on fundamental human right concepts, such as the right of people to follow their own faith or absence of faith, we will leave no place on the planet for terrorists to hide. For both of our countries, the journey to recognition of these concepts was challenging, but it is clear now that our obligation as nations is to ensure that all people who wish to live in peace and openness should have the right to do so."

"Do you think this will hold?" Defense Secretary Mendoza later asks the President after hearing of the quickly created accord.

"The Premier knows he will be pushed but he is sure he can gain support," the President assures him.

"Won't they have to make internal changes for the words to be more than hollow?"

"Perhaps," the President replies. "Our agreement has a side deal that China will make those changes at a pace controlled by China's leaders."

Secretary Mendoza looks at the President and nods. "Oh."

Ascending from the DUCC, President Phillipi enters the Oval Office to find Professor Stark waiting for him. Professor Stark finished his call with Brody Maguire to find an aircraft waiting to lift him from the Midway Plaissance at the University of Chicago.

"Thanks for coming on short notice, Professor."

"Certainly, Mr. President. We may have sent a few students scattering for shelter, but I know the University is willing to tolerate the disturbance given the circumstances," Professor Stark replies. "Before we conclude, I'll need direction from you and your staff on how you want me to respond to media inquiries."

"Fine. We have a problem," the President says, slowly circling to pull up a chair next to Professor Stark.

"That much I fully understand," Professor Stark acknowledges.

"Here's why I asked for your advice. You've spent time studying the interconnections of government and religion. If the United States were to consider military attacks as a response for the nuclear attack in Armenia, what do you see as the implications across the Islamic world?" the President asks.

"It's always complicated, but you're well aware of that, because you have to deal with both the reality of the rationale for U.S. involvement as well as the perceptions of why we are involved and how that will be distorted," Professor Stark replies, his favorite high-caffeine soft drink now in hand. "You have to start with an understanding of the Muslim faith. It is widely accepted across the Muslim world that Muhammad and the Quran have made clear that Muslims are allowed to fight in self-defense. Self-defense, though, can be defined very differently in the Islamic world. The most radical Islamic clerics and followers will contend that an attack on any Muslim for any reason is an invitation to holy war."

"We've certainly seen that multiple times just in my lifetime," the President replies.

"And we'll likely see a similar response from the radicals to whatever the U.S. does in response to Armenia," Professor Stark states.

"Why's that?"

"Particularly in theocracies, governments and state religions are so thoroughly intertwined that whatever the government sees as aiding its continuation is perceived by those running the nearly exclusive religious faith as also in their best interest," Professor Stark instructs. "It works the opposite direction just as clearly. If the mandated or principal religious sect is at risk, national leaders will worry about losing the power base created by claimed higher authority. Anything we do can always be twisted into, even wholly fabricated into, an attack on Islam in nations where the people have no connection to reality, where truth always filters through religious and government channels. We can't win any wars in these countries without an aggressive effort to first create religious, media, speech and other freedoms."

President Philippi paces around the office without needing help from his cane: "Is there any way to retaliate without triggering a holy war against the United States?"

After a short, audible exhale, Professor Stark responds: "Among the radicals, the small but dangerous adherents to Islam who create destruction in vast excess to their numbers, probably not. That terrorist threat has truly existed now for fifteen hundred years and is tied to how some clerics interpret Muhammad's actions during his life."

"How about the mainstream Muslim world, particularly to the extent it is intertwined with government and advanced weaponry?" the President asks.

"Not easy either," Professor Stark replies. "I'm not asking for details here, so let me ask the questions and you answer them to yourself if you prefer for national security. Can you narrow the response to the true decision makers? In other words, does intelligence tell you with certainty who most has earned retribution?"

Stark looks at the President, waiting for eye contact to signal that he's ready for the next questions.

"If you have definitive intelligence, can you share that publicly without putting your intelligence gathering capabilities at great risk for the future? If you can share it, you've got a chance to prove your case, but don't assume that even definitive proof of who ordered the bombing and who conducted it will be seen as true. Remember, academic research has proven that if you repeat a lie often enough and with total conviction, eventually people believe it. So your real risk here is that the politicians, clerics and media in the Islamic world will develop a story that suits their purposes and repeat it frequently enough that everyone in their society will believe it."

"I know that's true, a deep inherent flaw in humanity and politics," the President agrees.

"True. It's not like American politicians haven't been exploiting this concept at home. I'm always amazed how many of my students enter class reciting facts they are certain are accurate simply because they've heard them often enough without considering the biases and distortions of their sources," Professor Stark acknowledges.

"You think students are a problem. Try working with Congress," the President says, with both men exchanging their first smile since the explosion as he says it. "With the exception of Jill, of course."

"Oh, trust me. Jill has her views that she's certain about and she doesn't just buy that I know what I'm talking about because I say something," Professor Stark interjects. "But what makes her different than most is she will listen and consider evidence."

"Maybe my wife and I need to spend some time with you and Jill," the President states. "I sometimes wonder if I didn't run for President just so someone would tell me I'm right once in a while."

Professor Stark starts pounding his knuckles on his chair, up and down at a rapid pace. Despite the soft cushioning on the chair, the knocking sound is loud enough to irritate the President's ears. It's one of the Professors habits when he's on the verge of bringing a concept together.

"What if the U.S. does nothing on Armenia?" Professor Stark finally says.

"How can we do nothing? These terrorists, or whoever, just killed nearly a million people with the deadliest weapon release in a hundred years," President Phillipi replies. "We can't just stand aside and let these men get away with this."

"I understand that," Professor Stark continues. "If you can prove who did this, isn't the ideal solution to have people of their own tribe inflict retribution for the whole world to see?"

"Well, sure, but what chance is there that someone inside Iran, connected to the terrorist cells and the old Revolutionary Guard, will stand up in full view of the world and kill the people involved?" the President says. "We have absolutely no way to compel this type of response, or count on it ever happening."

"Don't you have ways to inspire behavior, without needing to order it?" Professor Stark asks. "Don't answer that. I actually don't want to know."

"I don't know that I even want to know," the President mutters.

"Just speculation, Mr. President. Trying to come up with an alternative that may not lead to an ongoing sequence of devastating events."

Rather than return home immediately, Professor Stark surprises Jill in her office after doing his best to evade being spotted, traveling through a series of underground tunnels before catching a taxi.

"Does she have anyone in there?" he asks the receptionist as he walks into Jill's Cannon Building office.

"Not, that I know, but is she expecting you?" the newly hired young man asks, not recognizing Professor Stark.

After a quick knock and invite to enter later, he walks in on Jill, who responds with dropped jaw, pitched head and raised eyebrows.

"Aren't you supposed to be in class now?" she asks.

"I was, but someone had other plans I couldn't turn down." Several minutes later, a summary story of his campus Midway extraction and discussion behind, Jill invites him to join her for lunch in the Member's dining room. Exiting her office door, they find themselves surrounded by more than a dozen reporters.

"Can you tell us, Professor, what urgent issue led to your airlift and meeting with the President?" one reporter asks. Since Jill was the only person who now knew about his meeting, Professor Stark was certain the leak of his meeting had to come from White House staff.

"I'm here to have lunch with my, uh, girlfriend now, so hope you don't mind giving us the chance to enjoy a meal uninterrupted," Professor Stark pleads.

"Sources have told us that you are being consulted on Armenia. Can you tell us what you recommended to the President?" another asks as the group of reporters continues to impede Jill and Professor Stark from moving.

"I think all of you know that the President and I have had a number of discussions in the past about the God's Law proposal," Professor Stark says. "And I'm here now having lunch with his chief House proponent. I'll let you draw your own conclusions."

After responding to or evading a dozen additional questions, Professor Stark and Jill walk down the hall with their arms around each other's waist. While public displays of affection aren't normally Jill's approach, they quickly decide that video of the two together will distract reporters from focusing on the Armenia angle since relationships trump policy in media coverage.

As the pair reach the Independence Avenue steps, Jill whispers in Paul's ear: "Why did you mislead reporters into thinking you were working on God's Law?"

"I'm stuck trying to keep my commitment to the President without lying. I couldn't think of any other response," he replies, whispering in her ear to reduce the ease with which their conversation could be intercepted. "I was simply stating a series of facts from which they could draw their own conclusions."

"I get that, but then how do I know you won't do this to me, answering my questions by stating facts that appear to answer the question when in fact they are simply intending to draw my focus elsewhere," Jill replies.

"The difference is that when I tell you I can't answer a question, you respect that, just as I respect it when you tell me you can't answer a question," Professor Stark says. "The media doesn't respect that. They speculate. Sometimes, speculation is worse than the truth."

Abdullah closes his Almaty bookstore to head for the fourth of his prayers, his favorite prayer session of the day because he shares worship with friends and fellow believers. The rest of his prayers, his worship to Allah and the Prophet Muhammad, are done from his prayer rug wherever he happens to be at the time. Typically, four of his daily prayers are done in his store, in his apartment or while making the rounds of contacts he's developing. Only six of his contacts realize they are involved in a professional relationship.

It's his first day in weeks back in Almaty. Abdullah is anxious to return to a normal routine, even if just for a few days.

He leaves the mosque quickly when prayers conclude, finding no response to the message he had left in a hidden pillar slit before departing to search the country for General Timur. He wants to be sure to get his seat at the hookah bar.

As he waits for a clean mouthpiece to be delivered, Abdullah reaches under the table, pulls down a note, sees it's not his paper and rolls it into a crudely sewn pocket on the inside of his shirt sleeve.

Back at the bookstore, after searching to ensure his security hasn't been breached and protecting himself from every possible camera angle, he opens the note, holds it above the stovetop burner and reads: "No known contact."

Then Abdullah lowers the note into the flame to set it on fire. He drops it to the metal surface to finish burning the last corners.

29 DISORIENTATION

Professor Stark is completely aroused as the morning sun pokes through a slightly open shade in Jill's bedroom. A quick mint spray later, he rolls to his side and edges his body up closer to Jill.

"Oh my God, Paul. Aren't you ever satisfied?" she asks.

"Satisfied? How can I not be satisfied? Uninterested is a state I don't seem to be able to reach with you," he replies as she rolls his hand away.

"Is that a no?" he asks.

"No, that's a close the shade all the way. I can keep cameras out of our house, but I can't guarantee some nut job isn't flying drones around our windows."

As Professor Stark stands to close the shades, Jill offers another admonition: "You should cover yourself until the shades are shut."

"I can't believe I actually found someone more paranoid about security than I am," Professor Stark replies.

"Yeah, well you're not a woman, in public office, seen as a threat by both parties and with a large following of male and some female admirers from television newscasting days who think of themselves as in a relationship with you since you were in their house every day for

so long," Jill replies. "All I need is someone with technology sophisti-
cation or a spy agency to want something to use against me."

"Well, at least you'd look hot if they did capture you," he tries to
assure her.

"Get over here," Jill replies, grabbing Professor Stark and throwing
him down on his back.

Later that morning, Professor Stark dresses in a professionally
appropriate sport coat and slacks with a white- and blue-striped
button-down shirt and a tie rolled up in the sport coat pocket as he
slowly, meticulously walks down the steps from their D.C. townhouse.
He holds the handrails to cushion each step. A grimace reveals pain in
his lower back, an ache he had been fighting to hide just minutes
earlier.

His mind drifts from his back pain as he spots an actual driver inside what would normally be an automated, software-driven taxi.
Only Members of Congress, a few members of the Executive Branch
and police, military and Secret Service personnel are able to drive uncontrolled vehicles inside Washington, D.C. limits.

When he makes it down to the bottom of the steps, the driver
steps out of the vehicle. "Professor Stark, the President asked me to
escort you to your air travel," states the driver, a tall, muscular and
clean-cut man who appears to be in his thirties at most. The driver is
dressed in suit and tie, looking every bit like a poorly disguised Secret
Service officer. Several blocks later, Professor Stark gets nervous that
the driver isn't heading southwest, the direction that would take him
to Reagan National Airport.

"I'm flying back out of Reagan, sir," Professor Stark points out.

"We've cancelled that flight, Professor. My instructions are to take
you to Andrews. You'll fly back from there."

Professor Stark looks around the outside of the vehicle, then looks
up toward the driver, searching for clues about what is happening.
"Do you know why? Who I'm meeting?"

"No sir, need to know only and I don't need to know," the driver
asserts.

"Well, then, can I ask who you are?" Professor Stark asks, worry
visible in his expressions.

"You can ask," the man replies, without making any further sound or motion to indicate additional information is forthcoming.

"Okay, if we're playing this game, I'm asking who are you?" Professor Stark inquires.

"Need to know, sir."

"I need to know," Professor Stark demands.

"The President thinks otherwise, Professor. My apologies, but I have clear instructions," the driver continues, looking at the now sweating academic through the rear-view mirror.

"So what are your instructions from the President if I jump from the car and run?" Professor Stark asks, deciding to up the ante on this cat-and-mouse game.

"If you hurt yourself, my instructions are to make sure you get medical attention and then get you to Andrews," the driver responds.

"What if I don't want to go to Andrews?"

"I've been assured that you want to go to Andrews but I'm not allowed to arrest you to insist that this happens if that is the answer you are seeking."

"So, I'm free to leave?" Professor Stark asks again.

As Professor Stark regains consciousness more than an hour later, he's sitting inside a small room. He counts eight small, oval windows to his left and an equal number to his right.

A mango-flavored diet soft drink sits in the cup holder next to him, still cold to the touch. On the table between him and a seat facing his direction rests a sweet potato and gravy hash and other favorite foods that appear to have come directly from the Heart and Soul Café he frequents on days he teaches. He smells the carafe on the table and determines it must be the hazelnut coffee he frequently drinks at Heart and Soul, with artificial sweetener packets and a pint of skim milk beside it. Whoever brought him here is interested in making him comfortable and knows him all too well.

"I'm so glad to see you alert," a deep, guttural and obviously distorted male voice states from behind Professor Stark. "I was worried that we might arrive in Chicago before we had a chance to speak."

"What happened to me and who are you?" Professor Stark asks as he feels control of his mind slowly return.

"Sorry about that," the distorted voice states. "Whoa, whoa, whoa. Don't turn around. It's better if you can't identify me."

"I'm lost. What's going on?" Professor Stark asks. "Is this one of Jill's pranks?" he asks as he reaches into a code-protected pocket in his boxers to set off a security alert signal. Ever since a series of muggings a decade earlier when Professor Stark led the effort to reform the nation's political system, he has been extremely nervous about security. At Heart and Soul, for instance, he sits in a back corner with quick access to two exits and visibility to the main entrance. He quickly taps in the code to his security alert pocket only to find it empty. Realizing that no one will know where he is, Professor Stark's internal panic sets off. He tries unbuckling his seatbelt, but can't get it to release. It's tight enough that he also can't wiggle out of the seatbelt either, though he realizes as he is squirming that the room is moving past clouds and he is clearly on some type of airplane.

"I'm sorry about all of this," the man behind him states. "We've obviously been watching you for a while and I figured you'd be very uncomfortable in a place where you had no control. We've taken some precautions for your own safety, and frankly so you didn't run and open the door and kill us all."

"What's going on?" Professor Stark asks while feeling around for his security alert button or any way to send a panic signal.

"If you can calm down for me," the man says. "I'll fill you in on why I needed to speak with you and you'll be in Chicago with your vehicle waiting for you at the airport in thirty minutes."

"Since it appears I have little choice, go ahead," Professor Stark finally relents.

"Great. And please enjoy breakfast as we speak," the man offers. "You are aware, Paul, if I may, that the world faces a constant series of dilemmas on how to deal with truly evil people who have both the authority and means to destroy large numbers of people and even whole countries."

"I'm aware of that," Professor Stark replies.

"People like this, when they achieve great positions of power, either within a government or within the protection of a government, can be very difficult to reach without causing great harm to many innocent people around them, in some cases through devastating war," the man continues.

"I understand that," Professor Stark agrees.

"So when these people order true atrocities, it's quite difficult to gain appropriate retribution without substantial collateral damage," the man says, pausing to allow each concept to be fully absorbed before continuing.

"I agree and have said as much myself," the professor states as he considers whether this trip is a direct outcome of the comments he made to the President.

"What if I told you that doesn't have to be the case?" the mysterious man blusters.

Professor Stark starts to turn his head toward the man before recalling he has been warned repeatedly: "What do you mean?"

"What if I told you that evil people can be forced to pay for their crimes without collateral damage?" the man suggests.

"Assassinations aren't anything new," Professor Stark states forcefully, again trying to turn his head to see who's talking to him.

"No, they're not, and assassinations have collateral damage, imposed on either the assassins or those surrounding the assassinated," the voice responds.

"If you're not talking about assassinations, how do you produce the retribution of which you speak?" inquires Professor Stark, his curiosity now aroused.

The plane is already beginning its descent as the discussion continues. "A fair question, to be sure, but one that's best that you not understand fully," the kidnapping host contends.

"So why am I here?" Professor Stark asks, anxious to figure out what is going on and angry that his security precautions have again failed to protect him.

"The world needs a court, uncorrupted by the political dealings that have destroyed the United Nations and all of the other judicial panels set up through treaty and brokered agreement. The world no longer is able to secure swift, appropriate recognition of justice."

Grabbing his drink to keep it from sliding, Professor Stark is intrigued: "What does that have to do with me?"

"We've picked you to establish a new global court," the man states.

After laughing vigorously for several minutes, Professor Stark catches his breath. "That's ridiculous. I'm a professor, not a judge."

"We've considered that. You won't actually have to determine verdicts. You'll just administer the judicial process," states the man still seated directly behind Professor Stark to ensure he can't be seen.

"I'm sorry, but I need to decline. My role is with my students," Professor Stark states, doing his best to retain a polite tone to avoid sparking an angry response.

"I'm sorry that I wasn't clear earlier," the voice replies. "We aren't going to distract you too much from your professorial duties, though you will carry a reduced class load to free you up for your new work. The university will announce today, with you at a public press conference two hours after you land, that you have agreed to take on the additional duties as director of the Center for Atrocity Studies and Justice."

Professor Stark can't help but chortle again. "I'm sorry, but there is no such center at the University of Chicago."

"There is, as of today," the man states, "founded with the support of anonymous donations of thirty million Euros and similar valued anonymous donations in reals, yens, RMB and dollars. You have proven a masterful fundraiser."

"But I have nothing to do with this," Professor Stark says, finally deciding to eat and drink a little now that his mental fog is lifting.

"Don't be modest," the man tells him. "I'm not saying this as a suggestion. I'm saying you must take credit for having talked about your concept in many forums over recent years. You were surprised to have received such sizable donations without having any idea who is funding the Center."

While the man talks, Professor Stark contemplates the visits from Cindy Colorado and that young guy who solicited him at Heart and Soul. The breakfast was meant to tell him that this man has his ways of making the professor pliable. He's been followed, tested or both.

"Why is everything in my intuition telling me that this will come back to bite me or kill me?" Professor Stark inquires. "I finally have a good life that I don't want to screw up."

Sighing heavily, the man behind the voice leans toward the back of Professor Stark's chair. "Paul, if it's okay that I call you Paul, let me be blunt. If you don't run this Center and conduct global court-like trials of the men and women responsible for inflicting the greatest atrocities on our civilization, the chances that your great life will continue for very long are very small."

Professor Stark leans over, clasping his hand behind his head, only to feel his back compress his lungs, forcing him to wheeze to exhale and take in oxygen.

"Are you all right?" the man asks.

"Back spasms?"

"You were fine yesterday," the man states, a clear sign to Professor Stark of the intensity of investigation under which he has been tracked. "What happened?"

Reopening his Almaty bookstore for the first time in several weeks, Abdullah finds a sense of peace. He hadn't realized the serenity he achieved from this part of his assignment until he'd been taken from it for so long.

Carefully, he peruses his bookshelves looking for just the right stories to send. The herder's family had been so kind to him. He writes and attaches a short note in Kazakh that interprets as: *"Stories I hope will delight a wonderful family. Signal on cousin was wrong. Still searching for him but happy to find you on my journey. Perhaps our meeting was Allah's purpose."*

Abdullah's work requires him to build an extensive network while remaining invisible. Easier said than done. Several of his best contacts were developed through happenstance, without any recognition that Abdullah's friendship serves a purpose.

Extensive new military weapons contracts are dramatically enriching New Rite founder and total owner JT Alton but the expanded wealth isn't bringing the serenity he was certain he would achieve when he destroyed the Castillo cartel.

Sporting a newly trimmed beard and mustache, JT's medium brown hair is freshly cut as well, producing the outdoor magazine cover look that JT has honed and maintained throughout his New Rite existence. It has been more than twenty years since JT fully shaved off his facial hair. Should New Rite ever come under attack, he plans to quickly alter his appearance to buy time until he can more dramatically, surgically shift his facial signature.

He paces the balcony of one of his oxygen-enriched homes, this one built of non-reflective glass, precision-cut boulders and bark-coated beams that ensconce it naturally at an elevation of nearly eleven thousand feet near Colorado's Byer's Peak. He has always wanted his contributions to blend into the natural surroundings in a way that would have made Frank Lloyd Wright proud, but without the arrogance-driven architectural flaws of some of Wright's most famous works. New Rite's new mission, the one he continues to perfect, must work in the same manner. His teams will have to blend into the surroundings so fully as to be missed. Presence without visibility. Beauty that won't draw admiration. Purposeful distractions that draw all the attention.

New Rite long ago bought extensive land surrounding this home, headquarters and survival training compound at a sharp discount as the U.S. government sought to escape massive debt obligations and associated interest. Most federal land buyers had come from overseas, with several land-starved countries paying handsomely for the right to also send citizens to live on these lands and become U.S. citizens. JT had been able to negotiate much cheaper pricing, given his interest in converting federal lands into survival training and competition centers with potential to create at least some employment.

Pacing along a balcony with a clear view up to the peak as well as down into nearby valleys, JT holds on to one end of the clear plastic railing to watch as a nearby mountain goat perches at the end of a cliff wall. The goat looks over to JT, seeming to nod his head hello, before descending down a sharp cliff face that JT could never survive without serious rappelling equipment.

He's still pacing and contemplating his next move when Ally waves from the automated sliding doors.

"The meeting's ready to start," Ally yells out to JT. "Are you ready for us, or should I tell everyone to hold?"

"I'm ready," JT replies. "The question is, are you all ready?"

Ally's special operations team leaders are assembled for this mission reassignment discussion. After completing destruction of the Castillo cartel with massive U.S. military backing, JT has been torn by doubts about continuing to put the vast majority of New Rite profits into special operations rather than pocket some personally and use the rest for social service and sustainability charities. Driven for twenty years by revenge for his brother's death, JT questioned whether any other initiatives warranted the type of investment and risk he took in going after Cesar Castillo and his cartel. He has already started to build his answer.

Inside the New Rite compound's most secure meeting room, nearly fifteen hundred feet deep inside the mountain, JT welcomes Ally's team. Everyone stands around the perimeter of the table, chairs all removed at JT's request.

"Cesar Castillo and Raul Hernández are far from the only men who killed mercilessly to enrich themselves," JT says to open the meeting. "I'm willing, if you join me, to help eradicate the world of the type of scum who use destruction as the path to power and wealth."

JT searches around the room, looking in the eyes of everyone there. "But," he continues, pausing enough to create discomfort.

"But," Ally finally says, realizing JT is waiting for interaction. "But, what?"

"But, I don't want to put your lives at direct risk as we did throughout our pursuit of Castillo," JT says. "We need a better approach, one no one sees coming. I removed the chairs to ensure you understand this isn't a normal meeting. I want this discussion embedded in your memory. I need you to view our work from a new perspective. If we move forward, we need to be invisible. Invisibility, though, doesn't mean risk is eliminated. If there's anyone you love, you'll never be able to rest comfortably once we start these missions."

"I don't get it, JT," Ally interrupts, clearly speaking for everyone in the room as all eyes turn to her. "How are we gonna accomplish what we did with Castillo, not take risks, and yet still have our lives threatened?"

"The right questions," JT replies, stopping to push a call button that connects to an office inside the compound. "Send them down."

"Them?" Ally asks as she instinctively moves to a better defensive position near the door jam. As far as she knows, there's only one new team member.

"Your new, special operations team members," JT replies to Ally.

"I haven't vetted anyone," the team's intelligence lead states. Other special operations team members look at each other, gauging their nervousness at their enclosed location. Two quietly inch their way toward JT.

Ally hadn't vetted anyone either, but wants to imply to the group that she was in on these hiring decisions to maintain her appearance of control. JT doesn't normally interfere with her team selections, preferring to rely on Ally's superior operations expertise. Being out of the loop about her team unnerves her.

As the elevator descends, Ally realizes her operations team leaders are all in the room unarmed, a perfect place to be permanently discarded. She edges closer to the door, backing up against the wall. Another does the same on the opposite side. Ally looks at the two closest to JT, who instantly blink back that they're prepared to grab him.

JT realizes what the team is doing and starts laughing out loud.

"Seriously, you have that little faith in me," he says, spitting as he tries to speak around a laugh so robust he feels twinges in his rib muscles.

"What do you mean?" Ally says, trying to relax the tension out of her posture.

"Come on. I see you all moving in on me and preparing your entry defense. Don't think I haven't been paying attention all these years," JT observes.

JT laughs again, and Ally and the team members all follow suit, though with much greater reserve.

As the door opens, Ally and her team members stare at people entering the room.

First to enter is a thin, blond-haired woman, wearing thick-rimmed glasses, a flimsy silk sundress and six-inch clear heels. She smiles at the team as she enters, does a quick princess wave and starts walking around the room shaking hands and introducing herself: "Carol. Carol Zrom."

"Good God, she's barely legal," Ally says under her breath.

"Next," JT calls out.

Tall, thin, speckle-haired and dressed in a button-down shirt with a thin leather tie, the man coming down the hall is clearly the oldest person in the room. Abhirim Roussard rolls his lips inward, further thinning his smile, and flexes to raise his right hand in a small wave before stopping just to the side of the door.

Ally keeps her eyes closely focused on Abhirim. He doesn't appear interested in connecting with anyone in the room.

"Next," JT calls out. Ally is still fixated on Abhirim, at least until she hears a collective "What the hell?" from her team.

Ally looks over, then walks over to shake his hand: "Glad you decided to join the team."

"I'm happy to be here," he replies, looking around the room at a dozen people who might easily have wanted to kill him yesterday, perhaps even still today. "I'm also happy to be alive."

For a moment, everyone in the room remains silent, eyes alternating between JT and Ramon Mantle, a man they last knew as the new head of the Castillo cartel after many years as its undisclosed technology guru.

"What's going on here?" Clint asks, while the rest of the team members nod their heads to suggest they also want the question answered.

After looking in everyone's eyes as he wanders the room, JT stops and moves to the front.

"What's going on is that we're changing our operating methods, which require new skills and capabilities," JT says. "These three individuals bring expertise we did not have dedicated to your team before."

"No, JT," Clint interrupts. "What is he doing here?" he asks as he points at Ramon.

"Fair question," JT acknowledges.

Clint is visibly tense, angry that someone who recently took over the cartel he spent the last decade trying to destroy is now part of their team: "Yes, sir. I believe so."

"You know this man under a name that will never be used in our interaction with him. As far as the outside world knows, he is dead. His value to our team is substantially enhanced by his anonymity," JT states.

"Understood, sir. But why is he here?" Clint asks, strong emphasis on the word "he."

JT walks over and put his hand on Ramon's shoulder: "Simply, his technology skills enhance our ability to accomplish our next series of missions."

"Which are?" Ally asks, though she already has a strong idea of where this is heading.

"The world is missing its ability to efficiently eradicate evil without serious collateral damage," JT states, arms crossed in front. "Creating this capability with no collateral damage is our new mission."

"What about the U.N.?" a team member asks. "Shouldn't eradicating evil be their responsibility?"

JT shrugs his shoulders. "They've been neutered by their organizational structure since they were established. Geopolitical enemies with seats on the Security Council use the U.N. to neutralize each other's power far more than they use it to promote human advancement," JT notes. "When genocides in dozens of nations can take place with no one on the international stage having the cojones to intervene—no offense ladies—the world has a gap to fill."

"So, you want us to be the judge, juries and executioners," another team member asks. "No offense to you, but I don't think this power should be concentrated with anyone, including and maybe especially me."

"I agree, wholeheartedly, and don't want that power myself either," JT replies. "Our work relies on clear separation of these roles. This team won't ever be judge or jury. But we will, from time-to-time, gather hard-to-capture evidence and enable verdicts to be carried out."

Several team members look at each other, hoping that they aren't the only ones who don't quite get it. Ally interjects for the group: "So who plays judge and jury?"

"That's being established at a new university center as we speak," JT continues. "Except that they don't know, and must never know, that their conclusions directly determine the fate of those they put on trial."

"I think I'm confused," Clint states. "How can they not know they are the judge and jury if the people they convict keep dying?'

"Another good question," JT replies. "Anyone care to hazard a guess?"

JT waits for several seconds. As he is about to speak again, Ally speaks: "I don't know that I can answer how this happens, but I'd be willing to bet that the new team members here are part of how it will happen."

"Right on the mark," JT replies, driving his right index finger straight into his open left palm.

"I don't mean to be stupid and if you don't want to answer, I'm fine with that," Clint adds. "But I'm still not sure how this all works."

"You'll see," JT asks. "You'll see. And, in fact, the whole world will see when we see, but if we do our jobs right they won't know what we know. For the time being, I'm going to suggest you all spend the rest of the week here getting to know each other and learning each other's skill sets. Then we'll start filling in the picture of what we're going to do and get our new operations center in working order."

The mixture of clean, modern, amenity-infused buildings with historical sparse stone structures can be disorienting to those who struggle to adapt. But the University of Chicago thrives on change, focusing on driving development of its students and leading expansion of knowledge. Progress isn't always easy.

"Traitor, traitor. Hero to a hater," a protest group cries out in front of one of the University's more antiquated buildings. "Traitor, traitor. Hero to a hater."

Juan Gonzalez hears chants of protest outside the entrance of every building in which he's starting classes. The Coalición por Revolución (CPR) sprung up immediately after the Honor to Mexico movement was exposed for its cartel ties. This splinter movement is continuing efforts to form a Spanish-speaking breakaway nation though now expanded to include South Florida, Puerto Rico and several cities in addition to the U.S. Southwest states. In its desperation to replace H2M as the primary voice for politically active Latinos, the CPR attacks Juan Gonzalez to attract media attention, a necessary precursor to its massive fundraising plans.

"Juan Gonzalez, once the darling of the Latino and particularly the Latina community in the United States, came under attack today as a sell-out on his first day of classes at the University of Chicago," news network anchor Brody Maguire proclaims at the start of his national news hour. "It appears a small, but growing segment of the Hispanic population is angry with Gonzalez for retracting his support for Spanish language mandates and Southwest secession following the failed Republic of Alta Texas secession war earlier this year."

Video accompanying the story shows hundreds of signs expressing anger at Juan. Most networks air clips of University police arresting protestors, stating that the arrests are part of a coordinated University effort to restrict free speech. Only the Republican News Network (RNN) and several conservative sites show video of the protestors urinating behind evergreens on the sides of the University buildings. All of the arrested protestors were charged with disorderly conduct for public urination.

Watchers or readers of only single broadcasts, radio shows or online publications saw widely divergent views of actual events, depending on which news outlet they used. On RNN, viewers saw that only forty protestors were holding two hundred signs on rotating sign carriers strapped over their shoulders and rotating around their waistline. Mainstream media outlets only displayed the large number of signs, never showing how many signs each protestor held. MSDNC also neglected to mention that more than half of the protestors were actually CPR employees.

Regardless of the divergent perception, Juan was still angry and frustrated by the protests—seeking out Professor Stark at his office after finishing classes for the day.

"I'm not sure I'm doing the right thing," Juan says after exchanging pleasantries with Professor Stark.

"Why's that? Because a couple of dozen protestors decided they don't like you anymore?" Professor Stark asks.

"Well, yeah. I mean these are my people. These are the people whose lives I want to make better," Juan affirms.

Professor Stark nods gently, knowing how difficult it is to accept that it is impossible to please everyone. "There's no way you'll ever make everyone happy, Juan. That's such a small group that I wouldn't worry about it."

"I know, but Mom and my friends at home saw this huge protest against me. Mom is worried," Juan notes.

"What version of the protest did she see, because I checked out a couple of different versions of the stories online after you called, and the protest looks dramatically different depending on the version shown?" Professor Stark inquires. "Here, let's look at a few of these."

Professor Stark flips around his monitor and plays several versions of the story. Juan quickly sees how widely different the fact base looks depending on who aired the story.

"It's amazing how much they edit what happens to fit the story they want to tell. Whatever happened to the truth?" Juan asks.

"The truth has become subjective, with perception of the truth often skewed by what attracts more interest, and ultimately, more revenue for the news outlet."

"I used to think you were just old and cynical," Juan says, relaxing his facial expressions substantially. "Now I realize that maybe you're not so cynical."

"But still old?" Professor Stark asks.

"Oh, yeah. Still old," Juan says with a wry smile and a wink.

30 SOLICITATION

As the group meeting breaks up, JT pulls Ally to the side.

"To improve the effectiveness and invisibility of your team, we're going to need a group of brave data collectors," JT tells Ally, "people who can make themselves welcome in places where strangers are never welcomed."

"What kind of data do they need to collect?"

JT crosses his arms in front of him before responding, "DNA samples."

Ally looks sternly at JT, attempting to determine if he is serious: "And who do they need to collect from?"

"Dictators, generals, terrorists, militia rulers, maybe even an elected official or two who can't be held to account within their nation," JT admits, though he's certain Ally would have guessed as much if she had thought it through.

"So . . . , easy targets," Ally replies, sarcasm evident in her tone.

"What do powerful, evil men share in common?" JT asks.

"Arrogance and raging hormones?" Ally replies.

"Exactly."

Ally stares directly into JT's eyes, trying to read where he's going. "So, what are you saying?" she asks after failing to internally identify the answer to her question.

JT knows Ally well enough to realize this is his toughest part of the sales pitch. He steps around and puts his arm across Ally's back to rest his hand on her opposite shoulder, then pulls her toward him: "We're going to have to play against their weaknesses."

Ally's eyes fully dilate as she pulls away from JT to look directly in his eyes. "You're not saying special ops is bringing prostitutes onto our team, are you?" she asks, elevating her voice sharply at the end of the sentence.

JT, neither nodding nor shaking, wobbles his head back and forth in his best "depends" motion. "Not prostitutes, of course. Mostly, we'll need candidates for single mission work who can't be tied back to us."

"And then discard them?" Ally questions.

"No, no, no," JT responds. "We can't do that. We'd be no better than the people we hate if we did that. I'm creating a haven for the ones who need to be extricated for safety. But some of what we need for a few of these missions may be worse."

"What do you mean may be worse?" Ally asks.

"We'll need young girls, and maybe some young boys, that these powerful men won't be afraid to be physically close to, and that the worst of them will even seek out," JT declares.

"That's simply disgusting," Ally replies, pursing her lips and face reddening as she speaks. "I can't be any part of sending children into the arms of tyrants."

"I know. It's going to be your job to get them close but keep them from being hurt," JT states, trying to put his arm on Ally's shoulder.

"That hardly seems possible given the likely targets," Ally barks emphatically. Ally's anger is clear. She hadn't signed on at New Rite to hurt innocent people and particularly not children.

JT isn't at all surprised by her response because she only knows part of the plan at this point: "Not impossible. Difficult, yes. Not impossible. That's why I want you to directly manage these operations."

"I really, really don't know about this, JT," Ally underscores, deeply torn between her complete admiration for JT and her disgust at what he is asking her to do.

JT knows he can't charm Ally. She knows him better than anyone. His strengths. His flaws. "Well, let me tell you what we need for our first mission. We need a young girl, 13, 14, 15 years old at most. Tall, slender. Attractive. Extraordinarily brave. And with good enough voice that she can be part of a girl's choir travelling to the Middle East to perform for someone I expect to be among our first targets."

"You're not expecting this girl to do some fugly perv?" Ally inquires, looking back at him and seeing no immediate response. "Oh my God. You are. I just can't do that to any girl."

"No, no, no, no, no," JT replies, motioning that he has an answer. "I was just thinking about how much to tell you now. The girl we need may have to kiss his hand and stick him with a bio-absorption pad."

"What are you talking about?" Ally asks.

"The new blond on the team, Carol. She'll explain how it works. It's one of her inventions."

"Okay, but how can we protect a kid we put in harm's way somewhere where we can't be seen?" Ally asks.

"Your best hope is to pick the right person and train her well," JT notes, running a thumb and forefinger through his beard. "Your back-up is you go in and retrieve her if it goes wrong."

"This is tough, JT," Ally says. "You know our Golden Rule talk?"

"I do," JT replies. "I think about it every moment I think about this mission."

"Does this really fit with the idea of doing unto others as we would have done unto ourselves, or with not doing to others what we would not want done to us?" Ally questions.

"Let me ask, Ally," JT replies, opening a closet to pull out a couple of chairs to sit down. The discussion is taking longer than he had hoped. "Put yourself in the boots of one of these teenagers. Would you be willing to take on a mission at that age knowing that you're being asked to touch someone with your hands or kiss someone to capture a DNA sample, particularly knowing that your work will save thousands and perhaps millions from death, torture, rape and every other kind of human misery?"

"When you put it that way, I would have wanted to do it," Ally responds. "But I'm not sure that every kid would, and I know that any kid's parents would be furious with us for putting their child in that kind of danger. Don't we also need to consider the reaction of the parents and the impact of our actions on people around us?"

"Of course," JT replies. "If we truly follow the Golden Rule, we can't base our decisions solely on a straight one-for-one swapping of positions. We have to actively understand the implications and consider them across everyone who is affected," JT replies. "We also have to consider alternatives that mitigate any risks."

"I'm not sure what you mean," Ally replies, with her pulse and adrenaline levels slowly returning to normal levels.

"I want you to find kids for these roles who are at the brink of despair, who need to do something meaningful to understand they have a tremendous value to the world," JT directs.

"So, you want me to find suicidal kids and send them on what could be a suicide mission," Ally replies, crossing her arms in front of her chest.

JT stands for a minute and paces, then sits back down.

"You can put it that way, I guess. I want you to find a few very select kids who need a reason to live and provide them with the opportunity to have that reason," JT clarifies. "We don't need to take a happy kid and create a risk in their world when we can find someone struggling and help them take pride in their life, perhaps even give them the reason to stay alive, something their parents would want us to do. When I think about the Golden Rule, it's about creating the best situation possible and I think this does that. Don't you?"

"Couldn't we provide these kids the same kind of meaning if we got them jobs at a food pantry or created a teen Peace Corps that gives them a chance to see they can make the world a better place through service?" Ally asks.

"I suppose we could, Ally, but taking out evil is our skill set," JT notes. "We need to stay focused on a mission that perhaps only we are capable of undertaking. If Luke were here today, being part of this could have saved him."

Ally knows JT well enough to know that when he invokes his long-deceased little brother in a discussion, the time for debate is over.

Later that afternoon, Juan walks toward his dorm room, head down, still mulling over the protest and how he feels about being vilified by a group of fellow Latinos. He's grown used to facing occasional vitriol, but it has always been from someone he doesn't see as one of his people. Now, he has to acknowledge that his change in position on language and secession issues has made him an enemy to many of those who thought his original position was right.

"Hey. Hey. Aren't you Juan? Juan Gonzalez?" a woman's voice echoes out as Juan nears his dorm.

Juan stops, turns around to look for signs of an impending physical confrontation, but relaxes as he spots a woman about his age, wearing only flip flops, short shorts and a tight peach bikini top.

"Damn," Juan says only slightly under his breath. He turns his eyes both directions to make sure he's not missing any cameras. As he does, the young woman with long red hair, blue eyes, a pert chest and a waistline so thin it appears her breasts had to have been artificially injected rises from her beach towel and walks toward Juan. He can't believe he hadn't noticed her on campus before.

"It is you," the woman says, looking up at his eyes from well within his personal space boundary. "I heard you were coming here. I'm Mariah. Mariah Barron."

"Hi, Mariah. I'm Juan, uh, but I guess you already know that."

"Wow, I always wanted to meet a celebrity," Mariah utters. "Wow, you really are as cute as you look on screen."

"Uhm, thank you. Damn. I can't imagine you have any problem meeting anyone you want to meet," Juan replies, stumbling over his words in a way he finds embarrassing.

"That's really sweet of you to say that. Hey, I was just going to head up to our rooftop pool to swim for a bit and cool off," Mariah says. "Do you want to come up with me?"

"Thanks for asking, but I have a girlfriend in DC and there's a lot of cameras tracking me around today, so I don't want to freak her out by being alone with someone who looks like you."

"I meant just as friends, Juan," Mariah responds. "I already know you have a girlfriend."

"You do?" he asks.

"Sure, it's more fun to follow your love story than to think about the war stuff, you know."

"Hmmm," is the only reply Juan can muster.

"Well, maybe some other time. Maybe even just for coffee or something that won't freak your girlfriend out," Mariah offers.

"Sure, we can do that."

Mariah taps her Lifelink up against the pocket where Juan's carries his device, immediately sending him all of her contact information. "Just let me know whenever you want to get together. Mind if I take a picture of the two of us together?"

Lying in bed later that night, Juan can't go to sleep as his mind races, panicking that Rachel will see pictures or film of him talking to Mariah.

"Hey, baby doll," Juan taps out in a message to Rachel. "Crazy day here with all the protestors saying they hate me now and classes getting started. You didn't warn me at all about how much work I'm going to have to do here. Profs dumped a load of work on us and aren't giving us much time to get it done. Tight, tight deadlines. But all is good. I love you and can't wait to see you next month."

"I bet it was an interesting day. Seems like the deadlines weren't the only tight things you spent time looking at today," Rachel replies, sending a photo of Juan with Mariah.

"Oh, that girl. She was just a fan who wanted to take her picture with me. Nothing to it," Juan says. "You're not jealous, are you?"

"Jealous, no, but it is curious that you didn't mention her in your note," Rachel states.

"Not much to mention. I talked to her for maybe five minutes."

"I thought you said she just wanted to have her picture taken with you?" Rachel asks, using some of the grilling techniques she had mastered from watching Professor Stark.

Juan had contemplated mentioning Mariah in his first note, but thought it might make too much of their brief encounter. He kicks himself, figuratively of course, for not having realized that mentioning Mariah right away might have been the smarter decision.

"Well, yeah," Juan replies to Rachel's latest message. "I was just trying not to be rude. If it makes you feel any better, I turned down her invite to swim."

"I thought you said she just wanted a picture?" Rachel continues.

"Sure, but she was just being nice. She knows everything about you and me already, so already knows I'm with you."

"Well, isn't that special. My boyfriend has a stalker."

"Mariah is not a stalker," Juan replies quickly, hitting send before thinking through his message.

"So, it's Mariah now. You took enough time to learn her name."

"Well, yeah. She gave me her contact info in case you were okay with me meeting her for coffee or something."

"What's the 'or something'?" Rachel asks.

Juan feels sweat building up on his brow and dread in his heart. "What?" Juan messages, before quickly sending another message. "I think we just need to talk. It sounds like this is all coming out wrong."

Ally goes back in to talk to her team members, though her mind continues to be distracted by trying to figure out how to do what JT is asking and whether she wants to be any part of it. Killing cartel lords is easy to justify. Putting teenage girls and boys at risk—not so much.

Days later, Ally stops by to talk to JT.

"I think I might have a DNA gatherer identified," Ally states, using the term she has decided to use for the people she brings onto the team. It's easier for her to think about the new people as DNA gatherers. It sounds less dangerous that way. JT invites Ally onto the balcony where the pair stands in an area carefully screened to block out any satellite picture or audio capture, along with any noise capture from anyone targeting him for surveillance from the ground.

"Who is it?"

"A girl, 15 years old or so, that Sarah told me about. Sarah said this girl was a young version of her, stayed calm under some pretty intense pressure at the Utah compound during the secession battles. We tracked her recent communications history. It turns out she's just the type of girl you described."

"Do you think she'll do it?" JT asks.

"Don't know, but I can send someone down there to find out," Ally replies.

"I'd rather you manage the relationships personally," JT directs. "Everyone on our team understands the risks we're taking. These kids can't possibly fully understand so we need to protect them from ever being discovered as connected to us."

"Okay, I get it. I'll head down now," Ally agrees.

JT smiles in appreciation. He had hoped Ally would come around. It's clear she gets what he's hoping to accomplish. "Let me know, and work on three backup plans if she isn't the right person," he directs as Ally heads toward her APB.

31 ACQUISITION

When John Coleman, Clarissa's father, installed fingerprint identification controls on the family's weapons, he did so to ensure a stranger couldn't turn the family's guns against them. He never predicted that the identification pad's ability to only accept a fingerprint directionally pointed to fire the gun from behind would end up saving Clarissa from herself. When Clarissa tried to turn the family's weapon on herself, she couldn't get the fingerprint pad on the trigger to release and fire.

John's expertise in real-time sensing and control for a waste recycling and recovery company made him particularly sensitive to the importance of linking fingerprint identification directly to the firing mechanism of his homemade weapons. Without the identification being simultaneous with the shooting, any weapon lost in a struggle with a criminal could be turned against them. Clarissa hadn't anticipated that her arm wasn't long enough to twist her fingerprint the right direction to fire her rifle with the barrel stuck inside her mouth.

Clarissa's long struggle with depression seemed to originate with a classmate's merciless ridicule of her for being tall and gangly early in middle school when many of the boys in her class were barely shoulder to hip with her.

Beyond her small group of friends, Clarissa escaped to the outdoors when seeking solitude and peace. Frequently panicking her parents, Clarissa disappeared sometimes for entire days on trails leading up to Humphrey's Peak north of Flagstaff, over to Walnut Canyon National Monument and to several other nature sites in the area. Hiking out on her own put Clarissa's life and virginity at risk with every departure. Trail paths around her offered enough seclusion that someone stalking her could easily gag and drag her to locations to do as they wished with her.

The Colemans tried grounding Clarissa after the first of these escapes, only to find that she could disable their home alarms and climb out while they slept, adding darkness to the list of dangers she faced alone. At least the first few times, Clarissa took her Lifelink with her, allowing the Colemans to get police approval to track her location and bring her home. Clarissa couldn't figure out how her parents found her so quickly, but she soon discovered the answer. She kept that knowledge to herself.

When grounding didn't work, the Colemans tried taking away Clarissa's Lifelink as punishment, knowing that she liked to be in contact with a couple of her friends. It didn't take long for them to realize they absorbed the worst of this particular punishment. When Clarissa disappeared without her device, the Colemans had no easy way to track her down. John and Clarissa's sisters would split up on Clarissa's favorite trails. Mrs. Coleman stayed home searching online paid satellite views hoping to find movement along the trails or in the forests that she could zoom in to spot Clarissa. For Clarissa, there was no escaping this search method, but she learned to obscure her identity, dressing as a boy on some trips, and otherwise trying to keep from being found when she wanted to be alone by hiding under cave-like overhangs.

Finally, realizing that punishing Clarissa when she ran off wasn't working, John taught Clarissa to defend herself. Clarissa had natural speed that was still increasing in pace as her body control caught up with her height. John enrolled Clarissa in self-defense courses, taught her to shoot, and ultimately designed weapons that Clarissa could use to protect herself. John's best weapon invention was disguised as a wood hiking stick when not activated, allowing Clarissa to hike without appearing to be a threat to other hikers. A quick flick turned the hiking stick into a rifle, a three-digit code snapped open a long switchblade-like device at the opposite end that converted the stick to a bayonet and a third configuration folded the stick into a spiked club. Clarissa was skilled in using each of the weapons.

Clarissa's comfort in the wild and confidence with weapons use served her well during the secession battle. Her response to potential attacks earned her the respect of New Rite compound leader Sarah Osborne, a former Navy Seal who was a national hero for a dangerous single-woman deep dive to destroy a terrorist threat. Though they only spent an hour or two together during those troubling days, Clarissa grew to admire Sarah. That admiration made Sarah's combat death all the more unbearable for Clarissa, particularly following her grandfather's death just a few days earlier. Those deaths triggered a deep dive into severe depression for Clarissa, a free fall she is only just now slowing and escaping.

Back on Humphrey's trail, Clarissa carries a thirty-pound pack up the mountain, alternating between walking and jogging as she attempts to rebuild her strength. In the immediate aftermath of Sarah's and her grandfather's deaths, Clarissa has stopped exercising, started drinking her grandfather's alcohol stash hidden inside their home and stopped eating. By the time she decided to pull the trigger, Clarissa had lost nearly twenty pounds, few of which she could afford to lose.

Months removed from that day, Clarissa's road to emotional recovery has been combined with regular exercise, better diet control and only a few slips back into heavy drinking. Her goal, identified during her recovery to help her focus on something beyond her sometimes day-to-day misery, is to become a Navy Seal. She hopes to be as good as Sarah, but worries that making it to that level might not be attainable.

At the first of three false peaks, Clarissa rests just ahead of a final ascent over moon-rock like surfaces when she notices a quiet whir. She turns to each side, checking for anything unusual. While converting her hiking stick into rifle mode, she peers up toward the second peak and then down the trail below. As she does, the brim of her baseball hat presses downward, causing Clarissa to look up in time to see an unusual aircraft settling onto a patch of flat, barren lunar landscape next to her.

"Clarissa? Clarissa Coleman?" a voice yells out through a loud-speaker as the whirring blades overhead come to a quick stop.

Clarissa steps back, moving slowly away from the aircraft until she recognizes its shape and size. Sarah had taken a trip in an aircraft just like this one.

"I'm Clarissa," she yells back as a woman steps out of the aircraft.

"Clarissa, nice to meet you. I'm Ally Steele. We have . . .. We had a mutual friend, Sarah Osborne," Ally says.

Clarissa turns the rifle barrel to the ground, doing her best to hold her emotions: "You know Sarah? You knew Sarah?"

"You could say that. We worked together for many years," Ally replies, reaching out to shake Clarissa's hand.

"How did you know that I knew Sarah?" Clarissa asks.

"She told me, on our flight down to . . .," Ally says, before turning her head to her side and biting her lip. "She was so excited to meet you because she told me you were . . ., you are just like her."

Hearing this, Clarissa can't control her emotions. Sarah's words, if they really are from Sarah, are simultaneously an uplifting compliment and a reminder of a potential real friend lost.

Ally walks over and hugs Clarissa for a minute while Clarissa struggles to regain her composure. "Do you mind if we go somewhere else to talk?" Ally finally asks. "I can't sit here too long without risking that someone will spot me."

"That's fine. My house isn't that far away. We can go there or something," Clarissa offers.

"I have something far more interesting in mind," Ally suggests. "I want to convince you to work with me so I'll show you where I work."

Clarissa looks around, not sure what Ally could mean, but knowing the aircraft in front of her had to be the way there. "That sounds cool."

"Are you afraid of flying?" Ally asks.

"No. I don't think so. I mean, I don't know," Clarissa replies.

"Give me your Lifelink," Ally directs.

"Why?"

"I need to disable it, so we can't be tracked," Ally says.

"Really?" Clarissa questions.

"You'll understand when we get there," Ally assures her.

Ally's APB carries an external gecko-like skin coating across all of its external elements to deter human detection by quickly converting its extremity colors to match the appearance of its surroundings. Satellite flying overhead can't see an APB in camouflage mode. Radar and other tracking devices are detected by the APB, immediately analyzed for type and either absorbed or rebroadcast at identical angles from the opposite side of the APB to further avoid detection.

"Where are we going?" Clarissa asks as she jumps into the APB, scoots around to the co-pilot seat and latches in. Ally hands her an oxygen-injection mask and shows her how to insert it over her mouth. "You're going to need this," Ally says. "To keep from passing out."

"Really?"

Seconds later, Ally has the blades whirring on the APB and elevates straight up to fifteen thousand feet. Clarissa looks around as she sees the blades sucking inside the APB.

"Ready?" Ally tests.

"Ready," Clarissa answers.

"Head back," Ally says, checking to make sure Clarissa's head is completely against the headrest. Seeing that it is, Ally taps three spots on the console and the APB immediately accelerates to more than seven hundred miles per hour, heading northeast.

"Make sure you breathe," Ally reminds Clarissa.

Clarissa tries to respond, but her cheeks are tapping against her ears. Catching her breath when the acceleration is completed, Clarissa looks toward Ally.

"You know, my parents will freak out again if I'm not home in seven or eight hours," Clarissa suggests.

"Not a problem," Ally replies, an answer Clarissa knows to be true as she sees Lake Powell already below. "Ready for some fun?"

Clarissa smiles, her initial panic fading: "This is already fun."

"You haven't seen anything yet," Ally contends as she takes the APB into a five-thousand-foot dive, stops it flat, accelerates to full speed again and then climbs to fifty thousand feet.

Clarissa is surprised she's not feeling sick as Ally comes to a flat hold again, so asks why she's not even queasy.

"I hope you don't mind. That oxygen has an additive to medicate your lungs and heart so you won't pass out or throw up on my baby," Ally notes.

"Oh my God. This is awesome," Clarissa replies, scanning the horizon to see the curvature of the earth for the first time.

"If you think this is awesome, you might be just the person I'm looking for," Ally states, looking over at Clarissa as she speaks. "Let's go to our Utah compound to talk. Then I can either take you back to the trail or somewhere close to your home so you can get back on time."

Whispering quietly, Clarissa mouths out words intended only for her own ears. "If I would have known I would have missed this . . . ," she begins, before her sentence trails off in a wistful stare.

32 EXPLANATION

Washington reporters for every major news outlet in the nation cover the White House south lawn, an expansive reporting audience that extends well beyond the typical White House coverage teams.

President Phillipi takes no chances that his principal second term pursuit will be mischaracterized by cynical White House reporters, who see every legislative battle as a clash between winners and losers rather than as debates between right and wrong, practical and impractical, and emotional or logical.

God's Law is fundamental to America's future in the President's mind. The Political Freedom Amendment enacted a decade ago behind Professor Stark's intellectual drive fundamentally transformed Washington in a way that most hadn't truly understood prior to its passage. That constitutional amendment shrunk election cycles to sixty days, with primary elections running immediately into the general election. With fundraising to cover all but the candidate's travel expenses banned outside of the election cycle window, Washington had gone back to spending the majority of every two-year election cycle governing. Tripartisan compromise (including true independents) had once again become common, as incumbents learned that their most favorable path to reelection came from keeping the country on the right path. Still, remaining veterans of the old system are discomfited by constraints that hold their reelection at risk throughout each term.

Many long-term politicians still seek and find creative ways to circumvent the Political Freedom Amendment, including a provision that allows only actual candidates to name opponents in advertising in the final thirty days before an election. This provision, along with banning campaign finance bundling and limiting a contributor's donations to no more than one-one-hundredth of one percent of the candidate's spending, were developed to counteract *Citizens United* and *McCutcheon* Supreme Court decisions that helped elevate crony capitalism to art form in both major parties. To circumvent the thirty-day advertising restriction, some candidates with little chance of winning run in the new open primaries for the express purpose of being able to attack other candidates by name. Since general election races consist of only the top two vote getters in the open primaries, these shenanigans play a lesser role in general elections.

Having seen the difficulties Professor Stark and his supporters endured in securing passage of the Political Freedom Amendment, President Phillipi wants to leave as little to chance as possible in his pursuit of what he still calls God's Law.

His speech is simulcast on multiple networks inside the United States. It also attracts extraordinary international attention because of the novelty of the President's approach in using what most have seen as a personal moral principle as a core national governing concept. Stepping to the podium, the President expressly thanks his principle advocates in Congress, including Jill. He applauds the hard work of White House staff and particularly expresses his appreciation to Professor Stark for his insights and contributions.

"'Congress and the states shall make no law that contradicts the concept of doing unto others as we would have done unto ourselves,'" President Phillipi says to open his press conference. "This simple idea can fundamentally transform the way the United States of America is governed. It's an amendment our founding fathers perhaps never considered to be necessary, but as America has grappled to maintain a separation between church and state, we have too frequently instead separated our laws from the moral and the just."

With hundreds of local news anchors, well-respected instant reaction commentators and local interest group organizers joining the White House press corps for the speech, the Secret Service are on edge. A dozen snipers line the south edge of the White House roof. Hundreds of other Secret Service and D.C. Police guard the perimeter of the south lawn fences. It hasn't been that long since the White House fences were overwhelmed. No one wants a repeat, particularly with the First Family in residence.

"Scholars of history have long understood that our founders sought to ensure that no single religion control our government. They recognized that when religion and national government are one and the same with interlocking bureaucracies, nations lose the progress that comes with competition—competition of ideas, competition over what constitutes justice, competition to identify and enforce right and wrong," the President states, pausing when momentarily distracted by a small security drone flying overhead. A few audience members turn to look as well, seeing his eyes look away from the crowd.

"Before I took office, our federal bureaucracies had long lost accountability to the American people. Bureaucrats were and still are protected by laws that prevent everyday citizens from securing justice when their land is taken without cause, when their assets are confiscated out of governmental greed or when lives are ruined through simple incompetence."

While some of the interest group organizers invited to this session loudly applaud this last line, most press corps members busily send short quips from the President's speech to subscribers or followers. Speed often trumps insight.

"Justice is our objective," the President continues. "Justice for those whose sentences are too long or too short. Justice for those who have had reputations and lives ruined by prosecutors seeking victory at the expense of truth. Justice, as Congresswoman Carlson has focused my attention, for the quarter of our population that finds themselves hamstrung by a vast assortment of federal anti-poverty programs that often dehumanize recipients, enforce processes designed around bureaucratic compliance and frequently fail to enable quality-of-life improvement."

Whether initially out of courtesy or political expedience, the President had insisted that House Judiciary Committee Chairman Will Henry have a seat of honor behind him to face the cameras during his speech, an invitation the Chairman gladly accepted as a tribute to his power. Being seen as critical even to his political enemies will boost his carefully crafted rebel image back home, the Chairman anticipated in agreeing to attend. Instead, his facial contortions as the President trashed the old political system made for the type of reaction shots the President wanted to use to define the God's Law opposition.

"Perhaps the most important concept, and the one I hope is best enabled by passing this constitutional amendment, is that Congress cannot pass laws from which it exempts itself. There is nothing that contradicts the Golden Rule more than imposing laws on others that one is not willing to personally follow."

Chairman Henry's unease at this last statement is evident in his reaction. Nearly every media camera juxtaposes his dismissive sneer against the President's words.

"This will have a profound impact on society. Congress will not be able to exempt bureaucrats and prosecutors from lawsuits when they abuse their powers. Government prosecutors who initiate endless lawsuits in attempts to destroy or extort from companies and others with little merit to their claim will be forced to pay their target's costs if they lose and a judge and jury find that the government could not reasonably have believed in the merits of his case," the President adds, accelerating his pace as he finally nears the end of his carefully prepared remarks.

"These are only some of the changes in our nation's laws that I believe will follow passage of the Golden Rule as a constitutional amendment. Many of these changes will be popular. Some will be attacked as leading to unintended consequences. But having our discussions based on right and wrong or fair or unfair is far better than having our debates centered around winners and losers," President Phillipi states feverishly.

33 DEVOTION

Years ago, General Timur dropped a four-man submarine-like living station and storage unit into twelve deep lakes around the world, all containing nuclear weapons he stole during his reign in the Iranian military.

Once Timur stashed the nuclear weapons in submarines at the bottoms of several lakes, his only fear of having the weapons stolen comes when he or someone on his immediate team prepares to use them. At each lake, Timur built extended piers from modest-sized storage buildings that house marine services businesses during the summer months. In the winters, these buildings provide launch points for a three-man submarine maintenance team that Timur trusts as fully dedicated to the creation of a global caliphate through whatever means necessary.

Long piers attached to each building are elevated enough that the maintenance team can hide the long, thin, three-meter high attachable submarine station sections stolen by General Timur and his men. He accumulated these sub-sea station sections over years, overseeing contracts that allowed him to ensure that he stole one section for every two delivered to Iran's navy.

The sub-surface program was cleverly designed for its intended purpose. Iran had long feared being caught off-guard if U.S. submarines reached the Iranian coastline through the Gulf of Oman. General Timur also worried that Azerbaijan or Turkmenistan would provide the United States or Israel with a way to get submarines launched in the Caspian Sea and to the Iranian shores just fifty miles from Tehran. Missiles launched from near the shore could obliterate Tehran in just seconds; before Iran's missile defense systems could fully activate.

General Timur created widespread fear of this potential capability using statements extracted from an Israeli spy who was promised leniency after being caught running agents inside Iran's nuclear armament program. In return for his life, the spy was required by Timur to tell the Iranian military court that Israel and the United States had developed a submarine-based missile launch plan that could destroy Iran in just minutes, with full confidence that the attack could not be stopped. The Israeli spy, seeing he had nothing to lose in communicating an attack plan that he didn't believe existed, testified to this threat in open court.

After the spy was found guilty and sentenced to death by public hanging, General Timur followed through on his commitment, ensuring a private pardon was granted by the Ayatollah. At a breakfast in advance of the spy's release, General Timur served him a bowl of blueberries. Within minutes, the belladonna berries mixed in with the blueberries began to take effect, beginning with slurred vision and ending in the spy's convulsive death.

The spy's testimony ensured that General Timur was assigned to oversee a program to protect Iran's shorelines from sub-sea attack. The fabricated pardon he showed the spy was quickly burned.

The system Timur developed with Iran's highly skilled engineering force was designed for flexibility. Individual submarine units run thirty feet in length, roughly ten feet high and only two meters wide. A thickly walled section of each submarine contains nuclear power devices, parts of which since have been modified to house the stolen nuclear weapons. Each unit contains its own living systems including a dual-purpose saltwater and freshwater filtration system so the submarines can be used either in the fully saltwater Persian Gulf waters or the more lightly salted Caspian Sea. Each submarine section also contains its own oxygen filtration devices that extend out into surrounding water to extract oxygen from the water. The unit's primary sub-sea time limitations are in its food storage capabilities.

Since General Timur designed the system for primarily defensive purposes, he insisted that sonar and other detection capabilities emanate from sources that aggressors could not detect. Each unit can rest underground on the sub-sea surface for up to a year, as long as it contains a sole occupant maintaining the twelve-hundred-calorie maximum intake. Recognizing that remaining submerged for a year in a vessel alone would drive most sailors crazy, General Timur had the submarines designed to connect. Each unit has the ability to link to up to four other submarines, seal together and then open passageways between the units that allows the submariners to create human connections during their extended sub-sea tours.

Submarine sonar could still have easily detected these units from their straight shapes if not for another capability General Timur insisted be added. Each unit has the ability to extend its top exterior shell into a variety of shapes for sonar to encounter, making the units appear every bit a collection of surface boulders from top view, particularly when multiple units connect together.

Over the years, General Timur and troops loyal to him had taken and stored dozens of these submarines to achieve their own long-term objectives of destroying the enemies of Islam. When several generals defected to overthrow the Supreme Leader of Iran and turn the nation into a secular government, General Timur used the confusion of those battles to steal dozens of nuclear warheads and other nuclear weapons, immediately spreading them out in submarine storage around the world.

To ensure the weapons remain safe and protected, General Timur and his most trusted leaders use small sub-sea command vehicles easily transportable by truck to launch inspections. In his prior official role, Timur had used these two-man submarines for surprise inspections. Now, these units are dedicated to maintaining unmanned sub-sea stations holding stashes of nuclear weapons.

"Do you remember the last time we were up here?" Jill queries Professor Stark as they stand near the top of the Capitol Dome, looking toward the Washington Monument.

"I certainly do," Professor Stark replies. "It was the night we realized that our country would stay united. In fact, that's why I wanted to come up here with you tonight."

"Really? Why's that?" she inquires.

"I celebrated with you that our nation was staying together, that we wouldn't be separated from friends and family by virtue of the state they lived in at the time," Professor Stark says. "I was certain then that I wanted the same for us, to always be together, to be able to be in your life for the rest of my own, and to never face a future without you."

Professor Stark reaches into his pants pocket, pulls out a distinctly colored jewelry box and drops down to one knee.

"Jill, will you honor me by agreeing to be my wife, my partner, my friend and my lover for as long as I breathe?"

Jill looks away from Professor Stark's eyes, looking back to the monuments and memorials in the distance, before turning her attention back to him.

"Paul," she says, reaching toward him with her left hand. "Yes, I will. Absolutely, I will."

He pushes the ring onto her finger before standing up for a long embrace and kiss.

"You had me worried for a minute, there, when you wouldn't look at me," Professor Stark says.

Jill looks at him and gives him a quick kiss on the lips: "I just wanted to remember this moment, to take a second to let it all sink in. Becoming engaged to you is a feeling I didn't want to pass too quickly."

Professor Stark presses his lips together and nods his head.

34 PROGRESSION

It hasn't just been JT's passion driving New Rite's success. He's an astute businessman who understands the importance of a bargain. Following collapse of the Castillo cartel, dozens of companies with large but previously obscured cartel ownership stakes began to panic about U.S. asset confiscation laws. JT is among the first to recognize this panic. He secures a deal to buy The Detroit Salt Mine from the Phoenix Mining Company by offering a take-it-or-leave-it deal that Phoenix's CEO can't pass up without risking having the mine simply confiscated. Because of the low-ball acquisition price, New Rite profits handsomely even if salt extraction drops in half.

Salt, though, isn't the real reason for JT's purchase. Operational security is his prime interest, including the ability to covertly connect the mine to an eight-thousand-acre Center for Urban Recovery of the Environment (CURE) created out of part of former ruins of Detroit.

Surrounded by thirty-foot high white walls, ceiling and floors roughly twelve hundred feet below Detroit city streets and urban reserves, Ramon and his handpicked team test new surveillance systems needed to support New Rite's reoriented special operations mission. Equipment for the large installation is brought in from the Canadian tunnel opening connected to the mine beneath the Detroit River. The tunnel had been part of the cartel's drug-running operations. Highly encrypted connections to the outside world are wired through that same Canadian passage as well as up three directions on the U.S. side of the border.

Huddled with his team for a mid-morning stand-up review, Ramon works and directs at a furious pace he hasn't matched since completing creation of his Easy Ride operating software that at one point controlled nearly the entire U.S. vehicle fleet. He alternates between being team maestro and dropping in as first chair on several technologies, sometimes simultaneously playing the tech equivalent of wind and string instruments as he builds the new system, writes code and creates integration points others might never even contemplate.

Ramon's system includes the capabilities to operate Center for Atrocity Research trials and investigations, in part by borrowing processing capability from a number of over-sized government and corporate installations that Ramon and his team easily hack. Once the system is completed, it will simply arrive at Professor Stark's office unannounced with clear but untraceable instructions on its use.

The tougher challenge for Ramon's team is to modify headgear containing neuron and pupil sensor technology in time for use in the first Atrocity Center trials.

The headgear has a serious purpose. JT insists that everyone acting as jurors in Atrocity Project trials be monitored continuously to be sure they have viewed, read and listened to all of the evidence presented in each case. Verdicts are still subject to human error, but JT wants to ensure that these trials take justice consideration to a new level before Ally's team carries out any sentences.

By tracking brain, eye, pulse and related activities, the Atrocity Project can immediately identify which portions of trial evidence have been recognized and contemplated by each of the one thousand global jurors. Since the trials will rely on translators to communicate evidence in the language of each juror, the sensors will also serve as a guide to determine when a particular language translation might have been in error, triggering a thorough computerized translation review.

Any evidence a juror doesn't comprehend due to exhaustion or distraction is replayed before that juror can start the next day.

At the end of each trial, JT wants Ramon's team to identify a verdict certainty calculation. Professor Stark has already stated that he'll announce the center's unofficial verdicts by conviction voting percentage. These verdicts aren't quite enough for JT. He wants Ramon to determine how certain jurors are of their own verdicts. While Atrocity Center trials won't lead to formal sentences, New Rite's special operations team plans to execute sentences based on those verdicts. JT decided on this approach for the next phase of his special operations team to ensure no single individual exercises unfettered power to kill.

The conviction standard Professor Stark announces for trials of the world's worst people is "beyond a reasonable doubt." But as JT establishes The Morality Project—his code name for the combination of Stark-led trials and punishment of the guilty by New Rite—he sets a higher death penalty standard for special operations action. JT determines that the death penalty will only be imposed if a jury decides that the accused is guilty beyond any doubt. To JT, that test is met when ninety-five percent of jurors agree the accused is guilty with at least a ninety-eight percent rate of certainty as judged by brain impulses at the point jurors vote. JT would have preferred to set the execution rate at one hundred percent, but agreed that juror screening won't eliminate jurors who won't consider facts in verdict determinations. It's Ramon's job to figure out how to quantify JT's certainty rate.

In many ways, running the Center for Atrocity is the greatest challenge of Professor Stark's career, given that it requires skill sets he has never tested. Knowing this, while aware that Professor Stark surpasses expectations on every project he undertakes, JT is careful to ensure that needed resources show up on a just-in-time basis. The jury tracking system is a component Professor Stark might have needed years or longer to create if left to his own abilities. In other areas, JT does his best to leave Professor Stark alone, watching mostly from a distance as the Center selects lawyers and investigators for the first trial.

The Center's first indictee is known as General Timur, a ruthless perpetrator of global jihad before Iran's Islamic theocracy was overthrown. When several members of the Iranian military joined secular forces to return control of the nation to largely democratic processes, Timur and his hand-selected members of the former Revolutionary Guard fought back, inflicting grave wounds on the rebel forces including massacres of the wives and children of several coup leaders.

When Iran fell, General Timur escaped. For nearly a year, hundreds of global intelligence agents tracked him with little success. The nuclear detonation in Armenia has been tied by a number of national intelligence agencies to General Timur, a factor that swayed Professor Stark's decision to use Timur as his test case trial. That General Timur is merciless comes as no surprise to those who understand the history of the name. During the fourteenth century, Timur, otherwise known as Tamerlane, was the greatest self-proclaimed Muslim ruler over mankind, gaining his success through slaughters that eradicated as much as five percent of the global population during his reign. More than a dozen nations now exist in land ruled by Timur during the Timurid Empire. Armenia is one of those nations and one of the few with a largely non-Muslim population.

Despite being hunted by dozens of nations, General Timur remains free, forcing his trial to be carried out in absentia. Professor Stark decides to personally serve as judge for the first trial.

With many international institutions discredited, or at least temporarily weakened, Professor Stark sees his Center as supplementing the role of the International Criminal Courts and International War Crimes tribunals, taking on trials these courts can't administer, at least not without undue political influence.

What Professor Stark still doesn't know is his funding source.

A long-time Castillo cartel employee, Max Herta, had been New Rite's most important informant inside the cartel prior to Castillo's death. He turned JT onto the Detroit Salt Mine. Herta's last cartel assignment—before his arrest, plea deal and quick pardon at JT's request—had been to build secretive tunnel extensions at the salt mine that run under the Detroit River all the way to a grain storage facility inside of Canada. Between barge and train traffic at the grain facility and massive truck and rail loads in and out of the salt mine, JT saw the mine as the perfect location to build a large, secure location for his expanded special operations team.

To provide security, JT is using the company that built revamped biometric elevator control technology for the White House Deep Underground Command Center. Devices similar to those used at the DUCC to control movement were installed inside the mine. Nature maintains constant temperature control at salt depth. Insects, snakes and other life can't survive at these depths and particularly within salt mine confines—an additional point of appeal to JT. Perhaps most importantly, JT's team can cross borders unchecked between the United States and Canada.

JT and Ally drop down into the salt mine's new protected laboratory research facilities to assess progress made by Ramon and his team.

"Show me where we stand," JT politely but hurriedly demands on entering the secured, isolated rooms enclosing Ramon and his team.

Ramon had prepared for the visit, treating his need to impress JT as just as critical to his survival as had been impressing cartel boss Cesar Castillo when the Castillo cartel first co-opted him and invested in his technology and businesses.

Having conducted a three-dimensional scan of JT's and Ally's heads in advance, new electrode-rich, helmet-shaped detection devices are quickly placed on them with wireless monitors wrapped around their wrists as well.

"Take seats here," Ramon instructs so that Ally and JT are quickly inside personal viewing stations similar to the ones to be shipped to each participating juror.

On the screen, JT and Ally watch a basketball player shooting free throws, dozens in a row. After thirty shots, Ramon stops the display.

"You missed it, JT," Ramon calls out.

"Missed what?" JT asks.

"You missed the streaker in the upper left corner of the screen."

"How do you know?"

"Simple. Your eyes never moved to her location and no neurons triggered in your orbitofrontal cortex. You think this is a simple screen you're watching, but behind the beams of light are analytical eyes that detect what you're focusing on," Ramon says. "Match that up with the electrode sensors and we know what you're truly seeing."

"How can that be?"

"As soon as you sat down, in the minute before I started the display, small shots of light are sent from each of the sensors. Through electrode monitoring, we detect brain recognition patterns and match that up with what science tells us about what parts of the brain process what types of information. From there, we analyze the extent of your peripheral vision and then analyze your likelihood of spotting a section of the screen depending on the extent of your concentration on the object at the center of your vision."

"So there's estimation involved?" JT questions.

"Marginally. The system teaches itself your peripheral acceptance range in a matter of a few hours," Ramon clarifies.

"That sounds good. Are you sure this can be replicated?" JT asks.

"I'm sure. By the way, we confirmed you didn't see the streaker with several other methods besides visual attainment," Ramon points out.

"Such as?" JT asks.

"No heart rate increase at seeing the naked woman. Every one of us who saw it had detectable additional heart and brain activity. For those who concentrated long enough, we could detect systemic blood flow adjustments as well."

JT turns his eyes toward Ally. "What about Ally here? Any blood flow shift for her?"

"I think I'll let Ally answer that question, if she would like," Ramon replies.

"I'm just kidding," JT responds. "What matters is that the system works."

"It's working," Ramon adds. "Not perfect yet, but it's working. Once we have this set, we can work on the individual replay requirements for each portion of any testimony missed."

"Sounds like progress," JT observes. "I'm beginning to think I might have been right about you all along."

Ally finishes detaching herself from Ramon's equipment. "How is progress going at ensuring that the trial technology can't be disrupted or its host locations identified?" she asks.

"We had a good head start with the capabilities New Rite gaming built over time," Ramon replies. "I've been able to add some tricks I used to circumvent detection of the cartel's law enforcement avoidance system. Not to be arrogant, but I don't think any government or dictator or whatever will ever be able to track down this system and get rid of it or identify its developers."

"You mean like how we couldn't track you down," Ally interjects.

"That was pure luck, and my discipline slip," Ramon contends. "Besides, these computers can't be found by facial recognition scans."

"Perhaps," Ally replies. "But every physical object has its tells."

JT pulls Ramon and Ally away from the rest of Ramon's team to the corner of the research and testing room.

"I don't think I have to say this but I will anyway, Ramon. We can't afford for any of the terrorists we're going after to find us, even with luck," JT states. "And we certainly can't afford a discipline slip."

"Understood, sir."

"JT. Please just call me JT."

"Okay, JT," Ramon says, transitioning to another topic on his mind. "Then can you tell me when I'll get to see Abril and whether I'll ever get to see my family."

"We're working on how to secure your family without being tracked. General Hernández may be dead but there are dozens of nations and terror organizations that can't be tipped off in any way that you're alive, including your own government," JT states, repeating information Ramon clearly understands. "So when we bring them to you, they have to leave everything else behind."

Ramon drops his head: "I understand."

"We're trying to get someone close enough to ask a bunch of 'what-if' questions without giving your survival away," JT adds.

"And Abril?"

"Still in treatment," Ally interjects.

"Can't she be treated here?" Ramon pleads.

JT gently shakes his head side to side. "Of course not and you understand why. If we bring her here under the same isolation restrictions, we can't bring the therapists she needs."

"It's just tough, because I think I love her. Oh good God, I do love her. Wow, I don't think I ever said that sober before," Ramon says, his cheeks starting to turn red from the embarrassment of making the statement in front of two people he barely knows.

Ally puts her hand on Ramon's shoulder; an effort to assure him that he has no need for discomfort.

"She may ultimately have to decide between you and her intention to serve God," Ally asserts, "but first she has to learn to love herself and recognize that those weren't her sins before she can give herself to either of you. Once someone has taken from you what you never offered, it's tough to feel like your life is your own to control again."

"I understand," Ramon replies.

"I do too," Ally responds. "If you truly love her, you'll give her time and perhaps make better choices if you are back together."

"Sure, like staying away from strange women in bars," Ramon notes, winking at Ally.

After finishing up with Ramon, JT and Ally move next to the nearby but even more thoroughly enclosed laboratories led by Carol. Both put on full body jumpsuits and full-face protection masks and air systems. They understand that exposure in this lab quickly turns deadly. Before JT enters the room, a scanner detects an air gap between his headgear and jumpsuit that is carefully resealed and rechecked. Inside the laboratory, everyone looks the same, a feeling that helped attract Carol to her profession. Carol wants more than anything to be respected for an intellect she works hard to develop instead of her birth-gifted and less meticulously maintained appearance.

Carol leads the special operations bio-insertion team, charged with creating a targeted disease delivery mechanism. JT's intelligence team discovered and New Rite funded Carol's work early in her academic career on the condition that publication of her results cease. Carol debated whether to accept, caught between desire to gain global notoriety and fear that her delivery system could easily be abused. Ultimately, JT promised that she would have veto power over use of the technology in his organization, something she couldn't be assured of in any other company. He also committed to fund adjacent technology projects to make Carol a global science superstar if she later decided she wanted that as well.

In much the way a time-release capsule injects medication inside a patient over a set period of time, Carol's DNA-trigger mechanism releases disease to specified targets. Carol originally developed her mechanism to stop black market use of prescription painkillers by ensuring that addictive pills only work in designated patients. When his intelligence team caught wind of Carol's research, JT recognized its potential power and reached his funding agreement with Carol. Now he sees an opportunity to slash risks to his special operations team when taking out individual targets.

"On track?" JT asks as he finds Carol strictly by narrowing laboratory researchers to only the three who fit her height profile.

Besides JT and Ally, only four other people in the salt mine have entry and exit privileges. Everyone else on the various teams was brought under sedation and cover to work in the lab for six months straight. During this time, they will see only the insides of laboratories, dorm-style rooms, a large fitness and relaxation facility and a well-stocked kitchen and greenhouse.

"On track," Carol replies, turning to JT. "Let me show you."

Carol takes JT and Ally through an adjoining enclosed hallway into a quadruple-sealed testing structure that contains rats in hundreds of entirely self-contained environments.

"Three days ago, we injected bubonic plague using the DNA-release delivery mechanism into the one hundred rats you see spread throughout these chambers. Can you guess which one of the rats was the DNA match for the plague?" Carol asks JT, who quickly points to an immobile rat near the edge of the grouping.

"Let's see," Carol says, pulling up the DNA of the intended recipient rat on a display screen, then setting in motion equipment inside each cage to pierce the rats and run DNA analysis. Within seconds, the DNA codes of each rat display on a grid to their right matching the grid of the rat containers inside the room. One more button push. The display confirms that only the DNA-targeted rat has bubonic plague.

"So, this is how you intend to take out our new targets," Ally whispers to JT.

He winks, giving her all the answer she needs.

"Isn't bubonic plague contagious?" Ally asks. "How can you be sure we won't contract it here? How do you make sure that others besides the intended target don't contract it from them?"

"Critical questions," JT acknowledges. "First, with our delivery mechanism, if the DNA of the victim doesn't immediately match, the mechanism destroys the disease. We've tested this one hundred different ways without a failure because we actually modify the disease so it only triggers in specific DNA."

"Well, that makes sense, I guess," Ally replies. "But once the target victim contracts bubonic plaque or any other disease, how do you keep the disease from spreading to others?"

"We think we have the disease modified so that it's not possible but you're here at the right time for our biggest test," Carol states, setting in motion the release of all of the rats from their individual cages so they can circulate with the plague-infected rat. "We'll know soon if the plague passes from the target rat to any other rats."

"My high school biology classes were a long time ago," Ally says, "but don't diseases naturally mutate to survive? These are living organisms as intent on assuring the survival of their species as we are at ensuring our own survival. How can we be so sure they won't outsmart us and come back in a form we aren't prepared to treat?"

"A legitimate concern and, believe me, one I stew about when I try to sleep," Carol replies. "We're testing here with contagious diseases, but JT assures me that when we actually go to field use, we'll only be inserting non-communicable diseases. We're also testing our ability to attach the DNA-trigger release to poisons that take immediate effect, the type of poisons that might replicate the experience someone would have in a gas chamber, for example, rather than the slow, torturous death of bubonic plague, smallpox or any of the other diseases that might be tougher to control."

"My God," Ally exclaims, realizing the implications of Carol's work. "If this capability falls into the wrong hands, a dictator, a company, any government, can you imagine the potential for evil?"

Carol's covered head nods. "JT understood it right away. That's why I came to work for New Rite," Carol replies. "We're working on countermeasures at the same time so we can protect the world if something that awful ever happens."

"Ally, you're onto the real reason we have to act now. It's unlikely that Carol's the only one trying to develop this capability. We have to identify and take out those who would use it maliciously," JT interjects, "but with the type of process controls to keep it from itself being a tool of control and manipulation."

Ally excuses herself and exits the lab. Taking off her mask, jumpsuit and boots, she paces down a salt-crusted channel to find solitude. Pulling the trigger herself to eliminate a monster from the world isn't a problem. She takes pride in her role in getting rid of drug kingpin Cesar Castillo. But being part of a team that could accidentally release a horror so great the human race hadn't seen it since the fourteenth century black plague has her questioning JT's sanity. If she continues, Ally will have to rely on someone she barely knows to care as much as she does and display the same capability in her field as Ally does in special operations.

JT knows Ally well enough to give her time to stew and formulate her questions. It's nearly an hour before he follows her to ensure she understands and approves of the plan.

"I don't know how I feel about injecting a disease into someone that could morph into a global catastrophe," Ally states as JT catches up to her. "I couldn't live with myself knowing I had any part in something that horrific."

"Nor could I Ally," JT replies. "We won't use Carol's mechanism to inject a communicable disease unless I'm absolutely certain that the mechanism kills the disease any time it hits a wrong target, including when passed from our target. My hope is we'll use Carol's mechanism to release fast-acting poisons so we can trigger them in public when only top aides or close friends are around the target. This way, everyone sees them die with no one except their inner circle to blame. The world sees these evil people as being taken out by their own."

Ally crosses her arms tightly in front. "How am I supposed to get my team in and out of these places when they're surrounded by aides and certainly by their best security teams?" Ally asks, now refocusing on how she can survive her part of the mission.

"That's just the point, Ally," JT says. "Your team won't be anywhere in the vicinity when the DNA release is triggered. In fact, you won't be injecting these targets at all. Your team will ensure we have a valid DNA sample, maybe even taking it yourself at times. But we want these people to die with absolutely no evidence that any outsiders had any hand in their death."

"How in the world are we going to make that happen?" Ally asks.

"That's the research bay we're headed to next," JT replies. "Disintegrating micro-drones."

Entering another security protected research bay deep inside the Detroit Salt Mine, JT and Ally feel an immediate prick on the side of their necks. Simultaneously swatting to kill whatever stung them in a deep underground salt mine environment where no insects or other animals survive unaided, they look up in time to see New Rite's micro-drone team exchanging high fives.

"What's going on here?" JT asks.

"The team again passed our insert-and-escape test," replies the soft-spoken Abhirim Roussard as he looks up to Ally and JT.

"What's that mean?" Ally asks as she peers around the room, trying to understand what she is seeing.

"Abe, why don't you answer but first tell Ally what your team is developing," JT directs.

"Well, Miss Ally, it's a pleasure to see you again. Hopefully you are a little less worried about how you are going to incorporate a meek old man into your team of elite special fighters," Abe says. "I know I would be scared to go on a combat field standing next to me."

Ally raises her eyebrows but otherwise doesn't respond.

"You've been aware of New Rite's spy drone technology," Abe continues. "You know, the Cooper's hawk drones we've been flying around all of the cartel targets."

"Yes, I've been aware. Remember, we used them in Monterrey. I'm guessing you're the genius behind these drones," Ally says.

"Probably better that you didn't know me until you needed to know me," Abe affirms. "So anyway, for our next missions, JT has given us a very small added challenge. We need to create drones with all the visibility, maneuverability and invisibility of a flea, and they have to be able to carry a payload."

"You're losing me. Visibility and invisibility conflict."

"I'm sorry I wasn't clear," Abe replies. "The visibility is complete data capture of our target sights. We need to see 360 degrees at all times. The invisibility is to be invisible to the people we fly around. We can't have metal or any other detectable components, a true challenge when we also want to forcibly disintegrate the micro-drones at our command. Our control directions to the micro-drones also can't be detectable, which means, in some cases, we also have to be able to program directions for every possible scenario into each drone before we send it off on its mission."

"That seems impossible," Ally replies. JT smiles broadly on the side as Abe and Ally discuss the micro-drone project.

"Difficult, yes. Impossible? I don't believe in impossible," Abe replies. "Some people get so stuck on jumping every hurdle that they don't realize the best option is to choose a path around the hurdle."

Ally shakes her head, looks toward JT, then turns back toward Abe.

"So this test you mentioned?"

"The insert-and-escape test?" Abe asks.

"Yes. That one," Ally replies.

"We programmed these drones," Abe says as he holds up what looks like a common flea, "to identify you from a facial recognition scan, fly around behind you, insert a small stinger in your neck and then evade contact when you swatted to kill whatever was pricking you. We did this same thing when we wanted to confirm where Ramon was in Mexico. Come and look."

Abe walks Ally and JT back to the control center and waves his arm at one of the research team members to call up the video for display. Zooming in on the actions of the flea at one hundred times actual size and one-tenth actual speed, JT and Ally watch as the flea identifies them from the front, flies behind them, injects a tiny capsule into their skin and avoids being hit.

"Is that capsule still in our skin?" JT asks.

"Oh, yes," Abe replies. "It certainly should be there but we need to do blood tests on you to be sure the capsule released properly."

"You injected us with something?" JT asks, his face reddening as he finishes his question.

"Ah, yes, but very innocuous. Just one of the many performance enhancing drugs we test for in athletes, in an amount too small to affect you and very difficult to discover. We have tested this on everyone here repeatedly, without any concern," Abe replies.

JT's forehead furrows. His skin turns flush. "I don't want you doing this to me again without my permission," he directs, making clear that he's upset at being used as a guinea pig for this aspect of his team's operations.

Abe quickly apologizes: "I was thinking you'd be okay because of your Golden Rule principle."

"How did you get so good at this?" Ally inquires, trying to reduce the tension level in the room.

"This whole team, everyone here has been part of the New Rite online gaming development team. Most of this technology was adapted from discoveries we used to develop the pod-based game competition modules as well as to cover the live survival competition games for the broadcasts. We didn't want competitors knowing when cameras were watching, so we developed drones made to resemble birds that humans would not find threatening. This team not only developed the drones, we operated them manually for a few years before we decided to create the technology to automate their flight patterns based on facial recognition readings and a series of complicated action-assessment algorithms," Abe continues.

"Is this all real?" Ally questions as she turns to JT.

"This is how we take our capabilities to the next level," JT insists. "But don't worry, we still need your team. There are some actions that simply require human intervention."

"Yes, yes," Abe adds. "Our fleas and wasps right now can only remain aloft for a short time. That means they need to release near the point of capsule insertion at a time that allows them to complete their mission and escape the search perimeter so the use of drones is not discovered."

"That's certainly easier than making real-time contact, but won't be easy in a lot of locations depending on our target," Ally suggests.

"What do you mean by target?" Abe asks, at which point JT grabs Ally's hand to make clear that he'll answer that question.

"Our reconnaissance target. Your drones will insert a tiny tracking device that we can use to follow game participants in the most hazardous of environments," JT says. After leaving the room, JT turns to Ally: "Abe and his team don't yet know the full scope of how their creations will be used."

Secure on JT's Colorado mountaintop guest home in what used to be the Arapaho National Forest, Abril's physical recovery is nearly complete after multiple breaks and fractures endured in the cartel pit have been re-broken and re-healed. As the re-breaks progressed, New Rite's surgeons used laser-micro-quilt skin graft techniques to replace the lava-pit scar tissue patterning of her back and buttocks with smoother skin. To accomplish this, skin in the pattern of a single color of a tiny checkerboard was taken from Abril's undamaged leg and abdominal areas, then implanted over skinned scar tissue areas and grown.

U.S. military-provided salve had only marginally reduced the roughness of the scar tissue after Abril's release. The pits, modeled after the rape centers employed by several Serb militia officers to torment Bosnian Muslim women and girls as young as twelve, were part of the cartel's efforts to subdue local communities and ensure employee loyalty. Every cartel employee learned that any remotely attractive woman or girl they were related to or even were friendly with would be sent to the sex-slave pits if they ever turned against the cartel or disappointed its leadership. Women who didn't meet the pit master's attractiveness standard completely disappeared.

Ally travels back to the guest home as frequently as possible to provide Abril with some non-therapist connection, since only she and JT know Abril's connection to Ramon. Ramon did everything he could to stay connected, manipulating JT's private satellite and subterranean cable communication relay system to be able to talk with Abril at least one hour each day. He enjoyed the irony of patching his contacts with Abril through government communications networks.

With Ally's help, Ramon rigged a male robot to serve as his communication and contact device. Ramon's words come out of the robot's mouth, his facial expressions read the electrodes hooked to his face, and his bodysuit allows him to manipulate the robot to hold Abril's hand, caress her hair and even kiss her lightly. It's a poor substitute for flesh-to-flesh contact, but Ramon takes it as his best alternative.

Six times a day at first, a nurse visits Abril to change bandages, apply a skin graft accelerant and slowly, methodically help Abril move her arms and legs to keep her muscles from atrophying during her recovery. Given the elevation of the New Rite guest room, an oxygen system helps keep the air rich. Once a day, New Rite's company psychologist spends an hour with Abril, listening to her story and trying to convince Abril that the shame she battles belongs to her attackers.

"It's hard enough to live with failing myself and my family," Abril tells the psychologist at the start of one session. "But what I'm not sure I can ever forgive myself for is failing God."

"Did you fail your God, or did God fail you?" the psychologist asks, before seeing from Abril's expression that she's vastly overstepped her bounds.

The psychologist struggles for words, understanding that faith and reason sometimes struggle to coexist and wondering which method of counseling was more likely to generate the intended progress.

"Let me ask you, Abril. I can't pretend to speak for your God and you wouldn't believe me if I tried," the psychologist says. "Your relationship with God is between you and your priest, or maybe, more importantly, between you and your God directly. So I'll tell you how

I've learned to handle the adversity in my life with the hopes that it will help you think about how to take back control of your life."

"How do I ever take back control when it's clear to me that other people can take everything from me anytime they want?" Abril replies.

"Not everything," the psychologist replies.

"How so?"

"You endured one of the most horrific experiences anyone could be forced to endure," the psychologist tells her.

"I know," Abril says, battling to keep her emotions from breaking her down.

"But when you escaped or were released, you began taking your life back," the psychologist noted.

"I did?" Abril questions.

"You did," the psychologist tells Abril, jamming her pointed finger into the table between them. "You tracked down one of the men responsible for your horror and began to extract retribution. That's a form of control; perhaps not a healthy form in the long run," the psychologist says with a shrug, "but a clear sign that the real Abril is still inside."

"What do you mean, the real Abril?" Abril asks.

"Everything you've told me about finding this man, capturing him, holding him accountable . . .," the psychologist begins.

"But he wasn't the one responsible. He didn't even know," Abril interrupts.

"Are you sure he didn't know?" the psychologist asks.

"I'm sure," Abril replies, turning to stare out of the floor-to-ceiling glass panes at the majestic view of snow-capped mountains and blue skies with gathering clouds.

"But you didn't know that when you took him, did you?" the psychologist asks.

"No, I thought he knew. I mean I saw him in the tunnels," Abril says.

"And you're sure he's not lying to you."

"I'm sure," Abril replies.

The psychologist nods her head, saying nothing for several seconds to see if Abril has anything else to add. "How can you be so certain?" she finally asks.

Abril peers down at the ground as she answers: "He wants to . . . he wants to . . . uhm . . . be with me."

"You know this?"

"Let's put it this way, when he sees me even sort of . . ., his, uhm, you know, responds even at the risk of terrible pain."

"What?" the psychologist asks.

"I didn't tell you the whole story. I can't, really," Abril admits. "I wanted to torture him, but I couldn't just bring myself to shoot him or stab him or skin him. I just couldn't do it."

"So what did you do?" the psychologist asks, wondering as she does if the question is driven by the need for clinical insights or simply prurient interest.

"I had him completely tied down, and, you know, exposed," Abril says with reddening cheeks.

"Oh. Okay," the psychologist says, leaning toward Abril and doing her best to pretend her curiosity is only professional.

"Then I put a board over his man parts with sharp nails and blades and glass shards that would shred him any time he got, uh, arised," Abril continues.

"And?"

"And, it wasn't difficult," Abril tells her. "He was physically attracted to me. You know, no control attracted."

Abril is among only a few patients to surprise the psychologist over the years, but she tries hard not to show any emotion. "So this makes you sure that he didn't know?"

"I know he saw me because he looked at me while I was down there and not at any of the other girls. If he knew what was happening, his attraction is so clear that he would have had me in the center. I mean, he could have done anything he wanted to any of us there and I never saw him with me or any of the other slaves."

"But you didn't know he was innocent when you took him, did you?" the psychologist says.

"Of course not. I wouldn't have done that to him if I knew then what I know now," Abril argues.

"I understand, but my point," the psychologist continues, "is that that your action shows you have the ability to take back control of your life."

"But I didn't find the people who hurt me," Abril responds. "I didn't make them pay like I wanted to."

"To me, it's not important that you gain revenge or retribution," the psychologist says. "It's important to me that you take ownership again of your body and your mind. You are asserting your right to control with your actions. Now I need you to make that assertion permanent; though perhaps healthier."

Abril nods her head, looks away and puffs out several breaths. Tears begin streaming down along her nose, mingling beneath her nostrils with running mucus. The psychologist grabs a tissue and hands it to Abril.

"So what do you want me to do?" Abril asks.

"I want you to decide what Abril wants and then take the steps to make it happen," she responds, "whatever that is."

"I wanted to be a nun and they stole that from me," Abril contends.

"Do you want to be a nun now?"

"I can't. I mean, my chastity has been stolen from me. I'm not even a good person anymore," Abril says. "Look what I put this man through. Jesus didn't tell us to seek revenge on our enemies. He told us to turn the other cheek. I couldn't turn the other cheek. I failed my Lord's test for me."

"I don't see that you failed at all," the psychologist says. "I mean, I'm not a religious person, but I don't see how what you did disqualifies you from returning to the convent and becoming a nun if that's what you want to do."

"You don't understand," Abril says, the corners of her lips turned down, chin quivering as she speaks.

"But you have a good heart. You didn't hurt the innocent. You just wanted someone to atone for the sins created at your expense. That's just human," the psychologist says.

"But I did hurt the innocent, can't you see? I mean, I tortured him. I mean, like, you know, shredded him," Abril states.

"Yet, he recovered and even he has forgiven you, so much so that he desires you. Do you believe that God has plans and that God works in mysterious ways?" the psychologist asks, clearly stepping outside her comfort zone and glad she isn't doing government psychology work where every session is taped and computer-analyzed to determine the risk to society imposed by the patient. Discussions of the role of God in state-paid therapy sessions are strictly prohibited as part of the government's insistence on maintaining separation of church and state.

"I do."

"Then, perhaps God sent you to test this man. Perhaps God sent you to help him understand that he needs to atone for sins he allowed, even if they weren't his own," the psychologist suggests.

Abril stares out the window again, interlocking her hands and praying for help. The psychologist sits silently, recognizing that the questions she has asked may not be easy to answer now, even for Abril, after the pain she has endured.

"Abril, you're a remarkable person who has so much to give this world," the psychologist asserts as she stands up and starts inching toward the door, connecting to the enclosed pathway over to the main home. "And just as importantly, I'm sure the world has something to give back to you. I don't know what it is yet, but I am sure you have moments ahead of you in this life that you don't want to miss. You need to decide what path you want to follow and you will find them."

35 Encapsulation

The University of Chicago's Barack Obama Hall, named after the first President with recent lineage tracing through his father to Africa, was thoroughly modernized years earlier with a death benefit from a man who amassed great wealth through his political connections over decades. His investment firm expanded through a complicated series of financial transactions involving energy, water and currency swaps and derivatives, often aided by a deep understanding of White House policy initiatives. The investment firm's owner gleaned his insights through constant attendance at political fundraisers. Often, he spurred the government moves he needed through well-placed suggestions to mid-level aides he knew would be eager to please him because of his well-known penchant for discussing staff quality with the President and cabinet officials.

The financier was much more clever than most who abused the political system to enhance their personal wealth prior to adoption of the Political Freedom Amendment to the Constitution. Once forced to play on an even-playing field, unaided by tips and comments that might not technically have been considered insider trading under the law, his returns dropped to just below average—still extraordinary wealth increases given his starting point, but nowhere near the out-sized gains he had secured when political accommodation aided his investment strategy.

To his credit, the financier hadn't directly asked for everything he wanted. Instead, he built a reputation with each politician he aimed to influence as someone who shared great insights and rarely asked for anything. Mid-level staffers, though, were terrified by his influence and bent over backwards to accomplish anything he suggested. In an era when his contribution bundling abilities could swing an election, the wrong action could cost an aspiring staffer his or her future.

The ability to use government to game the system created enormous wealth for so many, something this particular donor had little use for after his death other than to secure his legacy and the legacies of those he believed worthy of support.

Professor Stark's office is nicely situated inside Barack Obama Hall, one floor below the top. Many of his colleagues took Stark's agreement to not be on the top floor as deference to his more senior colleagues. Everyone knew he had the political sway inside the university to have whatever office he wanted. For Professor Stark, though, his decision to request an office below the top floor was borne from paranoia. He didn't want anyone trying to attack him to be able to enter through a simple cut and lift of the roof above him. His personally designed office comes equipped with an automated safe room; one that allows him to survive unharmed for days if he or the building comes under attack.

During the national campaign to pass the Political Freedom Amendment, an effort championed by Professor Stark, he had been mugged four times in four different cities. Police in all four cities, including Washington, D.C., concluded that he was just the unlucky victim of coincidental beatings. Professor Stark always believed the attacks had been warnings from someone with substantial political influence to back off from pushing the constitutional amendment. He couldn't determine who had been behind the attacks: political parties, labor unions, corporate executives, trial lawyers or any of the other dozens of interest groups who liked a system they could manipulate to suit their own purposes. All had reason to want him to fail. Because opposition to real reform was broad-based and crossed political circles, even the private detectives Professor Stark hired weren't able to narrow down connections between the muggings to limit the pool of potential instigators.

During the course of the Political Freedom campaign, the muggings energized Professor Stark and provided impetus to his cause. He wasn't alone in believing that entrenched political forces wanted him to go away. Backing down was never a consideration as a reaction to the threats. After the thirty-ninth state ratified the constitutional amendment, though, Professor Stark increasingly hid from public life.

His paranoia about safety complicated any efforts at real relationships. Never a ladies' man before the Political Freedom Amendment battle, he'd become too engrossed in winning the campaign to have anything other than a series of casual encounters with rabid fans early in that fight. After the third mugging, his fear convinced him that women he was dating were set-ups, sent to build a relationship in order to provide information on his location to whomever it was that wanted him dead or deterred.

Professor Stark had wanted to settle down when his campaign reform ideas gripped national attention. Instead, he focused on securing passage and implementation of his ideas, knowing that without reform the United States was headed on a path to ruin.

In the intervening decade, Professor Stark had only had a handful of short-term relationships before he met Jill. His efforts at attracting her attention had been stilted and awkward at times, with Professor Stark struggling to trust that someone as striking and intelligent as the independent Congresswoman from Indiana could be truly interested in him. Fortunately, she also had been wary of new suitors, learning the hard way that bagging a congresswoman was a badge of honor to some in the relationship-driven political world. She also knew about Professor Stark's backstory, having been scheduled to interview him with instructions from Republican News Network executives to shred his integrity during an interview canceled on the day of his fourth mugging. Her honesty in sharing that this had been her assignment helped build bonds of trust between the pair.

Still, for every bit of confidence he exhibited in his professional life, it took time to build that same confidence level in his relationship with Jill.

Just as Jill and Professor Stark were taking the next step in their relationship, agreeing to travel on alternating weekends to be with each other, the Center for Atrocity presented Professor Stark with another professional and moral opportunity he wasn't sure he could pass up.

Inside his Obama Hall office, he contemplates the added workload the center requires and wonders whether he simply can't effectively manage the center and his relationship.

Opening his device, he contacts Jill.

"Hey cuddles," she responds when clicking to open the visual chat, a nickname she gave him after several nights of wondering whether he ever intended to take their physical relationship to another level. As offended as he is by the nickname, he knows it's a sign of endearment, so no longer objects.

"Hi sweetie. Uhm," he begins.

"I hate when you start sentences with uhm," she replies. "It's never good news."

"You know this Center for Atrocity Studies. I put a project plan together to figure out what it will take to get this up and running on time to meet donor commitments. I can't do this with anything less than one hundred hours a week of work for the next several months," Professor Stark states.

"So, what does that mean for us?" Jill asks.

"I don't know. I want to stick to our plan, more than you possibly could know, but I don't know how to get this done without being fully entrenched in it," he continues before being interrupted by Jill.

"Paul, Paul, relax. Let's think this through. Is there anything in the donor agreement that says you can't hire staff?

"Well, I don't think so," he replies.

Jill closes out several of the documents she had been reading to concentrate on her discussion with Paul. "So one hundred hours a week of your time. Make it ten of your time and hire two or three capable staff to do the implementing. You do the thinking, with their help, then they execute," she suggests.

Professor Stark looks up at the monitors in his sub-basement bedroom. "Yeah, I guess I'm not used to the idea of managing people."

"Neither was I, but you'll figure it out," Jill argues. "Any thoughts of who you might hire?"

"Actually, two of my brightest graduate students are still undecided on their next role."

"You might want to think about a third person, someone with strong project management experience," Jill adds. "I would recommend you think about adding a woman to the team, particularly someone from overseas."

"You'd be okay with that."

"Yes, Casanova," Jill replies, unable to control laughter as she does. "I don't mind you working with women. I didn't suggest she has to be a bombshell."

Professor Stark stares at the screen for several seconds before saying anything else: "Then I guess we can still stick to our alternating weekend plans."

"I certainly hope so," Jill replies. "I'm not getting any younger, and neither are you."

Even as he settles out his administrative staffing needs, Professor Stark is certain that the first Atrocity Center trial has to be a high-profile figure with an extensive track record of violence against civilians. General Timur fits this profile perfectly, having drawn public condemnation of his suspected involvement in Armenia and various other atrocities. Perhaps as important, remonstrations against Timur have rarely been accompanied by hard, publicly available evidence.

Announcement of the Center's trial of Timur attracts exactly the type of media attention Professor Stark hoped it would receive. Dozens of scholars, criminal investigators, lawyers and espionage experts offer to support the trial at reduced-level wages in order to ensure they are selected. For these experts, involvement in such a high-profile case will pay off in future business.

As jury selection begins, more than two million online applications are received for the one thousand spots on the jury. Jurors earn three quarters of the median daily wage in each juror's home nation thanks to the large grants that fund the Atrocity Center.

A sorting and sifting program conducts detailed analysis of all of the applicants, pulling data from One World, other social media applications and even from crawlers developed and inserted into the Center's jury selection system by Ramon's team. The crawlers inject into national, provincial and local law enforcement systems around the world, searching for incriminatory data on potential jurors, particularly data that links them to the accused.

Once the project team narrows the list to one thousand jurors from a wide assortment of backgrounds, nationalities and religions, Professor Stark launches the trial's evidence-gathering phase. Technology that Professor Stark needs to run the Center often shows up unannounced with capabilities he hadn't always anticipated but is so far finding useful. Often, an untraceable suggestion or two is buried inside of these deliveries.

The stated objective of the Center's Morality Project, as an anonymous note suggested the trials be called, is to establish an international norm for morality and behavior. Professor Stark's hope is this norm will be identified and encouraged by increasing pressure on those operating at society's perimeter through international trials.

As the physical systems for the trials are developed, installed and distributed, investigators and lawyers studying General Timur gather evidence shared instantaneously with both prosecution and defense lawyers. Electronic evidence often shows up unrequested and with no clear point of origin, particularly evidence that likely originated with national intelligence and law enforcements agencies around the world. Unbeknownst to Professor Stark, Ramon's team is skilled at breaking highly encrypted firewalls and forwarding this data.

By the time the trial opens, the volume of evidence gathered overwhelms both teams until software to automate and categorize evidence shows up from nowhere for the legal teams to use. As he starts the trial of General Timur, Professor Stark's nerves finally begin to fray. In only a few months, he has taken an endeavor outside his expertise from concept to launch.

"What are we forgetting?" he asks his new project manager just ahead of the live launch.

"Nothing—and everything," she replies. "I think we're ready, but I'm certain we aren't, if that makes any sense."

From a studio built inside Obama Hall, he calls for the live feed of the trial to be turned on.

"Ladies and gentlemen of the world, welcome to a grand experiment. Together we will explore judgment of individuals in society whose evil knows no bounds, focusing time and attention on assessing whether those absent accountability are operating outside of human decency," Professor Stark begins. "Our objective here is simple: to identify those operating unimpeded by conscience and system of law. Once suspects are selected, we will conduct a trial of each person's behavior using every shred of available evidence so that the public may judge and hold these individuals accountable. We will act as judge and jury, but we will and we must leave punishment to society. We will act swiftly, yes, but remain cognizant that we must be accurate in our assessments or risk damaging the lives of innocents. So with that, the Morality Project opens."

Trial cameras turn to the prosecutor, a woman whose sweet, grandmotherly appearance belies her keen intellect and tenacious pursuit of justice.

She says nothing for several minutes, instead showing a cascade of photographs and short video clips of General Timur and his various alleged victims, sometimes with the general smiling next to many of those he had crucified, beheaded, mutilated and otherwise slaughtered. The last photograph is a satellite shot of Yerevan. The camera zooms in from the aerial view to show a group of victims lying scattered around a city street in what appears to have once been a street market. It pulls back to aerial view, down to the bones of what appear the meager remnants of children's bodies in a schoolyard. Back to aerial view, then down again to show a series of buildings against which a photograph of General Timur walking the week prior to the Yerevan blast is displayed, captured from images posted on One World, all taken by those likely unaware of his identification.

"During the course of this trial, we will prove that General Timur is personally responsible for a series of actions outside the norms of human morality with deadly consequences. General Timur personally ordered the massacre of more than one thousand Iranian democracy protestors during a peaceful Azadi Square demonstration," the prosecutor begins. During her remarks, the prosecutor displays sworn statements from several former members of the Revolutionary Guard, followed by both satellite- and land-based video of the Azadi Square massacre. Photos of the massacred dead rest on screen for several seconds. Professor Stark, serving as judge for the initial trial, can see immediately from the electrode response units worn by each juror that the photos, including those of more than a dozen beheaded demonstration leaders, are capturing juror attention.

"When this massacre incited the Iranian democracy movement and turned more than half of the nation's military leaders against the Ayatollah, then the Supreme Leader of Iran, General Timur responded by kidnapping dozens of wives and children of his former military comrades, crucifying them and displaying their crucified bodies on the roads into Tehran," the prosecutor continues, displaying photos, videos and sworn statements that Timur was personally responsible for the orders.

"When it became clear that a new secular government would replace the Islamist theocracy in Iran, General Timur disappeared, taking with him all the material he needed to produce nuclear weapons. We will show that two of the nuclear bombs placed inside United States borders last year—those in Los Angeles and Dallas, Texas—certainly originated with materials supplied by General Timur to the Castillo cartel's Protection Corps militia wing. Several members of General Timur's team have escaped and will testify at this trial that he intended to use his destruction of the 'Great Satan,' his endearing term for the United States, as his rallying cry to retake control of Iran under his leadership," the prosecutor continues, pausing regularly to be sure the visuals that accompany her words sink deeply into the memories of jurors.

"When the United States captured and neutralized these bombs prior to explosion, General Timur became anxious to identify another rallying point for radical Islamists to return him to power in Iran. We will show substantial evidence that General Timur ordered and personally planned the nuclear explosion in Yerevan, including surveillance video that shows Timur walking the very streets and buildings where the explosion originated."

Professor Stark checks the system and finds that 994 of the jurors are engaged and paying attention to the prosecutor's presentation. The system administrator sends an alert to the six who are not paying attention to their screen letting them know they will need to replay and pay attention to the opening statements in order to be paid and to be able to vote.

The defense attorney for General Timur, an internationally known and respected lawyer with substantial experience in front of the international criminal courts, makes his opening statements next.

"This entire process, I am sure you all must know, is a farce," the defense attorney bellows while staring straight into a camera trained on him. "We have a case in which circumstantial evidence is presented against a man who served his nation with dignity, honor and dedication for decades, only to now have his name smeared by an un-Godly alliance of Iranian secularists, American interventionists and global alarmists hell bent on preventing General Timur from returning to Iran with the popular support of the people of that nation.

"Most importantly, General Timur would almost certainly refuse to acknowledge the legitimacy of this organization, a self-serving university project funded by an anonymous group of donors we believe to be associated with this unholy alliance and Israel for the purposes of discrediting General Timur before his return. He will not participate himself and I have not been able to meet with General Timur to prepare an adequate defense, making this trial an abomination to the concept of justice."

At this point, Professor Stark, serving as judge, interjects: "We realize that this organization does not have the full legal authority of any national or international court. Our objective here is to identify the truth and start the path toward justice for those accused of conducting heinous crimes without any national or international organization having the ability or will to hold them accountable. This court will hear the evidence and render a verdict, but punishment is not our mission. Educating the international public is our goal, which is why these proceedings are being simulcast in nearly one hundred languages."

Inside the Detroit Salt Mine, Ramon's team is on full alert. More than a dozen national governments are trying to halt Timur trial feeds inside their borders. New Rite had developed technology allowing its signals to be disseminated from cable, satellite and deep underground locations throughout the world without interruption. Governments sometimes identified some of the New Rite broadcast locations, but JT and his team had always ensured New Rite could operate around any government control efforts, secretly using government communication networks as backup for standard distribution channels. He remained confident they would never suspect their own resources were facilitating the transmissions. Ramon and his team added to New Rite's capability, ensuring that Internet accessibility to the trials can't be government controlled without a complete shutdown of all broadcast communications capabilities, including those of each country's national defense systems. As long as each government's national defense communication systems remain in use, the Morality Project remains viewable inside national borders.

The Morality Project's administrative manager alerts Professor Stark to the system attacks. He decides to use these repressive government attacks to attract attention to The Morality Project. It works. Global media coverage of the government shutdown efforts attracts international media coverage, with most national media outlets outside of these countries cutting in to the trial broadcast as they show viewers what some governments are trying to shut down. Within an hour of the system shutdown efforts, viewership of the Morality Project trial increases one hundred fold.

Ally Steele and her New Rite special operations team depart for Almaty, in Russia's Kazakh province, flying north over Alaska, down through Siberia and landing along a small flat patch on a mountain ridge south of the city. New Rite's intelligence team, aided by information passed to them from the CIA, believes that General Timur is holed up in a cave just inside the Kyrgyzstan border. After landing, New Rite's mountain combat specialists begin a tedious ten-mile hike to the cave opening.

Two miles from the opening, the white-clad team is rappelling down a snow-capped cliff face when the first bullets hit nearby.

"Under attack," the team leader calls back to Ally. "Shots fired."

Ally immediately turns on the APB reactor and whirls overhead blades to pull up off the mountain before converting to jet mode. Less than two minutes later she comes to a halt above her New Rite team.

"Identify," Ally calls out. The four New Rite special forces members trigger their identification signals. Ally arms automated weapons that detect movement along nearby mountain ridges from individuals not identified as part of the New Rite team. Missile-launched rifles fire shots hitting targets as far as five miles from the APB, all without triggering any substantial noise in the area. Ally hovers above the mountain ridge waiting for signs of any further human motion. Thirty minutes later, she signals "all clear."

"Thank you. Moving on," the team leader calls back to Ally.

"Call me if you need me," Ally replies before returning to her safe landing spot to await an extraction call.

Another three days pass with Ally not hearing anything more from the team. One hour after their deadline to return, she risks communicating again, sending out a "call-in" signal.

"Thirty minutes out," the team leader responds. "Package delivered."

"Ready to go when you are," Ally replies. "Can't wait to see if he uses it."

Following the 2040 Harvard Square massacre, Congress and the President established new safety procedures across every education level. Within days of the deadly backpack bombings—originally blamed on radical Islamic terrorists but now tied directly to the Castillo cartel—Congress began debating every safety protection they could conceive.

After extensive debate on gun and explosives bans and control schemes, Congress settled on changes aimed at stopping violent intruders regardless of weapon. The new law requires installation of in-school movement tracking systems triggered by facial recognition scans. These systems are then linked to an extensive federal threat assessment database that uses mental health records, explosive device material purchases, criminal history, recent online statements and several other characteristics to identify high-risk individuals.

The scanning devices are tied into local law enforcement systems (university police in the case of Obama Hall) and send immediate alerts to law enforcement whenever someone recognized as high risk enters a building. Since the June 30 compliance deadline, local law enforcement agencies have struggled to respond appropriately to each notification. Criminal history data linked to the systems varies widely in quality by municipality and state sharing the data. In some cases, including within Chicago, no effort yet has been made to distinguish between violent and non-violent criminal convictions. In other jurisdictions, arrest is deemed enough to warrant inclusion in the database. Protocols to remove individuals once charges are dismissed or they are found not guilty have yet to be established. Countless other data quality errors permeate the system, leaving local police under such constant state of alert that they often can't respond to each risk alert call.

When incidents occur though, facial recognition systems make it easier to track down a killer's location and lock down an attacker through closing automated security doors. Beyond entryway scanners, most schools have set up scanning locations throughout their buildings, enabling faster response to specific locations should an incident occur and a perpetrator escape to move around the building. Some schools supplement local law enforcement with specially trained on-campus protection dogs that regularly wander the school, literally sniffing for trouble from outsiders and between students. The university hasn't yet made this move.

At each building entrance, scanners link to metal detectors and other visual scanners that ascertain whether an individual is carrying weapon-sized or shaped objects. The invention of Lifelinks has dramatically shrunk the amount of materials students haul between classes. Other than Lifelinks, food, art supplies, music instruments and sports equipment are typically the only objects needed for the standard school day. At the university level, hand-carried beverages and snacks are the only distraction the scanners typically must consider.

In order to secure quick passage of the facial recognition bill and to minimize risk that the legislation would be found unconstitutional as interfering with the separation of church and state, congressional leaders agreed to an accommodation with Muslim leaders. Muslim clerics feared that facial recognition systems would force Muslim women to unveil their faces against what some Muslims believe to be a requirement of Sharia Law. That accommodation provides Muslim students with the ability to have their identity certified by eye scanners inserted at each building. Once scanned on entry into a building, Muslim women who choose to wear full head coverings attach a computer-generated sticker to their garment that is read along with an assessment of the garment by other scanners throughout the building.

A Muslim woman entering Obama Hall either forgot to conduct the eye scan or isn't aware of the relatively new requirement for academic institutions. Within seconds of her entry into the building, university police are notified that an unidentified intruder has entered the building.

That alert is forwarded to the nearest officer, who walks toward the building to intercept what is likely the same forgetful student he has tracked down three times in the past two weeks and escort her back to the eye scanner. Before he arrives, the cloaked intruder ascends to Professor Stark's floor, triggering a special alert in Stark's office.

"Hold on Jill, there's someone unscanned on my floor," he says, looking up to security screens across from his desk. Seeing someone walking quickly toward his office in a burqa with full head covering and no sticker, Professor Stark triggers his security system, which immediately closes off his doors and windows with bulletproof material.

"Stop and raise your hands or I'll have to shoot," the responding officer yells at the intruder as the officer exits the stairwell just behind her. "You know the drill."

"Don't shoot or you'll set off bomb," the attacker yells back in an exchange Professor Stark hears through his monitoring system. This is not the forgetful student the officer expected. Professor Stark worries that an explosive device hidden by the burqa might be powerful enough to damage his office security. He goes to a corner hidden by the windows, pulls the wall panel aside and steps onto a small metal platform, releasing himself down several stories, where he opens an obscured panel to a sub-basement escape tunnel.

Back on Stark's floor, the unidentified attacker yells back at the officer.

"Must deliver package to Professor Stark direct. It is by General Timur," yells out a clearly masculine voice from behind his niqāb.

"Perhaps Professor Stark doesn't want your package. There are easier ways to get it to him," the officer yells back, his weapon still trained on the intruder while he alerts police headquarters to immediately evacuate Obama Hall with threat of a bomb.

The intruder's view of the officer is obscured by students rushing out of their classrooms and racing for stairwells, having been alerted electronically by university police to a bomb threat. Several departing students spot the burqa and the officer with drawn weapon as they exit and knock fellow students out of the way to escape the area. The intruder stands still, arms raised, until the hallways are cleared.

Minutes later, two others join the on-scene officer.

"I have video from General Timur. Must give to professor for trial," the man tells the assembled police.

"By now, we're sure Professor Stark is gone, so if you give it to us, we'll be sure to give it to Professor Stark," the officer tries to assure him.

"Can't. If I can't give to Professor, I must blow up. Someone else finds him with copy. He is inside here," the man says, slowly removing his head covering and pointing to Stark's office. "Tell him to come out. I know he is here. He inside."

Contacting his commander, the first officer to respond relays the situation to get instructions.

"Professor Stark is not in the building," the officer is told. "I've been told by our commander that Professor Stark is not here," the officer relays to the bomber.

"I don't believe you. I need to give this to him. If he not here, come arrest me and I will blow us up. Kill me and bomb explode," he threatens.

"I don't like either option," the office replies. "What other options do you have for us?"

"Bring Professor Stark here. Let me hand video. Then I disarm. You arrest me," the man says. "And my family live."

"We can't let Professor Stark put himself in danger like that. We can't allow people who want to hurt him to succeed. You have to realize how stupid we would look," the officer says.

"Stupid? Stupid is nuclear bomb explodes?" the intruder bellows.

"Nuclear?"

"Nuclear. Yes, nuclear. I take burqa off."

"Slowly," the first officer demands loudly, hiding himself behind a door jam.

"Commander," the officer says loudly enough that the terrorist hears him. "The man here says he's wearing a nuclear weapon. Looks like triggers tied to his chest and his hands."

"Can you shoot his hands off cleanly and stop the bleeding before his heart rate lowers?" the commander says back into the officer's earpiece.

One of the other officers nods his assent. The first officer ignores him: "We need a non-explosive option. Can you contact Professor Stark and see if he'll meet with this man?"

Several minutes later, the commander calls back.

"Professor Stark will meet with the man. If it goes bad, you need to execute the arm shots and disarm," the commanding officer directs from the comfort of his office.

What seems to be hours later, Professor Stark arrives up the stairs behind a federal tactical team, with several other officers in tow and a rounded clear plastic shield in front of him. Only the very bottoms of Professor Stark's feet are exposed. The shield requires a stability roller package to be moved at even modest pace by all but the strongest responders.

The sweat-coated intruder looks at Professor Stark. He yells out that he must compare him to the pictures given by General Timur. Finally convinced it is Professor Stark, he invites Professor Stark to come forward. Professor Stark does, slowly, methodically, watching for any evidence that the man will trigger the bomb strapped around his body.

With everyone staring at each other, even the sound of sweat dripping off Professor Stark's face and falling on the marble floor tiles in this hallway serves as distraction.

Finally, the terrorist takes the small object in his hands, places it on the floor and slides it in the direction of Professor Stark.

Stark stares at him, waiting for either a sign to pick the object up or an indication that he can safely step around the shield to retrieve it. Of course, a nuclear blast would destroy them all. The threat of such a blast was one of few reasons Professor Stark would have returned to the building.

Professor Stark stares into the terrorist's eyes.

"Okay?" he asks, pointing toward the object.

"Okay," the terrorist replies, motioning toward where a pocket would typically hold a Lifelink. "Play it on your device."

Professor Stark types in his code on the inner pocket of his shirt to unseal his Lifelink. He unfolds it to paper-sheet sized screen, taps the object from the terrorist against it and sees a video begin to display. The video is from General Timur.

"If you are seeing this, Professor Stark, I trust that you will have the integrity to play my full defense at this trial you are conducting. I don't know how your people found me to inform me of the trial but, since you did, I want to be sure the world knows who you are dealing with before you try to find me again," General Timur states on the video. Professor Stark tells the system to stop play and returns his eyes to the terrorist.

"You work for General Timur?" Professor Stark asks the man.

"I have been instructed by his people."

"What's your name?"

"Pablo, sir," the terrorist responds. "Pablo Crucero."

"Pablo?" Professor Stark adds, waving his hands to the police to hold back. "Where are you from, Pablo?"

"From Mexico."

"How does a Mexican get tied up with a man like General Timur?" Professor Stark asks, before making the connection himself. "Castillo cartel, right?"

"I was. I guess I still am," Pablo replies. "Do you mind if I unhook my vest before it explodes?"

Pablo unhooks the link he has been told will disarm the nuclear detonator. The police begin walking toward him, when a light begins to glow on the vest.

Seeing the light, Professor Stark grabs his shield and runs away, pulling the shield behind him.

"Run," Pablo yells out. "He doesn't want me alive."

"Who?" Professor Stark yells back, slowing only slightly to listen for the answer.

"I don't know," Pablo replies, dropping to his knees. "Ten piedad de mí, oh Dios, conforme a tu misericordia."

Professor Stark continues to run backward, pulling the safety shield with him. Pablo begins the sign of the cross. Before he acknowledges the Holy Ghost, the bomb explodes, sending parts of Pablo splattering against the walls. Professor Stark ducks and covers his head as he sees the explosion. His shield absorbs some of the impact of Pablo before lifting up and knocking him to the ground. Police, several of whom had a head start on Professor Stark, absorb some shattered glass from the windows in the stairwell doors.

Professor Stark checks to make sure the video of General Timur and his device have survived the explosion. Picking himself up, he begins walking down the steps, aided by an officer. A few flights later, he sits on the stairs, opening his Lifelink to call Jill.

"Oh . . . thank God . . . Paul," she says when she first hears his voice. "We saw the explosion. I thought. I thought. Oh God."

"I'm okay, I guess, but I need to talk to the President. The war might not be over," Professor Stark says, brushing something off his clothes. Realizing that the chunk he just brushed off was likely part of Pablo that had bounced down from the ceiling, he turns from his device just in time to vomit against the stairwell wall.

"You sure you're okay?" Jill asks.

"No, I'm definitely not okay. Far from okay," he says, oscillating between anger and sadness. "Why am I doing this again?"

"Doing what?"

Professor Stark doesn't respond to Jill's question, putting his head into his hands.

"Doing what, Paul?" she asks again, this time much more clearly demanding an answer.

"Getting caught in the middle," he finally replies after taking several seconds to regain his composure. "Getting hurt in the middle."

36 FIXATION

Top national security officials invite Professor Stark to Washington, D.C. to discuss his hallway encounter. Looking for an excuse to avoid traveling alone, he convinces the Administration to allow Juan Gonzalez to travel with him, knowing that Juan needs time with Rachel. Juan hasn't yet been forgiven for neglecting to mention his redhead bikini encounter and eagerly agrees to the travel.

While Professor Stark is involved in what turns into an interrogation aimed at identifying why General Timur would believe that Professor Stark tracked him down, Juan joins Rachel and Tamika for lunch. Discussions of the Obama Hall incident dominate the first thirty minutes of lunch, before Rachel and Tamika veer off into discussion of the work consuming their nearly every waking hour—passage of God's Law. Juan is also interested in how the Golden Rule would work in government and happily joins in.

"I understand the point of the constitutional amendment," Juan remarks. "There's a lot to be said about ensuring that our laws don't create separate societies for the ruling class and the peons to be governed. But as I'm thinking, it might not be enough to simply prevent Congress from imposing laws from which it exempts itself."

"It's certainly not enough," Tamika responds after looking up from clicking her part of the order into the ordering system built into the table. "But I'm wondering how broadly the courts could interpret the concept of not doing to others what one would not want to have done to itself. Could the courts interpret this inter-generationally?"

"What do you mean?" Rachel asks, having not really listened as she was scrolling through the menu to decide what to order.

"I mean, could the courts effectively decide that Congress and the Administration no longer have the right to impose laws where the benefits are gained today and the costs are borne by future generations?" Tamika questions.

"Without giving it a lot of deep thought, that seems to be a reasonable interpretation, at first blush," Rachel replies.

"If the courts interpret it from an inter-generational perspective, this could have the effect of constitutionally requiring balanced federal budgets. Right?" Tamika questions.

Rachel purses her lips, nodding slightly as she responds: "You know, you might be right."

"But, if that's true, won't that just bolster opposition to the whole concept," Juan interjects. "I mean most Democrats and way too many Republicans historically have liked being able to spend money we don't have today to build up their political support and pass costs on to people who aren't voting yet."

Tamika interrupts: "Or maybe are voting, but don't think or don't care beyond what happens to them."

"Well, that could be the case," Juan admits. "But if you've figured out that the concept could be interpreted to require a balanced budget, don't you think federal employee unions, defense contractors and everyone else who requires excessive federal spending to meet their annual goals will get up in arms and fight against this like their livelihood depends on it?"

"It's certainly a reasonable concern," Tamika acknowledges, "and one we'll have to think through. On the other hand, it could help mobilize supporters, the American people, and the states. After all, forty states already live with real balanced budget requirements, and almost all the rest at least pretend to want balanced budgets."

"I'd be worried about what this is going to do to government support for social programs," Juan remarks. "I mean, look how many people depend on government programs for their very existence."

"I'd have that same concern," Tamika acknowledges, "if Jill and I weren't already working on a way to dramatically reduce the cost of social programs and improve the outcomes for the currently impoverished."

"You have my interest," Juan says, nodding his head and pressing his lips tightly together as he smiles. Rachel can't help but stare at Juan when he smiles. He's so damn cute it makes her smile.

"Mine too," Rachel adds after refocusing on the discussion, still not entirely sure what Tamika is talking about.

"You know how we've talked about how bureaucratic government programs are today and how many different programs my mom had to work with just to help us get by as she was getting started in her career?" Tamika says.

Rachel and Juan both nod their heads.

"Well, we've figured out that state and federal spending on antipoverty programs adds up to three to four times the poverty level for a typical family of three or four," Tamika says.

"That's ridiculous. That can't possibly be true," Juan replies.

"Oh, it's true, but the people who need help don't see enough of this money. It gets eaten up by government bureaucracies, in wasteful distribution to people not in poverty, and in running programs that really don't help."

"No doubt that's true," Juan agrees, having spent long days waiting with his mother at agency offices throughout southern Arizona.

"Look at it, there are more than one hundred different programs that a welfare family needs to work through, apply for, certify incomes, get audited. The bureaucracy is mind numbing. So Jill and I are working on a program that aligns all of this spending and all of these programs through a single focal point group that gets resources to families and individuals and helps them get on the path to success," Tamika says.

"Congress will never buy it," Rachel says. "Isn't the reason we have so much program complexity that every committee in Congress wants to control its own piece of the pie? They guard spending turf like it's their own money from what I've seen so far."

"I know," Tamika replies. "That's what Jill is most worried about. That's why it will require presidential leadership to get this done."

"I don't even know if it's possible, but when you and Jill are ready, let me know and I'll help set up the meeting with the President and his staff," Rachel offers as the food they've ordered arrive at the table.

"Great," Tamika responds.

"Can we get back to the budget limit issue?" Juan asks as he picks up several fingers full of heavily seasoned curly fries. "If this is going to work like a constitutional amendment to balance the budget, then there are a lot of groups—not just the poor—who are going to take issue with this."

"You're obviously right, Juan, but what I'm thinking is that this concept might actually offer a bit more flexibility than a straight balanced budget amendment," Rachel notes.

"How so?" he asks with too many fries still stuffed in his mouth.

"Well, it lets the courts determine if any deficit spending has benefits for future generations that the future generation could find reasonable and willing to support. It might not prevent deficit spending, but it would give the courts broad power in a deficit spending environment to require Congress to eliminate deficit spending that is done without a clear investment case."

"Doesn't that just give the courts a substantially more prominent role in budgetary decisions?" Juan asks. "That's a huge shift from the Constitution. Spending bills must start in the House."

"Maybe," Tamika replies, slowing only enough to take a sip of water, "but the courts would only have power to demand that spending be cut if the budget is in deficit. This gives Congress an incentive to pass balanced budgets so the courts can't cut out their pork."

"And," Rachel adds, "it would mean that deficit spending for wars and other items that could be deemed as having next-generation benefits would still pass muster. We could argue that it's not as strict of a test as a constitutional balanced budget amendment, but it's sure an improvement over the repeated spending failures that sent us into the Second Great Depression."

37 CONDEMNATION

Days later and back in Chicago, Professor Stark reconvenes the Morality Project trial of General Timur. As he does, the lead defense counsel and the lead prosecutor are the only persons not startled by Professor Stark's news. The night before, he brought them to his office to watch the video in its entirety.

After playing the first few sentences, Professor Stark stops the tape of General Timur and tells the jury and everyone else watching the trial that he does not know what General Timur is saying about Professor Stark having found him.

"I want to be clear and transparent that I do not know who found General Timur, but as you listen to the remainder of the tape it will be apparent that he truly was found," Professor Stark states. "With that being said, I would ask that all jurists listen to the remainder of this video which I will play uninterrupted. After conclusion of the video, I'll stop the trial briefly for consultation with counsel but would ask your indulgence to remain available in short order during that consultation."

Having been alerted to the statement from General Timur, much of the world's news media networks tap into a feed from the trial and play it live, with translators doing their best to fix the English subtitles or translate Persian into each juror's native tongue.

The corrected English translation of General Timur's statement follows:

"I would like to commend you, Professor Stark, for having found me in the middle of nowhere, a place where no government has ever been able to track me down and where I expected to remain. I want to thank you for making it clear to me that I am no longer safe here. By the time you receive this confession, I will have disappeared to a location even more difficult for you to reach. I can assure you that by the time you have finished listening to this, it will become clear that no one will ever want to find me again without a direct invitation.

"I am General Timur, descendant of both the great Tamerlane and the Prophet Muhammad, and honored servant of Allah in imposing his will on earth. You, Professor Stark, and everyone else serving as lawyers or jurors, are conducting a trial with the intent of judging me. I will be clear. You do not judge me. Allah judges me. Allah also judges you and instructs me."

It's clear to everyone watching that General Timur has either constructed an elaborate set that appears to be a cave or is speaking from inside an actual cave. As soon as the tape begins playing, national intelligence agents from more than a dozen nations begin assessing the background, trying to ascertain General Timur's location at the time of the taping by attempting to determine the cave's rock type and structure.

"I want to spare you the effort of reaching conclusions on facts I already know and spare myself the indignity of hearing about your babbling judicial decrees reached in ignorance or condescension of Sharia Law. You are to me as worthy as the traitorous Jews at Medina were to the Great Prophet. The simple act of believing you are worthy of conducting a trial of me puts you in the same company as the Meccan rulers who thought they had the right to pursue the Prophet Muhammad before he subdued and converted or killed them. You, Professor Stark and everyone associated with this trial, are my enemy now. At a time Allah chooses, you will be punished for your insolence. Fortunately for you, it appears that time is not quite here."

The starkness of the background behind General Timur provides little distraction for the jurors, perhaps a benefit to ensuring they focus on what he says. Several, however, are distracted as the general frequently swats his hands at what appear to be mosquitoes.

"Why did I not kill you, Professor Stark, when I had the chance? This is a very important question. I do not want you to see your continued survival as either luck or mercy. Your survival is part of Allah's plan. You will continue to survive as long as you, your jury and the rest of the United States execute the plan as Allah instructs through me."

At this point, General Timur stands up and moves toward the camera, which zooms out as he moves forward. It appears that one other person is inside the cave operating the camera, though some cameras have automated settings to ensure a subject's frame-fill percentage remains constant even as the subject moves, an innovation originally developed for sports broadcasting.

"Allah has told me that America is attempting to build morality back into its government policies through passage of something you call God's Law. If it is truly to be God's Law, it must originate from the word of Allah, words that are contained in the Quran, and that form the foundation of Sharia Law. If the United States adopts Sharia Law in the next six months, Allah will spare all of you the horrific tragedy that awaits you for centuries of service to the false gods and to the immoral will of men and women acting in contradiction of Allah's will."

Professor Stark stops the tape briefly, breaking a demand to play Timur's remarks without interruption. "Before I continue with General Timur's comments," he states, "I want to let those of you unfamiliar with the God's Law concept the General is referencing know that this is really the proposed embodiment of the Golden Rule into U.S. federal law through a constitutional amendment. The Golden Rule, as you may know, is a foundational concept in nearly every major religion. The Islamic Hadith quotes Prophet Muhammad as expressing the Golden Rule to a Bedouin. Numerous passages in the Quran advocate Golden Rule behavior. Many question, though, whether the Golden Rule fits with Sharia Law as it exists today. Some in the United States, including me, are pushing the Golden Rule as a critical governing concept in an effort to unite and improve our nation through morals common across faiths and secular beliefs."

Professor Stark redirects the system to return to General Timur's taped remarks.

"I am sure you will argue that your God's Law idea links to the Prophet Muhammad because of his direction in the Hadith that, 'As you would have people do to you, do to them; and what you dislike to be done to you, don't do to them.' I will follow this up, as did Muhammad, by demanding that you let my stirrup go. I will not accept a partial, self-selected concept derived from the truth of Muhammad. No single concept of Islam can fix all that is wrong with America. Only full implementation of Sharia Law will suffice. You have six months to meet my demand. Why should you fear a simple man like me when I threaten you with punishment for your heresy?" Timur continues, stomping his foot to emphasize certain points. "Simply, you must fear me because I am the arm of Allah and Allah has provided me with enough nuclear material to destroy half of your nation and send the remainder into economic ruin."

Signals relayed by the evaluation system make clear to Professor Stark that every juror is fixated on Timur's every word.

"Six months from today," the general promises, "if Sharia Law is not your law, my troops will deliver nuclear punishment to your doorstep, just as my messenger did in bringing a tiny amount of nuclear material to your Chicago university to prove to your military that I have the capability to destroy you. By now, you know that had the messenger deployed a nuclear weapon, easily half of Chicago would have been sent to ruins. But, you would not be hearing Allah's message. Allah has instructed me that converting the United States to Sharia Law requires my patience and loyalty to him."

Professor Stark battles temptation to turn off the recording, fearing that he is providing a global platform for General Timur to spout his threats. That's not my role, he decides in letting it continue.

"In order to save you time that you might waste on continuing this trial, rather than on the work you must do to convince America to convert to Sharia Law, I will admit now that I have conducted all of the executions of which you accuse me, carrying out the will of Allah on each and every occasion.

"The nuclear attack on Armenia was my personal handiwork. I am proud that I have served as Allah's executioner of Christian infidels who refused for centuries to convert to Islam, even while surrounded by Allah's faith and knowing of its virtues. Those exposed to and aware of the magnificence of Islam must be held most accountable if they fail to follow the instructions Muhammad received directly from God and transmitted to earth. Two billion of our global citizens recognize the will of Allah. Allah has grown tired of you others who refuse to worship him as directed. The bombing of Armenia serves as punishment for centuries of arrogance and insolence by the Armenian people.

"I also take great pride in having eliminated the families of the heretical generals who stole Iran from Allah and are attempting to return it to the man-made failure that has marked the United States throughout its history. By all rights, all of these women and children should have been beheaded, with their heads displayed on pikes throughout the city," General Timur states.

Professor Stark receives hundreds of instant messages from jurors, asking for the opportunity to be heard. The vast majority of those seeking attention have identified themselves as followers of Islam from more than forty different countries.

"Professor Stark," one juror states, "I must beg to be able to speak here. With the world watching this trial, it is important that they understand that the ranting of General Timur is the ranting of a lunatic, not a true follower of Islam."

After considering the messages, Professor Stark decides to interrupt the General's testimony in order to bring in experts on Islam to discuss its faith. Trial staff scramble to identify individuals respected enough to speak for Islam. They are surprised to find that dozens they would want to consider have been listening throughout the trial and quickly settle on the best spokesman.

"Imam Aalim, welcome to this trial, or what is now a discussion," Professor Stark states as he clicks a couple of spots on the control screen—with some assistance—to display the Imam's voice and face.

"A number of jurors on this trial have expressed concern that General Timur's description of Islam could inflame already significant tensions around the world between Muslims and the rest of the world. If you wouldn't mind, please tell participants about your background before correcting some of the perhaps erroneous or at least questionable statements about the requirements of Islam as stated by General Timur."

"Certainly, Professor Stark. It is good to speak with you again, this time with a much broader audience listening in to our discussion," Imam Aalim begins. The Imam is wearing traditional western clothing, though with a taqiyah on his head. "As you know Professor, in addition to being the leader of a small mosque in West London, I am Director of the Center for Islamic Studies at Oxford University and have dedicated my life to deep reflection on the roots of Islam and its connections to other faiths in the world. I appreciate that you have interrupted this trial to allow me to clarify, and perhaps at times to confuse, the debate on what it means to be a Muslim in today's world."

"Thank you, Imam. I appreciate your willingness to take this time. The floor is yours," Professor Stark states.

"The fears many Christians and Hindus and Jews and others have of Islam are partially rooted in misunderstanding our faith. However, some misunderstanding derives from what I believe are substantial misinterpretations of the Quran and the Hadith by small groups of Muslims. There are still today groups of Muslims who believe it is their duty to impose Islam on others when the Quran clearly states that conversions to Islam must be free will decisions of the heart. Our obligation as Muslims, I believe, is to spread the word of Muhammad in an effort to convince others to join us. But when I fail to convince, the failure is mine. I certainly believe that the Quran is the true word of Allah, just as Christians believe the Bible is the word of God and Jews believe that the Torah provides God's guidance. So, if I cannot convince others of this, I must be doing something wrong and must work to fix myself, not force others against Allah's will."

Professor Stark holds his hand up, a gesture the Imam notices. "So what do you believe General Timur is misinterpreting in attempting to force Sharia Law on the United States and likely the rest of the world?" Professor Stark asks.

A floor-to-ceiling wall of printed books serves as the background for the Imam, a carefully chosen location to visually bolster his academic credentials.

"His misinterpretation is in the arrogant belief that Allah has chosen him to impose Allah's will on the world and to punish the non-believers," Imam Aalim notes. "I should point out that his failing is not unusual for deep adherents of other faiths, particularly Christianity. You will recall that we have discussed the Christian Crusades, the Thirty Years War, and even recent battles between Catholics and Protestants in Ireland as examples of violence begun by Christians to spread the will and specific teachings of a man many Christians refer to as the Prince of Peace. The utter incoherence of using violence to impose the will of a prophet whose life revolved around non-violent teaching seems ludicrous in hindsight, yet men still led such actions. I am afraid General Timur is engaged in just such self-deception and self-aggrandizement with his stated mission."

Professor Stark exhales audibly, fear diffusing through every nerve that wading into the Islamic versus Western values debate will earn him the scorn of many and a fatwa from fanatics. "What do you want listeners and jurors of this trial to take away about Islam?"

"I want them to understand that being Muslim does not mean being violent or that we must impose Islam or Sharia Law on the non-believers. Certainly, Muhammad and his men responded violently to attack, but Muslims for many centuries have lived and worked among Christians, Jews and others, calling them brothers throughout history. And yes, as we are working to secure in England, we want the ability to enforce Sharia Law among committed followers of Islam everywhere Muslims exist. We believe it is our right to enforce laws that require more of the men and women of our faith than is required of secularists and we believe we have the right to promote and defend this right."

"When you say you have to defend the right to impose Sharia Law, what do you mean by defend?" Professor Stark interrupts to ask.

"I mean we have the right, peacefully, to protest to ensure our right to follow Sharia Law," the Imam responds.

MIKE BUSHMAN

"So Muslims have no intent to impose Sharia Law on people who do not follow the teachings of Muhammad?" Professor Stark asks.

"I do not," the Imam replies, a statement the Professor considers interesting because of the singular nature of his answer to a broadly applicable question.

Because the response seems to be a deflection, Professor Stark presses: "So you will support an amendment to the English laws, and the Constitutions of other countries in which Muslims reside, that expressly prohibit the imposition of Sharia Law on individuals who are not Muslim?"

"I have not considered this question, so will defer a response," Imam Aalim replies. "But let me say this. The United States forces people to pay for and in some cases participate in actions that conflict with their moral conscience. But I have found in my studies that this was clearly not the intent of the founders of the United States, who sought to provide for religious plurality at a time when Catholics were vilified in much of the land and even prevented from holding office, Quakers were derided and persecuted and individual states imposed state-mandated religions and collected taxes to fund specific religions. It is my intent that Islam not be treated either like the Catholics or Quakers of the eighteenth century, or deeply spiritual Christians of today. We want to be able to live in our faith."

"General Timur seems to suggest that Allah believes the only way for his will to be achieved is to rid the world of all infidels. Is this your understanding of the Quran and the Hadith?" Professor Stark asks, knowing the Imam's answer but wanting to be certain it is heard broadly.

"I do not believe this to be true," Imam Aalim replies. "We have lived for millennia in tranquility, with only small groups of Muslims taking it upon themselves to spread Islam and repress other faiths through violence."

"But can you see how the silence of peace-loving Muslims allows these Islamic radicals to attack and destroy people of other faiths, so that to Christians, Jews and many secular governments, the appearance is that peace-loving Muslims are turning a blind eye to the violence spurred by their faith?" Professor Stark asks.

Imam Aalim expected nothing less than challenging debate with the professor, so welcomes the exchange. "A great misfortune, certainly, and a misinterpretation that will continue until Muslims who know our faith to be built in peace take up arms against the radical Islamists who bastardize and shame Muhammad's teachings," the Imam states.

"And that type of intra-Muslim settlement will occur when?" Professor Stark asks.

"Perhaps never, as you fear, Professor," the Imam replies. "But perhaps very soon. Soon enough that General Timur will feel the wrath of his brethren."

A discussion of what constitutes the true meaning of Islam continues for another thirty minutes before Professor Stark returns to playing the remainder of General Timur's message. "In the nation some now call Persia," the General continues in his taped message, "we had in place a system of government that matched the will of Allah and the teachings of the Prophet Muhammad. Muhammad was not just Islam's spiritual leader. He was also the ruler of Medina, then Mecca and then vast territories. He left to his followers the job of completing conversion to Islam of all nations. In the Islamic Republic of Iran, we had the perfect system, with the leader of the proper Shia branch of Islam as the Supreme Leader and earthly men running the government under direction from Allah's representatives. Only under this style of government, blending religion and government, faith and implementation, loyalty and submission, can Allah's blessed world emerge.

"We were approaching our nirvana when several generals decided to ally with the Great Satan and destroy all we had built in Allah's name. Under Sharia Law, their punishment had to be death. Because the men who created this failure ran and hid, that punishment was shamefully passed on to their wives and children," General Timur argues, his voice fully raised and his face twisted in anger. "I had wished to do as Muhammad had done, to allow the beheading of these traitors while enslaving the women and children. Instead these generals ran in shame and left their families to suffer their punishment. Mercifully, I had them crucified instead," General Timur adds, a statement that clearly agitates jurors if the real-time reaction system worn by jurors provides any indication. Heart monitors of nearly ever juror detect elevated rates.

Professor Stark interrupts the display to interject a few comments.

"I would just point out that I have received a flurry of messages from jurors objecting to the characterization of Muhammad's actions, with some references to his dual role as spiritual leader and head of state coming into conflict, some references to his actions being merciful for the era in which he lived, and other questions suggesting that a true prophet would instead act in a manner that is timeless in its morality. These concepts and questions are too complex and time-consuming to debate and resolve here, so we'll come back to them only if necessary to reach a verdict. However, I can assure you that the debate on the proper interpretations of the Quran and Hadith has been occurring for centuries and will likely continue as long as we have centuries. Having said that and with much appreciation to Imam Aalim for his illuminations, we'll continue with General Timur's message."

A quick wave and the message from General Timur begins again to display. Another twenty minutes of boisterous recitation of his involvement in atrocities listed in the indictment against him takes place before the general reaches his conclusion. "You may, as a jury of infidels and effeminate intellectuals, find me guilty of any crimes you wish to convict me of doing. I have made clear that I have taken part in all of the actions you condemn, proudly and freely admitting that I am responsible for implementing the will of Allah as directly told to me by Allah and preached by his great Prophet Muhammad. So convict me if you must. But I will warn you today. Fail to impose Sharia Law as the law of the land in the United States and I will punish America. Fail, among the other nations, to force the United States to accept its punishment for replicating the sins of Sodom and Gomorra and I will hold you accountable as well."

Response signals make clear that every juror is fully focusing on General Timur's statements. In addition to measuring a drop in prefrontal cortex activity, a drop normally associated with a rise in aggression, facial analytics conducted real-time on all one thousand

jurors determine that more than nine hundred of the jurors are consumed by a combination of fear, anger or hatred as the General
speaks. Professor Stark is surprised to find, however, that dozens of
jurors brain activity and facial analytics suggest they are responding
to the General's threats with a mixture of contentment and outright
joy.

"Within my network, I have enough nuclear material to create
weapons that will destroy far more than the five percent of the world
population killed by my namesake. I promise, if you fail to comply
with the will of Allah, to surpass his sacrifices to Allah," General Timur continues, causing fear levels to rise even among jurors who had
shown contentment with his earlier claims. "In case you are one of the
billions of ignorant people who do not understand, I will cause the
death of at least one billion heretics by detonating my nuclear weapons if the Great Satan fails to follow Allah's order."

38 CLARIFICATION

As General Timur's remarks conclude, President Phillipi's Director of National Intelligence (DNI) runs to the Oval Office, alerting Chief of Staff Vijay Chinh on the way.

"Mr. President," the DNI says as soon as he enters. "Vijay. I think we need to get the President into the DUCC immediately and get your family, Mr. President, to a secure location."

The President responds slowly, particularly juxtaposed against the urgency of the DNI's demands: "Why now?"

"We have reason to believe that most of the lost nuclear material we've been chasing the past twenty years is with General Timur," the DNI states.

"Any imminent threat?" President Phillipi asks.

"By the time we have any, it will be too late," the DNI replies.

"Understood, but if I head underground now, right after General Timur's threats are aired, it will tell the American people that we know an attack will take place any minute and it will send our nation into physical and economic chaos from which we may not recover," the President states. "General Timur will succeed in destroying the United States without ever firing a weapon if I act rashly now."

"Understood, sir," Chief of Staff Vijay replies. "I'll order a drill to be sure all systems are ready when we need them."

"Not now," President Phillipi orders. "Word of the drill will leak and even a few seconds of delay in communicating that a drill is being conducted could destroy many lives. Leak at the end of the day that a drill will be conducted next week, just as a safety precaution. Be sure to leak it to enough reporters that everyone will believe it."

Several miles away, a group gathered outside Jill's home sings: "Oh, deep in my heart, I do believe, we shall live in peace someday." Jill recognizes the lyrics from childhood church services and from use in several movies and documentaries highlighting Civil Rights era struggles. She finds it ironic that the protestors are singing a civil rights protest song to object to broader constitutional embodiment of the very principle that makes clear that slavery, segregation and degradation are wrong.

Nevertheless, Jill quickly makes several pots of coffee to bring out to the protestors and throws together a quick batch of banana-chocolate-chip-whole-wheat muffins using a bunch of stale bananas she might have otherwise tossed. Less than twenty minutes later, the protestors take a break from their singing and marching as Jill asks if they are willing to talk to her.

"What's your biggest concern with what we're doing?" Jill asks a woman who appears to be the protest organizer.

"There's a lot of people who believe crazy things and we don't want to have to treat them the way they want to be treated," she replies.

"Have you studied the Golden Rule in depth, to really understand how to apply it to the kinds of situations you're afraid of encountering?" Jill asks.

"I don't know about in depth, but everyone knows the Golden Rule," the group's leader replies.

"I might just suggest that most people have heard of the Golden Rule. That doesn't mean that most understand it. It's not as simple as it might seem," she replies before suggesting several books to read and excusing herself to finish preparing for the day.

Nearly twenty percent of the House Judiciary Committee, led by Chairman Henry, voted against sending the God's Law amendment to the House floor, a percentage Jill can't afford to let grow. In fact, to give the amendment the momentum she thinks it needs, Jill's goal is to take the winning margin to ninety percent on the House floor. Constitutional amendments require passage by two-thirds of the House and two-thirds of the Senate, with ratification by three-quarters of the states.

As sponsor of the resolution, Jill opens debate on the House floor. She carefully considers this moment. Her words certainly matter, but Jill knows that appearance affects public opinion almost as much as substance. Before going to the floor, she adds mascara, eyeliner, a soft terra cotta eyeshadow chosen to convey genuineness while matching her blue eyes and a soft coating blush to her normally sparse makeup use.

Her preparation intensity helps Jill stifle her nerves as she launches three days of debate in advance of a final vote. As she steps to the podium to start debate, Jill looks to the ceiling, making one last request to her long-deceased mother to watch out over her through this challenge.

"In recent decades, America has suffered from the pains created when our nation became divided," Jill says to open the floor debate. "Divided by race. Divided by religion. Divided by language. Divided by party. These divides have led to violent massacres, an invasion and a brief civil war, impacts of which we are all acutely aware. However, the divides have also caused extraordinary personal pain for millions of American in less noticeable ways, suffering caused by leaders in Washington who no longer attempt to understand each other and find common ground. We cannot and must not allow this to continue. By passing this constitutional amendment, we will start down a path of barrier destruction that truly embeds the concept 'that all men are created equal' into our laws. With this amendment, decency and common sense force their way into our system of justice and, over time, will improve our everyday interactions," Jill states, physically speaking to only two dozen members and several employees of the

Clerk of the House and its parliamentarian. Some lawmakers and millions of citizens watch from the comforts of their homes and offices.

"It seems such a simple concept," Jill continues, including several pre-choreographed gestures as she speaks. "The idea that we should treat others as we would want to be treated under similar circumstances is common sense, but often neglected by our laws and enforcement. As President Philippi has stated, it is a universal concept, discussed in every major religion and even fitting the conceptual framework of secular humanists interested in creating lasting societal peace. It is so universal that our nation's founding fathers did not explicitly state the concept in our Constitution or in the Bill of Rights. Perhaps this neglect was the result of believing it unnecessary," she continued, "or perhaps because they recognized that its inclusion would have ended slavery far sooner than was finally achieved or prevented the creation of the union. Who knows?"

A few of her fellow members of Congress are paying attention to Jill. Most of the others on the floor are engrossed in their Lifelinks or in finalizing preparation of their own remarks.

"But we must understand a few critical points about the creation of our nation. Many of our framers initially thought that the Bill of Rights was unnecessary; that explicit protection of free speech, freedom of worship, the right to bear arms and other divinely granted human rights would simply be understood. They believed that remaining silent on these issues would make clear that the federal government had no authority to impose restrictions. We have learned through the years that those founders who believed the government would not take rights unless explicitly granted have repeatedly been proven wrong."

The gallery above the House floor finishes filling as Jill continues, though a small section remains open to a constant rotation of waiting tourists. Jill's aides finish carefully placing visual aides behind her so the public sees something other than row after row of empty seats when the cameras are focused on Jill.

"Even after explicitly protecting many rights, these Constitutional blessings have come under continuous challenge throughout our nation's history. Imagine the arrogant injection of federal authority that would have been pursued had our rights not been explicitly noted and granted," Jill adds. "Despite flaws, our founders proved their genius by making the Constitution an amendable document, able to mature with the nation. The ability to amend the Constitution ensures its vitality and continuity long after other constitutions from even subsequent eras required wholesale replacement in other countries. Perhaps the most important signs of maturation were the Reconstruction amendments, which put an end to slavery and began the hundred-year process of converting the concept of 'all men' being created equal into reality for those who had been confined as slaves. The nineteenth amendment, granting women the right to vote, continued us down a path toward treating all Americans as equal."

Jill's cadence accelerates, tone deepens and volume increases as she drives her admonishments home.

"Despite these improvements, the federal government still routinely flaunts the Golden Rule. Congress passes laws that it exempts itself from following, creating a political elite segregated from the nation's citizenry. This must stop. Our business laws and regulations are too frequently written in a manner that confers a government-granted advantage to some businesses over others, creating a crony-based playing field that stifles competition, harms consumers and unfairly enriches those who use government to insulate themselves from competition. This must stop. Our criminal and civil justice systems create win-lose battles, ensuring fair justice only to the properly resourced, putting people of different races or even people in front of different judges in prison for vastly different lengths of time even when the circumstances of the crime are nearly identical. This must stop. We create bureaucracies to manage the impoverished that invest far more resources in supporting dependency and testing eligibility than they do on the mentoring, guidance and personalized support individuals need to escape poverty. This inequity must stop. We too often treat each other in everyday life on the basis of what is legally required rather than the basis of what is right and just. This must stop."

"Will the gentlewoman yield?" a loudly yelled interruption comes from the other side of the House floor.

House Judiciary Committee Chairman Will Henry, the leading opponent of the constitutional amendment, asks to speak. Jill controls the time and considers whether to yield time away from her supporters to someone she knows opposes the measure.

"Will the gentlewoman yield?" Chairman Henry requests again, making clear he'll interrupt incessantly if she doesn't.

"I yield to the gentleman from Tennessee," Jill relents.

"Thank you, Congresswoman. The pretext, or perhaps pretense, of this God's Law message is that the Golden Rule is a concept shared by all of the nation's religions and even by atheists and agnostics. Today, Islam is the second largest faith in the world and I would suggest that Muslims do not believe that the Golden Rule applies to their treatment of anyone other than Muslims. So, that being the case, it seems to me that this proposed amendment directly contradicts with the freedom of religion clause of the first amendment and ought to be rejected on that basis as it does not allows Muslims to pursue their faith as they desire."

Jill had prepared vigorously for a wide range of arguments against embedding the Golden Rule into the constitution. This one, though, hadn't been on her radar screen, particularly coming from Chairman Henry who she had expected to focus on maintaining the prerogatives and privileges of being a member of Congress, the motivating factor that drives a substantial amount of his attention.

Jill scrambles through her notes to find a specific quote.

"You certainly have heard the quote from Muhammad, the prophet of Islam, in which he told a follower, 'As you would have people do to you, do to them; and what you dislike to be done to you, don't do to them,'" Jill notes.

"I have heard this, but the quote is taken out of context, something that is easy to do for someone with only a passing knowledge of the Quran," Chairman Henry states.

Jill hadn't known Chairman Henry to be a student of the Quran, and was near certain he was not a faithful adherent to Islam or any other religion, despite his oft-public statements to the contrary.

"I would ask the gentleman, then, to put the quote in context for me to improve my understanding," Jill says.

Chairman Henry glares at his staff director, who sits next to him feeding notes and displaying on-screen information as quickly as possible. This particular attack was designed to divide the interfaith coalition supporting the amendment.

"It's very clear, from reading the Quran, that Muslims are instructed to treat others differently, that People of the Book as it calls Jews and Christians deserve mercy only to the extent that they pay a protection tax to Islamic rulers, and that those who believe in more than one God have no rights whatsoever. There is even a divide within Islam, with Sunnis believing the Shia sect to be the result of a divisive plot coordinated by the Jews and therefore Shias are unworthy of equal treatment. Without taking too much of your time, then, it is clear that Muslims do not believe that Muhammad's statement applies to all. Therefore, President Philippi's primary argument, one you mimic, that all major religions believe in this idea is inaccurate."

Jill considers the Chairman's intrusion into her time irritating but is delighted to engage in this debate.

"I appreciate the gentleman's educational initiative today. I'm quite aware that the Quran itself contains many contradictory messages, having read it and studied it somewhat intensively in recent months," Jill replies.

"Has the gentlewoman converted to Islam?" the Chairman heckles.

"The gentleman's comment is out of order. The gentlewoman has the time," a legislator acting as temporary speaker interrupts.

Jill sees now what Chairman Henry is attempting to do, trying to link the amendment to fears of Sharia Law and concern that the God's Law effort is being redirected to accede to General Timur's demand.

"The Chairman is correct on one point," Jill comments, causing heads to turn as other supporters fear she is about to derail their momentum. "Not everyone who follows the Muslim faith believes that all men and women are created equal and that we must do unto others as we would have done onto ourselves. But many are able to distinguish between the words of Muhammad as prophet and those of Muhammad as ruler of a nation. Many followers of Islam are again turning to ijtihad, an historic Muslim practice that enables them to filter faith through their own reason rather than through the self-interested teachings of clerics seeking assent within their bureaucracies."

Chairman Henry turns to his staffer. "How come I've never heard of this ish-tee-hod?"

Fortunately for staff, Jill provides the answer: "Ijtihad drove Islam's growth until theocratic governments mandated that only clerics aligned with the government had the right to contemplate and understand the Quran. Many faith leaders, when pressed, acknowledge that sacred texts provide a basis for continuous faith exploration, not a strict set of rules to follow mindlessly."

Jill is now certain that Chairman Henry's understanding of the Quran had been exhausted by his earlier comments so she decides to press her advantage.

"When you speak of your understanding of Muslims and the Quran, from which sect is your interpretation derived?" Jill asks. "I yield such time as necessary to respond to the gentleman from Tennessee."

Chairman Henry leans toward the staff member assisting him on the floor. The two exchange whispers.

"The Saudis," he finally replies, before being poked by his staffer. "I mean the Sunnis."

"Would it surprise you then, Mr. Chairman, that not all followers of Islam share identical views, just as not all Christians think the same and not all Hindus believe in identical concepts," Jill inquires.

"Of course, it would not," the Chairman replies.

"So let me return to the central point of this debate, which is whether the concept that we should do unto others as we would have done unto ourselves should be embedded in our Constitution. This is a concept that our founders might have thought self-evident and unnecessary to write out at the time, but the self-indulgent rulings of our bloated political class since then have made it clear that our founders were overly optimistic in believing public servants would serve rather than rule the public," Jill states, holding her hands in front of her stomach as she uses the word "bloated" in a manner that sets Chairman Henry off away from the microphones.

As morning sun sprays above her nearby mountain panorama, Abril pulls two pillows over from the empty side of the bed and shoves them under her head. It's her new routine, allowing her to comfortably gaze outside while the rest of her body fully awakens. For several months now at night, the king size bed has overwhelmed Abril. She conforms to its edge despite constant restlessness. Even as she flips from left side to right side, or from stomach to back to stomach, her body never strays far from the edge. Now long-removed from pain medications and with her skin grafts nearly healed, her tossing creates less pain and more repetition most nights.

Morning sunrise is the most stunning time of day in this secluded cabin; painting a color array as beautiful as any she had ever seen in her childhood. More importantly, the first rays let Abril know another darkness has passed. After months in the cartel's underground slave pits, Abril craves daylight, not wanting to miss even a moment to absorb or view its glow.

Night is another story. Alone most nights in New Rite's guest cabin, set near the tree line on the eastern edge of Byer's Peak, Abril's mind races quickly to her darkest thoughts and memories. Even her nightly snuggling and handholding session with Ramon, or at least the artificial replacement for Ramon, isn't enough to assuage her fears once back alone in the dark. The comfort robot Ally secured for Abril—with its ability to replicate Ramon's physical movements, serve as his eyes and ears, and move its mouth to match the movement of his own—helps Abril maintain a connection with Ramon while he does the same wherever he is located with a comfort robot replica of Abril.

But it's not the same. His face wasn't customized on the robot she has—perhaps to minimize the risk of Ramon being discovered as alive. That alone is enough to turn Abril off. She won't willingly share her physical affection with someone she doesn't love, let alone something. But it's more than that. The robot's body temperature always seems a bit off. The give on the skin isn't quite right. The lips and tongue are just mechanical enough in movement to make kissing less enjoyable.

And she refuses greater physical intimacy despite the physical pressing she frequently feels as Ramon's reaction to any contact from the comfort robot he had made of Abril is replicated by his replacement. He's clearly not as discouraged that the skin touch isn't real through her replica. With its customized face and body measurements, the artificial Abril is close enough to stimulate him.

Couples used to being separated by countries or continents use comfort robots to keep their physical connections, some even using the male robot's storage and injection capabilities to conceive despite physical distance. Abril finds the prospect too creepy to consider.

It's far from the worst thought that infiltrates her mind, especially while sitting up and staring out at the distant stars or moon when repeatedly awakened by nightmares. New Rite's guest cabin is attached by enclosed walkway and tunnel to New Rite's compound main home, but Abril feels completely alone when she closes and locks the door to her cabin at night. If someone wants to keep her here, they only have one pathway to block. The only other alternative is over the railings and down the mountainside.

JT and Ally are the only routine residents of the main home and its stunning sunset views. For Ally, the home holds all of her possessions and is her only temperature-controlled residence. JT uses the home only when he's working out of New Rite's headquarters or attending survival gaming competitions at the company's Colorado compound.

With Ally out of town, Abril's only break from loneliness today will come from her time with Ramon and his stand-in and another draining session with New Rite's corporate psychologist. By the time the psychologist arrives, Abril decides she's ready to leave this camp whether the psychologist thinks she's ready or not.

"Can't I see him yet," Abril demands to know from the psychologist. "I need to be certain that I'm more than just a distraction from whatever he's working on. I need to know that he forgives me for the pain I caused him."

"I understand that," the psychologist replies, leaning forward on her chair across from Abril as the sunlight shines onto her back. "But I need to know first that you forgive yourself for causing that pain, that you recognize the suffering you endured was not your fault and that you have figured out how to love yourself enough to be part of a loving relationship, whether with this guy or your God or whoever else you allow into your life."

"I know. I know. But I need to know if what he tells me is real or if he's just using me," Abril argues as the two go back and forth while on the balcony overlooking the natural surroundings, sharing freshly gathered rainwater and snacking on vegetable slices.

Abril's physical recovery is nearly complete. The patchwork skin graft has successfully taken, replacing the scar tissue covering her back with smooth skin grafted and grown from her legs and stomach. Four bone fractures and breaks have also been reset. All are nearly healed. Abril's physical therapy sessions, another gift from New Rite, helps restore her strength and shape. JT insists that her mental recovery efforts run in parallel.

"I understand your frustration, Abril," the psychologist says, speaking softly and calmly. "But I need you to feel good about you and only then add whoever to your life. You're close. You're close. We just need a little more work."

"But I just need to leave. I need to get out of here," Abril demands. "I feel like I'm in prison again, just a nicer, less violent prison."

"You're free to leave anytime you want," the psychologist offers as she places her hand on top of one of Abril's hands. "In fact, now that you're physically healed, I think you should be spending far more time hiking outdoors and getting away from the machines you've been using. Getting into the sun will aid your physical and mental recovery."

"Are you kidding me?" Abril replies. "I'm not going out there alone. I can hear the wolves at night. And I know there are bears and moose and plenty of other things out there to kill me and eat me."

"Oh," the psychologist replies. "I hadn't really thought of it, but this isn't your neck of the woods, is it?"

"My neck of the woods?" Abril asks.

"Your home. Your comfort zone. A place where you know how things work."

"No, definitely not," Abril agrees.

"Well I'll report that then and I'm sure we can find you an escort who can protect you," the psychologist replies.

"Okay, okay," Abril replies, standing up and looking down over the edge of the balcony before stepping back to feel safer. "But how can I be sure he won't hurt me."

"It doesn't have to be a he," the psychologist replies.

Abril stares at the psychologist. "No?"

"No. The goal is to make you feel safer. Not to unnerve you."

"Unnerve?" Abril asks.

39 SEPARATION

Professor Stark had alerted his new class of graduate students that they would have an unusually early opportunity to make an impression on a national audience. For years, his integrated studies courses had tackled subjects so controversial that they attracted substantial media and public attention. Several times each semester, he turns on the broadcast system in his state-of-the-art classroom to provide students with exposure to potential employers.

It's a high-risk adventure for the students and for the university. Students sign waivers before taking his class to allow the university to freely disseminate their intellectual property. In return, students gain a forum that none could create for themselves.

The broadcast system inside his classroom automatically focuses camera and microphone pickup on students as they speak, unless Professor Stark specifically cuts a student off. He has only done this on a handful of occasions over the years, always with the purpose of protecting the student's future from their poorly considered thinking in the process of being expressed. His room is also designed to make course discussions an integrated learning experience. As he speaks, projection systems that circle the room search for visual objects he has personally uploaded or that the system finds through the internet, taking statements he or other students make and displaying items that illuminate each point. Video, still pictures, definitions and other objects appear as each person speaks. To make the discussions easier to follow, Professor Stark enables the note-summary function on his Lifelink, a function that provides a running organized summary of key points made during each debate.

"We're going to test a concept that has often been misunderstood by generations of the most educated jurists, lawmakers and thought leaders during the past 250 years, so I hope you came prepared to argue your perspective," Professor Stark says as he opens the class. "I also welcome journalists from more than one hundred different outlets around the world who are listening in to this discussion and remind each of you that anything you say can and will be used both for and against you throughout your life. With that as the opening, let's jump in and start the discussion with your high-level perspectives on how morality should affect our laws, with particular attention to the role of religious dictates on our legal system."

Looking across the room, he sees no hands raised, so reaches to his desk and grabs the tattered childhood foam rocket into his hand. Turning away from the class, he tosses it over his head, swinging around just in time to see where it lands.

"You appear to have been selected by the spirit of the foam football to open the debate, Insha," Professor Stark says, looking toward Insha, a Muslim student from Mumbai, India. Insha tightens her hijab, running her fingers along the rim of the cloth headscarf to be sure that no hair is displayed. She doesn't make eye contact with Professor Stark, a behavior that he found initially discomfiting. He now understands it is the only way Insha feels comfortable in interacting with men.

"It would be far easier on society if our religious laws and our government laws were uniform," Insha begins. "For some Muslims who follow Sharia Law, it creates great difficulties when government laws do not conform to the laws under which we live."

"Explain what you mean," Professor Stark directs, not giving away that he had purposely thrown the foam football in Insha's direction with the hopes she would either catch it or be brushed by it. He had even arrived to class early to take a few practice tosses to increase the odds she would be the first to speak.

"Sharia Law is very clear about what behaviors are acceptable and what behaviors are not, prescribing specific penalties that all followers come to know and accept as the way Allah has prescribed," Insha adds. "Obviously, I don't believe in all aspects of Sharia Law as practiced by many or I wouldn't be here unescorted, but I do believe that followers of Islam should be able to subject themselves to Sharia Law instead of government law."

"An interesting proposition," Professor Stark says. "So, let's take your concept to practical application in the United States. We do agree that Sharia Law is not defined identically in every society, don't we?" he adds, looking back to Insha.

"Yes, there are different interpretations," Insha agrees.

"Okay, and under some of the strictest interpretations of Sharia Law, women who commit adultery can be stoned to death. Correct?"

Insha normally would dismiss someone asking such a question, but feels compelled to engage Professor Stark in debate. "That is still true in some countries, yes. But not everyone in Islam believes this," she notes.

"I understand that, but you have already agreed that some followers of the faith of Muhammad have reached the conclusions that women, but not men, can be stoned to death for adultery."

"Yes, I have agreed to this," she agrees.

"So a woman commits adultery with a man, who is also married. Both have committed sins of equal weight in the eyes of most here, correct?" Professor Stark says, looking around the class to find almost all heads nodding in agreement. "Okay, and after being found guilty by a Sharia court in some countries, she is sentenced to be stoned to death, taken to the public square, dropped in a stoning pit and the men of the town gather to throw heavy stones at her until her skull and bones are crushed, blood oozes from every pore, her internal organs are mangled and she dies an excruciating death. You agree this could happen under Sharia Law?'

"It could, but not every Muslim believes this is right," she responds, still looking down, but the darkening of her face still evident.

"You've already established that point, and you have also agreed that some Muslims agree this is acceptable, so my point is that if this happened under Sharia Law in the United States, every man who took part in the stoning would be indicted for the murder of this woman. Adultery is not illegal in most of the United States. Murder, however, is illegal in every state, and prosecuted whenever evidence exists as to who committed a murder," Professor Stark states.

"That is my point, though," Insha interjects. "People who truly believe in Sharia Law will not inform the legal authorities of who participated in these executions, because they know the executions were authorized by Allah and conform with the law to which they all follow."

"Okay, another interesting twist," Professor Stark states. "Let's say the adulterous woman was not a Muslim and that the Muslim man she had an affair with is married to a Muslim woman who insists that the woman who slept with her husband receive her due punishment. Which system of law should be followed?"

"That's exactly my point," Insha argues. "When religious law and government law are not one and the same, an unhealthy dichotomy is created that secures different outcomes for different people depending on their faith or lack of faith. You would agree that it is fundamentally unfair to have people treated differently for exactly the same actions, wouldn't you Professor?"

"I would agree with that, as I'm sure would every adulteress. Could someone else in the class tell me how they would solve this conundrum?" Professor Stark asks, letting Insha off the hook from having to answer her own question.

Looking around the class, Professor Stark spots a student lifting his hand half-heartedly: "Go ahead, Saul."

"I don't believe there is a God and I certainly don't believe that the self-aggrandizing proclamations of a bunch of narcissistic religious clerics have any authority over me, ever, in any way, especially when it's clear to me that the laws they propose are designed to aid in controlling a populace rather than serving the people," Saul begins, standing and walking around the room as he talks, with visuals of clerics from multiple faith and a definition of narcissism displaying automatically behind him. "If I did believe that God existed, I certainly wouldn't believe he gave some men the power to kill and maim others. If my sister wanted to ride a married Muslim, and he wanted it, no religious cleric has any right to kill her for something that doesn't harm anyone."

Standing and turning toward Saul, though still with her head down, Insha interrupts: "You think it doesn't harm anyone for a woman to have sex with a married man and try to lure him away from his family, his commitments and his attention to Allah?"

Saul looks toward her and motions to suggest she pick her head up, a motion Insha ignores.

"Certainly, not to the extent that the woman should be killed, when in this case it would be the man who is breaking his vows," Saul replies. "Murder is murder. The only legitimate reason to kill another person is in self-defense and there is no self-defense when a bunch of men stone a woman to death."

"What about killing people in war? Is that acceptable to you?" Insha asks.

"Let's get back to the topic we're debating," Professor Stark says. "Thank you, Insha. Thank you, Saul. I think you've illustrated the point here, that in a society where people are able to choose their faith or choose not to have faith in a higher being, religious law and government law must be separated. So the question now is how do you ensure that laws reflect the sometimes competing concepts of fundamental human rights, community mores, functionally stable societies and moral principles?"

With announced support for God's Law growing as day two of congressional floor debate begins, House Judiciary Committee Chairman Will Henry is desperate to destroy the diverse coalition now supporting President Phillipi's hoped-for legacy achievement. As previously agreed, he opens the day two floor debate.

"With this constitutional amendment, we are vesting every judge in every district and every appeals court and ultimately, the nine justices appointed, let me repeat that, appointed to the United States Supreme Court, with the authority to strike down every law, every regulation, every action of this Congress and the President of the United States," Chairman Henry says. "This isn't the fox guarding the hen house. This is giving nine roosters unfettered access to every hen in the nation to do as they wish with them and I do not wish to be the hen forced to endure whatever the Supreme Court shoves down our throats. Does the gentlewoman have any understanding of the power we are transferring to the judicial branch with this proposed amendment, in clear violation of the intent of our founders?"

Jill stands and moves to a podium area as Chairman Henry speaks, planning to interrupt but delighted he invites her to respond.

"Thank you, Mr. Chairman, for the question. It's a wonderful irony to me that after decades of encouraging the judiciary to reinterpret Congress, and even reinterpret the meaning of the Constitution and the Bill of Rights themselves, you are now concerned that we provide guidelines for such reinterpretations embedded in our governing document," Jill replies. "The Supreme Court has clearly had the ultimate ability to determine the constitutionality of the laws we pass since *Marbury v. Madison*. This amendment does not change that."

"But, reclaiming my time," Chairman Henry contends, "we have such an open-ended concept, the Golden Rule means something fundamentally different to different people. The Supreme Court will be able to essentially do whatever it wants to whatever law it wants and I, for one, find this prospect of nine unelected jurists essentially ruling the nation frightening and appalling. Never in my decades as a legislator have I seen an executive branch and many members of Congress so anxious to give control of the nation to others in a way that is almost treasonous."

"Thank you, Mr. Chairman, for bringing hyperbole into the debate. What would a good congressional debate be without hyperbole?" Jill says, doing her best to keep control of her emotions, but the blushing of her cheeks and neck making clear that Chairman Henry is getting to her. Still, she knows that if she can keep control, she can goad him into losing his composure and making statements he is certain to regret later.

Just as she considers this, Chairman Henry obliges.

"You clearly don't know the people of America as well as I do," Chairman Henry continues. "If you did, you'd know that some people would tell you they'd kill themselves if they were gay, so could the Supreme Court decide that we must impose capital punishment on acts of homosexuality even though Congress and the President would never impose such a thing. How could you let this happen?"

Jill looks at Chairman Henry, shaking her head, taking a few seconds to contemplate her response.

"The Chairman clearly must have misspoken in his last question. I will give you a minute to retract and restate your question in a manner that is appropriate to the floor of the House of Representatives," Jill finally says, the chamber now silent and everyone on the floor and in the gallery intently watching this exchange.

"That's my damn question," Chairman Henry says, banging his hands down on the podium. "If you don't have the . . . the . . . the . . . . guts to answer the question, at least admit this is the fundamental flaw of this proposed constitutional amendment. Don't show up to this dog fight with a poodle unless you're prepared to be torn apart."

Jill steps back from the podium, turning to a Democratic colleague supporting God's Law who is now torn between seeing an opening to secure its passage and needing to rescue Chairman Henry from himself. "I have to shut him down," Jill says to the colleague, who nods his head in agreement.

"Let me understand your premise, one I will argue is entirely false," Jill says. "You are suggesting that, of the nine Supreme Court justices, it is plausible that five will be appointed who would kill themselves if they were gay and believe that the death penalty for homosexuality makes sense, that Presidents would appoint these five despite such deep character flaws, that majorities of the Senate would consent to these appointments having either not understood or actually having supported such a mindset."

Chairman Henry's agitation remains evident in the cracking of his voice. "Well, if you don't like that scenario, maybe you could see that the five Supreme Court justices might support a gay activist agenda in which people whose faith teaches them that homosexuality is bad are forced to serve the gay activist agenda by a Supreme Court that decides that part of 'doing unto others as we would have done unto ourselves' is that we would never want anyone to not support everything we do because it would hurt us to know that others don't like us. Perhaps this is a more likely scenario that your religious right might find objectionable," Chairman Henry continues, attempting to imply that Jill is aligned with the religious right and anti-gay causes.

"Mr. Chairman, I appreciate the opportunity to clarify legislative intent on this concept. As you know, Mr. Chairman, Congress, various Presidents and various courts have not been kind to people of faith, particularly during the last seventy years," Jill states.

As Jill speaks, Chairman Henry turns away as he tries to hide a smile. "She's gonna do it," he whispers into the ear of his floor aide.

Jill continues: "Congress, the Administration and the courts have played loose with our First Amendment religious protections for too long. Clearly, we have an interest in protecting citizens from religions that preach the rights of believers to kill or mistreat non-believers. But, we have taken to compelling believers to act against their faith in manners wholly unnecessary to protecting the rights of others, simply because the majority has determined the believers to be wrong. We have even gone so far as to compel people of faith to fund actions they see as murder."

Chairman Henry waves his right hand in a circle, encouraging Jill to continue and suggesting he doesn't want to interrupt. He turns to his staffer with a broad smile. He has succeeded in bringing wedge issues into the debate.

"To fix this, we have to clearly define what is a civil right," Jill argues. "I suggest that a simple question leads to the answer. The question is: "Does the imposition of equal treatment harm others in a manner they cannot mitigate?" How does government find the right balance on controversial issues such as racial equality, gay marriage and gender equality? The correct answers—achieved by questioning whether 'the imposition of equal treatment harms others' in ways they can't offset—must be based on a consistent conceptual underpinning that doesn't neatly align with the current perspectives of the Democratic and Republican parties. Let's use the LGBT issue you raised, Mr. Chairman."

Chairman Henry turns again to hide a smile as Jill continues. She's biting the tangent bait.

"Does requiring that the government recognize gay marriage harm others? I can't find any convincing evidence that it does. How could the marriage of two people who love each other create harm when, even if I were not already married, either I would certainly not be interested in both participants or they would certainly both not be interested in me? The mitigation to gay marriage is the same as for any other heterosexual marriage; find a partner where one's attraction is shared. Nothing in equal treatment of gay marriage would prevent anyone from seeking this alternative," Jill contends. "The best argument for suggesting there could be a societal harm in allowing gay marriage is that gay couples cannot reproduce without the assistance of someone outside the marriage and that it is in a nation's best interest to facilitate reproduction to create cultural stability and facilitate self-perpetuation. Using this argument as the rationale to deny gay marriage raises the question of what should be done with infertile heterosexual people. If the outside-agent-required-for-reproduction argument provides the reason to deny gay marriage, would it be fair to also suggest that heterosexual individuals who are infertile should be prevented from marrying? I believe I don't have to explain why this concept is nonsensical."

Chairman Henry has his back turned to Jill and the cameras. He tries to hide his glee that Jill is allowing the debate to take a turn into other controversial issues.

"A second, and more vocal, argument against gay marriage is that homosexuality is viewed as forbidden in the Bible, Quran and other religious texts," Jill says in expanding her views. "As a firm believer that the nation's founding fathers acted properly in preventing the government from establishing a state religion, this means that no single religious text should define our national policies and, more importantly, no single religious bureaucracy should drive our government. The founders also recognized that many human rights emanate from a higher power, not the text of a religion that claims ownership of such a higher power. This means the nation has the right to define what we believe is truly right, in conformance with the foundational idea 'that all men are created equal.' As a society, we now recognize that 'all men' means 'all men and women.' We should also recognize that 'all men' does not read as 'all heterosexual men' or 'all heterosexual men and women.'

Chairman Henry turns to his aide, covering his face as he laughs at how easy it was to goad Jill into this debate.

Despite noticing the Chairman's inattention, Jill continues undaunted: "Though government should treat gay and lesbian marriages the same as heterosexual unions, religions that object to gay marriage should not be forced to conduct gay marriage ceremonies. Government should not be able to mandate that any specific religious institution conduct homosexual marriages or individuals be compelled to provide private services for religious ceremonies they find objectionable. Government compulsions to do so compel harm on those who would be required to participate in activities directly contradicting their moral beliefs. Recognizing that gay couples have the right to hospital visits, wealth transfer at death, health care coverage and other elements of government recognition of marriage doesn't otherwise compel behaviors that one could reasonably argue threaten the moral creeds of others. This concept has relevance to a number of other issues worthy of reconsideration that I won't explore here.

"I'm convinced that faith—and belief in a being greater than any human who will hold us accountable for our actions—is important to building a better society, but when elements of particular faiths contradict human reason, we must allow reason to alter our actions," Jill finally concludes her long statement.

As she concludes, Chairman Henry turns back to his floor staff. "That'll tear a gaping hole in her coalition," he whispers in his staffer's ear. "If the people don't get now that there's a wide divide in how others will desire to be treated, and that we are giving the Supreme Court's nine justices the chance to define right and wrong over the objections of the elected Congress and President, they'll never get it."

40 REHABILITATION

Clarissa stops after another two-hundred-yard sprint toward Humphrey's Peak, drops to the ground and begins a set of twenty push-ups. Jumping to her feet, she sets off on another two-hundred-yard sprint before leaning up against a spruce tree missing its low-lying branches, doing a handstand against the tree and fighting through ten upward pushups, the last few of which she can barely bend and re-straighten her elbows. Sit-ups, push-ups, leg lifts, fallen tree branch lifts and stretches to build flexibility add to her workout. Driven by hearing her mission from Ally, the high school student continues pushing for nearly two hours every day, stopping only to catch her breath at the oxygen-deprived elevation.

It's also cathartic to Clarissa to be in her preferred outdoor setting, focusing on recovering her health, building her strength and, perhaps most importantly, restoring her will to live. This mission, her assignment from Ally, frightens Clarissa but she's at a place where death isn't scary as long as it isn't accompanied by torture. Having stared down the barrel of death earlier in the year, she finds it much easier now to take risks she might have been afraid to take a year earlier.

But she understands that she has to prepare hard in order to have a chance of accomplishing her goal.

Failure in her mission frightens her more than death. It's not just fear of disappointing someone else she is starting to admire and who believes in her. It's the thought of being confined by a South Yemeni prince, held as a slave or worse as a sex slave, with no one alive knowing what is happening to her. Ally has her convinced that New Rite's plan will work and that it will be the first of many missions they intend for her, so Clarissa is focused on making it happen.

First, though, she needs to complete her day's training run.

Up amidst the bristlecone pines, near the tree line, oxygen runs thin. Clarissa's pace slows substantially. Despite this, she presses on, knowing she only has weeks remaining to prepare, to look as hot and fit as possible.

Later in the day, Clarissa endures a far more punishing grind—voice lessons. Clarissa's cover requires her to be part of a girl's choir travelling to perform in the Middle East. Clarissa doesn't have to be a great singer to be in the choir. Ally has assured her of that. But she has to avoid being noticeably bad. Her voice coach assures her she has more work to do to reach that goal.

41   EVISCERATION

House floor debate on God's Law, the Golden Rule constitutional amendment, erupts into an intense battle over the future of Islam in the United States, a debate Chairman Henry consciously spurs. Henry watches from the sideline with mischievous glint in his good eye as dedicated Muslim and Christian members of Congress attack each other.

"How can you believe for even a minute that the Quran is the legitimate word of God when it embeds slavery as a natural human condition?" inquires a conservative Republican congresswoman from central Missouri.

"The Quran says no such thing," argues a Muslim member of Congress from Maryland's outer suburbs, a mid-life convert to Islam.

"Well then, tell me what verse 31 in Surah 24 means, when it instructs women to 'not to display their beauty except' to related men 'or their womenfolk, or what their right hands rule,'" demands the congresswoman, making quote marks with her fingers around relevant passages.

"I don't even get how you say this means the Quran endorses slavery," replies the Muslim congressman.

"Don't you get that 'what their right hands rule' is a reference to slaves, stating that women don't need to be modest in their dress around slaves they control," the congresswoman argues. "How can you, of all people a descendant of African American slaves, endorse a religion that glorifies slavery and suggests it is directly approved as the word of God?"

"You pull bits and pieces from our scriptures. How about your own? Have you read what Leviticus and Ephesians say about slavery? You dare to denounce my faith. Not only is use of slavery embedded in the faith of Christians and Jews, but you believe that God would demand a man sacrifice his son in order to prove his love. What kind of horrific man would slaughter his own son and what kind of tormented, brutal God would demand such a sacrifice?"

The Missouri congresswoman begins walking toward her verbal opponent but her voice continues to be picked up by a mobile voice capture system.

"First, God stopped the slaughter and many scholars believe Abraham mistook the instructions he was given. Second, Islam also traces its religious foundations to Abraham and Jesus so every attack you level against Christians and Jews, you level against your own faith," she says as she stands looking up at her Muslim colleague. Chairman Henry is seated fifty feet away, but the glow from his smile is captured as the camera pulls back to scan the House floor.

"Muhammad never instructed anyone to kill his own children," the Maryland Muslim argues.

"Is Muhammad your God? Or is it Allah?" the Missouri Christian congresswoman retorts. After his dismissive wave, she continues her argument. "Muhammad added his views to the faith of Abraham, views constructed during the brutality of life in the sixth and seventh centuries, and views that many adherents take as direction from God. The Hadith considers the views and actions of Muhammad during his life as direction from God, but Muhammad was not just a prophet during his life. He sought power and ruled over others, supporting the beheading of Jews and killing enemies in the process. Isn't it clear to you that religion and government must not intermingle?"

DOING UNTO OTHERS

The Muslim congressman stares down his Midwestern colleague, moving closer to her until he is looking directly down at her forehead. She doesn't back away. "It's clear to me. What I don't understand is why it isn't clear to you," he states, before sitting down and releasing tension that built high enough for the floor audience to now include a dozen members of the Sergeant at Arms staff.

Jill recognizes that allowing the debate to focus on religious scriptures and practices could destroy her coalition, which includes hundreds of key Islamic leaders and organizations and five of the seven Muslims in the House. She refuses to allow more of her time to be used on this topic. Having started this morning with more than eighty percent of House members in favor of the constitutional amendment, Jill decides to switch the tone of the debate and put Chairman Henry back on the defensive.

"Will the gentleman from Tennessee agree to engage in dialogue?" Jill asks.

"I will," Chairman Henry replies, moving to one of the floor podiums. His staffer flips open the Chairman's congressional Lifelink and taps to a screen that includes key message points. After a few misstatements in recent years created political turmoil, Chairman Henry has adopted a more cautious communications style. He agrees with his staff on message points in advance and then, often regardless of question, repeats those message points. Usually, he takes the time to cleverly bridge between reporters' or colleagues' questions to his message points. Sometimes, he simply ignores any surrounding context and simply repeats his message points. Jill has seen this practice in action in committee hearings and markup sessions. She's determined to get him off script and knows she'll have to work carefully.

"Mr. Chairman, do you agree that our nation's founders were right in stating that all men are created equal?" Jill asks.

Seeing a soft lob pitch over the middle of the plate, the Chairman can't resist. He winks at his staffer.

"I'm surprised to hear such a question from you, the gentlelady from Indiana," Chairman Henry says. "I would have expected you to be more sensitive to one of the key failures of our founders. Clearly, the Constitution, read literally, correctly acknowledges that all men are created equal in our rights. However, the Constitution failed to acknowledge that all women are created equal as well, even going so far as to deny women the right to vote."

Tempted to interrupt and assure the Chairman that she is aware of this failing, Jill knows it's better to remain silent. Still, she can't resist pointing out that the "all men are created equal" statement is contained in the Declaration of Independence, not in the Constitution.

The Chairman is unimpeded by her interruption.

"Perhaps even more important than denying women the right to vote was that our founders, in stating that all men are created equal, failed to acknowledge that all men should include all men, property owner or employee, black, white or otherwise, native or immigrant and that all men must mean all men and women and everyone in between. I would assume that the gentlewoman agrees with my remarks."

"I do, from the perspective of human interest," Jill retorts. "I might narrow the definition somewhat from the perspective of protecting national sovereignty to those immigrants who enter legally."

Chairman Henry senses another opportunity to tear support away from Jill's coalition. "Ah, I see that you don't believe that all men and women are created equal, wanting to treat some people who come here simply to feed their families differently than people who were born here." Immigration has long been a critical Democratic Party wedge issue. Every time the issue settles, Democrats offer new proposals for Republicans to oppose and then characterize their opponents as anti-immigrant. At times, elements of the party make the characterization easy.

"Just to make sure I understand you clearly," Jill counters. "You're saying that all men and women are created equal, or at least with equal rights, with no exception."

"That is exactly what I am saying," Chairman Henry responds, turning to smirk to his staffer.

"And under no circumstance, if I hear you correctly, do you believe that one class or race or sex should be treated in any way differently than any other."

"Clearly, that is correct. I think anyone who argues with this concept is a misogynist or racist or worse," Chairman Henry replies.

"So you would think poorly of any individual, myself included, if a person suggests that one class of person deserves to be treated differently than others?" Jill asks.

"The gentlewoman from Indiana has found the proper understanding. I would look at such ignorance as certain to be coming from leeches, usurpers or worse; people who latch onto the underbelly of a society and suck its nutrients until the society is malnourished and shrivels away," Chairman Henry replies.

"I would like to thank the gentleman for his apt and colorful description, a skill for which I am immensely jealous," Jill says, doing her best to maintain as neutral of facial expressions as possible. "Now if the gentleman would agree to continue, I would have a small set of additional questions I believe are relevant to the debate."

Chairman Henry agrees to continue, seeing the discussion as continuing to work tremendously in his favor.

"As a form of government, does the gentleman believe that anarchy is destined to fail in any large society?" Jill asks.

"I do. Most certainly," Chairman Henry replies. "I can think of no examples in the history of man in which anarchy prevailed as a form of government over any reasonable length of time and number of people."

"So do you believe that men and women, left to their own devices, are unable to create and build a peaceful, prosperous society without the establishment of some form of government?" Jill asks.

"I do, and assume you and everyone else in this chamber would agree with the proposition that the structures of government are necessary to create a free and fair society," the chairman responds.

"I certainly do agree with your statement, Mr. Chairman, and appreciate the clarity of your response," Jill notes. "Do you agree that the Constitution and its amendments provide the underlying structure for our form of government, a form that is essential to protecting the people of this nation from the perils of anarchy?" Jill asks, winking to reassure several of her colleagues who aren't sure where she is going with this argument.

"I do," Chairman Henry responds, after stopping for a few seconds to try figuring out where Jill is taking him.

"And do you agree that embedding the right to free speech, the right to assembly, the right to practice our own faith and other measures in the Constitution and its amendments have improved the nation's governance, to the benefit of the people of this nation?" Jill inquires.

"Certainly, as I suspect you and everyone else in this assembly would agree," the Chairman replies, surprised Jill is still tossing such softball questions during a debate of this significance.

Jill looks around the room at the dozens of members milling about on the House floor during the discussion or preparing for their chance to speak either for or against the God's Law amendment.

"Conceptually, do you believe in the Golden Rule?" Jill asks. "Do you believe that we should treat others as we want to be treated given an understanding of the circumstances and that we should not harm others in ways that we would not want to be harmed?"

"Of course I do," responds Chairman Henry. "This is the basis of common decency and I believe it is only decent to behave this way. However, as you know from our myriad of discussions, I don't believe this concept is workable in government because it subjects our people to constantly changing societal norms with no clear-cut yes-and-no rules on which people can rely to live their lives."

"Yes, Mr. Chairman, I understand that has been and is your concern," Jill says. "So, let me ask just one final question and I will turn the debate over to our next presenters."

Still formulating the question in her mind, Jill pauses for a couple of seconds. Chairman Henry grows impatient: "I'm ready," he states, attempting to spur her to speed up her pace of questioning.

"The people who would be held most accountable by the imposition of God's Law are those of us in government," Jill finally suggests. "I count dozens of laws that still exempt Congress or have modified impact on us. On top of this, many of the laws we set for political activity, including clarity of recognizing government obligations, are far looser than similar laws for business operations."

"The gentlewoman knows that those exemptions are in place to protect the separation of powers that is enshrined in our Constitution and to prevent abuse by the Executive Branch in enforcing laws in a discriminatory manner that could be driven by political purposes," Chairman Henry interjects.

"Yes, Mr. Chairman, I'm aware of the stated intent of these exemptions," Jill says. "But you would agree that, with these exemptions, Congress is imposing laws on the nation that it finds too onerous to comply with itself."

"Perhaps, but to protect the separation of powers," Chairman Henry responds.

"But, the Golden Rule, which you suggest is important to abide by in your life, says we should not do to others what we would not want done to ourselves," Jill states, opening her hands up and turning them out in a way many preachers would gesture when inviting their congregations to pray. "Do you agree?"

"That's what it says," Chairman Henry replies, exasperation clear in every word.

"Yet Congress often passes laws that exempt us from compliance and we hold ourselves to lower standards than the standards needed to have a fair and functioning government," Jill continues.

"To protect the intentions of the Constitution," Chairman Henry interjects, not waiting for time to be ceded.

"In doing this, we are saying that all men and women are, in fact, not . . . created equal, that there is a class that needs to be treated differently, are we not?" Jill asks.

"All men and women are created with equal, inalienable rights. Period," Chairman Henry contends, his voice rising in both volume and pitch.

Jill smiles at the cameras, reminding herself that appearance is critical during a discussion she hopes will be shown repeatedly. "So we would not want to create a political class with rights that are over and above the rights of the people?"

"Legislators are servants of the people and enjoy only equal rights with the people we represent," Chairman Henry argues in response to Jill's question.

"But it's true, is it not, that Congress is exempt from many of the regulations we've imposed on society?" Jill prods.

"I've already explained the purpose behind those exemptions and do not need to repeat myself," Chairman Henry replies in elevated voice.

Jill intentionally pauses. "Did you not say earlier that all men and all women are created equal, imbued with the same inalienable rights?"

"I did," the Chairman replies after failing to find a way to answer the question any differently.

"And did you not say that you would consider anyone who does not share your view as, open quote, leeches, usurpers and worse, people who latch onto the underbelly of a society and suck its nutrients until the society is malnourished and shrivels away, unquote?" Jill inquires.

"Perhaps something to that effect, though you have clearly taken my words out of context," he argues.

Jill doesn't give him time to continue: "Then, would you not be describing members of Congress and members of the executive branch who impose requirements on the American people while exempting ourselves from compliance with those same laws as leeches and usurpers?"

"I do not," Chairman Henry bellows, clearly seeing now where he is being taken and angry he allowed it to get to this point.

"Well, I would describe us in that fashion," Jill says, "if, when presented with the opportunity to pass a constitutional amendment to embed the fair and equal treatment of everyone in our society as a principle on which this nation should be governed, we decide to take a pass. Congress must be subject to the laws, ethics and morality we impose on others or we should not impose them. We must be accountable for the statements we make or we should not make them. We must allow fair and reasoned jurists an outlet to erase unfairness and incivility where it exists, even when Congress does not have the political will to tackle these issues. And we must ensure that, when confronted with the idea that all men and women are created equal, we not impose a form of governance that creates a special political class conferred with advantages and rights and priorities that do not exist for the rest of the American people."

Jill is on a roll, speaking at a rapid pace: "We must pass this constitutional amendment and start behaving as a society in a manner that those of faith and those who do not believe in a higher authority understand is the world in which we want to exist. Utopia cannot and will not exist on this earth. But we should not sprint from an opportunity to make this a better nation, to set an example of the decency that can be created in laws, in order to protect the rights and privileges of a select few in the political class, the 'leeches and usurpers' who destroy nations," Jill concludes. "With that, I yield back the balance of my time."

42 ATTRACTION

Clarissa is surprised her parents generate tears as they drop her off at the airport. The choir trip is just seven days. Two days to get to South Yemen, one day to take an escorted tour of the country and its capital, two days of public and private performances and two days to return. It's a long way to travel to perform in a few concerts, but the honorarium the prince pays covers all of the group's operating costs. Choir members train and perform free all year in return for this performance.

None of the choir members, and certainly not their parents, realize that the prince they are set to entertain was the last man convicted by an international war crimes tribunal for his roles in funding terrorists.

After a series of coincidental overlaps triggered an investigation, New Rite's intelligence team broke through the prince's cover story. JT invested significant resources to discover that the terrorist-supporting prince had taken over the identification and physical appearance of one of his well-respected brothers, a man as loved in the global interfaith community as Prince Taban is feared.

Changing planes at New York's JFK International Airport, Clarissa is struck by how large the plane is that will carry the group to South Yemen. Even with the size of the plane, she's also struck by how little legroom exists in the back of the plane. Getting her knees comfortable, though, is among the least of her concerns.

When she looks up, she sees a familiar face she hadn't expected.

"Al . . .," Clarissa starts to say, before seeing Ally raise her index finger to her mouth. Clarissa looks around, trying to figure out why Ally shushed her. As Ally waits to move back toward Clarissa, she sends Clarissa a message. Clarissa opens her Lifelink to read the rapidly disappearing message: "You don't know me. Name is Alycia. I'm the new travel planner and manager for the choir this week."

The reason for the message becomes clear as Ally sits next to Clarissa, displaying her passport. "Alycia Dunn," it reads.

Clarissa looks at her quizzically. Then Ally does something Clarissa rarely sees. She pulls out a pen and starts writing on paper.

"My cover," Ally writes, pointing to her passport. "Here as backup. Change in sample recovery strategy too."

Ally reaches into her backpack and pulls out a matchbook. Clarissa reaches over to put her hand to stop Ally from striking the match.

"Oh yeah. You're right," Ally says.

Ally looks at the paper for a couple of minutes, turning her head to see if she can find a disposal method that couldn't possibly be found by South Yemeni authorities. She rips the part of the paper where wording appears, puts it in her mouth and starts to chew. Then she gets out of her seat, walks to the back of the plane and spits the mashed wad around the catering truck and onto the tarmac.

Taking her seat again, Clarissa leans over and whispers to Ally: "What was that?"

"No evidence. Safe mission," Ally whispers into her ear.

Clarissa shakes her head, clearly not getting it.

Ally leans over to whisper again in her ear. "We'll be under constant watch. Even our garbage on this plane will be searched when we land and we'll be tailed the whole time we're in South Yemen."

Clarissa looks at Ally.

Other choir members haven't yet filled in the seats around them but Clarissa sees several now making their way down the aisles.

Clarissa spots her last chance.

"Is that why you wanted me to work out so intensely? And doing the splits during choir practice?"

"Your choir director is probably a scout for the prince. She'll get paid extra for sending you his way. I was worried you might be too old for him if she didn't see something to spark her interest."

Clarissa shakes her head, staring at Ally with her jaw dropped, trying to make sense of everything she has just heard.

"Remember," Ally says. "It's Alycia. We never met before."

As she finishes the comment, Ally and Clarissa stand to let one of Clarissa's choir mates take the window seat. Clarissa scrunches in next. Before Ally sits down, she asks another girl on the flight to point out the choir director and then introduces herself as the substitute travel manager for the choir's travel agency.

At London's Heathrow Airport, a New Rite team member bumps into Clarissa, handing her a small sheet of paper with instructions to follow Ally from a visible distance. Clarissa flips open the folded note, reads it and looks for Ally, who she sees waiting two hundred feet away past their new departure gate in front of the women's restroom. She follows her, but Ally walks farther away, not looking back for Clarissa. Ally takes an escalator down, turning around another hallway and stopping in front of a security door. She waits for Clarissa to see her, punches in the security code and steps through the door. When Clarissa reaches the door, she pushes on it. It won't open. Looking around, she sees no one looking at her and tries to push harder, still not opening. Then Clarissa flips open the note again, realizing the number 1791 is depressed into the note. She enters the code, walks through the door and sees Ally and the man who handed her the note with several items spread on a desk top in front of them.

"Quick, Clarissa, we only have ten minutes before we'll be missed for boarding the charter," Ally asserts. "I need to show you how to use a new DNA capture technique we've created in case you don't get a chance to take a sample with the hand stickers I showed you earlier."

Clarissa looks around the room, checking the ceilings, walls and corners.

"That noise you hear is an audio scrambler, if that's what you're looking for," Ally states.

"I was wondering what that was," Clarissa replies, turning her head back toward Ally and her colleague.

"Anyway," Ally continues. "We've found out the prince doesn't let new women touch him with their hands. As you approach to meet him, you'll be instructed to hold your hands behind your back and to kiss his hand. Even though these stickers are clear, you can't have it visible on the outside of your lips as you approach or you'll be discoverable. So we've worked to make sure the back stickers work in a wet environment."

"What?" Clarissa says, clearly confused.

"You'll need to place it on the inside of your bottom lip, then as you kiss his hand, you roll your lips up so that the inside of your bottom lip comes into direct contact with his skin. The tiny prick will inject as soon as it recognizes it is in contact with DNA other than your own and take a tiny skin sample from the prince."

Clarissa shakes her head again and takes a deep breath, trying to make sure she understands the instructions.

"I'll show you," Ally continues. She taps her finger on a button on her blouse, a blouse similar to the ones Clarissa is wearing along with all of her choir colleagues for the flight and later under her robe for the performance. As she does, she shows Clarissa that she had pulled off a clear covering on the button. She takes this covering with her index finger and presses the tip of her finger to the inside of her bottom lip. A second later, she grabs her colleague's hand, pulls it up to her mouth so Clarissa can see, kisses his hand and gently rolls her bottom lip up to bend over on the man's hand.

"Felt it," he says.

"Now your turn," Ally states.

"Wait, if he feels it, won't the prince?" Clarissa asks.

"Good question," Ally says, "but the prince will be so delighted that your lips are lingering on his hands that he won't be thinking about the tiny little prick he feels."

"If I wasn't focusing on it, I'm not sure I would have noticed," Ally's colleague adds.

Clarissa's eyes are fully dilated. "Are you sure this will work?"

"We certainly hope so," Ally's colleague interjects. "It's the safest capture method we've been able to contemplate."

"Can you tell me yet why you need his DNA?"

"We'll tell you once we get you home," Ally replies. "It's better that you not know until then or you'll risk being exposed. You're not a trained liar yet."

The day of the private Prince Taban choir performance arrives. Clarissa makes sure she is wearing the right blouse under her robe as a series of seventy-two-foot stretch limousines arrive to pick up the choir from the hotel. The girls all line up in the hotel lobby. It's beginning to make sense to Clarissa now. The choir is based in New York. Clarissa has practiced with them only by remote. She had thought they were able to see her during practice but none of the girls on the flight recognized her or even realized she was part of the choir until they saw her uniform.

Now Clarissa is traveling with the choir director in a separate car for the performance, again keeping her separated from the other girls. At first, she thought she was receiving special treatment. Now she understands she is being isolated.

After the first day's performance, the choir members line up for the chance to kiss the prince's hand, all delighted for the opportunity to meet a prince who is younger and more attractive than any of them had expected, and with a reputation as one of the world's most caring leaders.

When Clarissa's turn arrives, she is fully prepared but the line moves too quickly. She has little time to think when her turn arrives and she realizes he is wearing a glove that covers all but his fingers. Her chance to capture the DNA passes without success.

Disappointed in herself, Clarissa begins to tear up as she walks away, turning back to look at the prince as she does. She realizes now that his eyes have continued to follow her. He walks over, takes her hand to walk outside of sight of the remainder of the choir. Once out of sight, the prince grabs Clarissa, pulling her head down to his shoulder, rubbing his hands through her hair and down her back.

She feels pressure against her thighs and backs away startled. Seeing the prince shocked that she has backed away, she reaches out, pulls his hand toward her, removes his glove, grabs his hand with hers and kisses around his index finger, rolling her bottom lip to trigger the DNA capture device.

"I think we need to spend some time together," he tells Clarissa.

"I can't on this trip, but if you invite me back, I can come back alone. Soon," Clarissa tells him, just as Ally had trained her to say if she was caught alone with him.

"And, I guess I'll be back tomorrow," Clarissa says as she backs away from the prince and makes sure she is back in sight of the other girls, all of whom are now trying to determine why she is getting special attention. Clarissa walks back to her place in line, knees shaking nearly uncontrollably. She looks over toward Ally, who is sitting in the back of the room and making facial motions to remind Clarissa to breathe.

Back at the hotel, the choir director calls all of the girls in for an impromptu practice before the next day's performance.

"I'm very proud of the performance today," the director says, "with one glaring, embarrassing exception. Our new girl chose this day to make a spectacle of herself, drawing attention away from the rest of this team. Choirs can only perform at their peak if everyone acts with mutual understanding and respect for the other members of the team so we are sending the new girl home tonight."

Seated in the back of the room to watch the rehearsal, Ally realizes the plan is about to go bad.

"I've had your new travel arrangements made," the director says to Clarissa without ever using her name in front of the group, a statement Ally is almost certain is not true. "A car will be out front for you in two hours. Go to your room, shower and pack your luggage for departure tonight."

Clarissa runs out of the room, ashamed that she has disappointed the choir and runs up to her room. Ally searches for a chance to escape the room without being noticed, waiting for more than ten minutes until the choir gathers on stage to rehearse and the director's attention refocuses on music.

Ally calls in to New Rite command for an immediate roof extraction. The unusual number of reported private plane crashes with American victims in recent years now makes sense. The crashes were all covers for kidnappings. A New Rite team, waiting offshore, launches an APB from inside a fishing vessel and races for the hotel.

Ally waits down the hall outside Clarissa's room, knowing Clarissa's room is almost certainly bugged and equipped with multiple video cameras. Hair still wet—Clarissa was in no mood to dry her hair knowing all she would be doing is sitting on a plane for more than a day—Clarissa spots Ally as she walks out of the room.

Ally points to the exit stairs. Clarissa follows.

"To the roof," Ally says. "We're being extracted now. You are about to be taken if we don't."

Clarissa follows Ally, who stops Clarissa long enough to put her luggage on an elevator and send it down to the ground floor. Ally scans Clarissa for any evidence of other tracking devices.

"You're clean," Ally says.

"I just showered," Clarissa replies.

"That's not what I mean," Ally responds, waving for Clarissa to follow her.

After ascending three flights of steps, Ally and Clarissa are at the rooftop exit, 120 floors above ground. Clipping off the lock and opening the door, Ally realizes they've triggered an alarm.

"Five minutes max," Ally whispers into a communication device.

On the roof, Ally constructs a bar from rooftop cooling unit metal to keep the access door from opening easily, then walks toward the edge of the roof. Lying flat, she pulls her head over the edge to see dozens of police and military vehicles racing toward the hotel.

"They found your luggage," Ally says. "Now they're coming for you."

"Who's coming for me?"

"The prince is coming for his prize. You're this year's prize."

"What?"

"For the last four years, this choir has been coming to perform for this prince," Ally tells Clarissa. "Every year, one girl has died in a plane crash and it's always the out of town girl nobody else knows."

Clarissa is stunned, and angry: "You knew he was going to kidnap me?"

"We figured that out part way through the mission. That's why I had to inject myself into the trip," Ally says. "We couldn't figure out how none of the other girls noticed or complained when the extractions happened."

"Is that why you need his DNA?" Clarissa questions.

"The prince never leaves his compound anymore. His security is too great for us to rescue the girls he kidnaps unless we get him and his main security out of the compound."

Clarissa looks back at the roof door, hoping it's still shut. "So how does having his DNA help?" she asks.

"I'll tell you once we're out of here," Ally offers.

Seconds later, Ally wraps on an extraction jacket clipped to the end of the dropped rope, latches Clarissa to her, pulls on the rope and starts a rapid upward climb.

Clarissa screams out: "Holy . . . ."

43 LIBERATION

It's a quick turnaround before Ally's next mission for New Rite, returning to South Yemen to release micro-drone fleas over Prince Taban's compound. New Rite's Red Sea fishing boat is one of only two naval vessels in New Rite's arsenal. Designed to appear every bit a fishing vessel to anyone passing by or even boarding and looking around, the boat has a sub-hull door below which one of New Rite's APBs is stored, along with any equipment that wouldn't normally be found on a fishing vessel. Sonar would normally detect the large below-boat protrusion, but the same gecko-like skin on the sub-hull and detection avoidance technology that protects the APBs in flight has been modified to protect this vessel from sonar.

The primary challenge in preventing detection of the boat is getting the sub-hull in and out of ports during fishing runs as well as protecting the crew from pirate raids that continue to plague the Red Sea and several other areas. Pirates never make it close enough to attack, having their hulls shredded by New Rite missiles and captains taken out by New Rite snipers well before they ever get close enough to raid the vessel. Only a few have tried, as most pirates search for bigger scores than the modest fishing vessel offers. Those who have tried disappeared with their boats into the sea or ocean.

Once Clarissa and Ally land on the fishing vessel, Ally and her mission team check every aspect of the APB, waiting patiently for launch time. When an opportunity opens, Ally and her three-person crew launch, sprinting toward the prince's compound. Hovering ten thousand feet above the compound, her crew releases the micro-drones and the salt-mine-based operating team takes manual control of all ten drones. They have a limited window to complete their mission, a time span that shrinks as strong winds require flea drone operators to use more power than planned just to drop down into the prince's compound.

Once inside the compound, the micro-drones follow pre-planned routes to ensure the target is identified and attacked. The flea drone first reaching the prince finds him, as expected, in his massive bed-room wing. Rather than in bed, the crew manning the drones, including New Rite drone master Lou, is startled that the prince has a young girl's arms tied up to a rope over her head. Her robe is tattered and lying at her feet on the floor. The prince winds back, holding a horse whip in his hands and swings mightily, striking the girl across her back, drawing blood and screams of pain.

The drone operators try to stay focused on the mission, a challenge made difficult by the adrenaline surging through their bodies. Lou flies her flea drone to ceiling height to avoid the lash of the whip before dropping down to the top of the prince's head.

A translation program prints what the prince is saying: "Beat your disobedient wives, Allah instructs. Did I give you a choice? You will take me when and how I want you to take me."

A New Rite drone operator who is also a Muslim reacts in fury, pounding on his desk: "Fool. He thinks Allah made him God."

Lou guides her flea-drone down the back of the prince's head, set-tling on the back of his neck, before taking a bite. The prince feels the bite and stops whipping the girl long enough to swat at his neck. Lou darts the drone sideways and up, trying to avoid capture. The prince takes his whip and begins whipping into the air, narrowly missing the flea-drone before Lou guides it down the hallway and out an open window.

"We need to send your team back to stop the prince now, before this girl is killed," the Muslim drone operator argues to JT after maneuvering his drone into open air and flying as far away from the compound as possible before its energy source drains.

"We can't," JT says. "It would be a suicide mission for now. That's why we need to make him sick."

It will take six hours before the prince feels the full effects of his virus, but the first signs of weakness cramp him in just a matter of minutes.

"We just have to hope this girl is taking a normal beating, that he thinks of her as a believer worthy of some mercy rather than an outright infidel," JT states.

With the fleas safely released, Ally's APB pulls up fifty thousand feet, above the level any commercial aircraft is expected to fly. She hovers, watching from above, until the prince departs the compound.

Ally's anger encourages her to disobey orders and drop into the compound right away, but Ally's team is too small to extract the girls safely with Prince Taban's full security force in the compound.

Prince Taban does not relax, even after slapping his whipped wife unconscious. He sits on the throne-like chair beside his bed, still angry that this girl he honored by taking her as his fourth wife resists his affection. It's not that he hasn't taken her, of course, but it's always a fight that leaves him not feeling fully appreciated.

"Can she not see that her arguments force me to hurt her," he yells at a guard. *"I honor her and she disrespects me. I give her one more chance. She has no right to play with my emotions."*

While waiting for another of his wives to be brought to him, sweat forms on Taban's face and brow. Rumblings from his stomach tell him all is not right. At first, he figures the nausea is residual anger at having to endure the insolence of his youngest wife. The desire to vomit grows. His energy drains. By the time his first wife arrives to his room, he has lost interest in sharing his gifts with her and sends for the compound nurse to take care of him.

Arriving in the bedroom, the nurse runs to the beaten wife.

"*Not her. Leave her,*" he orders in Arabic, his voice noticeably weaker than he expected. "*Me.*"

The last of the drone fleas departs as a doctor arrives, its energy down to its last five minutes, perhaps just enough time to get outside the compound wall before imploding. Thirty minutes later, all but two of the prince's twenty-four-man security force leave the compound, two flying by helicopter with Prince Taban. The doctor barks instructions to keep him cool as his temperature soars past 106 degrees. The other guards race toward Dhamar General Hospital to set up a security perimeter.

As Ally and team descend, sharpshooters on the APB use traditional rifles to take down two remaining guards who had come running to the helicopter pad assuming Prince Taban had quickly returned.

With the guards down, the New Rite team faces little resistance from the servant staff, only a few of whom leave their assigned quarters or work stations to figure out what is happening and whether they are under any threat.

Entering the room where the American girls are held, Ally yells out: "Americans, here to rescue you." The girls stare in bewilderment, still escaping the depths of sleep.

Ally searches the room. Three heads pop up. "Only three here? Where's the fourth?"

One of the girls, captive for just two years, is the first to figure out that the words from this strange woman and her soldiers are in English.

"Yes, yes, four. Serena with prince. Her night," the girl says. "You take us?"

Ally waves at the soldiers to take the three girls to the APB. She sprints toward the prince's bedroom, stopping only when encountered by three fully covered women who are most likely the prince's public wives. She looks at them, points her assault rifle toward them and all three quickly turn and run.

Inside the prince's bedroom, Ally tries to control her anger as she finds Serena passed out, hanging by her wrists from the ropes, streaks of blood running down her still-bare back.

Ally kneels under Serena, lifts her by pressing her shoulder up into Serena's gut, then reaches up and slashes through the robe. As she does, Serena screams as the wounds on her back rip further as her body bends over Ally's shoulder. Ally grabs Serena's robe from the floor, throws it on top of her and begins sprinting toward the APB.

"I'm taking you home," Ally says, as Serena pounds on her back in agony as her wounds tear apart. "American," Ally continues. "Rescue. Home to America."

Before she reaches the APB, a black clad woman, wearing full hijab to deal with the stranger in her home, steps out from a bedroom door. Ally quickly spots her pistol. Before the woman can fire, Ally unleashes a barrage of gunfire, sending her body splattering to the ground.

Ally throws Serena roughly to two of the New Rite soldiers, drawing another scream from Serena as Ally jumps to the pilot's spot. She triggers the APB to lift up. Seconds later, the APB is ten thousand feet in the air, the girls on board have all coated the floor of the APB with vomit having not had time to be equipped with oxygen support masks and Ally sets the APB toward the fishing boat for a quick refueling before beginning the long flight back to the United States.

"Where are we going?" one of the girls, now nearly seventeen, asks.

"We're taking you home," a New Rite soldier replies.

"Where's that?" she replies.

"America."

"Allah be merciful," the girl replies.

An expansive site lies empty in Detroit's night except for coyotes, rats, deer and other wildlife that are returning this one-time urban wasteland to a more natural state. Nature makes inroads day-by-day, night-by night. Time-series photography captures the natural reclamation efforts as part of a charitable foundation's project to determine how long it takes the planet to recover from various levels of human impact.

The Center for Urban Recovery of the Environment (CURE) bought the homes, parks, long-shattered industrial buildings and other sites in the eight-thousand-acre center over a period of more than a decade, hiding their desire for complete control of the land until the last of the territory had been purchased. Dilapidated homes were bought for thousands and sometimes only hundreds of dollars from owners who abandoned Detroit for the sole purpose of survival. Industrial sites were gifted to CURE in part so prior owners could escape the range of environmental liabilities they could have incurred if they remained owners and, in part, so the owners could avoid exorbitant property tax increases as the Detroit City Council scampered to unravel nearly a century of mismanagement, corruption and cronyism that had left its citizens waiting for basic police and ambulance services so long that few survived serious criminal encounters.

Once it had acquired all of the land for its study project, CURE built a series of fortified walls around the site, ostensibly to ensure that the study's results could be proven as pristine over its one-hundred-year span before CURE would be converted into a permanent nature preserve as directed by its founder. Openings in the walls allowed animals to enter and leave at will during the initial years of the project, but are now completely closed as the city around CURE is recovering and wants to avoid wildlife roaming its streets. Two openings into CURE remain. The main entrance, the one known and visible to people who come to see the Center, accepts as many as five thousand people daily who come to take the center's recently completed treetop walking tour of the environment.

The three-hour tour begins at an education center outside the wall, and continues along fortified, often tree-top-level enclosed clear walkways that allow visitors to walk through homes with plants growing through the floors, rats taking over guest rooms and beehives taking over pantries. Inside former industrial buildings, baby coyotes fight and tumble in play, resting only for sips of mother's milk. Tree roots shatter building foundations. Molds and mildews spread through remnants of homes.

Halfway through the tour, visitors drop into the centralized research buildings, which biologists, entomologists, and other CURE researchers use as the base to conduct their research.

Three of the scientists visiting the center today aren't here to study nature. Instead, they are here to meet JT Alton, Chairman of the Board and the largest funder of CURE's mission.

"We need to be sure that this is written on paper he would have, with a writing instrument he would use, in an exact replica of the handwriting samples we have and in perfectly rhythmic Arabic, as he would use to communicate to the prince," JT says to Ramon, who is wearing cheek and nose implants, colored contact lenses and a wig to disguise his appearance for this aboveground meeting. When Ramon tires of the confines of the salt mine, needing to see the sky and breathe fresh air, he ascends the two-man elevator to the bottom of the research center, entering JT's private office and walking out to his patio. Even in this protected environment, JT insists that Ramon remain disguised and Ramon complies readily, knowing the risks he faces if found alive.

"I'm certain this is the right paper," Ramon replies, holding up a pink piece of construction paper, "and this ink is just as thin as the writing the cartel received from General Timur. General Hernández used to keep these sheets in his office, I presume to be able to use them against General Timur if he ever needed to. General Timur was the only man Hernández feared. He knew Timur saw him as an infidel and would come after him when he no longer served Timur's goals.

"Then my friends next door will do their best. Stay here so I can show you the results of their work and get your approval," JT tells Ramon.

Next door, JT works with three experts, a handwriting reconstruction expert and two experts in Arabic. It takes hours to perfect the message, most of which is consumed with the Arabic experts contending they have created the more rhythmic Arabic version of the message JT asks them to create: *"Your betrayal of Allah exceeds that of the People of the Book. Shirk warrants none of Allah's mercy."*

All of the experts believe JT is working on a children's book about Allah. He has studied English versions of the Quran and the Hadith for years, but his knowledge of Arabic is barely infantile. He has consulted the Arabic experts on many occasions, paying them handsomely for their time, in an effort to understand the Quran unfettered by the alterations of the cleric class that has constrained Islam since early in the twelfth century. It was then that Islam's golden age ended when ijtihad, the direction of Muhammad to each believer to personally discover Islam's meaning, was frozen so that only the cleric class was allowed to define Islam in most Islamic sects.

The handwriting reconstruction expert has been told the handwriting he is attempting to replicate is similar to the writing done for one of Islam's earliest ruling caliphs.

When the note is finished, JT brings it back to his office, where Ramon pronounces that it looks to be an original note like the ones Hernández received from Timur in English.

Ally and her team must launch one more mission to South Yemen; to ensure this note is delivered to Prince Taban in his hospital room.

Ally and her team consider alternate methods to get the message to the prince. New Rite can't directly deliver the note to Taban and have it be taken seriously. General Timur's courier will be frightened by the message and would be sure to reach back to the general to confirm its authenticity.

In the mine, they test whether the note is light enough to be transported to the prince by micro-drone, then debate for hours how to get a drone carrying a message this large past security particularly without the drone being spotted.

"Is there any chance a drone can move the paper without being spotted?" Ally asks Abhirim Roussard, leader of the drone operations team.

"Sure, with a little fairy dust," he replies.

Ally paces for a moment.

"Great idea," she says after several seconds of silence.

"What?"

"Attach the paper to the bottom of the drones and then we'll fly them so that only the paper can be seen," Ally says.

"Them?" Abe asks.

"Yes, we'll need backup, in case the first doesn't get through," Ally replies. "Can you add an exploding component to the drone so it looks like it's being delivered in a puff of fairy dust?"

After an extended, heated debate with his team, Abhirim returns to tell Ally: "We can do it but you know these drones aren't cheap. I mean, it's not easy to put something that small together and we're just going to blow them up?"

"A little fairy dust. What makes a message more believable to someone in a delusional state than seeing it delivered in a puff of fairy dust?" Ally asks.

Modifications to the micro-drones take weeks to finalize and test, with detonator controls added to the operating controls.

Inside Dhamar General, Prince Taban lies flat, sweating profusely with fluids pumping into his body to try controlling a temperature that continues to exceed 106 degrees. The prince is fully delusional, struggling mightily to survive what doctors tell him is a new, previously unknown version of swine flu.

Looking up from his bed, he sees a sheet of pink paper flying over him. He tries reaching for it, but doesn't have the strength. He stares in awe as the paper floats down to rest on him, while a tiny bug hovers above him.

"Guards," he whispers, the microphone attached to his lip ensuring he is heard. Six guards race into the room. "Flea. Swat."

The guards look for the flea, trying to hit it with their hand.

Finally, Ally makes the call.

"Blow it," she orders.

A quick press later, the fleas explode, dropping what looks to be tiny metallic dust.

"What . . . was . . . that?" the prince whispers.

"What is that?" one of the guards asks, pointing to the paper on top of the prince's chest.

"This . . . flew . . . in," the prince whispers, catching his breath between each word.

"From General Timur," the prince's chief bodyguard calls out, before grabbing the note to read it.

"What . . . does . . . it . . . say?"

The guard looks at the paper, looks at the prince, looks back at the paper and then turns back to the prince.

"Your disease," the guard says, "appears to have been a gift from General Timur."

"What?"

"He says you have turned from Allah, that you worship other gods," the guard says. "And that you must die as Allah commands."

Even more frightened now, the prince looks at his guard. "You . . . know . . . this . . . is . . . not . . . true," Prince Taban argues meekly, fighting exhaustion with each word. "Before . . . I . . . die, . . . revenge . . . on . . . Timur . . . and . . . whoever . . . secures . . . it . . . will . . . have . . . my . . . wealth, . . . my . . . wives . . . and . . . my . . . servants."

Exhausted by the surge of exertion, Prince Taban falls asleep. His guards argue among themselves whether the prince's commitment is likely to be honored and worth going after General Timur to secure.

The last flea drone is flown out of the hospital room. The note appears to have done its job.

Following House passage of the God's Law amendment with nearly ninety percent of the vote, the Senate follows suit with only two dissenters.

44 · REJUVENATION

When General Timur's guards return from scouting surrounding mountains, they again bring disturbing news. The mountain borders with the Kazakh province have been breached again. Fresh tracks. It's not clear if it is the same people who found them earlier.

"*One hour until departure,*" General Timur announces in Arabic. A team of his twelve most trusted soldiers pack up gear, burying anything they need to leave behind in case someone finds the caves. Still, General Timur worries that the team will be tracked by satellite, easily distinguishable from the snow-capped mountains at the beginning of their hike. He can call for helicopter pickup but that will only increase the number of people aware of this location.

The group separates, hiking out in three directions. General Timur travels in one of the groups of four, hoping that the largest group will be the one that attracts any attention as that group hikes toward Almaty. General Timur and his three guards travel south, crossing rough, snowy terrain on their way toward Issyk-Kul, the second largest mountain lake in the world.

General Timur is heading to the certain safety of the submarine-station units parked at the bottom of Issyk-Kul.

"No one will find us or reach us once we are at the bottom of the lake," he assures his three traveling companions as they extract themselves from their inconvenient mountain residence.

"It'll be good to be safe, but we'll be alone with just four men," the guard replies. *"Allah is testing our faith."*

"It's no different than being in the caves," the General dismissively reassures him.

"Perhaps," the guard replies, thinking but not saying anything about his frequent encounters with an older woman tending to her sheep that he encountered during his patrols. *"Will we be able to visit town if we need?"*

General Timur wouldn't normally tolerate expressions of timidity, but he only has a handful of troops on whom he can rely. He can't afford to execute any more. *"Only at certain times of the year. Otherwise, we'll be detected."*

A fairly uneventful trek leads Timur's group to Cholpon Ata, a resort village in Kyrgyzstan beautiful enough to house a summer home for the tiny nation's President and small enough that newcomers are quickly identified. Timur and his three travel companions follow a mountain stream the last several kilometers as they descend from snow caps into the edge of town, stopping where the steppe mountains edge along small farm fields. Only after nightfall makes spotting their unconventional arrival less likely do they walk the final two kilometers to the marina, where the marina's full-time operators have prepared their arrival.

One of the general's travel companions will head down first, connect and ensure that the water and oxygen stations are fully operating. Once opened, he'll head back to the below-pier launch to pick up the general for a quick inspection run. Two more food re-stock visits will take place before he brings the fourth in their group to the sub-sea station. They will return from the station to civilization just in time to change it, forever.

"Our prayers, our reading and our planning will keep us very busy," General Timur assures them before the first submarine dive. *"We must succeed to assure that Allah opens his kingdom to us for eternity."*

Another guard gleams. *"Is it time? Is it the day of reckoning for the infidels?"*

"All will soon face Allah's wrath," General Timur states. *"But we can have no more mistakes like we had with the Great Satan. We cannot involve infidels in our plans."*

"Do we have enough men to execute your plans, General?" the guard asks as he leads him to the underground launch. Even in rapidly approaching winter, the lake remains unfrozen. In English, Issyk-Kul translates to "hot lake."

"Focus on where you're going first. Allah will provide us the resources to do his work if we focus our full attention on executing his plans."

"Yes, General," the guard replies, focusing on his control panels.

Mid-term elections in 2042 deliver a stunning victory to President Phillipi, one that is clearly unusual in American history. Presidential parties typically lose seats in mid-term elections taking place just two years after their election. This is particularly true of presidents who've been reelected to second terms. By the time a president has spent six years in office, the national political pendulum has generally plateaued and begun to swing rapidly the opposite direction.

As an independent, President Phillipi's policies seem to attract alternating opposition from either the Democratic or Republican party infrastructures, and sometimes from both. To offset this structural intransigence, the President has become the ultimate retail politician. He actively endorsed and campaigned for legislators from both major parties as well as a large number of independents who supported sizable portions of his agenda. His political calculus was complex. In a heavily liberal district, he would endorse Democrats closest to his positions with a chance to win in the open primary. President Phillipi went so far as to campaign with Democrats he endorsed if they were one of two candidates to advance to the general election. He did the same for many Republicans, always with an eye toward securing support for his upcoming legislative initiatives as well as rewarding those who had supported him in the past. The mid-term elections brought an unprecedented number of independents into the new Congress; twenty-one in the Senate and 173 in the House of Representatives.

Remarkably, President Phillipi supported fully two-thirds of the new Senate and three-quarters of the incoming House in their most recent elections. The President's popularity as a war hero—personally participating in the effort to destroy the cartel and anti-American nations who had invaded the Southwest United States—made him the most trusted President since President Dwight D. Eisenhower and a welcome endorser by nearly every candidate.

His popularity was further aided when he came out in strong opposition to a grassroots campaign to eliminate the twenty-second amendment, which would have allowed him to run for a third term as President. He neither wanted a third term nor thought it was a wise idea to allow third terms for future presidents.

"Even though I came to office fully willing and perhaps even desiring to be a one-term president," President Phillipi said in a nationally broadcast speech in which he announced his opposition to the grassroots campaign, "it has become abundantly clear to me that thousands of staff who serve this country with honor also harbor their own personal desires. In many cases, those personal desires include maintaining their positions of power as long as possible. As I strengthen my relationship with staff, I felt an increasing tug during my first term to emphasize reelection considerations, sometimes at the expense of what I believed to be in the best long-term interests of the nation. It's human to feel this tug. We don't want presidents to feel this tug as an endless cycle. It's also critical that our nation be in a continuing pattern of growth and rebalancing. That growth, that rebalancing may not occur fast enough when power is held by too few for too long."

After extensive reflection, President Phillipi decides that as he steps aside, his legacy must include leaving the nation in the hands of a leader he can trust.

Vice President Marcia Wilt and Congresswoman Jill Carlson receive invitations to join the President for a weekend in the wooded hills and resort-like comfort of Camp David, just an hour outside of Washington, D.C.

When Jill arrives, she finds that the President and Vice President have pulled chairs up near the fireplace, President Phillipi sipping a cold, low-calorie beer and Vice President Wilt resting a glass of cabernet sauvignon on the table between them. A platter of fruits, cheeses, dips and thin crackers also sits between them, with a glass of pinot grigio brought to Jill as she takes a seat to join them.

"It truly is a special treat to be invited here," Jill says as she sits, crosses her legs, sips from her wine and places it on the table. "I'm anxious to know your purpose but I trust you'll tell me when the time is right."

Vice President Wilt often displays the wear of decades in national politics: a few more wrinkles than the average Social-Security-collection-aged American, grey increasingly allowed to accent her shoulder-length sweep as she acknowledges that middle-age is in her past, and shapes inverted from concave to convex where she prefers concave and from convex to sagging where convex would be welcome. Perhaps it's the light, but she appears more youthful than she has in at least a decade.

"One of the characteristics I love about you, Jill, is that you're always a straight shooter and don't waste time playing games," Vice President Wilt interjects. "The President and I have discussed the nation's future extensively over the years, but even more so in recent weeks with the mid-terms behind. We wanted to discuss one of the conclusions we reached in a setting where you would have time to reflect on your answer before responding."

Jill sits up even straighter than her normally strong posture before leaning toward the Vice President, turning her head back and forth between the President and Vice President. Instinctively, Jill clasps her hands in front of her, resting her elbows on her knees as she does.

President Phillipi puts his hand lightly on Marcia's hand, letting her know he wants to speak. The President has a stronger personal relationship with Jill than does the Vice President.

"Jill, I'll be endorsing Marcia to be the next President. For me, it's an honor and privilege to support Marcia after so many years in which she has been an extraordinary, trusted advisor," President Phillipi states. "Besides, she's the only candidate who has experience as President," he continues with a wry smile, referencing that Marcia's presidency during his temporary cartel compound raid incapacitation.

"There's only one way I could be more proud and honored on that day," the President continues. "That would be if I could also announce my endorsement and support for you as her running mate for Vice President of the United States."

Jill is frozen in her seat. Of all the topics she contemplated might be raised at Camp David, this is one that hadn't even crossed her mind, even after stewing about why he had not invited Professor Stark to join her. Looking over at Vice President Wilt, she sees a broad, beaming smile on Marcia's face, one that wipes away every wrinkle that accumulated on Marcia's face during her decades of public service.

"Jill, I've given this great consideration," the Vice President adds. "I know of no one who can better assist me in keeping our nation together, fixing our intractable problems and preparing for a generation of peaceful prosperity than you. I knew, though, that this offer, actually this request, would come out of the blue for you and that you would need time to contemplate it before deciding. Marc was very generous in bringing us here to have this discussion."

Jill grabs her wine glass, taking a less-than-lady-like gulp. She presses her hands together at her lips.

"I'm truly honored, and perhaps shocked more than anything," Jill responds. "I, . . . I don't even know how to respond right now. I haven't ever even thought about the possibility of serving in the White House . . . "

"Well, to be clear," Marcia says with a wink, "your actual home will be up the street a bit, but you'll be working in the White House as my closest advisor."

"I understand, but, whew," Jill exhales. "I'm so honored. But I hope you won't mind if I take some time to wrap my mind around this?"

"Not a problem at all," Vice President Wilt responds. "Marc had suggested to me that you might be too stunned to answer right away.

He suggested that we come out here so we can talk, so that you can reflect and ask questions."

Jill rests her elbows on the arms of her chair, makes loose fists with both hands and starts pumping her hands up and down so rapidly that President Phillipi is distracted.

"What is this?" the President says, pointing toward Jill's hands.

"Oh, my God," Jill replies. "Sorry, when I was a kid, the milking machines broke down sometimes. I've milked a lot of cows by hand. I did a lot of thinking when I had to milk. I thought I'd broken that habit after so much teasing in high school."

"Teasing?" the President says, asking for an explanation.

Marcia replicates the motion with one hand. "Get it?" she asks as she looks at the President.

"Oh, got it," he replies, turning bright red. "Yes, you definitely need to lose that motion."

After nearly an hour of discussion on what Marcia expects her Vice President to work on, Jill feels her brain ready to overheat. "Do you mind if I take a walk for a bit?" Jill asks. "My heart is racing a hundred miles a minute and I need to think."

"I figured that would be the case," President Phillipi responds, standing up to show Jill where she needs to head. "There's a walking path around the grounds, boots to keep your feet warm and jackets if you need one. An agent will show you the way and then walk behind you to make sure you don't get lost or anything."

Jill excuses herself and changes into warm jogging clothes she brought with in case she ended up with free time.

Stretching as soon as she steps outside, Jill looks around to find the Secret Service agent assigned to her waiting just at the corner of the house.

She's shaking a bit in the cold during the first few steps, but knows her body will warm up soon enough as she runs. Her Secret Service agent jogs ten steps behind, yelling out infrequently to ensure Jill sees which way the path turns.

The timing of a run for Vice President couldn't be better. It also couldn't be worse.

Only days earlier, Jill and Professor Stark decided they wanted to adopt. They are already working on adoption papers, wanting to submit them before they leave on their honeymoon. Though he would be happy to take the risk of having children themselves, Jill is worried she'll pass on the cancer gene that killed her mother when Jill was a teen. Besides, though Jill and Professor Stark both think of themselves as young, Jill's biological childbearing capabilities are already into the years when added complications can crop up.

"Does this mean putting off a family even longer? Can I be Vice President and raise young children properly?" Jill questions herself as she runs, while acknowledging that raising young children while having to travel back and forth to a congressional district might be even more of a burden. "What about the wedding? Will Paul and I have any chance to really be husband and wife if I'm in this job? Would he quit his job and move with me?"

Jill desperately wants to talk to Paul, her father and her sister before making a decision. Before making those calls, ones Marcia already encouraged her to make, she needs to get straight in her head whether she wants to do it and, if she does, what she is really asking of them.

At various points during her run, Jill's thinking grows so intense she doesn't realize she is barely moving. Cold, chill winds remind her when she isn't jogging fast enough. Jill picks up her pace for another stretch before another deep thought strikes her, her legs slowing down as the synapses in her brain increase their connection rapidity.

Back inside the compound home, Jill showers while continuing her internal dialogue.

After cleaning up, Jill's first call is to her father, who for twenty-five years since Jill's mother's death has kept the family dairy farm going despite enormous struggle. Jill's sister and husband are with her dad when Jill calls so he quickly puts the call up on screen.

"Dad, I called you through a government encryption service to make sure our call isn't overheard. Is there anyone else there besides you, Jane and Walt?" Jill asks, wanting to be certain no one else overhears the discussion. A sure-fire way to cut short a political career is to be caught leaking information. It's not the leaking that does the damage. It's getting caught. Jill needs to be sure her father, sister and brother-in-law will maintain the confidentiality of the discussion.

"Then I need you to take this call down to the basement and turn music up loudly upstairs, in case someone has parabolics aimed at our house," Jill says.

"Parabolics?" her father asks.

"You know, the microphone equipment that can pick up discussions from a long way away," Jill replies.

"I'm scared now," her dad states.

"What's going on Jill? Are we safe?" Jane asks.

"You're safe," Jill replies. "Just tell me when you're all in the basement and have music cranking upstairs."

Several minutes later, her father tells Jill they're all set.

"Okay," Jill starts. "I haven't talked to Paul about this yet, so I'm not certain I'm going to do it, but Vice President Wilt has asked me to be her running mate in the next election."

"She wants you to run for President?" Walt asks.

"No. Marcia is running for President, with the endorsement of some very important people. She's asking me to run for Vice President of the United States of America as her running mate."

For several seconds, Jill sees and hears only silence on the other end of the connection. Her father turns his head, trying to compose himself.

"Your mother would be so incredibly proud of you—both of you," Mr. Carlson states. "We were just talking about Walt and Jane taking over the family farm so I could retire. It sounds like you might not object, since you're going to be mighty busy for a long time."

"Not only would I not object, I'd be delighted to know that the farm is going to be in the family for at least another generation. You and Mom put so much of your heart and soul into it that I can't think of anything better," Jill says.

"Well, I can," Jane interjects. "The only thing better to me than be able to say we're running our family farm is that my sister is the Vice President. Holy crap. That's just crazy. I mean. We're nobody and one day it turns out you make us somebody."

"Well, running for office. Nobody's going to just give us the job," Jill says.

"So, you're okay with it, knowing reporters will be breathing down your necks trying to get you to say something horrible about me?" Jill inquires.

"I won't tell 'em that you slap like a girl or that you belch when you drink milk too fast," Jane offers.

"Don't say anything about this to anyone before it goes public," Jill instructs the trio. "That way we'll also have more time to talk about what might be good for you to forget."

With the call to her family concluded, Jill connects to Professor Stark.

"Professor Stark here," he answers, not recognizing the number connecting to him.

"Paul, it's Jill. I had to dial you through encryption," Jill says. "Can you set up so that no one can overhear? Maybe even head to your little basement thing if you're not already there."

Jill and Professor Stark have had dozens of conversations one or the other wanted to ensure wasn't overheard.

"Okay, all set," he finally tells her after heading to his basement security room and putting on headphones.

"I have interesting news that might be either good or bad, depending on your perspective," Jill tells him.

Professor Stark takes a deep breath and reminds himself to filter his response through his brain before speaking: "What's going on?"

"It's pretty shocking, really," Jill tells him. "I've been asked to run for Vice President with Marcia. Marc is gung-ho behind us."

"Wow, I can't say I saw that coming," Professor Stark says while checking out the security monitors in his back basement bedroom, "even though you certainly will be a great Vice President."

"I didn't see it either, Paul, but I'm worried that this could interrupt our plans," Jill says. "And I don't want to ruin what we have."

"Why would it ruin it?" he asks, though fifty potential sources of ruin immediately start rummaging through his brain.

"Well, you know our marriage and the adoptions and being a good mother. How can I do that and be Vice President?" Jill considers.

"It's a hard job, I'll grant you that, but could it possibly be worse than you flying back and forth between cities every three or four days?" Professor Stark asks, now sitting at the desk with the monitor in front of him simultaneously broadcasting several news channels. "Let's say we're married and we have children and you are Vice President. You'd probably be able to have more time with the children than you do serving in Congress, at least given how dedicated you are to actually getting things done."

"You think so?" she wonders.

"Am I going to get less one-on-one time with you while you're campaigning and once you win? Maybe. But we can make the family work if it means having the right person in the second highest office in the nation, can't we?"

Jill's fists are pounding up and down as they talk. "Are you sure you're okay?"

"Yes, under one condition," Professor Stark replies.

"What's that?"

"We get married and file the adoption paperwork before your announcement goes public," Professor Stark suggests.

"Really, Paul?"

"Really."

"But that's like in two weeks," she notes.

"Nothing wrong with a shotgun wedding. Everyone will assume you're pregnant," he says while smiling.

Jill smirks and shakes her head. "I don't know if that's the image I'm looking for."

"Maybe, but the tabloids will eat it up," he adds. "Then you can announce that we've filed to adopt right whenever the media attacks start to get rough."

"Why would I want to do that?" she asks.

"Remember President Obama. Part of his political genius was not releasing records—birth certificate, academic records—that really are inconsequential to voters and letting his opponents focus their energy on beating him up over relatively meaningless issues," Professor Stark observes.

"So, you're suggesting they should beat me up for having pre-marital sex with you and getting pregnant," Jill says. "I'm not sure I like that."

"Maybe, but it does do something for my reputation," he says, laughing, but only lightly to be sure he hasn't pushed the wrong button. "No, seriously and if you really want to still marry me," he begins to state.

"Good God, Paul. When are you going to figure out that I am madly in love with you?" Jill responds.

"I know it," he replies. "It's just, well, well, do you want to speed up the wedding? I can do next weekend."

"Are you saying you're okay with this because you want to speed up the wedding or because you're really okay with it?" Jill inquires.

"I'm really okay with it," he assures her. "Besides, with the way things have been going and the work I've been doing, it might be nice to have a little Secret Service protection around."

"Then what about actually getting your work done?" Jill asks, wanting to be sure she's considered every possible consequence.

"I'm pretty sure I can convince a university in the D.C. area to bring me on, one way or another, if Chicago won't work with me on my location."

"And your trials?"

"Well, I can do that from anywhere. DC might actually be a better host city in terms of resource connections. But I think we need to talk some more about that issue, in person, securely," Professor Stark says.

"A line secure enough to talk about me being Vice President isn't secure enough to discuss your Atrocity Center project?" Jill asks.

"Maybe not, I'm afraid. That's why we need to talk, and why the security might be more crucial than ever for us."

45 DETECTION

Ramon's encrypted communications and surveillance team picks up a series of electronic messages and disturbing movement patterns linked to now-deceased Prince Taban.

"JT, we've found a lot of traffic leaving South Yemen. Taban's former security guards," Ramon says in a short, secure exchange with the New Rite founder. "I don't know that we have the resources to track them all down physically. We know they all ended up on flights headed to various 'stans, but we won't be able to find them there unless they communicate electronically again."

"Okay," JT replies. "I got it."

"What are you doing next?" Ramon asks.

"I got it. Track them as much as you can, but we need to call in help. This might be too big an opportunity to pursue on our own."

JT and Ally leave minutes later on an APB to Washington, D.C., calling in advance to let JT's newest friend, Secretary Mendoza, know that they have an urgent threat to relay in person. Pentagon troops meet JT and Ally at a private hangar attached to Reagan National after Mendoza orders their flight cleared so they can be sped to Mendoza's underground office bunker.

"We have a bead on General Timur," JT tells the Secretary, skipping any attempt to exchange pleasantries as they meet. Secretary Mendoza calls in three top aides to join the discussion.

"Where?"

"Somewhere in the 'stans."

"Well, that's not very specific."

"Four teams headed to four airports, all arriving in the next few hours."

"We can't track them any further with our resources but they're either going to join back up with General Timur or to take him out," JT predicts. "Every one of them has substantial extra luggage that was carried around airport X-rays without inspection."

Secretary Mendoza turns off the treadmill he had been walking on when they entered. "Who are the teams?"

"Prince Taban's security forces," JT replies.

"I hear he doesn't need security anymore," Secretary Mendoza states, looking into JT's and Ally's eyes to see if he can read anything into their response.

"Actually, my guess is that he needs more security than ever where he's going but it still won't do him any good," Ally interjects.

"Gotcha. What do you want from us?" one of Mendoza's aides asks while the Secretary dries his face.

"If they're going after or to meet up with Timur, they're also going after or to connect to the stolen nuclear weapons," JT states, running his fingers and thumb through his beard as he's talking.

An emergency inter-agency call is triggered with the heads of all U.S. intelligence organizations. Within minutes, on-the ground operatives head to the airports with JT's photos and backgrounds in hand.

"We'll talk about how you know this later," Secretary Mendoza states to JT, making clear that he has his suspicions.

CIA and NSA surveillance teams immediately retrace historical satellite records with the supercomputer systems quickly identifying abnormal events once they knew where to search. Before the meeting concludes, Secretary Mendoza receives an alert from CIA Deputy Director Branch.

"Ally," Mendoza says as he looks back up from his screen where urgent information has been relayed to his attention. "Is it okay if I call you Ally?"

Ally nods her head yes.

"Intel tells me that they found you showing up at the dead prince's compound a couple of times recently. You extracted some people from his compound, right after the prince turned ill," Mendoza states.

Ally looks at JT, who nods at her to go ahead. "Yes, sir," she states.

"Purpose?"

"Kidnap victims," Ally replies. "His victims. We brought them home."

"And, I suppose, we were hoping to set these contacts in motion," JT acknowledges. "The prince was the only person alive we knew was in semi-direct contact with Timur. We've traced tens of billions moving from Taban to Timur over the years."

"Did we know this?" Mendoza asks his CIA colleague.

"We knew Timur had a benefactor on the peninsula. We suspected South Yemen, but only recently identified Prince Taban."

"You should have gotten this to us earlier, JT," Secretary Mendoza states emphatically.

"We didn't have anything actionable earlier. Now, we do. Now, we're here," JT replies in matter-of-fact manner, without feeling any need to consider whether Mendoza has a point.

Before they depart, Secretary Mendoza pulls JT aside: "Can you tell me anything about Ramon Mantle, the Castillo cartel guy. He had to be in New Rite's surveillance scope. The President's hot on us to find him."

"Well, sure. Brilliant guy. Created the tech that helped Castillo consolidate. Not a willing participant though. Father was held captive. He and the rest of his family were surrounded by Protection Corps guards," JT replies. "Wasn't he killed in the compound attack?"

"We thought so," Mendoza states, raising his eyebrows as he responds in a way that makes JT question what Mendoza knows. "Well, anyway, thanks for the Timur lead."

CIA undercover agent Abdullah Raheem arrives at the Almaty airport with simple instructions. Find the four individuals, identify their departure vehicles, send that information back to headquarters and track from a secure distance.

Not sure where to expect them to exit, he moves to elevated ground, setting up area scanning equipment loaded with facial recognition capabilities. Loading in the facial details he just received, Abdullah pulls his car off to the side on a hillside road, jacks it up and deflates his rear tire. He pushes the scanning equipment underneath the jacked up car to prevent it from being detected by satellite.

The equipment is coated in light-absorption rather than reflective material to make it that much more difficult to spot. Abdullah opens his Lifelink and makes calls to several local contacts to support his cover that someone is bringing him a new tire. Before parking, Abdullah had already pulled out the spare tire and left it in a ditch a mile away from the car. He hides the hand air pump to re-inflate the flattened tire when he's done in nearby weeds. Abdullah superglues two sawed-off nails tightly inside the treads so any passersby will instantly recognize the source of his flat tire.

Hours pass with Abdullah sitting along the side of the road, facing the airport with a book in front of him, trying to not make it easy to determine that watching the airport is his actual mission. Hundreds of cars pass by during those hours, with at least a dozen stopping to offer assistance. Abdullah tells each that he's already called for help.

Finally, the scanning software alerts Abdullah that it has spotted a target. Abdullah opens a scanner disguised as a Lifelink device and zooms in. Four men leave down a back ramp from the plane, jumping immediately into a luggage transport vehicle that also holds their uninspected luggage. Abdullah watches as the luggage transport heads under the airport terminal.

"Uh, oh," Abdullah says to the open air around him. He retrieves the air pump, pretends to pull the nails from the tire and patch non-existent holes, before inflating the tire and pulling down the jack. He keeps his eyes on the airport, but alerts CIA headquarters that he might not be able to determine the group's departure vehicle.

Just then, a military transport truck drives east from the luggage area, racing at high speed across all three runways. "It could be a dummy, but I'm guessing they think they're safe here," Abdullah tells his agency handler. "I'll chase this one, but have HQ keep eyes on anything else unusual."

Abdullah doesn't know the full extent of his mission, but the Jersey-born Muslim suspects he's getting a chance to pursue what he joined the CIA to accomplish, to retake control of Islam from terrorists who abuse Muhammad's teachings to suit their own purposes and try to destroy his home and family in the United States.

"Allahu Akbar," Abdullah says to himself. God is greater. It's a phrase Abdullah instinctively repeats to himself whenever a mission becomes challenging.

Nearly twenty kilometers pass before Abdullah realizes that he is approaching the Kyrgyzstan border. Traveling several vehicles back, Abdullah regularly slows to stay out of sight of the transport vehicle he is trailing. As the border approaches, Abdullah stops to watch. The vehicle drives straight through, with only a cursory wave from the driver.

"It's them," Abdullah communicates back to his handler. "I'll lose them at the checkpoint. Make sure intel has eyes."

As night arrives, Abdullah arrives at a small motel looking out over Issyk-Kul, an unexpected, pleasant diversion from day-to-day life.

His next orders arrive at nearly the same time. Eyes on the lake. The four he tracked are ensconced in a home near the Islamic cemetery.

The next morning, Abdullah wakes early and decides to take a run and short cooling swim in the lake. He doesn't know when he'll get his fitness regimen in next, so needs to act while he awaits more detailed instructions.

While running near the lake, he spots something unusual, another group of men being dropped off near the marina. None look like the men he followed. Rather than return to his hotel and check for instructions, Abdullah follows his well-trained instincts and walks down to take a short dip into the lake.

Stepping into the lake, Abdullah gives himself no more than ten minutes in the water before he'll start to lose function in his limbs. He swims as fast as he can to warm his body up, but has to turn around sooner than he had hoped and doesn't get within underwater sight of the marina.

Leaving the water along a rock-strewn section of the beach, Abdullah is greeted by an unwelcome sight.

Two men confront him, asking him in Kyrgyz what he's doing. Abdullah shakes his head. They ask him in English, clearly suspecting that something is wrong. Abdullah shakes his head again, pretending to not understand.

Abdullah finally asks them if they understand Arabic. Both men nod and Abdullah greets them warmly, reaching toward them. As he reaches, one of the men pulls a gun from his back holster. Abdullah drops to the grounds, rolls toward the man, springing up with a crunching palm into the man's nose, shoving the nose back into his brain and leaving him at least unconscious.

As Abdullah reaches for the pistol, the other man tries to wrap his arms, dropping both men to the ground with Abdullah on the bottom. Abdullah grabs the pistol and fires three quick shots into the man's side, turning his mouth away as the man spits blood onto his face.

Now blood-soaked and having attracted attention from passersby, Abdullah picks the gun back up and surveys the area. Four men armed with automatic weapons sprint toward him from the front and back of the marina. Abdullah doesn't recognize any of them, but he isn't waiting for formal introductions. He takes off running at full speed, not even feeling several bullets graze his body—knowing that capture assures a death far more painful than simply being shot.

A few buildings help to obscure him from his pursuers as Abdullah runs. He doesn't even look for traffic as he runs out between buildings to cross Sovetskaya Street. He looks behind as he runs onto the street, looking to see if his pursuers have eyes on him when a car coming from the other direction flies past him, slams on its brakes and turns toward him. Abdullah reaches for the pistol to take shots at the car and realizes he has exhausted his bullets.

The driver yells at him in a language Abdullah struggles to process until he hears it a third time. "Get in," the driver yells again, reaching over to fling the door open without coming to a stop. Looking back, Abdullah sees three of his pursuers stepping around the corner of a building and realizes he has no choice. He jumps in, falling clumsily to the seat and feeling his right foot explode before he can get his leg fully into the car.

"Duck," the driver says, keeping his head below the dashboard as he drives several hundred feet before lifting up, seeing where he is on the road and ducking back down again. Seconds later, they no longer hear bullets crashing through glass or pinging into the antique car's thick steel frame.

The driver sits up, looking back and seeing that the men are standing a mile away in the middle of Sovetskaya Street, firing automatic weapons.

"Hope they don't have snipers set," the driver methodically states, adding to Abdullah's long list of concerns.

Speeding away, the driver heads toward what he hopes is an abandoned farmhouse building he spotted while setting up a safehouse east of Bosteri.

"I know you're one of us," the driver says to Abdullah.

"Meaning?"

"CIA."

"Who are you?" Abdullah asks.

"Muhammad. Muhammad Medina."

Abdullah glares at him. "You're kidding, right?"

"No, that's my actual name. Mother's Muslim. Father is Spanish. Medina is from the Spanish side," Muhammad says.

"Doesn't that attract extra questions?" Abdullah asks.

"I don't use Medina normally. Look, you're in rough shape. Save your energy," Muhammad says. "I'll get you to safe house and patched, then figure if you've blown the mission."

"What do you mean?" Abdullah asks as he takes off his shirt, rips it in half and ties a tourniquet just above his right ankle to stop the blood dripping onto the car's floor.

"You were directed for no contact, right?" Muhammad asks.

"Right. I'm not the one who made contact. They found me."

"Of course they found you. You swam right by their operations center," Muhammad informs Abdullah.

"I just went . . . to work out. I had no idea they'd be there," Abdullah argues.

Muhammad stops the car, opens the door and turns to look behind him.

"What are you looking for?" Abdullah asks.

"Just to be sure I'm not dropping glass or oil to create an easy trail to follow," Muhammad responds, tension still fully apparent in the brisk pace of his speech.

"And?"

"And, I think we're good," Muhammad says, pulling the door closed, driving past a dirt road and then backing the car down the dirt road until the road is consumed by trees and bushes on both sides. Several hundred feet later, Muhammad jumps out of the car, runs to pull open doors to a dilapidated barn, pushes aside rusted-out farm implements and pulls the car into the garage. As soon as the car is inside, he checks to make sure Abdullah has the blood flow stopped, then lies down on the ground to look under the car.

"What are you checking for now?" Abdullah asks.

"Make sure blood wasn't dripping through floor," Muhammad says, struggling to speak English again. "I could miss when I checked road. They won't miss with time to track."

Muhammad codes into his pocket, pulling out his modified Lifelink and connects through encrypted code to the mission lead at CIA headquarters in Langley, Virginia.

"Agent hit. Contact with targets," Muhammad states emphatically after coding in. "One tracker spotted and shot. Rescued, but we may be followed. Need medical extraction ASAP."

"Which one?" the CIA team lead asks.

"Almaty," Muhammad responds.

Muhammad walks outside the barn and out of earshot of Abdullah. "Are you hit?" the team lead asks back.

"No. Need to launch on marina ASAP. I'll steal transport and head back as spotter now," Muhammad says.

"No. Stay put. Saw battle. Teams already launched. Won't get there in time," the coordinating agent states. "Satellites confirm no follow."

"I didn't spend thirteen years in nowhere to miss my shot at something real in my back yard," Muhammad yells back at his team lead.

"Treat your man. We'll take the rest from here."

As Muhammad disconnects, he turns to see Abdullah right behind him with a knife in his hand.

"What mission?" Abdullah inquires.

"If you don't know, I can't tell you," Muhammad responds.

"What mission?" Abdullah asks again, this time, holding the knife closer to Muhammad but without posing any physical threat to him.

Muhammad ignores the implied threat. "My new mission is to take care of your wounds," Muhammad directs, simply walking away from Abdullah and struggling to open the car trunk. "Not sending anyone for you or me until mission over so put knife away and let's patch you up." Once he forces the car trunk open, Muhammad pulls out the medical kit from his nearly trunk-sized weapons case.

Abdullah hobbles behind him as he pulls out the medical kit.

"Clearly, you get all the good stuff," Abdullah notes, pointing toward a weapon he hadn't seen before. "What's this?"

"New rifle. Bullets missile propelled, up to five miles. Once locked, bullets stay on the target no matter how much or where target moves," Muhammad replies.

Abdullah looks outside, but doesn't have any bearings on where he is. "How far are we from the marina?"

"Has to be 10 kilometers, at least," Muhammad estimates.

"Then patch me up, and we'll hike back until we're in range if no one's coming to get us," Abdullah suggests. "Besides, if someone is coming to get us, we sure as hell don't want to sit around here. Let's get into the mountains and move to range."

"You won't be able to move even after I treat that," Muhammad predicts, pointing toward Abdullah's foot.

Abdullah cuts through the blood-soaked material and laces atop his shoe. He cuts the top of the shoe into quarters to make it easier to pull off straight down, then cuts the sock down the middle to remove it.

"Great. The shot didn't even hit much bone," Abdullah notes. "Looks like a crucifixion wound."

"Oh please," Muhammad responds. "Who do you think you are?"

Muhammad helps patch the hole in Abdullah's foot, dumping wound sealant around the inside of his foot and shoving gauze into the hole while Abdullah bites through several tongue depressors. Once he thinks the wound is sealed, Abdullah unties the tourniquet. Only a few blood drops press through the bandage. Muhammad fixes that with more wound sealant.

"Think you can walk on it?" Muhammad asks in hopeful tone.

Abdullah waits for a modest amount of feeling to return to his foot, then stands up and puts pressure on it. "I'm going to need some pain suppression, but I can do it," Abdullah says.

"Without a shoe?"

"If we can't find anything else, we have gauze and duct tape," Abdullah says. "So, what's the mission?"

Muhammad reconnects to his CIA team lead, coding in once again.

"Wounds treated. Ready to assist mission," Muhammad states.

"You're too far. Stay put," the team leader orders.

"Negative. With weapon, we can reach elevated spot to provide support," Muhammad contends.

The team coordinator re-checks a map of the area and considers the shooting distance.

"You're right, but you need to get one mile west and eight hundred feet of elevation without being spotted and be set in one hour. Can you both make it?"

Muhammad looks at Abdullah, who nods his head in assent.

"We'll be there," Muhammad says, seeing a message with the coordinates of his exact location target as he talks. "Can I educate Almaty on mission?'

"Confirmed," replies the team leader before disconnecting.

"What are we doing?" Abdullah asks.

"Saving the world from nutjobs who keep trying to control our faith and blow up the world at the same time," Muhammad says. "I'll give you more as we go, but we don't have any time to waste."

Muhammad pulls out the missile-bullet rifle and several other weapons from the case. Abdullah grabs a rocket-propelled grenade launcher and the rest of the weapons he can carry, then both look for trees to hike out under and start a steady march westward and upward.

Muhammad sends Abdullah ahead. With Abdullah's injury, he knows he can catch up.

Opening the car trunk, he pulls out plastic explosives, trip wires and detonators, then sets to rigging up the barn to blow if anyone finds them.

46   TRANSLATION

New Rite's intelligence and technology teams independently track movement of known CIA and Defense Department assets, particularly those heading to the parts of the world where JT and Ally had suggested that Prince Taban's security forces are gathering. Ramon's team hasn't yet been able to break through CIA encryption to identify contents of conversations between headquarters and field agents, but Ramon has developed a method to triangulate field agent locations, with capabilities stolen from New Rite's breakthrough into China's defense satellite systems.

"We're getting a bead on U.S. military asset movement," Ramon tells JT through New Rite's secure communication system. "There's a bunch of words on the screens with the maps. It would sure help to know what they say."

"What do you mean?"

"They're in Chinese, I think," Ramon says.

"Mandarin, or something else?" JT asks.

Ramon shakes his head. "How would I know?"

"Okay, send a screen shot, but just the words. I'll have intelligence figure out the language, but I don't want them seeing the source."

Ramon complies, cropping tightly around the art-like strokes.

Fifteen minutes later, JT messages Ally.

"Trust anyone who knows Mandarin?"

"Expert, or not?"

"Probably not expert, but trusted," JT replies.

"The kid," Ally suggests.

"You mean JG?" JT asks.

"Yep."

"Do it. Deliver to special ops HQ ASAP. Can't risk using external translation programs for this, in case they're tracked."

Ally sheds her black jeans and sweater as she walks toward the front door of the New Rite Colorado compound director's house she shares with JT whenever he's in town. Inside the hall closet, she keys in her entry code, grabs her flight suit, and climbs down into the tunnel system that runs below the house. Minutes later, she's below the helipad surface, warming up the APB and turning on its gecko-skin and other detection avoidance technologies. An automated scanner checks for any sign of human movement or body temperature within visible radius of the helipad. Finding none, Ally opens up and moves into jet mode immediately to race to Chicago.

"Is this Juan?" Ally asks after a New Rite intelligence team member makes an audio connection between her APB and University of Chicago student Juan Gonzalez.

"It's Juan," he replies.

"Juan Gonzalez, right?"

"Yes. Who is this?" Juan asks.

"Do you remember your last flight out of Mexico?"

"You must have the wrong person. I've never flown out of Mexico."

"Monterrey?" Ally asks.

"Oh," he responds, his voice lowered in town and volume.

"I'm not talking commercial flight," she adds for clarity.

"Yes, I remember," Juan acknowledges.

"I was your pilot. My name's Ally."

"Oh, yeah. I'm sorry. We didn't really talk much. Thank you again for saving me. I never really fully got the chance to say thank you."

"Well, maybe you can now. I need a favor," Ally states.

"Sure, what?" Juan asks.

"I'll explain when I see you," Ally notes.

"Okay, when's that?" Juan asks.

"I'll be there in just over an hour. Meet me at the ice rink," Ally directs, speaking with an unmistakable sense of urgency.

Reluctant to agree at first, Juan realizes that he owes his life in part to this woman and decides he can adjust his plans: "Uhm. Okay. I can do that, I guess, but I have an exam tomorrow."

"Bring your reading, then," Ally recommends unnecessarily since nearly all of the resources Juan needs for his courses are contained on his Lifelink.

"Why?" Juan asks.

"I'll explain when I see you," Ally adds.

After racing to Chicago at full speed in the APB, Ally sets it down gently on the Midway Plaissance. Running over to the ice rink, it takes her only a minute to find Juan.

"Juan. Ally," she says, extending her hand.

"Hi Ally. Good to see you again."

Ally swivels her head around, looking in every direction. "I hate to be a pain, but I need you to follow me quickly."

"Where are we going?" Juan questions.

Ally grabs his hand, pulls it lightly and then releases it. "We have a flight to catch. Same vehicle you took before."

Juan is too stunned to do anything other than follow Ally. Crossing the street, she warns him to slow down.

"We're almost to it. You don't want to hit it hard."

"I don't see what you're talking about."

Ally clicks off the gecko-skin camouflage just long enough to be sure she doesn't hit it. Juan is startled.

"That's why I didn't see anything except the rope and the people when you were coming in down there," Juan comments.

"Load up. Once we're airborne, I'll fill you in," she orders.

Entering the APB, Ally hands Juan a helmet and an air mask.

"So?" Juan asks, once strapped into his seat.

Ally blasts straight up five hundred feet before turning the jets to propel them forward across Lake Michigan.

"Where are we going?" Juan asks.

"That, I can't tell you," Ally replies, taking time to look over at Juan so he'll see the intent in her response.

"But what do you need my help with?" Juan asks, his heart rate elevation telling Ally that he's beginning to get nervous.

"You can read Mandarin, right?"

"Yes, pretty well, anyway," he replies. "Though I've let my skills go soft over the last year or so."

"Good enough for what we need," Ally assures him, the opposite shore of Lake Michigan already in view. "We just have some words we need help with," Ally tells him before medicating him into unconsciousness.

Only after landing on the CURE research center helipad, holding Juan at her side as she walks him still unconscious into JT's office and then down into the Detroit Salt Mine does Ally wake Juan up.

As he begins to regain consciousness, Juan mutters: "What? What happened?"

"I think you passed out from the speed," Ally replies, not feeling any need to tell him that she drugged him through his oxygen mask. "Don't worry, a lot of people can't handle our acceleration."

Ramon is carefully kept away as Juan interprets screen after screen in a makeshift room adjacent to the New Rite's special forces operations and command center. Buried deep in the Detroit Salt Mine and hidden behind a series of false mine faces, the command center now houses hundreds of New Rite employees, only a few of whom know where the center is located. Most are transported to the command center through a tunnel linked on the Canadian side of the border to a grain storage facility, following thirteen hundred miles of unconscious transport from Colorado.

"What am I looking at?" Juan asks Ally.

"Probably best that you forget you ever saw this," she recommends as a way of telling him that she's not going to tell him.

Thirty minutes later, Juan has translated several dozen screens. Team members note the translations, doing their best to not show their concern as they realize that in the past twelve hours, China has elevated its military to the U.S. equivalent of DEFCON 2, meaning they expect imminent hostilities.

After a team member pulls Ally aside to let her know, she messages JT: "It's going down. We need to get there."

JT leaves his CURE office and races down to the salt mine control room. As he exits the tube tunnel down, he makes split-second eye contact with Ally.

"I don't have time to deal with the kid. You'll need to figure it . . .," she yells to JT as they exchange positions on the tunnel tube, a small two-person elevator running off its own power source through a compression-drilled tunnel to the bottom of JT's office that few know exists.

Even before finishing her comment to JT, Ally begins her ascent back to the CURE surface and out to her APB. Seconds later, she's back in the air, racing back to New Rite's Colorado compound to pick up her crew for the long flight to the Far East.

"New Rite's moving," an analyst tells Secretary Mendoza in the DUCC situation room. "The new air displacement detectors around their survival compounds tell us we've had five move in just the last hour. We confirmed this with satellite in three spots. Detection between opening and closing of helipad doors."

"Where are they headed?" the Secretary probes.

"Don't know, sir. All we could tell is all headed west," the analyst responds.

"From?"

"New Rite compounds in Hawaii, Colorado, Alaska and Utah, plus the site in Detroit you asked us to survey."

"Whatever's going on, JT Alton knows more than he let on. Find him. Bring him in for questioning," Secretary Mendoza directs.

"Involve the FBI?"

"No time. Go."

Juan sits quietly but uncomfortably. Ally asked him to wait here for her, but she left in a hurry. Looking around, he sees nothing familiar. No sign that he's in a U.S. government installation. But the wall of monitors outside the room he's locked in all display screens with information written in Mandarin.

Juan instinctively drops to his knees, leaning over his chair with hands clasped. He can't escape. He doesn't know where he is. As he thinks about what he's just translated, it's clear that it's Chinese military systems he's been reviewing.

When the door to the room opens, Juan rises and stands behind the chair, taking position behind the only bit of shield separating him from whoever is walking in the door.

Muscles tensed, Juan looks up, hoping to see Ally coming back to get him. Instead, it's a man coming up, his right hand outstretched toward Juan. Juan's eyes expand and his breathing stops until he sees that the hand contains no weapon. The outstretched hand is reaching to shake Juan's hand. Only then does Juan look up.

"Ramon," he mutters, shaking his head back and forth. "Uh. Uhm. I thought. I mean. Aren't you dead?"

"Clearly not," Ramon replies, grabbing Juan's hand to shake it, with Juan still too startled to move voluntarily.

"I'm lost," Juan says.

"That's probably just as well, Juan. It's bad enough now that you know I'm alive. It would be worse for me if you knew where we are."

"But isn't this New Rite? I mean, Ally the pilot brought me here. Right?"

Ramon puts his hand on his old ally's shoulder. "It is."

"But, but you're their enemy, aren't you," Juan inquires, still looking in every direction for clues as to what is going on.

Ramon smiles: "Life isn't always as simple as it seems, Juan."

Juan sits down, propping his chin up to continue looking at Ramon. Juan tries to be sure he's not suffering some type of delusion.

"Ally had to leave. As much as I would prefer that you not know I'm alive, I didn't want you freaking out here. The monitors Ally placed on you during flight showed you were starting to lose it."

"The what?" Juan asks.

"Don't worry. I've convinced the team that you may as well join us for the next day or two, to see what we're going to do with the information you translated for us."

"I have a test tomorrow," Juan replies. "Ally promised me I'd be back in time to take it. I really should be studying."

"Don't worry about your test," Ramon replies. "If we don't succeed with this, there might not be a tomorrow that anyone wants to live through."

Juan's face tenses, eyes watering, lip quivering. "What the hell?"

"We're trying to avert World War III," Ramon states. "You're going to help."

"Ay dios mío," Juan replies, as Ramon puts his arm around Juan and brings him over to the control room.

"Right now, the U.S. is positioning hundreds of military assets to take out a terrorist target they think is about to move or launch dozens of stolen nuclear weapons," Ramon tells Juan as they stare at the monitors. "The problem with this is that China sees these assets, many of which are moving in their direction, and thinks that the U.S. may be about to launch a military attack on China."

Ramon leads Juan into the command center, where he points to a map showing that U.S. submarines and aircraft carriers are moving into the Persian Gulf, approaching Pakistan through the Arabian Sea, eastern India through the Bay of Bengal and both the South China Sea and East China Sea out of the Philippines and Japan, respectively. In addition, U.S. bases throughout Asia have moved to full alert.

"China thinks this is all headed toward them. They've put their forces on alert for imminent war, as you've just confirmed for us. We've triangulated U.S. movement and believe it's centered on an area in Kyrgyzstan. You're going to ask: why would China have a problem with a U.S. attack on Kyrgyzstan?" Ramon continues. "Well, the answer is because it's on China's border."

"How do you know that Kirgistan or whatever is the U.S. target?" Juan asks.

Ramon shrugs. "They're going after a target we pointed them toward."

"What?" Juan asks.

"That nuclear explosion in Armenia," Ramon begins.

Juan invites him to continue: "Yeah?"

"We've been tracking the general who did it," Ramon continues. "We believe he's in one of five spots. We gave this to the DoD to see if they could lead us to which one of these spots is the right one."

"How do you know it's this one?" Juan asks.

"We don't know for certain, but we do know that if the U.S. launches a military attack, it'll almost certainly draw a response from China. Accidents launch many wars, so we're trying to keep this from happening," Ramon replies.

"How can you do that?" Juan asks, dripping in sweat as he reconsiders whether he had properly translated all of the screen shots he viewed.

"We're going to try to take down the target quietly," Ramon states, moving Juan to shake his head in confusion.

"Wait, are you talking about General Timur?" Juan finally asks.

"You know about him?"

"Yes, from the trial, from Professor Stark's trial."

"I suppose you would know," Ramon says. "Now you know why we need you to interpret these words as they pop up."

"But what if I'm wrong?" Juan asks, the effects of being drugged now fully mitigated.

"Don't be."

Ally and her team break the sound barrier all the way through their overnight flights, stopping to refuel and coordinate in Japan before launching for Kyrgyzstan.

Detailing the mission plan, Ally makes clear that they have to physically locate General Timur before sending in the flea drones. An APB filled with Cooper's Hawk drones will be sent to search in and around Issyk Kul, an area that has drawn extensive CIA communication and appears to be the focal point of U.S. military asset movements. To further verify this is the right spot, Ramon's team traces adjustments in U.S. satellite orbits to identify global spots of intensified interest.

47 INFILTRATION

With Juan's help reading screens, Ramon and his team identify China's military asset movements.

"They're leaving the north open, taking everything south and east. Let Ally know to come around from the north," Ramon directs his communications lead.

JT is back seated inside his office at CURE's research headquarters when a half-dozen choppers land around the perimeter. Seeing them come in, JT stands up with his hands raised in the air, walks out toward his patio overlook of the renewing urban forest and waits for someone to approach.

"JT Alton," a soldier asks as he comes up to JT with his missile-bullet rifle pointed at JT, a move JT finds ironic given that New Rite invented the advanced rifle technology the U.S. military is now using.

"That's me," he acknowledges.

"I need you to come with us," the soldier orders.

Taken at combat speed to Wright-Patterson Air Force Base, JT is led as fast as he can move to the base command center and seated without explanation. After everyone leaves the room, a screen turns on with Secretary Mendoza at the other end.

"I thought it might have been you who sent for me," JT states.

"No time for small talk. Tell me where your people are going," Secretary Mendoza orders.

"What people?" JT asks.

"Your APBs. We don't have time for this, JT. We have new technology to track the APBs. We know they left. What we haven't found yet is where you're headed. Spill it."

JT sits and takes a breath, considering the legal implications of disclosing his operations, along with the moral considerations.

"Now, damn it," Mendoza screams. "China's prepping to intervene."

"I know," JT replies. "They're on DEFCON 2 equivalent now."

"How do you know?" Mendoza asks.

"We watch, just as you watch, when our people are in harm's way."

"Who are your people, JT?" Mendoza forcefully demands, fists visibly clenched on the video feed.

"My people. Everyone's my people, everywhere. At least as long as they're not taking life and liberty from someone," JT tries assuring the Secretary.

"Hmmm," Secretary Mendoza mutters, rolling his upper lip inside of his lower lip. "Is there a threat in there?"

"You don't need to worry about me," JT replies. "I wouldn't be coming to you with this if you were my problem."

"You're not coming to me," Mendoza yells. "I came to get you."

"Sure," JT counters. "But you wouldn't even be thinking about me if I hadn't come to you on Taban and Timur."

"What are your people doing?" Mendoza barks, loudly enough that the speakers vibrate inside the room in which JT is being held.

"Trying to take out the threat quietly so you don't have to move," JT states. "Back up and give us twenty-four hours. If you start to pull away, China will pull back."

"Yes, but twenty-four hours gives them time to position to stop us if we need to launch," Mendoza responds.

"Perhaps," JT counters, pausing for several seconds, "but once you start flying over and shooting missiles their direction, you won't get measured response. Trust me, Xavier. You need to give us a chance to do this."

JT asks to be flown to New Rite's Colorado mission command. He doesn't want his salt mine operations center to attract any attention. JT is certain that investigators are pulling apart his CURE office, but equally sure they won't find the entrance into the elevator tunnel and down to the salt mine operations. Even if they do, they won't get past its security measures. JT knows fully that the CIA is already aware of his Colorado-based command operations and will assume he's going there to lead mission command for New Rite's attack in Kyrgyzstan.

New Rite zeroes in on its tracking of two of the CIA's agents near Issyk-Kul. To New Rite, Abdullah and Muhammad are known as nothing more than CIA assets in transit, but they happen to be the assets nearest to Ramon's triangulated estimate of where the U.S. government thinks General Timur is located. Ramon's team track the pair using its gaming satellites to watch them slink through low-lying mountains. Intermittent communications origination intercepts confirm for Ramon that they are tracking the right people. Ramon built a massive logistics optimization company from the concepts and technologies he created to help the Castillo cartel evade law enforcement detection. Now, he and several encryption evasion experts are working for New Rite using these same skills in combination with several of JT's most trusted intelligence team experts.

"We need to get word to Ally that the feds think the target is in this boat house," Ramon says to one of the long-time New Rite intelligence team members as he points to a map. "The logical center action is in range: 42.6307 77.0491."

Ally notes the coordinates. As she flies, other team members design the attack. "We have a thousand drone fleas broken up between five teams," Ally is told after landing along with New Rite's other APBs on a plateau south of Almaty. "We're planning to go in up to ten waves, one hundred drones at a time, flying in off the lake to seem like a mosquito infestation. We can only manually control twenty between the team here and the HQ team. Plan is to insert visual code into the other eighty in each wave and have them search till they drop and disintegrate."

"Target bite only?" Ally asks.

"Permission to prick everyone and let the DNA trigger sort out which one's Timur?" drone operations leader Abhirim Roussard asks, now fully informed on the details of this mission.

"Permission granted, given high likelihood of disguise. He has to know someone is out there," Ally replies. "We have to trust our team. No second chances if we don't succeed. Did we set alerts on the DNA trigger to signal if it finds a match?"

"Done."

After a five-minute leg stretch while remaining inside the APBs to avoid being detected, Ally orders the team up to twenty thousand feet before heading south to their target location on Issyk Kul. Ally drops to one thousand feet above the boathouse before her team releases its drones, including twenty micro-drone fleas and two Coopers hawks. Two other APBs hover at ten feet above the lake, just one thousand feet away from the boathouse before releasing their drones while the remaining APBs release from just east and west of Cholpon Ata.

"Go," Ally orders as the team lifts back to the Kazakh plateau. Drone operators inside the APBs along with the salt mine team go to work. A Cooper's hawk finds three openings through which the fleas access the building.

Lou, on board Ally's APB, guides her micro-drone through each room traveling along ceiling corners, looking for anyone who vaguely resembles Timur. Room by room, she and the team search, covering off the main boat repair bays. No evidence of anyone located there.

Spotting no one on the main floor, Ally agrees to take a risk, triggering the heat detection scan on one of the Cooper's hawks. Once triggered, the scan quickly turns up three heat signatures coming under the marina main floor, at lake surface level. Lou flies her drone flea out and under the boathouse, spotting three men, of which two have automatic weapons on their backs while they work on a small submarine. When one of the men enters the submarine, Lou dashes one of her drones in to join him. Recognizing that she has little power left and that the man is not her target, she shuts the drone down inside the submarine.

"Get the rest into the water," Ally orders, wanting to be sure the drone fleas aren't discovered before they can disintegrate. "Lou. How long do we wait?"

"What would a sub be doing in a lake?" Lou asks rhetorically.

"Good question," Ally notes.

"Do we know the depth? How about sub speed? Need to figure out how long before reactivating." Lou demands,

"We don't have this," Ally replies. "Calling in to intel."

Ramon and the intel team get to work.

"East to west is 178 kilometers, with drop spot near the middle. North to south is sixty-four km. Max depth says 668 meters. It's the distance, not the depth that drives this," Ally replies.

"Sub speed?" Lou asks.

"Intel says these are stolen Iranian inspection subs," Ally relays. "Max speed approaching eighty km per hour."

"So likely one hour max east or west, and less than one hour max to south. Add in a fudge factor for max depth and we wait 150 minutes," Lou states. "Agreed?"

"Agreed," Ally replies, identifying two raid participants to stay on guard. "Everyone else, two hours sleep. It might be your last for a while."

Ally can't sleep sitting up, so lies curled around her seat. Four others on board, including Lou, split between trying to sleep with their restraints holding them into their seat and lying down on the floor.

As the minutes tick by, Ally grows angry at her inability to sleep. She's exhausted, even after getting three hours of fitful sleep on the flight from Detroit to New Rite's connection spot in Japan. Ally climbs back into her seat, attaches the restraints and tries relaxing her shoulders and easing her neck tension. It works. For fifteen minutes.

On landing at New Rite's Colorado headquarters and descending to its special operations command center, JT can't hold himself back from demanding an update. His alert triggers Ally to semiconsciousness.

"Yes, sir," she responds.

"Update," JT orders.

"Nothing to report," Ally quietly replies.

"Haven't found him yet?" JT asks.

"No, sir."

"Where are you looking?" JT inquires.

"We have a lead but have to wait."

"You're sure there's nothing to do while waiting?" JT suggestively questions.

Given her exhaustion, Ally realizes she hadn't fully pondered what he's asking.

"Will reconsider, sir," Ally replies, with a formality she only uses with JT in mid-operation.

Ally turns to look at others in her APB, not wanting to communicate across the group and wake up the rest of the team. She sees Lou seated with seat restraints attached and fingers tapping rapidly on her thighs.

"Lou," Ally whispers.

"Yes, ma'am."

"Anything we should do while we wait?" Ally asks.

"I was thinking about that. Is intel watching the site with the hawks?"

Ally calls in, reaching Ramon.

"You have eyes on the full target?" Ally asks Ramon.

"He does. Circling at a distance. Abe doesn't think the hawk is native there, so we're trying to avoid getting too close," Ramon replies, looking over at Abhirim for confirmation that he agrees with Ramon's assessment.

"Any movement?" she asks.

"Nothing since launch. We'll let you know," Ramon assures Ally.

Ally and Lou try to get back to sleep. Even a few minutes of rest can sharpen their decision-making.

Ally's alarm alerts her that the two-hour rest time is over.

"Everyone up. Three minutes to departure," she orders, taking the APB through its pre-launch checks.

Checking back with salt mine intel, Ally is alerted that an armed guard has moved back below the boathouse to the surface level.

"Lou, reactivate your drone. The sub might be on its way back already."

Lou reactivates her drone.

"I can't move it," Lou tells Ally as the APBs elevate to return to Issyk-Kul.

"Why not?"

"Don't know. No sight line. All dark," Lou replies.

"Are you on?" Ally asks, a question Lou considers the equivalent of "is it plugged in?" Lou lets it slide given the critical nature of the mission and the importance of checking everything multiple times.

"I'm on, but can't move," Lou finally responds.

"Switch to listen only. Let's see what you hear," Ally suggests.

Lou sets the drone to listen mode.

"I'm not getting anything. We might be too far away. Have intel hover a hawk at lake surface level for signal relay."

Ally connects to intel. The adjustment is made quickly.

"Got anything?"

"Garbled, yes. Not sure the language. Not one I know. I'll relay to intel," Ally states.

Another team member interjects. "That's Persian. I recognize some of the words."

"Can you translate?"

"I might catch one of every twenty words, not enough to help," he replies.

Before he's finished responding, Ally relays the signal.

In a matter of minutes, Ally hears back.

"We don't have it translated yet," Ramon notes.

"Then what?"

"Voice pattern match," Ramon states.

"To?"

"Target. Matches audio he sent to trial."

"We sure it's him?" Ally probes.

"Certain. Tested every way from Sunday," Ramon responds, a clear overstatement.

"Signal location?" Ally asks.

"Nearing marina. Approaching surface," Ramon responds before disconnecting.

"Full speed everyone. Drone launch immediately after reaching release spot. Target coming out," Ally orders.

Ally accelerates the APB full speed until directly above the marina, before dropping back to the one-thousand-foot hover. Lou and the crew release the next wave of drone fleas, flying some manually while the rest have been programmed for patterned search.

A guard for General Timur exits the marina, searching the perimeter to be sure no one is in range to spot the submarine as it breaks the water surface below the boathouse, particularly not whoever took down two of their outside security team. The underwater station isn't ready yet, forcing the General to return to the marina. As a guard walks the perimeter, he feels wind thrusts from several nearby APBs. One is so close that discrepancies between his memory of the elevation of surrounding ridgelines and those displayed on the APB gecko-skin camouflage attract the guard's attention, even if he's not yet sure why. Ally spots the guard as he reaches for an automatic weapon, pointing it in the general direction of one APB hovering northeast of the marina.

"Ready," she calls to the marksmen on board her APB, who spots the same movement and is already in motion.

"Ready," he responds, pulling his missile-bullet rifle to his shoulder.

Before Ally's next word, the guard collapses to the ground, a large hole through the middle of his chest instantly outlined in red.

"Who shot?" Ally asks.

"Not me," her on-board marksmen respond.

Checking with the other APBs, no one claims responsibility.

Lying prone along a ridgeline eight kilometers northeast of the marina, Abdullah asks Muhammad, "Why'd you shoot?"

"Orders to protect the invisible," Muhammad responds. "Choppers we can't see hold the good guys. He was aiming at empty sky."

"Now what?" Abdullah asks.

"We wait to see if any more come out," Muhammad replies, "or to see if our orders change."

48 ELIMINATION

Ramon alerts Ally that a submarine is now satellite visible as it nears the water surface. Hawk drones spot two more armed men below the boathouse at surface launch level, not yet noticing they have a man down.

"Be ready when he comes out. Let's get eyes on and be sure skin is exposed before we bite," Ally directs her team.

As the submarine comes to surface under the marina, two men exit. Only one had been in when the submarine went below surface. When one of the men grabs a military suit from behind him, Lou's first drone flea regains visual site. The second man is fully clothed, with a full beard and sunglasses hiding his facial features.

"Is that target?" Ally asks no one in particular, looking at a screen display as she slowly moves the APB back to thirty thousand feet.

"Has to be," Lou replies.

"No skin surface open behind him. I have to go for his cheeks," Lou reports as she maneuvers two micro-drone fleas simultaneously to come at the target from the right and left.

The target moves quickly, running up the stairs into the street level floor and into an office before Lou can catch him. None of the other fleas signal injection confirmation either.

"Damn it," Lou says as her first wave flea loses the last of its power, drops to the ground, and disintegrates.

"Max ten minutes on wave two," Lou reports as she tracks after the target with her second wave flea. Two guards take up position outside the office door facing out. Trying to avoid detection, Lou flies her drone up to ceiling and comes straight down the wall and door between the two guards before wedging under the office door. "Three minutes left," Lou states.

Flying straight up the door to the ceiling, Lou flies along the wall in an effort to circle at the target from behind. "He's screaming about something," Lou says just as a coffee cup thrown by the target crushes her drone flea.

"Merde," Lou yells. "He got me."

"Damn it," Ally utters intending to say it only to herself, but instead talking loudly enough that everyone on the APB hears her. "If we run out of time to get this done, all hell's gonna break loose. Wave three now," she orders, with the APB dropping quickly back to the one-thousand-foot level.

"We need to get him out of that office," Lou suggests. "Hawk attack on the guards ought to do it," a message Ally quickly relays to salt mine intel and drone operations to execute. Two minutes later, a dozen Cooper's hawks dive bomb the two guards outside the office, with drone operators doing their best to avoid fast moving swats from the guards. The guards step away from the door as they swing at the hawks, before one of the guards pulls out his pistol and starts shooting at the birds.

"*What's going on?*" General Timur asks as he steps out of the office. "*Put your damn gun away before you shoot one of us and the police come to search here.*"

"*You don't have to worry about the police, General,*" a guard replies.

"*But I do have to worry about you shooting me,*" he replies as he spots dozens of bugs circling around, biting him more harshly than he remembered mosquito bites. *"Who brought the damn cave bugs with us?"*

Ally and other team members hearing the discussion break into broad smiles when the general's last sentence is interpreted for them.

JT connects with Ramon.

"You were right, Ramon," JT states.

"About?" Ramon asks, only to clarify what part of what he has said that JT has decided is correct.

JT responds: "About Timur thinking the video equipment was sent to him just so the world could hear his musings."

Pods injected into the target trigger their DNA analysis sequence. Four confirm that the target is General Timur and confirm through electronic signals that the poisons have been released.

Eighteen other drone fleas biting others in the marina send signals that the DNA sequence has been rejected, triggering a pod destruct sequence that injects a strong antidote and a strong multi-hour sedative as well.

"Everyone out," Ally orders, with all five APBs hovering on the northern side of the snow-capped mountains behind Cholpon Ata, awaiting indication that it is fully safe to return.

"Get injection team lead on," Ally requests, wanting to confirm with Carol how long it should take for the injected toxin to take hold.

Several minutes later, Carol responds. "It's me," Carol says.

"How long before we know if it worked?"

"Thirty minutes, from bite. Maybe sixty until full paralysis," Carol replies.

"And from there?"

"Another thirty, max, depending on how much reaches his system."

"Four confirmed target bites," Ally replies.

"Well, then, you might be able to confirm now."

A hawk drone rests on top of a shelf inside the marina, sending back live visuals. Ramon forwards the feed to Ally and the other APB teams to obtain visual confirmation.

All of the other bitten soldiers are passed out on the ground, the sedative combined with the antidote having knocked them unconscious.

General Timur writhes in pain, rolling side to side, scratching so intently that he is shredding his skin with elongated, ragged fingernails. While the audio feed isn't working, Ally can see he's screaming as he squeezes around his abdomen.

"Why isn't he knocked out?" Ally asks.

Carol bites the side of an index finger. "We couldn't figure out how to deliver the sedative with the poison," she meekly replies. "The sedative is triggered to the antidote release."

"So not a disease," Ally confirms, worried about exposure to her team if a contagious disease had been injected.

"We made it work with straight poison," Carol confirms.

"Looks pretty cruel," Ally notes.

"Yeah. It's not ideal," Carol agrees.

Carol and her New Rite team set up the sea snake poison to inject with every micro-drone bite. If the micro-drone analysis determined that the recipient was not the DNA target, the antidote and sedative automatically released.

"Really?" Ally asks. "I thought we had this set so only the target would be hurt."

JT jumps into the discussion. "That's right, but we needed to knock the rest of his team out. This was the best plan we could execute given the time we had."

Ally demands that the remainder of the micro-drones be evacuated or detonated before her team goes in, not wanting to take the chance of an errant bite leaving them sedated with Timur's team, and waking up after them.

"What poison?" Ally asks.

"Sea snake," Carol replies. "Belcher's sea snake. Concentrated."

"Do they live in that lake?" Ally asks.

"Not as far as I know," Carol replies.

Ally raises her arm and calls out orders. "Retrieval and delivery, execute," she orders as the APBs return to the marina.

Surrounding the marina from both the land and lake, eight of Ally's team members enter the boathouse, quickly tying up and hauling the four bodies onto four different APBs.

Once loaded, all elevate to fifty thousand feet before accelerating at full pace to a little-used U.S. air base in Uzbekistan. At the air base, Ally and her team drop the packages on the tarmac. Before they can be identified and stopped, they depart for Japan to refuel and head home.

Once package delivery is confirmed, JT calls Secretary Mendoza.

"Packages delivered on tarmac in Uzbekistan. General Timur is dead. Three guards will recover for questioning," JT tells Mendoza.

Mendoza immediately contacts the CIA Director to take control of the live packages, while an Air Force jet is detailed to fly General Timur's body for forensic analysis and cremation.

"It scares me that you're able to do whatever you just did without us tracking you," the Secretary states after returning to the exchange with JT.

"It scares me too, Xavier, but not as much as it would scare me if you or another government had this capability," JT replies during their encrypted discussion. New Rite adds an encryption layer to JT's voice to ensure his comments digitally implode upon capture.

"We can't afford for what you do to get in the wrong hands, JT," Mendoza states. "I appreciate what you've done for us, but I think we need to bring the rest of this capability in house."

"I don't think I can let you do that, Xavier," JT replies, his matter-of-face tone belying an immediate elevation in his fear.

"It's too late, JT. Our troops are surrounding your headquarters to take control of all undisclosed capabilities. If you give these up willingly and fully, we won't press charges," Secretary Mendoza states. JT checks his security team, confirming that four thousand Marines are surrounding New Rite's Colorado headquarters and its prior special operations control center.

"I'm going to give you time to reconsider, Xavier. Are you sure that every administration that follows you will use what we can do responsibly?" JT asks, with the message clear from his tone that he intends the question to be taken as rhetorical. "Besides, if it's the military surrounding our headquarters, you're already in serious constitutional breach.

Secretary Mendoza considers JT's objections for less than a second: "Those aren't my concerns. My concern is national security."

"Everything you're looking for is already gone, Xavier. I figured that once you couldn't figure out our next technology, you'd come looking to take it. But don't worry," JT assures the Secretary of Defense. "It only works against the truly evil. I don't think you're truly evil. Perhaps a bit misguided, but not evil."

As soon as he shuts off the call, JT runs out from his Colorado compound home to the edge of his patio overlook. He's already completely encased in heat absorption clothing to obscure his nighttime descent down the cliff face. He clips on and jumps over the ledge, dropping rapidly, feet intermittently pushing off the cliff face on the decline. Eight hundred feet below his patio, JT's rapid plunge halts. His automated belay pre-set to stop at his target elevation slows and then stops him, swinging JT against the cliff wall to ensure he doesn't bypass his opening.

He grabs at nearby rocks, poking his hands into every ridge opening, trying to remember how he had positioned the fingerprint ID pad. He knows he's at the right altitude. Perhaps he's in the wrong crevice.

Feeling nothing familiar, he decides his descent had to have been off-center from straight vertical. He can't swing his rope enough to release whatever has thrown him off center. Plan B.

Pushing off, he circles around into adjoining crevices, searching for and shoving his hand into every hole in search of a grip he hasn't felt in several years. Finally, he finds something familiar—shoving his hand inside until it's fully absorbed. Running his index finger up and down inside the gulley, he finds the fingerprint ID pad.

A four-foot-by-four-foot section of the cliff pushes out, attached at the corners by three-inch metal beams with a metal shelf between the bottom beams. JT pulls himself up above the section and drops down onto the shelf, sliding his feet forward inside the cliff face until he is lying flat. He unlatches one portion of the rope from his belay and pulls it vigorously until the rope passes through the anchor ring on his patio and begins descending rapidly toward his face.

As soon as he feels it release up top, JT pulls himself under the protection of the cliff wall, stands up in its inside cavity and pulls the rest of the rope in as rapidly as possible.

Finally, with the rope all drawn in, JT taps another fingerprint ID pad to shut the cliff face opening. From the outside, nothing about the surface appears unusual.

Inside, JT goes to work on preventing heat detection and radar gap technology from discovering his security cubbyhole, putting up insulation and reflection padding to buttress the cliff wall protection around this tiny but well-stocked holding room. Originally designed as an escape pod to protect JT in case the Castillo cartel discovered his attacks against them, the cubbyhole has gone unused since JT tested it and had the connection to his headquarters from which it was constructed sealed off.

He messages Ally that he'll be waiting for her inside his "security blanket." He hopes she remembers where it is. He also hopes no one in the U.S government thinks to check old satellite images of when the cubbyhole was under construction or new images to pick up his nighttime descent. He hadn't anticipated needing to hide from U.S. government attack when he built his escape.

49 RECRIMINATION

From prone positions elevated eight hundred yards out, Abdullah and Muhammad survey the barn where Muhammad's bullet-riddled vehicle is stashed, looking for any signs someone tracked them. The barn remains intact. Muhammad searches to be sure his trip wires are still in place.

Electronically, Muhammad turns off the detonator mechanisms before approaching the barn. As he walks its perimeter, be unhooks trip wires from the electronic switches, then slowly removes detonator blasting caps from the clay-like bricks before placing the bricks back into the bullet-proof equipment case. The vehicle remains as they left it, each of the four doors one-half inch ajar. Anyone checking the interior would have been unlikely to re-close the doors with identical precision.

Abdullah remains in cover position until waved in. Once waved in and below any sight line, he uses his rifle as a cane.

"We have new orders, Almaty," Muhammad tells him.

"What's that?" Abdullah replies, putting all of his body weight on his non-punctured foot.

Muhammad continues to survey the area, looking for signs of any surveillance devices. Not wanting to take a chance, he softly whispers into Abdullah's ear: "Marina cleanup."

"What's that mean?"

Muhammad rubs at his beard. "Good time for prayers. Care to join."

"That's fine," Abdullah replies, a bit bewildered at the suggestion given the intensity of recent hours. "Why now? Why here?"

Muhammad waves to take their discussion outside, still concerned that whoever shot at them might be clever enough to be more interested in what they know than in killing them quickly. "New instructions. Men we chased were leading us to weapons stored here," Muhammad states, taking another visual search of the perimeter. "Extraction team is on the way. We need to secure the marina for entry and we can't go back in this car since we don't know that everyone who shot at us is gone."

"How many bodies did you count being carried out of the marina? I counted five," Abdullah states.

"Five. Five?" Muhammad considers. "Could be. Not sure there weren't more shooting at us earlier, though."

"Hiking into town then?" Abdullah asks.

Muhammad looks down at Abdullah's foot. "Better idea," Muhammad offers. "Drive east. Steal boat. Loop around the lake back to the marina. Should be safer to go around anyone looking for us."

"Let's go for it," Abdullah agrees, before they both prostrate themselves for quick prayers.

President Phillipi bypasses the White House Rose Garden and all of the other traditional signing spots. He wants this signature to be one to remember, something that has never been done before and with a background that is certain to catch the eye of even casual viewers. He's certain this occasion is important enough that the White House press corps will withstand a little discomfort. Reporters who insist on wearing high heels may be a bit perturbed, but his press staff will make it up to them with luxury buses, gourmet box lunches for the ride and temporary ramps and platforms for members of the press corps with physical disabilities.

Secret Service teams have spent the past week preparing the sight, setting up mile-long security perimeters upstream and downstream, blocking entry into the parks on both sides of the Potomac River for forty-eight hours and setting up military sniper teams along the cliff ridges that overlook the signing platform.

Reporters are dropped off at the main parking lot to assemble for the signing ceremony with camera operators scrambling to gain the most spectacular shots. One cameraman comes fully prepared in a wet suit with watertight camera equipment and gains permission to shoot the event from just below a cascading waterfall, looking up to the President, shooting him through the clear glass table on which he will endorse God's Law. Technically, his signature isn't required, but yesterday's ratification in Texas went as expected and President Phillipi is anxious to claim success for what he believes will be his most enduring legacy.

President Phillipi arrived two hours earlier than any of the press corps, joined by fourteen of the twenty-two people who will stand behind him as he signs the Golden Rule amendment. Fresh from their small family wedding in Indiana and shortened five-day honeymoon sunbathing, ATV riding and jet skiing off the coast of Aruba, Jill and Professor Stark are among the fourteen who arrive in cars as part of the President's motorcade.

Exiting the vehicles, it looks to Jill like some of the participants have their instructions wrong. She'd been told to come prepared for physical activity, but nearly half of the group is dressed in either suits or dresses, with only a change of shoes. Professor Stark and Jill are dressed in unintentionally matching jogging suits, with complete changes for the official ceremony.

Gathering around the front of a short gravel entrance, President Phillipi calls the group together.

"With your help, we've accomplished something that few thought even possible, passing and securing ratification of a constitutional amendment to require that the nation's laws conform with the idea that we must do unto others as we would have done unto ourselves," the President says, dressed in the tattered, blood-stained military fatigues he wore during the raid on the Castillo cartel's Sinaloa Province compound. "While we can take pride in what we've accomplished, the reality is that what we have really done is to restore the natural order of governance so I wanted to honor this achievement with a hike to our signing platform."

"A hike?" asks a senator who arrived in skirt, blouse and jacket, with flat shoes.

"Yes, Jennifer, a hike," he replies. "You did get our message about activewear clothing for the first part of the event."

"Well, yes. Yes," the senator replies. "I'll be fine," she adds as she pulls out her Lifelink and sends an emergency message to her chief of staff to be sure someone meets her at the other end of the hike with fresh clothes, fresh makeup, a flatiron and a brush.

The President turns and leads the group, making a short turn onto a well-worn path, before stepping off into a small trail entrance. Jill notices that several spots on the trail remain muddy from recent rains and does her best to walk around the spots. Secret Service agents lead and trail the hike. It's not long before the group reaches an outcropping of large boulders, jutting out over the Potomac River. President Phillipi walks up and over several of the boulders before reaching one that remains slippery. He scoots himself backwards up the rock, a movement that those in skirts, dresses and suits decide they'll wait to follow. Several minutes of hiking up and down rocks later, the President takes a seat on a large boulder.

He stares at the Potomac River, looking up at clear blue sky interrupted only by stacked white lines of jet exhaust to the west. The sun shimmies off the surface of the water, darting and dancing oblivious to anyone in the surrounding area. Waving to those who followed on the rocks, he asks them to sit beside him.

"We have to take our moments some days," the President says after Jill, Professor Stark and a half-dozen others are seated in his vicinity, "to look around at the world and see what we were sent here to serve and protect. When I look into children's eyes, I see my responsibility to make this a better place for them. When I see the beauty of the world that existed long before we were ever conceived, I'm reminded that we are caretakers. With God's Law, I think we have really upheld our responsibility. It's the natural state of the world that people need to treat each other with respect and decency and our laws need to encourage that respect, rather than setting a legal standard that diverges widely from decency as our government has done far too often in the past."

"Why here?" Jill asks. "Why this hike?"

"Fair question," President Phillipi replies, standing up on the boulder and looking around.

Several seconds pass as the President looks around and everyone else in the group looks at him.

Finally, he looks back at the group. "Before we sign this amendment, we will trample through mud, climb up rocks, edge along on the face of a cliff and walk up to beautiful overviews and down into hidden valleys. We will be scratched by sticks, poked by weeds, nicked by falling pebbles. We will feel thirst and hunger for sustenance. We'll see magnificence as far as our eye can see at some moments and, at others, be so focused on our next step that we won't have the slightest concept of our surroundings. Some of us will stub our toes. Others will twist ankles. A few may even fall, with others around us here to help pick us up. We'll get our hands dirty when we reach down to keep from falling or as we pull up to get over the next long step. We don't know what is around the corner, but we'll keep pressing forward because we have confidence in our ability to overcome obstacles. We won't play it safe, turning away at the first sign of difficulty," President Phillipi concludes before he starts walking back over the boulders.

A step later, he stops and turns back to the group. "Most importantly, we'll hike this Billy Goat Trail together. The hike is a metaphor for what we've accomplished together, something to remind us to be proud of what we've achieved."

As the hike continues, Jill ensures that her foot is secure in the next foothold before stepping up. She reaches up another eighteen inches and secures her other foot in the next tiny ledge in the rock that serves as the natural ladder up this forty-five-degree-angled section of the hike.

She has been thinking about the President's comments and turns to Professor Stark.

"I don't know if I'd be ready to replace him," she says quietly, making sure that the rest of the group is out of earshot. "I'm not sure that I'm ready. I mean, could I ever have thought of doing this? It's clearly perfect. I'll never forget this."

Professor Stark waits until he's on level ground before responding, walking side-by-side with Jill as the trail opens up for a time into a forested patch.

"The good news is that you don't need to replace him and even if you did become President, you wouldn't need to be Marc. You would need to be Jill," Professor Stark whispers. "And best as I can tell, you've always taken risks, pressed on over obstacles, dealt with adversity, and always come out stronger and better prepared for the next challenge."

"You love me, don't you," Jill says, clearly more of a statement than a question.

"I think that's pretty clear. But I mean it," Professor Stark says, whispering quietly with his hand around her waist. "I wouldn't support you doing this if I didn't think you were not only ready, but clearly the right person for the job."

"You're sure?"

"I'm sure," Professor Stark says. "And I'm also sure you're not going to want that dirt on your face when we come out at the end of the trail to a collection of waiting cameras," he adds, licking his fingers and wiping the dirt off her cheek.

"Do you think that fits with God's Law?" Jill asks. "Do you want me licking my fingers and rubbing you?"

Professor Stark looks at Jill and smiles.

She shakes her head back: "Don't answer that. You're such a boy sometimes."

Jill shakes her head and speeds up her pace, catching back up to the rest of the group just in time to run into dozens of video and still cameras taking the group's pictures as they emerge from the Billy Goat Trail.

After fifteen minutes to change, the full group is escorted across the temporary walkway to a temporary platform built in the middle of the Potomac River.

President Phillipi takes a seat at the table.

"It's not by accident that references to the Golden Rule concept are embedded in every major religion created and followed throughout the history of the world and that humanists understand the importance of this philosophy. God's Law won't prevent our government from imposing unnecessary and overbearing laws on Americans, but it will help minimize the damage done by flawed government."

Once the press event ends, President Phillipi asks Jill to travel back with him to the White House and to stay for meetings.

"I hope you don't mind if I steal your wife for a bit," he says as they part.

"That's fine," Professor Stark replies. "She's safer driving with you than she is with me, especially given my apparently rusty driving."

Once in the White House, the President walks with Jill to the Oval Office, where Vice President Wilt is waiting. The public announcement that Jill will be Marcia's running mate in the open primaries one-and-one-half years from now is rapidly approaching, though delayed to not compete with the God's Law ceremony for media attention.

A fourth person is also in the room.

"Jill, you know our CIA Director," the President says.

"Yes, Mr. Director," Jill replies. "Good to see you again."

"Jill, the FBI has completed a background check on you and everything is clean, with one exception," the Director states.

"Which is?" Jill asks.

The Director looks at the President and Vice President, looking to see if either of them will take this burden off of him. It's quickly clear that neither will.

"Why isn't the FBI part of this if they've discovered a problem?" Jill asks, filling silence in the room.

"I'll answer the easy question first," the Director says. "The FBI identified an anomaly. That anomaly is linked to information held at the very highest levels only in the government, and not something anyone in the CIA is authorized to share with any other agency."

"Okay," Jill replies, her curiosity fully aroused. "And the exception is?"

"The exception, Congresswoman."

"Jill, please call me Jill."

"The exception, Jill, is your husband."

"Paul?"

"Yes, Professor Stark."

"I'm speechless. How could Paul be a problem?"

"Jill," Vice President Wilt interjects.

"Yes, Marcia?"

Dejection is clear from Vice President Wilt's expression. "I'm afraid it's a serious enough issue that I'm going to have to withdraw my offer to have you as my running mate."

Jill shakes her head side to side, doing her best to project an exterior calm while everything inside her churns.

"Wow," Jill responds. "Wow."

"I know," the President states. "I'm truly sorry, Jill."

Jill clasps her hands over her waistline and drops her eyes to the ground. The corners of her lips press downward, cheeks tightening, forehead furrowed.

"Can you tell me what it is?" Jill asks. "I think I deserve to know."

"It's probably better that you not know," the CIA director states. "From a security perspective."

"If it's a security issue and my husband is the reason that the nation feels threatened, don't you think I have a right to know the risks I'm under and that my child is under," Jill says, unclasping her hands and holding them flat against her belly.

"Oh, my God," Vice President Wilt says. "You're pregnant?"

"Yes, and obviously with Paul's child."

"I thought you were planning to adopt," Wilt says.

"Yes, we were. We are. Well, I need to understand we, but this was clearly not in our planning or I would have told you when you offered," Jill says.

"So, I hate to be crass about this, but I just want to be sure: Is divorcing Paul out of the question?" the President asks.

"Yes. I mean, unless you tell me something truly awful about him and I find out he's been lying to me about who he is and what he does," Jill says. "I need to know. I need to know what it is, for me and for my baby."

"You have the authority, Mr. President," the CIA Director re-marks.

The President stands up and walks over to Jill, sitting on the couch next to her. "If I tell you, you need to be prepared to keep one of the nation's most important national secrets from your husband under risk of spending the rest of your life in prison, away from your child. Are you sure you want to take that risk?"

The little remaining color in Jill's face drains away, adrenaline surging through her arteries at levels so great that Jill's entire body begins to shake. She looks at the ceiling. Seconds later, she drops her focus back to the floor.

"I need to lie down for a few minutes," Jill says. "I'm getting dizzy. I'm sorry. I can't stop it."

"It's okay, Jill," Vice President Wilt says. "Pregnancy will do that to a woman."

"I don't know what it is. Tell me I'm not just a naïve farm girl who got played by a city boy. That would just kill me."

"If this turns out to be what we think it is, you're not the only one who's been played," the President says. "This plot goes all the way up to the top, and I certainly never saw it coming."

"Most importantly, Jill," Marcia adds. "We still don't know what your husband knows about what is happening around him. He plays a role but we don't know what he knows about what is going on."

Jill glares in each of their eyes. "I have to know what this is."

"Your decision, Mr. President," the Director reminds President Phillipi.

The President relents. "Bring her in, if she wants to know."

"I want to know," Jill replies. "I need to know."

"Okay," the Director says. "Follow me to the DUCC, the deep underground command center."

"Why there?"

"It's something we can openly discuss only in optimized security settings. The Oval Office isn't clean enough," the President notes.

Jill follows the CIA Director down to the DUCC, stopping per security protocol at every hundred-foot interval to reconfirm identification through eye scans, facial recognition and fingerprint.

Once settled into a thick, closed conference room situated more than one thousand feet below the bottom of the Potomac River, Jill prepares for her world to be shattered.

Though not sure she wants to know, she asks anyway, "Okay, what is the problem with Paul?"

"Whew," the Director exhales, doing his best to ensure he doesn't say too much. "You are aware of the Morality Project, the Atrocity Center trials, he has been leading at the University of Chicago?"

"Of course," Jill says. "The whole world is aware."

"You also are aware that three trials have now been conducted under the auspices of the Morality Project, with Professor Stark acting essentially as the judge in these three cases."

"Of course," Jill replies. "The trials are fascinating. I've watched portions of them."

"You're also aware that two of the men who were tried by the Morality Project passed away of sudden illnesses within weeks of the jury convictions of those men."

Jill turns her palms up and shrugs. "Yes, again, global news which anyone would know."

"Okay, now my next statement gets you to the point of no return. Once I make it, you are forever bound to confidentiality, a confidentiality you cannot break even in tiny doses to your husband," the Director states.

"I understand," Jill confirms.

"General Timur was just found dead three days ago, also, it seems, from a mysterious poisoning."

"That's certainly an interesting coincidence, or maybe I should say providence," Jill replies. "But what does that have to do with Paul?"

"It appears that all three of these men weren't just unlucky, though we do not have access to two of the bodies yet in order to conduct thorough autopsies to be certain."

"And you think Paul executed them?" Jill says, trying to control her laughter. "I have to kill the spiders in my home, even when he's the first one to spot them. He can barely kill a cold, let alone a person."

"Perhaps not directly, but he's part of what appears to be a broad conspiracy aimed at undermining international law by trying and executing people with extensive track records of violence," the CIA Director adds.

"The men Paul tried are nothing more than mass murderers, every one of them conducting crimes against humanity, and the evidence has shown it so overwhelmingly that they were found guilty of genocide, mass murder, systematic rape and just about every other heinous crime one could imagine," Jill argues. "All Paul did was put these men on trial, ensure that the evidence against them was gathered and presented, give them a chance to defend themselves and then tabulate the votes from jurors around the world. I don't see how his involvement in this disqualifies me from running for Vice President or is so serious that I should even consider divorce."

"It's not just what you see in public. Funding for The Morality Project comes from anonymous sources, as far as you know. Correct?"

"That's right," Jill affirms.

The Director looks to President Phillipi, who has since joined, for confirmation it is okay to continue. He gets approval. "We've put considerable effort over the last eight months into investigating the sources of these funds and we've found a connection between these funds and the Castillo cartel."

"You've found what?" Jill asks.

"The funding for The Morality Project comes from accounts that we have been able to link to the Castillo cartel. We had been tracking these funds to seize them after we brought down the cartel, but they've been kept moving at a pace and through techniques so sophisticated that we weren't been able to track and confiscate them before they were used to fund the Morality Project."

"But why would the Castillo cartel, or whoever controls that money now, want to fund something like the Morality Project that stands for everything the cartel tried to destroy?" Jill probes.

"We're still trying to figure that out, but the political and physical risks to you and your husband are substantial when that is discovered by others," the Director contends.

"Well, as soon as Paul finds out the funding source, he'll shut the Morality Project down that minute," Jill asserts. "There's no way he would ever do work he knew was funded by a drug cartel."

"That's part of the issue and why this is confidential. He's conducted three trials. Three times, the individuals were convicted. Three times, they died under mysterious circumstances, the last being General Timur who was poisoned by a sea snake that doesn't swim in the waters near where he was found."

Jill can't believe she's having this discussion. She's equally troubled that they think anything she's been told disqualifies her from executive office. "Should I tell Paul to stop doing these trials now? He can't possibly know or take part in plans to actually kill the people once they're convicted."

"No, no, no," the Director says. "You cannot say anything to him. If he's not involved in the killing, he can keep holding these trials until the world's terrorists figure out that they need to kill him and his trials to keep from dying themselves. Eventually, no one will believe these deaths are coincidental."

"So, what he's doing is so destructive that I can't run for Vice President but you want him to keep doing it?" Jill asks.

"Jill, what he's doing may be a service to humanity, but if it's tied to the U.S. government, the consequences to the nation could be disastrous," the President states. "I know that's a tough pill to swallow."

"Sure," Jill replies. "Just a tough pill to swallow."

50 RECLAMATION

"Who's after you?" Ally asks JT as he climbs into her APB from the coffin-like extension jutting out from the cliff face.

JT doesn't hear the question, focusing instead on ensuring he is safely inside the APB and triggering closure of his cubbyhole before his mind has any capacity to consider anything else.

Tapping the fingerprint ID pad one last time, JT sends the four metal bars back inside the cliff wall until the exterior rock covering blends seamlessly into the remainder of the cliff. Finally, he latches into his seat. Ally turns the APB camouflage skin back on; having turned it off to be sure JT didn't miss his climb aboard under the already difficult night sky. She shoots the APB quickly up to fifty thousand feet and heads east.

"Who's after you?" she asks JT again.

"I'm not sure, but it sounds like the U.S. government is coming for me and for New Rite. I just didn't want to take any chances of being taken before we could finish a few jobs."

"Do you really think you can hide from the government?"

"Sure. If I need to, until I can do something to eliminate the risk."

"Eliminate?" Ally asks.

"Maybe eliminate isn't the right word," JT replies. "Perhaps mitigate is more like it."

"While I've got you alone, can we talk?" Ally asks.

"Of course."

"I'm getting worried about what we can do," she states, dropping the APB back down to thirty thousand feet for transport over the plains and enabling her and JT to both take off their oxygen masks with the APB now enclosed and pressurized.

"I've always had those worries. The ability to kill is not something to take lightly," JT acknowledges. "I never have and I never will."

"I take it the government has figured out our role with Timur by now."

"I'm sure. That's why I went to the blanket," JT says.

"So what are they going to do about it?" Ally asks.

"That's the big question, isn't it," JT responds. "They could decide that because New Rite is based in the United States that they have a responsibility to regulate us—or even send us to prison."

"But we haven't done anything against any Americans. Do they really have jurisdiction?" Ally asks.

"It's less a question of jurisdiction than a question of fear of our capabilities," JT states. "I think they know now that we have the power to eliminate without anyone being able to detect us."

"So, I guess my question is do you think they're gonna want to stop us?" Ally asks. "Do I need to be able to disappear?"

"I sure hope not. I've been trying to be sure we have relationships with people in government to protect us from being feared," JT says, looking down to see a scattering of lights projecting up from farmhouses and then up to see a profusion of stars.

Ally allows silence for several minutes before asking, "So, let's say they leave us alone to finish what we've started. How do we make sure that this ability doesn't fall into the wrong hands?"

"As long as I've got control, we're doing it this way. Trials. Juries. Verdicts. Then elimination. And we do it only if no one else shows initiative and capture isn't possible," JT notes.

"Yeah, I get that, but there's likely fifty people now who know what we can do. How do we make sure none of them, including you and me, use this capability to settle our own scores?"

"I've tried to accomplish this through segregation of duties. Carol and her team know how to control the DNA triggers. The capsules need to be tailor-made for each victim. Inside Carol's team, you need three different experts to get the capsules made. Abe's team manages micro-drone control. Ramon and his team deal with intelligence and systems execution. Your team does operations. No one of you can execute this on your own and I can't do any of it without the full team. That's the way it needs to be," JT states.

"Not to be morose, but what happens if you die?" Ally asks.

"In terms of?" JT asks.

"In terms of whoever replaces you as owner keeping the rules of engagement in place," Ally states.

JT looks toward Ally, making sure to make direct eye contact. "Good question, of course. I'm sure you'll know what to do."

"What do you mean?" Ally asks, clicking the APB into autopilot and looking directly at JT.

"I'm not turning New Rite over to just anybody."

"What does that mean?" Ally asks.

"Don't even think about it. I need you to focus on the next target," JT says, doing what he can to change the conversation.

"Which one?" Ally asks. "The Morality Project is finishing four more trials, three expected with conviction rates that meet the standard."

"I guess the question is which one is the nearest term threat to more people?" JT asks. "All of these were trial targets picked without any help from us."

"Personally, I'd prefer to go after the junta leader targeting women and children through the Congo and CAR," Ally says, "but there's already government forces mobilized against him."

"What about that kid trying to lead a rebel force to retake control of North Korea?" JT asks.

"He's certainly proven as ruthless as everyone in his lineage," Ally responds, "but we've got to believe that China, South Korea and the

U.S. governments have him on their target lists. We have to leave some of these people to be killed in a way that doesn't always draw attention to us."

"Well that only leaves one target," JT says.

"Yep."

"Agreed."

"Agreed."

"We might need your girl again," JT notes.

"Clarissa?"

"Yes."

"But if he gets ahold of her, we may never see her again," Ally argues. "This is even riskier than the last one. At least with Taban, we knew what he did with his girls."

"True. That just means we'll have to be even tighter with our planning and back-up plans," JT insists.

Ally's face crunches and contorts as she thinks about her new target. "This man, this thing, makes me sick. If it's true, and the trial seemed to prove it, his depravity is beyond human comprehension."

"Can you find him?" JT asks.

"Eventually, sure, but we've got to figure out how to draw him into the open," Ally replies as she slows the APB to a stop, slowly dropping down to the helipad next to JT's office at CURE headquarters in Detroit.

JT knows he doesn't have long before Secretary Mendoza sends a team to grab him if he really wants control of New Rite's capabilities. Waiting in his office is a man he once thought at least partially responsible for his younger brother's death.

"You wanted to see me?" Ramon asks, careful to stay away from visibility to anyone outdoors until JT turns on the visual obscurity screens and turns on a sound-proofing system that ensures any sound heard from outside the room is so distorted that neither the voice patterns nor words can be detected.

"I'm afraid, Ramon, that we're fully exposed," JT tells his new friend. "The U.S. government thinks you're controlling and funding The Morality Project. And they now are pretty certain that I'm in cahoots with you."

"Well, at least they're partially right," Ramon responds. Several hundred million dollars from various accounts Ramon once controlled around the world have been used to fund Professor Stark's Atrocity Center and Morality Project trials. As carefully as he had protected the accounts, he knew it was only a matter of time before the link between him and the funding was exposed.

"So, now what?" Ramon asks.

"It's time. You have to disappear."

"With my family?"

"I'm afraid not," JT responds.

"No?" Ramon pleads.

"No. It's not safe. Too many people to hide at once and I'm sure the government has every one of them under constant surveillance trying to find you," JT replies. "They'll be taken care of, but they have to still believe it's possible you're dead, for now."

"And Abril? Do I at least have her?" Ramon pleads, clasping his hands in front of him as he looks down at JT reclining slightly in his simple, black, ergonomic chair.

JT creases his lips, looking with head titled toward Ramon. Slowly, he shakes his head side to side in ever-so-slight motion.

"Abril wants to spend the rest of her life seeking salvation . . . ," JT states, a morose expression clear on his face. Ramon drops his head down, shoulders slumping and skin turning pale. " . . . with the man that she loves."

Oxygen returns to Ramon's lungs. He visibly exhales, shaking his head side-to-side. "You're cruel, man. Cruel. How could you do that to me, making me think I would be empty and alone the rest of my life?" Ramon pleads.

"She wanted to be sure."

"Sure, how?" Ramon asks.

"Sure that you truly loved her before she abandoned everyone and everything she knew to be with you," JT says.

As JT finishes his statement, Abril steps out of JT's bathroom and runs to Ramon.

Lifting her in his arms, Ramon holds Abril in a deep embrace, lost for several minutes before noticing as his hand caresses her back that the gravelly welts that had built on her back through months of captivity are now gone.

Pulling away from the hug to see her real face for the first time in months, he sees the ebullient smile and vibrant eyes that had occasionally poked through her hardened mask during their initial encounters.

"How can we ever hide with Abril's beauty?" Ramon asks JT, looking only briefly at him as he asks. "She'll be stared at wherever we go, and not just by me."

"I agree with you, Ramon, if people see her like this," JT responds.

"So, how do we hide?"

"We've found a convent in Caracas to take her, a convent where her hair will be covered. With the right face-distorting prosthetics, she'll be able to avoid too much attention."

"Where does that leave me?" Ramon asks.

"With her, as a deacon in training for a nearby parish where you'll work together, sometimes even visiting an elderly gentleman who looks a lot like I will in thirty years when I need ministry in that home. It's the best I can do, and your safest escape."

"When do we leave?" Abril asks.

"Ally is outside waiting."

Holding Ramon's hand, Abril turns to JT. "I haven't packed anything."

"No need. What you need is waiting for you," JT assures them.

"But why would a convent take me?" Abril asks, still struggling with her worthiness.

"Some people compromise themselves for enrichment. Others are willing to take risks to save lives and save souls. Ramon's generosity to the convent made this happen," JT acknowledges.

"But what about The Morality Project?" Ramon asks. "Are you shutting it down?"

"Far from it," JT replies. "We've taken out some of the people who might be able to go after you but the world's still full of monsters. If we can convince these monsters that God is exercising selective, excruciating wrath against the sons of Satan, I'm hoping more and more will opt out of the violent control and confiscation racket."

"What are you doing with Juan?" Ramon queries. "He knows I'm alive and he's bound to spill it."

"True. True," JT replies. "Worse yet, he knows the connection between you and New Rite and he's now part of Professor Stark's trial management team. This adds a complexity that won't be good for us. We'll just have to deal with it," JT adds.

Abril sits down on the chair across from JT's desk. "How can Ramon; no, how can we be sure that you won't use the power Ramon helped provide in the wrong way?"

"That's the right question, Abril," JT replies, standing up and moving closer to the pair. "We've set this up so it isn't my decision or any single person's decision. We have to protect against such ultimate abuse."

"But you have all the capabilities to kill today and no one will ever know," Ramon states.

"Ever is a long time, Ramon. An eternity in my mind," JT replies. "It's my eternity that I'm not willing to risk."

"So you won't hurt the kid?" Ramon questions.

"Of course not. That's not the way we will ever do things here," JT responds. "If we go that route, we'll need to be the targets of our own technology. How would we be any different than Timur?"

"Timur?" Abril asks.

"Damn it," JT whispers under his breath as he turns and walks away, pretending not to hear Abril's question and hoping she'll just let his reference go.

Abril grabs Ramon on both sides of his cheeks and turns his face to look directly into his eyes. "I heard about him. Wasn't he that terrorist killed and turned over to the Americans by his own . . . by his own . . . by his own guards?"

Ramon turns away from Abril to glance at JT, now standing several feet away and kicking himself for his slippage.

"You couldn't look at me?" Abril contends, pulling Ramon's head back toward her. "Tell me the truth."

JT recognizes he needs to step in and, at least temporarily, save Ramon from having to construct his own truth.

"I was just referencing how Timur thought he could act as judge, jury and executioner, and that no man should ever have that power, right Ramon?" JT argues.

"Of course not," Ramon says. "I saw with General Hernández what happens when a man acquires unchecked power. And you saw it too, Abril."

Abril lets Ramon's hand go, steps back from him and looks between him and JT. "So out of these—out of judge, jury and executioner—which one are you?"

Ramon stares back at Abril. JT comes over to Abril, asking her and Ramon to take a seat.

"She needs to know, Ramon. If she can't live with what we do, and how it works, it's better that you know now before both of you regret it," JT states before proceeding to explain the Morality Project process and the safeguards in place to ensure that even he can't terminate a target without trial.

A short time later, with the sun setting and no clouds to obscure the horizon, Ally takes off with Abril and Ramon inside. After they depart, JT walks out to the helipad deck and calls Defense Secretary Xavier Mendoza.

"One demand, Xavier," JT states as the men connect through a secure device.

"Don't make it unreasonable," Mendoza replies. "You know I can't promise the world."

"I want one hour with the President before you decide to make any public announcements of what New Rite has done," JT requests. "I have a deal for you that I don't think you'll want to refuse.

"Fair enough," Mendoza replies. "Turns out, he only wants to meet with you. He's as scared of us being able to do what you do as you are and doesn't want it brought in house. And he's buying into your God's wrath deterrence concept. What's the deal you want?"

"The deal is you leave us alone and I deliver you a list right now of where Timur's stolen uranium and nukes are sitting," JT says.

"We've already captured it from three spots," the Secretary replies, wanting to avoid giving JT any upper hand in negotiations. "Issyk Kul. Caspian. Geneva."

"Then you have eight more to go," JT tells him, intending to add the twelfth storage location, the one inside U.S. borders, to the list only after it's clear the President and Mendoza are holding up their end of the agreement. "The sooner the better. We had drones sending back images as Timur wrote up and burned daily lists of his storage locations. I can give you amounts and locations."

As the Secretary contemplates his response, JT hears him walking on his office treadmill. He knows he's seriously focusing when he turns the treadmill off. He places JT on hold and makes a quick call to the President.

When Secretary Mendoza comes back to JT, he jumps right back to the middle of the conversation. "Deal. You give us the material. The President lets you all off the hook and signs a presidential order allowing you to continue as long as no execution action is taken against U.S. government. You can have your trials, but final decisions have to go through U.S. courts if the target is inside our borders."

"So the President is letting us continue?" JT asks.

"He is."

"That's good news," JT replies. "A little separation is a good thing. We can only do one-offs. If we do the wrong one-offs, you can destroy us. But if you do the wrong one-offs, who holds the U.S. government accountable without war? Who can keep the wrong people from using this capability to steal our country?"

"Apparently, the President likes the structure Stark has set up with the global trials. Thinks it's better control than our single-panel drone kill review policies, not to mention cleaner with less likelihood of anti-U.S. retribution," Secretary Mendoza acknowledges.

JT rubs his thumb and forefinger through his beard, a slight smile and glint in his eye making clear his satisfaction. "I hope you all don't mind giving me a lift to DC. I'll be on the CURE helipad in Detroit, staring at the stars. My rides are all out of pocket."

"I know," Mendoza replies. "You have to know we've been watching you."

"I assumed as much," JT responds. "So, what's next?"

"I'm not sure I want to know which of the Morality Project convicts are falling next, but I do know I'll still be panicked if I ever end up on trial," Secretary Mendoza states.

"It certainly will be better for all of us if you don't do anything to earn such attention," JT responds, pulling up a chair to look over his balcony, thinking back to how much the site has changed since nature started reclaiming the long-ignored and abandoned surroundings.

51 RESTORATION

Jill and Professor Stark walk toward the national monument holding hands. She had waited to share her bad news until she could do it in person.

The two were so lost in joy at her unexpected pregnancy that Jill hadn't even gotten to the point of sharing that she wasn't running for Vice President anymore. Truth be told, she can't wrap her head around the rationale. As they loop around the monument and head back toward the Capitol building, three black sedans drive up the wide walkways to the monument and stop just in front of Jill and Professor Stark.

Vice President Wilt steps out from the middle sedan.

"Jill."

"Marcia?" Jill replies in surprise, before recognizing there are dozens of people with cameras around, now being turned on and focused on them. "I mean madam Vice President."

"Have you told him, yet?" the Vice President says as she pulls Jill away from Professor Stark.

"About the baby? Yes, of course," Jill responds quietly, hopefully quietly enough to not be picked up by any of the devices now filming them.

"The baby?" the Vice President asks. She hadn't even considered that Jill wouldn't have told Professor Stark about that. "Well that's not what I was talking about," Marcia states, clear now that Jill hasn't said anything to Professor Stark about the upcoming campaign. "I was referencing our earlier discussion."

"No. Not yet," Jill replies. "I was getting to that."

"Then don't," Marcia Wilt directs, now noticing that people are walking toward them with their Lifelinks open and pointed at them. She points toward one of the sedans and Jill steps in with her before they continue. "I've talked about it with Marc and Xavier."

"And?" Jill asks.

"And, they agreed it's my call," Marcia replies. "I want you on my team. Just as importantly, Marc and I think Professor Stark should continue doing his work. What he's doing fits with the Golden Rule agenda. If we were monsters, we'd expect to be held accountable. The Morality Project does it more fairly than anything we have in place. Better yet, now that a few of the people he's put on trial have been taken out by their own people—you know what I mean. Anyway, it's got these people fighting internally instead of plotting against the good people."

Vice President Wilt leaves out that the President has since confirmed with JT that Professor Stark knows nothing about the deaths that have followed Morality Project convictions. Marcia has also considered and decided that Professor Stark would never undertake a trial of her as President if Jill serves as her Vice President. If she ever worried that she might be taken out to elevate Jill to the Presidency, she would just have to act first.

It's made clear to Jill that she still can't let Professor Stark in on what she knows.

"What was that all about?" he asks after the Vice President exchanges pleasantries with him and quickly departs.

"Just some strategy discussion," she replies, buying time to figure out what to tell him. "I'll fill you in when we can talk."

Professor Stark puts his arm around her waist and pulls her in tightly as they walk, then leans over to whisper in her ear.

"It's really coming together," he says softly.

"What's coming together?" Jill asks.

"All of it really," he responds. "But I was thinking about us."

As they get further from the crowd gathered around the monument, Professor Stark leans back toward Jill. His expressions turn serious as he looks at her.

"You really need to win the next election," he tells her, careful to choose words that won't be fully understood by anyone trying to listen in.

"Why's that?" she asks, stopping and turning to look at him.

"Because we've had many of the greatest leaders from all over the world making clear that the Golden Rule is the right way to live for thousands of years. This is our chance to ingrain it in the government and maybe even the world our children will be raised in," he says as the tense expression transitions to a broad smile. "And our grandchildren too."

"You dare to utter the word 'children' when you know how miserable I've been," Jill asks.

"Oh. You caught that," Professor Stark replies, attempting his best innocent boy gleam. "Just trying to seed the concept."

Jill contorts her face. "Don't even right now, unless you want me to puke on you."

On her way back from Caracas to New Rite's Colorado compound, Ally pulls up her APB to a false crest near the top of Humphrey's Peak, just a few hundred yards away from where intel tells her that Clarissa is hiking.

Ally waits, stretching out her legs on a boulder as Clarissa approaches. Slowing as she sees another person in this usually serene area, Clarissa finally recognizes that it's Ally and runs up.

"Good morning, Clarissa."

"Good morning, Alycia, or is it Ally?"

MIKE BUSHMAN

"Ally. Ally," Ally responds as she hugs Clarissa and points to invite Clarissa to sit down with her. "Just wanted to check in and see
how you're doing. Are you ready for your next mission?"

"Ready? Of course I'm ready," Clarissa replies. "But you promised
to tell me what was really happening to that prince once we were safe.
We're safe now, right?"

"Safe, yes," Ally replies, holding her finger out in an effort to get
Clarissa to stop talking. "But we can't talk about it here. We don't
have the security.

"So, where and when?" Clarissa asks.

"One of our compounds. We'll go to the one in Utah. We have a
discussion safe zone there," Ally replies.

"Like, at the New Rite compound in Utah, where I camped with
my family?"

"Exactly," Ally replies as she clicks the gecko-skin camouflage off
to allow Clarissa to safely board the APB. Twenty minutes later, the
pair set down at New Rite's Utah compound east of Kanab.

Ally leads Clarissa to sit on a flat surface under an elevated rock
that hangs over and blocks an upward view.

"I've been here before," Clarissa suggests. "This is where Sarah
found me when I got lost."

"Could be," Ally replies, sitting on a flat rock surface under the
overhang. "Our sounds are distorted out of here. Even someone tracking us can't capture audio when we're under here."

"Great, so can you tell me now what happened?" Clarissa asks.

"You've already read about or seen what happened to everyone
affected by your bravery," Ally states.

"I have?" Clarissa replies, voice elevating to punctuate "have."

"Yes, but tell me you haven't done any searches for information,
like I asked," Ally says.

"I can take orders," Clarissa asserts.

"That still stands. Don't ever. Not from your Lifelink and not from
anything that can ever be traced back to you," Ally directs.

"What?"

"And for that matter, not even from anywhere in Flagstaff or any
city where there's any other evidence you are there."

"Then you'll tell me?" Clarissa asks.

"You already know. The four girls rescued from South Yemen. You heard about that, right?" Ally asks.

"I did. How scary is that whole thing," Clarissa notes.

Ally looks directly into her eyes: "You were going to be target number five."

"Seriously?" Clarissa asks, eyes expanding as she shakes her head.

"What you did gave those girls their lives back," Ally assures Clarissa.

Clarissa looks at Ally: "It did?"

"You captured his DNA," Ally states. "That allowed us to identify and remove him from the scene long enough to rescue the girls he had already taken."

"Really," Clarissa responds. "Well, I guess that's pretty cool."

After a lull in the discussion during which they both look off in the distance, Clarissa turns back to Ally: "What happened to the prince?"

"Turns out, he became very ill and didn't make it. No loss there," Ally states.

"Was he really that evil?" Clarissa asks.

"Does it help knowing he was convicted in a global trial of rape, torture, kidnapping, murder and financing an extensive terrorist network that killed more than a million people?"

"Seriously?"

"Seriously."

"I should have been way more scared," Clarissa states as they start walking back to the APB.

"Better that you weren't," Ally assures her. "Now, can we talk about our next mission, to see if you're interested?"

Near Puerto Vallarta, Juanita returns home after another twelve-hour extended hospital stretch. Her feet are aching as the kind, stocky nurse walks the last several blocks from the bus stop. Nearing her home, she sees three men standing outside in front of a moving van.

Immediately, her mind races with a list of potential problems. "I paid the mortgage," she reassures herself as she tries to remember exactly when she last forwarded payment from her bank account.

Making the sign of the cross as she slowly approaches the men, Juanita works up the nerve to approach them.

"*Can I help you gentlemen?*" she asks in Spanish. "*Are you lost?*"

"Señorita Juanita Méndez?" one of the men asks.

"Si."

"Tenemos regalos para ti," the man replies, as the men open the truck and start walking boxes toward the door. We have gifts for you, they say, adding that they don't know who bought them after Juanita inquires.

Juanita walks into her modest home to open box after box of clothes, electronics and cooking pots and utensils before seeing one man installing a new oven in her kitchen and another installing a washer and dryer in a room she is just seeing has been built onto the back of her home.

With the truck now emptied and boxes filling her home, the man who greeted her hands her an envelope.

"*I was told to give this to you last,*" he says.

She opens to find the deed to her house. Her mortgage has been paid off.

She turns her translation program on and takes a picture of the note, written in French.

"Vous avez aide de nombreux. Merci beaucoup."

Checking her translator, she sees it is telling her that this is appreciation for helping so many as a nurse. More important though is what it really tells her.

She hugs the movers, walks to her bedroom, drops to her knees and prays.

"Abril vive," Juanita cries, dropping to her knees in prayer as she recalls the man she treated who spoke French and left under Abril's care. "Abril vive."

Abril lives.

52 ANTICIPATION

Rachel thought it would be cool to duplicate the President's Billy Goat Trail hike. She wasn't among the fortunate few to have been invited to accompany him, but that doesn't mean she can't follow in his footsteps. With Juan visiting and Tamika anxious for a break from the office, the trio climbs off trail across a span of large boulders, jumping over crevices and climbing around ankle-twisting gaps to sit uncomfortably on a large boulder near water's edge.

Soft rumbling whitewater nearly drowns out the tweeps, caws and rhythmic whistles of birds perched and soaring along the trail, each searching for enough sustenance and same species connection to convert mere survival into memorable passage of time.

Juan unloads a beach towel from his hiking backpack—he's the pack mule for the day—flipping it open on a flat section of the boulder. Next, he opens the small cooler inside the backpack, pulling bottled waters, sliced Granny Smith apples with a cup of peanut butter dip, small containers of Tamika's homemade apple cider vinegar slaw and a bag full of Juan's peanut butter/roasted poblano/brown rice balls to set between them. Having forgotten forks, he breaks the two plastic knives in half so they each have part of a utensil to help in lifting the cabbage, apple and green onion mixture from their small cups.

For nearly ten minutes, the three eat, watch and listen. Juan reaches over to Rachel's hand, finding the reception he hoped for his fingers. Tamika lies flat across the boulder, looking up at the sky through her tinted lenses.

"Do you think this Golden Rule amendment is really going to make a big difference?" Juan asks, interrupting a long stretch of silence. "I mean, do you think people will start treating each other better, caring for each other, working to honestly solve problems and respect each other?"

Juan looks at Rachel as she scoots over closer to him. Tamika's head doesn't move. Seeing no answer forthcoming, Juan turns back to watch the river flowing over the random collection of boulders that lines the river bed, watching as some of the waves twist into rotating pools, other waves jump up and over rocks in their way and still other waters rush past small eddies, sealing somewhat stagnant water in its place.

After he's given up hope of an answer, Tamika pulls up her sunglasses and turns toward the pair. "It has to be better than how we have been treating each other."

Rachel nods gently. "Just recognizing that there is a common moral concept that binds us is progress," she comments, looking to see Juan and Tamika both nodding agreement and Tamika rising to a seated position. "Everyone ready? We still have a long way to go."

53 GRATIFICATION

Compared to surrounding favelas, the deeply impoverished areas on the outskirts of Caracas, Abril finds relative comfort inside her new convent home. Her small room is shared with three other nuns, all born and raised within walking distance of the white, stucco-crusted walls that house the sisters when they are teaching, nursing, praying, cleaning and tending to the deep emotional needs surrounding them.

From their convent's perch at the top of the western edge of a large coastal hill, the Caribbean Sea glimmers in the distance, a beauty betraying the squalor of life on the hill. Winds move eastward at strong enough pace to carry away much of the stench of the adjoining favela, the stacked layers of hillside homes constructed from waste cardboards, metals and plastic materials scavenged from city dumps. Inside the favela, children run and play jumping over open sloughs that carry household wastes down the sides of the hill. Pumps to carry ocean water to the top of the hill and carry the wastes down the slough run just one hour on the days the pumps work at all.

In her first days at the convent, Abril struggles to fully switch back to her native Spanish, and particularly struggles to adjust to the Venezuelan dialect and idioms that are such departures from her

Mexican speech patterns. It's quickly clear to the other nuns, however, that she belongs and will earn her place among them. She cooks and cleans inside the convent walls at a pace and with skill that draws their respect. When asked to lead prayers, her knowledge of the Bible and depth of compassion becomes evident to all taking part.

Outside the walls, Abril is already a magnet for children who depend on the convent for bits of food and the education that inspires their hopes of escape. She tells them about parts of the world they might only dream of seeing one day even if she can't acknowledge her true name or origins. Her smile alone brings the children peace, warmth and a measure of hope. She runs and plays with them, not resting until dusk when all of the nuns are required to return inside the convent's walls.

A month passes before she is finally asked to work with the new deacon at an adjoining church. He's having trouble with the language, she has been told: speaking too much Spanglish and not enough Spanish. Abril is selected as Deacon Rey's tutor, an assignment she gladly accepts to finally have time alone with the man she knows as Ramon.

After moments of passion once safely protected from anyone else's eyes, Abril backs away from Ramon, putting both hands on his shoulders. Ramon is ready to burst, having dreamed about being with her every minute since they were separated after Ally dropped them outside the city. Abril's mind, though, has been occupied by other thoughts as well.

"Who's that girl?" she asks, pointing at a picture of a young Latina woman, likely a few years younger than Abril, that caught her eye on Ramon's desk as he tried to encourage her physical desires. "Your sister's not that old, is she?"

Ramon had sketched what he remembered of the girl from the alley, the one who goaded the gang into beating him. A few clicks of a facial imaging program converted the drawing into a realistic picture. The additional time for reflection he's had in the past month hasn't all been put to productive use.

Sheepishly, Ramon responds. "No, Celia's still a few years from that."

"So what's this girl's picture doing on your desk?" Abril probes.

Ramon quickly considers several different responses, trying to figure out how to assuage Abril's fears while still being honest: "She's the gang leader I told you about, the one who ordered the attack on me."

"And?" Abril presses.

"And, I couldn't get her face out of my head," Ramon admits.

"So. So, you want to keep her picture on your desk? I'm not enough for you?" Abril counters.

"No, no, no. Nothing like that," Ramon responds, deciding to come clean. "At first, I was sketching it to make sure I didn't forget her when I had the chance to take revenge."

"And?"

"And, now I use it to remind me that sometimes what we endure brings us to the people we are supposed to meet," Ramon replies, putting his arms around Abril. "If it weren't for this girl, this hateful, malicious thing, I wouldn't be with you. So I decided that she's my reminder to look for the good in life, even when life isn't good."

Satisfied that Ramon is telling the truth, Abril decides it's the right time to press for something she has contemplated ever since the last discussion with JT.

"I need to know Ramon. The work you do," Abril states, turning and staring directly into Ramon's widely dilated eyes. "I want to do it too."

Ramon grabs her hands, pulling them off his shoulders and holding them on the tops of his thighs.

"Are you sure?" he asks, shaking her hands up and down as he inquires.

With a half smile and a nod, she responds: "I'm sure."

Ramon stands up, walks to the corner of his room and puts his index finger on an edge of tile. He walks to the opposite corner, placing his right eye against a deep red mosaic pane of stained glass. Abril watches him carefully as he turns back to the initial corner, where the corner tile is now elevated. Ramon reaches in to withdraw his Lifelink, along with other devices to securely contact JT and New Rite.

"JT thought you might want in," Ramon acknowledges. "He has a mission for us, but he admitted to me that you could be in real danger of being hurt or worse if you are part of our work. I begged him not to ask you to do it."

"Why? Shouldn't my life be my choice?" Abril contends, extremely sensitive to the idea of being controlled in anyway by anyone.

Ramon covers his eyes and looks away. "I want to be with you more than I have ever wanted anything in my life," he admits. "I can't stand the thought of finally finding real joy, only to have it torn away from me."

Abril steps to Ramon, pulling his head down onto her shoulder. "I don't need you to protect me," she murmurs. "I just need you to love me. Now what's the assignment?"

Ramon flips open a screen, showing photos of six targets, all wearing different types of religious garb.

"We'll be attending an interfaith conference in Jerusalem, meeting up with close friends of a man we now know as Prince Taban," Ramon tells her. "If you would have me, we can get married in the Holy City while we're there, where no one will know us."

"Yes, I want to marry you. Without blowing our cover, of course," Abril replies, kissing Ramon gently, both hands holding his face. "Now what's the mission?"

"Well," Ramon replies. "That's my simple mission, getting you to agree to spend the rest of your life with me. Our New Rite mission will be far more complicated."

ACKNOWLEDGMENTS

I remain forever grateful for the support of family, friends and colleagues in all of my writing. Once again, Dick Riederer, Bryn Collman Henning, Christine Hudzik and Bill Bushman provided invaluable guidance throughout the process of writing and editing *Doing Unto Others*. While I ascribe no responsibility for the contents of this book to them, I would also like to thank Golden Rule expert Professor Harry Gensler, Arizona Interfaith Ministry Executive Director Paul Eppinger, Paul McKenna of Scarboro Missions, Moral Courage Project Director Irshad Manji and so many others for contributing to my education as I conducted research on the issues explored in this story.

ABOUT THE AUTHOR

Prior to turning to writing full-time, Mike served as Washington Director for a U.S. Congressman, was head of global policy for a multi-billion-dollar sustainability services company and held executive responsibility for investor relations and global communications at that company. The father of two young adults, he has been married for twenty-six years. Mike earned his MBA from the University of Chicago, with honors, in 1997. His undergraduate journalism degree was earned in 1986 from the University of Illinois at Urbana-Champaign, where he served as Editor-in-Chief of the student-run *Daily Illini* newspaper.

Doing Unto Others is Mike's third novel in a series questioning the consequences of an increasingly divided United States of America and an even more disjointed world. *Melting Point 2040* and *Secession 2041* tell stories describing the painful effects of this division. Once deadly lessons of allowing and even encouraging division are clear, *Doing Unto Others* suggests a path to renewal that builds on the central uniting Golden Rule theme often taught to elementary school children but somehow ignored by national leaders.

Mike's fourth book, *Suicide Escape*, is a unique combination of novella and memoir in which Mike reveals his painful struggles with deep depression as a teenager in a story interwoven with the struggles of Clarissa Coleman, a character in both *Secession 2041* and *Doing Unto Others*. All of Mike's stories are set in the future, reflecting his view that the best method to understand the right decision today is to deeply consider its long-term consequences.

Made in the USA
Charleston, SC
18 December 2014